Sanctuary

By Helena Harte

2024

Butterworth Books is a different breed of publishing house. It's a home for Indies, for independent authors who take great pride in their work and produce top quality books for readers who deserve the best. Professional editing, professional cover design, professional proof reading, professional book production—you get the idea. As Individual as the Indie authors we're proud to work with, we're Butterworths and we're *different*.

Authors currently publishing with us:

E.V. Bancroft
Valden Bush
Addison M Conley
Jo Fletcher
Helena Harte
Lee Haven
Karen Klyne
AJ Mason
Ally McGuire
James Merrick
Robyn Nyx
Simon Smalley
Brey Willows

For more information visit www.butterworthbooks.co.uk

This trade paperback is published by Butterworth Books, UK

CATALOGING INFORMATION
ISBN: 978-1-915009-59-3
CREDITS
Editor: Victoria Villaseñor
Cover Design: Nicci Robinson
Production Design: Global Wordsmiths

Acknowledgements

I've loved every second of writing and producing this book, and that process has been made even more enjoyable with all the wonderful people who've helped me make it happen. One of the great things about creating a series is the ability to explore all the side characters you bring to life, characters who normally get short-changed and don't get their own stories. And that's one of the main reasons I wanted to start a series—to give me the flexibility to play with all the people who inhabit the world of Lori and Gabe. And I enjoyed it so much that I'm already working on book two; when you've finished reading this, will you be able to guess who's getting their own book next?

Anyhoo, a huge thanks to my beautiful and talented wife, my editor and cheerleader, for helping me through this book. For understanding that I have to squirrel myself away instead of adventuring with you. For loving me the way you do. For being my everything.

Thank you to Margaret Burris, for polishing the Britishness out of my phrasings. I enjoy working with you all the way over the ocean!

Thanks to my amazing team of ARC readers—I really appreciate every one of you and the time you take to read and review my words.

And to the reader out there now with this book in their hands, thank you. I hope you enjoy getting to know all the lovely people in the Windy City Romance books!

Dedication

To my wife,
you are my sanctuary
in this and every life.

Chapter One

"*THIS* IS WHY THE lawyer cheated on me with her assistant."

"Katherine is a poor excuse for a butch who submitted to becoming a patriarchal cliché. That's not your fault," Rosie said between over-dramatic chest heaves.

Lori frowned and gave her best friend *the look*. "You know I love how much you hate her on my behalf, but you also know that we don't say her name out loud."

"Are you worried that if I say it three times, she'll poof here out of thin air?"

Lori huffed and prodded the pile of excrement a little more fervently. The pungent odor that rose up in response to her agitating it got her thinking that she should bag some up and smear it on the windshield of the lawyer's prize Porsche. "No, I don't. She's not Lucifer, though she did a damn good job of impersonating him in those last few weeks. It just helps me keep emotional distance if I just call her *the lawyer*. You know that too. Why are you being so obstreperous?"

"Ooh, stealing that for my word of the week," Rosie said then rattled the tripod in her left hand. "Because I came to help you shoot a new video. I didn't come here to watch you play with poop. It's gross."

Lori didn't feel the need to point out that Rosie had practically wrestled the tripod from her hand and insisted on tagging along after they'd had lunch. She assumed Rosie was working up to something she wanted to talk about. A favor, maybe. Whatever it was, it must be pretty big for her to traipse out in the mud, risking her white sandals. "I'm going to have to call the vet. One of the horses must have a gut infection."

"Then we should definitely get this video done before it gets dark. You'll need some more donations to cover their fees."

Lori tossed the stick to the ground and sighed heavily. "You're right."

"I usually am."

Lori rolled her eyes and pointed toward the kennels. "I want to do a video with Max. The fireworks freaked him out, even with the special ear defenders."

Rosie started toward the large building. "You don't have to ask me twice. I need to get away from this stench before it infiltrates my clothes, and I have no choice but to burn them."

Lori shook her head and followed. "Maybe you shouldn't always come here in such fancy threads. I can loan you something from my wardrobe."

Rosie flicked her gaze over Lori's outfit of tank top, jeans, and work boots and looked vaguely mortified. "You do somehow manage to look adorable in your thrift-store ensemble, but I need all the help I can get."

Lori hooked her arm through Rosie's and tugged her close as they walked. Rosie didn't often let her dirt-poor upbringing vulnerabilities show, but Lori's heart ached for her when she did. "I call BS. You'd look amazing in a trash bag tied at the waist with twine."

"I hear that's the latest fashion in Milan." She winked and nudged her shoulder to Lori's.

"I can't wait to see you pull it off."

Rosie laughed, her sadness apparently gone as quickly as it had surfaced, and Lori pulled her toward the increasingly deafening sound of barking dogs, already alerted to their approach.

Lori headed toward the rear of the building where the individual outdoor runs extended fifty feet from each in-house sleeping area. Max was at the end of the building, as far away from the main entrance of the farm as he could be. His hearing seemed even more finely attuned than the average dog, and he reacted badly to any and all noises, which was no surprise given what he'd gone through.

She'd had him for over six months now, and he'd been doing well, improving steadily after the two months it had taken her to get close enough to put a leash on him for a walk. But the Fourth of July celebrations a few days ago seemed to have set him back, and he'd regressed to spending most of his time cowering in the corner of his sleeping area. Seeing a magnificent Belgian Malinois act that way was heartbreaking, but she wasn't about to give up on him. It didn't matter what some of the trolls on her TikTok said, Max deserved a chance to live a happy life after what he'd done for his country, and she would do her damnedest to make it happen.

"I saw that Toni did a duet with your last video of Max," Rosie said, flicking her bangs from her forehead with a flourish. "That was sweet of her..."

"You're so subtle." Lori chuckled. "But you should douse your torch for Toni in my duck pond. She's still all loved-up with her British soldier."

"The language barrier's bound to kick in soon enough." Rosie extended her hand and inspected her nails. "I'll bet soldier-girl will realize she's out of her league eventually, and Toni can run into my arms for comfort and understanding."

"Except the soldier-girl is exactly Toni's type, and you're exactly *not* her type."

"I could be... Maybe. I'd draw the line at power tools—I'd hate to break a nail—but I could butch it up."

Rosie tensed her arm, but Lori didn't see any discernible difference in bulk. She poked Rosie's skinny excuse for a bicep and raised her eyebrows. "It's that easy, is it?"

Rosie nodded. "I just need to add a little plaid flannel to my wardrobe, buy a ball cap, and constantly tie my lovely locks up in a ponytail. Easy peasy."

"Wow. If you do all that, I might not be able to control myself around you."

Rosie swatted her shoulder. "You'd take more convincing, I'm sure. And I'm not cutting my hair for anyone. Even you." She flicked her hair dramatically again. "There *was* a time when I might've considered it, but I'm no longer a foolish girl-child, and I've grown accustomed to you as a best friend. I don't have time to audition anyone else for the job."

"You don't *want* anyone else for the job." Lori grinned and turned to open the gate to Max's run. "I'll take a little footage of Max first and then I'll do a piece to camera." She closed the gate behind her and walked slowly toward the half-size opening to Max's sleeping space, softly calling his name. He'd never shown any aggression toward her, but she didn't want to risk him reacting badly if she spooked him. In the six years that she'd been running this place, her vet hadn't been forced to euthanize any healthy dogs because of violent behavior. It was a record Lori was proud of and wanted to keep in place.

She heard Max's low whine before she saw his nose twitching quickly. "Hey, handsome boy," she said gently and crouched down slightly to crawl into his indoor area.

His sleek black ears, which should've been standing erect were pinned flat against his head, and his eyes were so wide, she could see a sliver of white edging them. He was sitting on his haunches, pressed back into the farthest corner of the kennel, but his furrowed brow relaxed a little when he was sure it was her, and the whale eye effect disappeared. He would've recognized her scent—she rotated blankets from the chair and sofa in her office to the dogs' beds—way before Lori had even opened his gate, but he clearly no longer trusted his instincts.

She sat beside him, moving extra slow, then lifted her hand even more gradually to stroke the top of his head in deliberately long motions. He sank into his shoulders only slightly before craning his neck to push back into her touch. "That's it, Max. You can relax." She continued to rub his head for a while, letting him get used to the steady rhythm of her touch.

He moved his snout toward her a tiny bit and sniffed the air rapidly. He glanced up at her briefly before averting his gaze again. Lori smiled and moved her hand marginally closer to one of his ears so she could graze her thumb over it. "Smell something you like, huh?"

He repeated the sniffing and the furtive look and pushed his head against her palm again. Lori lifted her right hand and moved carefully toward the chest pocket of her dungarees to retrieve a beef cube. She held the treat in her palm and lowered it gently. Max didn't move toward it, but his nose went into overdrive. "Go ahead," Lori said.

He moved his muzzle toward the chunk of meat and took it from her tentatively. He barely chewed it, gulping it down like he hadn't eaten in a month, then looked at her again, this time holding her gaze for a little longer.

"Another one? I suppose it takes more than one little cow chunk to sustain eighty pounds of Belgian beefcake, huh?"

Max lowered his head and prodded her pocket with his nose. Lori took out a handful and held them out for him. "One at a time."

He whined in a tiny show of petulance. Usually, she'd discourage such behavior but with Max, it was a tantalizing glimpse of his personality, and she wanted to draw out as much of that as possible. Still, he took the treats individually, though the time it took him to swallow them got less and less with each piece.

"Are you camera-ready? Or do you need more bribes?" She ran her hand from the top of his head and along his back. His tail twitched so minutely that she wouldn't have registered it had her hand not been as close. "Okay. One more, and then you'll be ready for your close-up."

He licked his lips as if he understood every word she was saying. For all she knew, maybe he did. Max had been trained to detect bombs; was it that much of a stretch to think that he had a rudimentary grip of human language?

After he'd munched the final offering, she took out her phone and got them both in frame. "You remember Max, our hero who came home from Syria six months ago? He was an explosive hazard expert, but he couldn't do his job anymore after being injured in a bombing. Well, he's been doing really well, slowly getting better with each passing day. And thanks so much to everyone who's sent in money, and food, and gifts for our little place and especially for Max." She panned the camera to a small collection of partially destroyed chew toys. "Oh, and BlueEyedHusky, the monkey you sent is his favorite—it may have a couple less limbs than it started with, but it's still going strong." She put them back in the shot and smiled. "But we've had a setback."

Lori hit pause on the recording and slipped the phone back in her pocket. "Good boy, Max. The camera loves you." She got up in a low squat position and gave him one last head rub. "Beth will be in soon with your dinner. Make sure you eat it all up, or I'll get into trouble with her for ruining your appetite with treats." She crawled out of the opening and turned back one last time. She swallowed her gut reaction to the bereft look in Max's eyes. She'd been looking after animals of one kind or another her whole life, and she'd loved every one of them, but that love had always been temporary. Somehow though, Max had burrowed deeper into her heart, and she knew she was going to have a hard time letting him go when he was fully recovered. "I'll be back to take you for a walk in an hour or so."

"Why so sad?" Rosie asked as she opened the gate.

Lori locked it behind her and sighed. "I'm going to miss him," she said and handed Rosie her phone before locking the gate behind her.

Rosie frowned and fixed the phone onto the tripod. "Really? It's not like you to get attached."

She nudged Rosie gently. "That makes me sound like a monster."

"Oh, yeah, a monster who uses all her money and time to save ex-service dogs and horses. And wolves. And elephants. You're a poor example of empathy and humanity." Rosie pointed back toward Max's kennel. "Seriously though, you shed a few tears for all of the animals who leave here for shiny new homes, but I don't think I've ever heard you say that you'd miss them."

Lori shrugged. She supposed she hadn't. "Ignore me. I'm just being hormonal," she said and prepared herself for the predictable speech.

Rosie arched her eyebrow. "Don't you–" She narrowed her eyes and tilted her head. "You're just trying to get a rise out of me, aren't you?" She turned her attention to the phone. "Not today, Lori Turner. I won't be wasting my precious feminist words on your ungrateful ears."

Lori grinned. "Can ears be ungrateful?"

Rosie tapped her watch then gestured to the camera set-up. "We're losing the light. Best get your message recorded and out in the world if you want to stop your horse from pooping nuclear waste."

"Okay, okay. Let's do it. And then you can tell me why you really tagged along and risked ruining your beautiful clothes."

Chapter Two

GABE JACKSON BOLTED UPRIGHT in her bed and looked around the room frantically, trying to get her bearings and situate herself in the moment. It took a while before the environment became vaguely familiar; she'd been in this motel for five days. Five days too long, but she didn't have a choice. She blew out a long breath and shook her head before dropping back into the softness of the pillow. Twenty years of service relatively unscathed, and an insider attack ended up being the one thing that occasionally dragged her out of a deep and restful sleep.

"Are you okay?"

Gabe half-turned toward the whispered voice. "I'm fine."

"What time is it?" Solo asked.

Gabe glanced at the neon-blue display on the side table clock. "Nearly 0600." She turned the phone's alarm function off. Her body was so used to getting up early, she didn't really need it, but it gave her the illusion of a normal life. "I have to go for a run."

A low grumble followed her statement. "*Have* to go for a run? You can tell you've only just gotten out of the service."

She pushed the sheets off and swung her legs out of bed. "Twenty years of habits are going to take more than a few weeks to break."

"But we drank so much last night, you're probably still buzzed."

Gabe gave a short chuckle. "You're probably right, but a run will wash it out of my system."

"How come I ended up here instead of going home?"

Gabe laughed again as she recalled the phone conversation she'd overheard at around one a.m. "Because your wife locks you out if you're not back by your curfew."

"Damn it. This is going to cost me a fortune in forgive me flowers, and it's all your fault."

Gabe leaned back and punched her buddy in the gut. "Don't blame me, Solo. I would've been just as happy to have swung by your place and had dinner instead of whatever the hell it was we got up to."

"True, but I wouldn't. I need the occasional night out for the sake of my sanity. You have no idea the effect triplets have on your life."

"And I never want to either."

"What *did* we get up to?" Solo asked, sounding a little sheepish. "I really don't remember."

"You're not likely to after everything you put away." Gabe pulled on her shorts and replaced her tank top with a sports bra and running tee. "But you don't have to worry; I kept all the local talent away from you."

"You mean you kept them all to yourself?" Solo threw a balled-up sock, but Gabe caught it before it hit her head.

"Nope. You and I were talking business, so I was pretty well-behaved actually." Which had been a shame, because there'd been some seriously sexy women at the bar they'd gone to after dinner. She threw the sock back at Solo. "If you get up, I'll drop you at home before I hit the lake."

"Are you sure? It's kind of far to drive for a run," Solo said.

"It's no problem."

"Still, you need to get out of old habits, bud. You're a civilian now, and you don't have a job. You should be sleeping in while you've got the chance."

Gabe dropped into the chair by the desk and pulled her socks and sneakers on. "I'll sleep when I'm old and don't have an empire to build. Wait." She flicked the light on and looked at Solo. "You remember you said you were in, don't you?" Panic flared in Gabe's gut. Solo was the final piece of the financial puzzle.

Her brow furrowed as if she had no idea what Gabe was talking about. "I told you already; I don't really remember anything about last night."

"Don't fuck with me, man. You said Janie had given you the green light. I'm all about the green lights. You can't take it back." Of course, Solo *could* take it back even though they'd made a gentlebutch's agreement, which was as good as a legal document, but their friendship would take a serious hit if she did.

"I'm shitting you. Of course I remember." Solo burst into laughter and jumped out of bed, before she dropped back onto it gingerly, looking particularly pale even for fluorescent motel lighting. "Damn, I'm out of practice. I shouldn't have tried to keep up with you, and we should've given up at midnight."

"Sure thing, Cinders. And I should've driven you home in the pumpkin waiting in the alley behind the bar." Gabe blew out a long breath as she tied her laces tight. She hadn't needed the near heart attack, but it reminded her how much she'd missed Solo's sense of humor over the past few years. She'd missed all of the old buddies she'd recently reconnected with, but Solo had been separated from the military the longest.

Solo pulled on the clothes that she'd dumped on the floor beside the bed before crawling back under the covers. "You're an asshole. Are you going to be an asshole when we're working together again?"

Gabe laughed and nodded. "You wouldn't want it any other way."

"I forgot to tell you that Janie invited you for dinner tomorrow night. You can meet the triplets, and then maybe you'll go easier on me when you realize what I have to go through at home."

"I have no sympathy," Gabe said before heading to the bathroom. "Your wife is beautiful, and thankfully, your kids have gotten her looks instead of yours. You're blessed." She didn't know whether Solo actually *was* blessed by having kids—the thought of trying to raise mini people in this world terrified Gabe.

"Maybe now you're settling here, you can babysit."

Gabe nearly choked on her toothbrush. "You want your kids to live, right? I'm way too stupid to be trusted with the well-being of tiny humans."

"You'll be fine. They're practically unbreakable. I think they're little superhero kids. And besides, it's part of the deal, and I want it written into the contract."

"Not fucking likely," she muttered and washed her mouth out. She was about to run some water through her hair to pull it into some vague style, but when she looked in the mirror, it was in almost the same position as it had been when she styled it last night. The new product that the barber had given her had set hard enough that it looked like she could cut glass with the spikes. It was a bit flashy for an early morning run, but maybe no one would be around to see it.

Gabe walked back into the bedroom and wafted her hand in front of her nose. "Christ, you stink. Open the window."

"That'll be the Buffalo wings; I can't handle spicy anymore." Solo got up to let fresh air into the room.

Gabe grabbed the stuff she needed for her run and motioned toward the door. "Let's go."

Solo took a short pull from the beer on the side table and swished it around her mouth before swallowing it.

"I have gum in the car, nugget head."

"I'm gonna need bleach to clean out my mouth before I go anywhere near Janie."

"I don't doubt it."

Gabe pulled the motel door closed behind them and took a gulp of warm air into her lungs. It was already maybe seventy degrees and would hit eighty by lunch, but it was nothing compared to the sweltering July temperatures she was used to in al-Tanf. By comparison, this felt like autumn.

She and Solo jogged down the metal staircase to the parking lot and got into Gabe's truck.

"I assume this old beater will be the first thing we restore?" Solo asked as she pulled her door closed with a creak loud enough to wake the whole motel.

"You know I'm a sucker for a classic."

"What's under the hood?"

Gabe grinned. "V8 396."

Solo whistled. "Nice."

The engine growled into action on the fourth attempt. "Our shop can't come a minute too soon," she said and pulled out into early morning traffic to head to Edison Park. "I'm desperate to get started on her."

"No doubt. Are you restoring the original color?"

Gabe raised her eyebrows, already knowing where Solo's line of inquiry was going. "What would you do? You're the paint technician."

"I've always liked the sage green, but I'd add the cream detail along the sides and on the cab." Solo nudged Gabe. "Is that your deal-sweetener? I get to choose what color to spray your truck."

"You'd change the red?" she asked, feigning incredulity.

"Red's overdone. Cream and sage are more understate—ah, what am I thinking? I'd forgotten that you don't do understated. How about electric purple in a metallic finish with a gold cab?"

Gabe punched Solo's shoulder hard. "Now *you're* being an asshole." She liked garish colors on cars about as much as Superman liked kryptonite. "Cream and sage sound perfect, bud." She turned onto North Lake Shore Drive and smiled at the view of Lake Michigan on her right. She'd always dreamed of living in Chicago. She liked the combination of big city and nature, but it was her dad's bizarre fascination with gangsters that had first gotten her interested in the city.

"What time is dinner?" Gabe asked. "I've got an appointment at the Sanctuary at three, and I don't know how long that's going to take. It's forty minutes outside the city."

"Around eight, so don't be late. Janie's more of a stickler for punctuality than any of our COs ever were."

Gabe nodded. "I'll be there. I need to thank her for letting you join us on this adventure."

Solo made a disapproving noise. "For your information, Jacko, I didn't need my wife's permission to come in on your crazy plan. I make all my own decisions, especially the ones that involve—"

"Your wife's money? Bullshit. You need Janie's permission for everything but your bodily functions, and that's as it should be. You wouldn't survive without her."

Solo feigned a look of offense for a millisecond before breaking into a belly laugh. "I've been ordered around by all manner of people, but I never enjoyed it like I do with Janie. She always looks so damn hot when she's in full-on feminine power mode."

Gabe had met Janie briefly, and it wasn't a stretch to imagine her in that role. She was a beautiful woman and a high-flying lawyer at a top city firm. "You're a lucky son of a gun. She's way out of your league."

Solo pushed up her shirt sleeves and tugged on her collar. "I still have no idea why she chose me, but I'm damned glad she did. So don't go working your charms on her at dinner."

Gabe gave Solo a hard shove. "Like you need to tell me that. I take the bro honor code just as seriously as my oath to serve my country. Seriously though, I'm so fired up that you're on board. I texted Lightning, RB, and Woodchuck last night; they'll all be here by the end of next week, so I'm going to sign the lease on the four-bedroom house today."

Solo shook her head. "I can't believe you're all bunking together. It'll be just like old times."

"Aw, you can come over any time. You don't have to miss out on all the fun."

"I don't really have time for that. The triplets took their first steps a few months ago, and Tia keeps trying to climb on Griff's back. Once she masters that *and* they start walking instead of stumbling, all hell will break loose."

Gabe didn't try to stifle a laugh at her friend's situation. "Rather you than me. I can't believe you've settled down *and* had kids. I was sure you, me, and the rest of the team would end up in a gay version of *Golden Girls*, still single in our sixties."

The smile on Solo's face expressed her contentment more than a million words ever could. "Me too, buddy. But I got pulled into Janie's tornado, and I haven't touched the ground since." She unwrapped a stick of gum and folded it into her mouth. "Maybe the same thing'll happen to you."

"Yeah, right." Gabe scoffed. "Is that why they call this place the Windy City?"

"Could be. Could be that there's a stunning, long-haired beauty in killer heels and a power suit waiting for you to sweep her off her feet. Especially once we get the shop open." Solo swept her hand across the air, setting the scene. "Her Aston Martin DB12 is going to break down in the middle of the city in rush hour, and you'll drive to her rescue. There'll be sparks—and they won't be from the engine—and she'll hop in your cab so you can tow her to safety. She'll be in love with you before you even get to the shop."

Gabe stopped at a red light and stared at Solo. "Who the hell are you? And what have you done with Hannah Smith? Jesus Christ, it's like you've swallowed a dump truck full of Hallmark movies."

Solo tilted her head from side to side. "Janie does like her romantic comedies, and I've grown to appreciate them. You will too when you fall in love."

"Huh. That's the litmus test, is it? I'll know I'm in love the moment I subscribe to the Hallmark channel."

"You mock, but I'll bet you a hundred bucks that's how it happens."

"The car breaking down or the movie subscription?"

"Both."

"That's gonna be the easiest one hundred dollars I ever make." Gabe pulled away from the light and couldn't stop chuckling. "Man, you've changed. Just know that I don't want you painting hearts and flowers all over my truck when I let you loose on her."

"Hey, I'm not that far gone."

What little traffic there'd been virtually disappeared as they got closer to Edison Park, and they continued to chat about nothing and everything. The three years they'd been apart melted away like the fog dissipating over the lake. Everything Gabe had dreamed about for the eighteen months it had taken to separate from the Army was finally in motion. The Famous Five were reuniting, and the plans they'd always talked about on those long days and nights out on patrol in Syria were coming together. Solo's buy-in was the last chunk of finance in place, but really, Gabe was the final jigsaw piece they'd all been waiting for. Now they'd get to see what their picture was going to look like for real.

And Gabe couldn't wait to get started.

Chapter Three

LORI POLISHED THE EDGE of the glass and set it back on the table before she glanced up at the grandfather clock. She really didn't like when people didn't show up on time. If her visitor was going to be delayed, why hadn't they texted or called to let her know? Unless there'd been an accident on her way here from Chicago and they *couldn't* let her know. She suddenly wished she hadn't entertained the unkind thoughts about not letting her see Max... if she ever arrived.

But she'd assured Toni that she was more than happy to let Sergeant Gabriella Jackson visit her old canine Army buddy. Lori had been running this ranch as a sanctuary for ex-service dogs and horses long enough to know that the bond between a handler and their animal was often very strong, so she wasn't about to deny Ms. Jackson the opportunity to see how Max was doing.

She glanced at the clock again just as she became aware of the sound of a throaty engine and gravel crunching under tires. She leaned over the dining room table to peer through the window and saw a truck that had obviously seen better days roll to a steady stop. Only feeling a little bit like a peeping Tom, she waited to see Ms. Jackson exit from her vehicle. Toni hadn't sent an actual photo of Max's Army friend from where she'd been reporting on a military base, but she had taken the time to describe her in detail. In such technicolor detail, in fact, that Lori had teased Toni about her loyalty to her new girlfriend, Jo. Lori and Toni had discovered early on in their friendship that they shared the same taste in strong, butch women, and Toni had been overly eager to tell her everything she knew about Ms. Jackson. Her zeal to impart all that information was probably due to Toni's belief that Lori should get over the epic failure of her marriage to *the lawyer* and get back on the horse, but on this matter, their opinions were polarized. Lori was nowhere ready to even polish the saddle, let alone strap it to a stallion and jump on for the ride.

But she wasn't dead, and appreciating a fine woman from a safe distance *was* permissible.

Lori shouldn't have doubted her friend's journalistic ability to accurately describe the acute hotness of her temporary colleague. As promised, Ms. Jackson did *not* disappoint. The faded red door of the truck opened, and a deliciously tall drink of water stepped out onto Lori's gravel drive. Boots; tight, tapered jeans; a T-shirt that hugged and accentuated all the important places; and close-cropped hair—not military-cropped but not far off: the kind of hair that felt so sensual when you wrapped your hand around the back of her head. Dark sunglasses completed her outfit and added to her overall rugged sex appeal.

She let out a long, contented sigh, filed away the vision of satisfyingly clichéd near perfection of butchness for later use, and stepped back from the table to go to the door. She paused briefly by the hallway mirror to check her overall appearance; she wasn't on the market, but it didn't hurt to look good on the shelf. Happy with her reflection, she opened the door and stepped out. The pleasant afternoon heat ramped up twenty degrees when Ms. Jackson smiled and took off her shades to reveal beautiful baby blues. Damn the lawyer for breaking her so bad that all she could bear to do was look.

"Lori Turner?" Ms. Jackson asked and held out her hand.

"That's me," she said as coolly as she could manage. It had been too long and not nearly long enough since she'd been around this kind of temptation. "And you're Ms. Gabriella Jackson?"

There was that smile again, only this time just the left side of her lips and cheek joined in, somehow making it an even more appealing gesture.

"Yes, but please call me Gabe. And I'm so sorry I'm late. There was an accident on the I-65. All the lookie-loos slowed down the traffic."

"Would you like to follow me?" Lori asked, appreciating the prompt explanation of her tardiness, but there was no way she was about to start calling her hunky guest Gabe. That was *way* too familiar and way too soon. Ms. Jackson was a visitor. Gabe would be a friend. She gave a mental shrug; another friend wouldn't be so bad, especially one that looked like her. Then she shook the thought away. Toni had said she was just passing through on her way to start a new life, and Lori couldn't remember where. She was sure it wouldn't be Gary, Indiana. Starting a new life here hadn't worked out well for her, and she didn't know why anyone else would choose it.

That wasn't completely true. She was being harsh. The sanctuary had been all kinds of successful since she'd gotten here. She stopped and turned around. "Sorry, I didn't offer you a drink. Would you like some fresh lemonade?"

Ms. Jackson wrinkled her nose. "Maybe after I see Max? Would that be okay? I'm eager to see how he's doing."

"Sure," Lori said and continued along the path to the kennel building.

Ms. Jackson took a couple of long strides to come alongside her. "Toni said you've been rescuing and rehoming ex-service animals for six years."

"That's right." She didn't offer any more information, and technically, Ms. Jackson hadn't asked a question. But she didn't have to be an asshole to maintain her professional distance either. "She said you'd been in the Army for twenty, and you've come out to start a new life." Nope, maybe that was too much. It implied she and Toni had talked about Ms. Jackson's personal life, and that wasn't professional at all. Lori racked her brain to think of how she could backtrack and came up empty, so she stayed silent and hoped Ms. Jackson wouldn't pick that thread.

"Yeah? What else did Toni tell you?"

Lori didn't miss the raspy playfulness in Gabe—dammit—Ms. Jackson's voice. More importantly, what had Toni told her about Lori? "That's about all," she said, affecting a breezy nonchalance she didn't feel. "She did say that you were both injured in the same attack. Is that why you left the Army?" *Oh, Mary, mother of Joseph*. Avoiding the personal didn't include outright questioning about trauma and possible PTSD. What was she thinking? It had been a long time since she'd had to disguise any kind of attraction to a woman, and she was sorely out of practice. She should've just let Beth take this visit; she was the most heterosexual person Lori had ever come across, so she'd be immune to Ms. Jackson's charms. Lord only knew what Toni had revealed about Lori's relationship situation in a misguided attempt to interfere. She could only hope that Toni hadn't taken it upon herself to play Cupid.

"No, that wasn't the reason," Ms. Jackson said. "It was time for me to follow my new dream."

Lori bit back a number of questions begging to be answered. Answers led to more questions, and when they were answered, they inevitably led to more questions, and before she knew it, they'd be getting to know each other better. None of that mattered. Ms. Jackson was here to visit Max and then she'd be leaving to follow her new dream, like she'd just said. "Dreams are important." Duct tape. That's what she needed. A roll of duct tape for her mouth, which apparently had no intention of listening to the logical side of her brain.

"Was this place your dream?"

"Beth!" Lori waved and gestured for her to join them, praying she didn't appear as manic as she felt.

Beth wandered down the path toward them, clearly in no hurry. Lori hadn't noticed she had one of their other charges straining at the leash in the opposite direction. That would make her planned request awkward and obvious.

"Boss?" Beth asked, stopping ten yards in front of them.

Honeycomb sniffed the air but didn't growl, which was a first since they'd taken him in; he didn't take kindly to any new visitors. His unofficial canine seal of approval was another check in Ms. Jackson's boxes—not that Lori was keeping score.

She backtracked on her original reason for calling Beth over. She'd pony up and be an adult instead of a teenager crushing on the hot new student. "How was Max when you fed him?"

Beth's frown was infinitesimal and disappeared as rapidly as it had appeared... Once she'd taken the time to appraise their visitor, Beth smiled widely. Why was everyone Lori knew invested in the ongoing drama of her personal life?

"He was quite engaged actually," Beth said. "I think he's back on track."

"Back on track?" Ms. Jackson glanced between Beth and Lori, concern instantly etched in her expression. "Has he had problems?"

"The Fourth of July fireworks messed with his rehabilitation," Beth said. "He'd been progressing pretty well up to that point. You know, as well as can be expected given the state he came to us in."

Ms. Jackson's concern clearly deepened. "The state he came in? Did he have a bad flight? Did something happen?"

Lori shook her head and placed her hand on Ms. Jackson's arm before quickly retracting the over-familiar gesture. "It was nothing bad, and nothing we weren't expecting. The journey from Syria to Chicago took nearly seventy-two hours, and Max was alone for a lot of that time. It exacerbated his condition a little, but that's something we anticipate for all the dogs that come in from overseas." She smiled, hoping to calm Ms. Jackson's fears. "Beth isn't one to sugarcoat things."

Beth raised her eyebrow, and Lori knew she'd have to endure a full-on interrogation once Ms. Jackson was gone. Which couldn't come soon enough. Sort of.

Honeycomb's attention drifted from the boring assembly of humans, and he pulled in the direction of the stables.

"If there's nothing else, Honeycomb wants to go visit Cash," Beth said, holding him with apparent ease.

She was powerful for her diminutive frame, something she'd demonstrated on the day of her interview by transferring twenty haybales from Lori's truck to the stables ten times faster than Lori had ever managed. They were about the same size, but Beth put her to shame in terms of physicality. She imagined it could be quite intimidating to any man lacking in self-confidence.

Lori shook her head. "No. I just wanted to see how Max had been before I took Ms. Jackson to see him."

Gabe took a half-step forward and held out her hand. "Just Gabe. Ms. Jackson sounds weird."

And now Lori couldn't continue to use her formal name or she would seem weird too. Gabe did sound nice when she said it in her head though, and calling her Ms. Jackson *was* weird. Using *Ms.* just didn't suit her at all.

Beth shook Gabe's hand. "I'm sure Max will be very happy to see you."

Then she headed off to the stables, but not before she'd winked at Lori and wiggled her eyebrows, which was just overkill. Lori got it: Gabe was hot, and everyone knew she was exactly Lori's type. She'd made a problem for herself by being so open about her private life, but everyone who worked here was like family, so the teasing was to be expected. Still, she would avoid Beth's inevitable interrogation by heading to the vet for their weekly medicine supplies after Gabe left.

Lori turned back to Gabe to find her looking amused. Or smug. Of course someone who looked like Gabe would *know* she was catnip to a woman like her...and to anyone, really.

"Honeycomb and Cash—did they come to you with those names?" Gabe asked and smirked slightly.

"Yes and no." Lori gestured to the path and started walking again. "Beth named the horse Cash because he's jet black."

The way Gabe tilted her head slightly indicated she hadn't made the obvious connection. Well, it was obvious to her and Beth anyway. "After Johnny Cash. He always wore black." Lori shrugged, thinking that it sounded silly when she said it out loud. "She's a big fan of old country music, or real country music, as she calls it."

"I like a lot of the country artists from this century," Gabe said. "Like Carrie Underwood. Miranda Lambert. Ashley McBryde. Kacey Musgraves. Kelsea Ballerini."

"Hm, you have good taste," she said. That was a lot of very beautiful women. Very feminine women. She stopped herself from asking if it was just their music she was so enamored with and tried to think of something Max-related to talk about. "Max has gotten himself quite the fanbase since he arrived."

"You mean the kids on their field trips?"

Lori hid her surprise at Gabe's knowledge. Had she done her homework on the Sanctuary, or had Toni told her all about their operation? "Oh no, Max isn't ready to be with the children yet. I meant his TikTok fans."

"Oh, of course. I watched some of your videos."

Gabe smiled a little, and Lori swooned a little more. *Some* videos? Or *all* the videos? If Gabe had her own thirst trap TikTok channel, Lori would be all over it in the privacy of her bedroom. Had Gabe just been interested in where Max was staying? Or had her interest been piqued by Lori? "It's a useful way to secure donations to help with our ongoing costs."

"I saw the link to your website and all the stuff you need every week. It must be crazy hard to keep this place going."

"It has its challenges, that's for sure." Lori stopped at the far end of the kennels. "This is Max," she said, but there was no sign of him. "Oh." Actually, there was his muzzle poking around the corner of his inner sanctum. And then his eyes. And the rest of his head. Lori's heart raced, and she grabbed Gabe's forearm without thinking, excited to see Max venturing out of his safety zone.

The flexing of strong muscle beneath her fingers drew her attention back to Gabe, and she withdrew her hand. "Sorry. I'm just so happy to see Max interested in something on the other side of that little door."

"Definitely no need to apologize," Gabe whispered.

Lori opened the gate slowly and ushered Gabe in, ignoring the husky tone of her response, and closed the gate behind her. Before Lori could give Gabe any instructions, Gabe had already dropped to her knees. "Hey, boy. It's me," she said gently. "Do you remember me?"

Oh, wonderful. An incredibly handsome butch carved out of God's own granite, combined with a gentle heart of gold. The Almighty had sent this woman to torture her, that much was obvious. Lori pulled her gaze away from the wide expanse of Gabe's back and glanced up the run. Max was inching his way out, his whole body shaking with the intensity of him sniffing the air.

"That's right, boy. Come on out," Gabe whispered. She sat down, stretched her legs out in front of her, and held her hands, palm up, on the ground. "You can do it, Max-a-million."

Lori smiled at the same nickname she'd been using and wondered if that's why Max had responded to her better than he had to Beth or anyone else. She crouched down herself and pulled in her breath, not wanting to do anything to spook him.

"Come on, Max-a-million." Gabe eased back against the short brick wall that formed part of Max's run. "Come say hi, old buddy. I want to see how your war wound's doing."

Gabe hadn't asked Lori about the wound, but it had been fully healed before Max had even arrived at the Sanctuary and hadn't been an issue. His mental war wounds were the thing she and the rest of her team had been most worried about.

Max was fully visible and in his run now, and Lori had to tamp down the urge to open the gate and join them. This wasn't her moment; it was theirs. Two war heroes reunited. It was the kind of thing they made movies and wrote books about; who didn't love a human/dog friendship that had survived the trauma of battle? But this was going to be a short-lived reunion, and she couldn't help the stab of sadness at that notion, though she couldn't say with total authority that her emotion was purely for Max and not for selfish reasons. Eye candy like Gabe didn't come along on a regular basis, and even though Lori was in no position mentally or emotionally to delve into anything deeper, having a hunk like her visiting on a weekly basis until Max was ready for a normal civilian life wouldn't hurt.

"Who's my brave boy?" Gabe whispered as Max took a few more tentative steps forward, still sniffing the air like crazy. "You know it's me, Maxi. Trust your nose."

Lori nodded slowly. Gabe had somehow divined exactly what was happening with her canine colleague: he'd been having a crisis of confidence in his instincts. And then it was like a switch flicked in Max's mind, and he quickened his pace until he was almost within touching distance of Gabe. He dropped to his belly and stretched out his neck until his nose touched the middle finger of Gabe's left hand. She didn't move at all, impressing Lori still further, and Lori held her breath for fear that even a loud puff of air might make him bolt back to his kennel area.

"Hey, buddy. Have you missed me as much as I've missed you?"

At Gabe's quiet words, Max stuck out his tongue and ran it along the length of her palm, like the taste of her would confirm her identity. It must've done exactly that because he immediately drew himself closer to Gabe, sitting to attention and as close to her as he could without actually sitting on her. Lori had no doubt that Gabe's thighs would be more than strong enough to take the pressure of all eighty pounds of the pooch, but she suspected that might be a level of affection and familiarity that wasn't encouraged in the Army. Not that she really knew, of course. Almost every dog or horse that had left the Sanctuary had gone to regular civilian homes, and she'd had little contact with actual Government personnel, other than when they dropped the animals off with her.

Still, Lori decided that since Max had shown that he was happy to see Gabe, she should give them some time together. "I'm going back to the house. When you're ready, just make sure you close the gate properly, okay? I'll have the lemonade and some homemade cookies waiting for you."

Gabe glanced across at her briefly and nodded, the joy of the reunion shining through in her grin. "I can stay a while? You're not in a hurry to close up?"

"No hurry, I don't have any plans," she said and backed away quickly to head up the path. For Pete's sake, why tell her that? For the few minutes it had taken Max to emerge from his kennel, Lori had just about managed not to have sexy thoughts about her visitor. Now she was back to oversharing. The fact that she had no plans on a Saturday night, even with friends, tugged at that part of her she'd been valiantly trying to hide away. She hadn't been out with Rosie for about three months since their last night out turned into an unauthorized double date. Lori hadn't forgiven her. Nor did she trust her not to try it again. Which was what Rosie's visit a couple of days ago had been about: a night out with a promise not to push Lori into anyone else's arms.

She got back to the house, pushed the door closed behind her, and rested her head on its stained-glass window. The warmth felt nice, but she pushed away from it at the memory it evoked: the last time she'd done that had been when she closed the door on the lawyer as she left with all of her belongings and half of everything else. Half their tableware, cutlery, even three of the dining table chairs. Lori had glibly suggested they flipped a coin to see who would get to keep the actual table, but the lawyer had pulled up a spreadsheet on her iPad with the costings of every *single* thing they had ever bought together. She'd pointed to the matching sideboard, which apparently was exactly the same price, and suggested that Lori keep that while she took the table. By that time, Lori had lost the will to fight over furniture and simply let the lawyer take whatever she wanted.

She took a deep, cleansing breath and let it out slowly, completing the box breathing her therapist had suggested she try whenever she had these kinds of thoughts. *Chocolate cherry cookies.* Lori headed to her kitchen to bake, something that always cleared her head better than any breathing exercise.

It was two hours later when Lori heard a knock on her front door. She made last-minute adjustments to the freshly baked assortment of cookies on her new dining table before letting Gabe in. Her well-pressed gray marl T-shirt that Lori had admired earlier—though obviously, it was what was underneath that she had actually admired—now looked like Gabe had been rolling around in the muck of Lori's stables.

Gabe tugged at the neck of her tee, having clearly spotted Lori's gaze sweeping over her. "I've got a fresh shirt in the truck if you want me to change before inviting me in."

A ridiculous, and particularly vivid, slow-motion movie of Gabe stripping down so Lori could launder the offending shirt played in her head. "Don't be silly. Come on in... I just won't invite you to sit on my cream couch." She chuckled, and Gabe laughed too. "This way." Lori tried not to swing her hips as she walked to the open-plan dining and living area, and she resisted casting a backward glance to see if Gabe was appreciating the view. "No upholstery for you to get dirty." She pulled out a wooden chair and gestured for Gabe to sit then poured her some lemonade.

Gabe smiled and nodded toward the cookies as she sat. "They smell really good. Did you just bake them for me?"

"No," she said, praying her nose didn't grow an inch or two. "I make a big batch every weekend for the field trip kids. You just got lucky with your timing, that's all."

Gabe's smile twitched and her eyes narrowed slightly for the briefest of moments, perhaps embarrassed at her assumption. Or perhaps not buying Lori's story.

Gabe took a long drink from her glass. "This might be the best lemonade I've ever tasted," she said and wiped her mouth with the back of her hand. "Did you make this yourself too?"

Lori didn't have a quick answer this time. She was too busy watching the trajectory of the errant lemonade drop that had escaped and was about to drip from Gabe's chin onto her chest... where it would travel down that deep V of muscle—

"I bet the kids love drinking this as much as they love coming to see the animals. What's your secret?" Gabe asked, when Lori didn't answer the first question.

"Yes, I make it for the kids. And my secret is years of patience," she said finally and pointed toward the plants lining the deck beyond the double doors. "I planted those six years ago when I first got here. I keep them in pots and bring them indoors during the winter. This is actually only the second year of them bearing fruit." Too much information, Lori thought, but at least it wasn't inappropriate information. She hadn't missed Gabe's smirk when she'd raised her gaze from Gabe's muscular chest to meet her eyes. Since Gabe was just passing through, maybe Lori *could* indulge in a one-night stand. The lawyer might've broken her heart and her spirit and everything else she could break, but Lori still had needs she'd ignored for nearly a year now, and it had only been a few months ago that she'd even started to touch herself again. How the lawyer had managed to get in her head to stop that too was beyond Lori's comprehension.

Gabe inclined her head. "That *is* patient."

Lori widened her eyes. Had she said all that out loud? Nope, Gabe was still talking about her lemon trees. "I have to be."

Gabe took a bite of a chocolate cherry cookie and made a sinfully delightful sigh, the kind Lori could imagine herself making as she slowly stripped Gabe's clothes from her insanely strong-looking body. She mentally kicked herself; she was out of control. It had been a long time since someone had stirred this kind of interest, and she was overreacting—that was all. And after all the hurtful things the lawyer had said about Lori's lack of prowess in bed, she definitely wasn't ready even for a meaningless fling. Best then that she gently encourage Gabe to leave, watch her fine ass walk away, and then run upstairs to bed to take care of herself.

"Thank you for letting me spend so much time with Max," Gabe said, looking serious for the first time since she'd arrived. "I really appreciate you giving me the opportunity to see him."

"You're very welcome." Lori was glad that the conversation had returned to Max; perhaps she could stay focused on the safe topic and stop her mind from wandering around fantasy land with a half-naked Gabe. "It looked like he was very happy to see you."

Gabe took a breath as if she was about to speak then paused. She rubbed her hand over her short hair and seemed to be studying the rest of the room rather than look at Lori. Her sudden change from being completely self-assured to slightly hesitant intrigued and baffled Lori, and she had no idea what could've initiated it. She ran her nails along the intricate pattern of the crystal glass in her hand and waited.

"When Toni told me that she knew of a place that Max could go to instead...instead of the alternative, I can't tell you how relieved I was," Gabe said.

Lori was glad for the break in the extended silence that was almost becoming uncomfortable, but Toni had also told her what the "alternative" had been, and the same anger stirred her again. "I'd hardly call destroying a perfectly healthy dog an alternative."

"You don't have to tell me that." Gabe clenched her jaw. "I'm sorry, I shouldn't have used that word. But Toni... I think I'll love her forever for what she did for Max."

Lori relaxed a little and smiled. "She's a good person."

"What does that make you for running this place? A saint?"

Gabe placed her half-eaten cookie on a side plate and eased back in her chair. "Honestly, what you're doing here is amazing."

Neither she nor the rest of her family ran their sanctuaries for compliments and praise but hearing it occasionally didn't hurt. "Thank you. That's nice of you to say."

"How long do you think it will be before Max is ready to be adopted?"

"That's like asking how long a piece of string is, I'm afraid. He was doing well, but like I said, the Fourth of July celebrations didn't help at all. It could be a couple of months. It could be a year or more." She shrugged. "Why do you ask?"

Gabe did the breath and hair thing again, and it was adorable the second time around. Was there anything sexier than a stronger-than-Hercules woman showing vulnerability?

"I was wondering if you'd mind... I was hoping that you'd let me visit Max again."

"Oh. Are you staying in Chicago for a few days?" With that prospect, Lori's decision not to follow through on her frankly outrageous notion of a one-night stand with Gabe was even more sound.

"A few days?" Gabe frowned then grinned. "Didn't Toni tell you? I'm starting a new business with some old Army buddies, so I'm staying in Chicago for good."

Lori gripped the wooden seat of her chair tight. *Lord help me*.

Chapter Four

GABE DROVE MOST OF the way to Solo's house on autopilot. Between the emotion of her reunion with Max and her instant attraction to the compassionate and philanthropic owner of the Sanctuary, her mind had little space to contemplate anything else. It was good that she'd had the forethought to get flowers and champagne for Janie before going to the Sanctuary, or she would've been late. As it was, she'd been forced to run out on Lori right in the middle of a very promising conversation, and she was sure the fascination had been mutual.

Now that Lori had given Gabe permission to visit Max again, she'd find out in good time. But while patience was clearly one of Lori's virtues, judging by her lemon trees, Gabe had always been one for instant gratification and hated waiting for anything. Still, the possibility of something developing with Lori would make the sixty-mile roundtrip to see Max even more worthwhile.

Solo stood in the doorway as Gabe pulled onto their drive. Gabe double-checked the time to see she was four minutes early, but in army time, that was considered late. Lucky for her, Janie worked on civilian time, so Gabe wouldn't have already irritated one of her new business partners.

She put the truck in park and got out as Solo hurried across to her.

"You're cutting it close, Jackdaw." Solo held out her arm to pull Gabe into a bro hug then pulled back and waved her hand in the general direction of Gabe's torso. "What the hell happened to you?"

Gabe looked down at herself and chuckled. "Max happened.

Don't worry, I've got a clean shirt." She recalled the look of pure desire on Lori's face when Gabe had offered to change her shirt after her time with Max.

"What're you grinning like a maniac for?"

"Am I?" Gabe grabbed her shirt from the back of the truck and quickly changed.

"Jesus, you could've done that inside," Solo said. "You'll have all the bored housewives swarming around you."

Gabe wiggled her eyebrows. "I don't mind some gay-for-you action."

"Then maybe you don't remember the trouble that got you into last time."

Gabe waved Solo away, uninterested in a trip down that particular memory lane. As she retrieved the gifts from the backseat, her watch beeped. "Better get inside; it's twenty-hundred hours, and I don't want to upset your beautiful wife."

Solo led the way back into the house, and Gabe followed her into the dining room where Janie was placing a sizzling dish of something tasty onto a hot plate in the center of the table. Once her hands were free, she came over to Gabe and kissed her cheek before embracing her warmly.

"Welcome to our home, Gabe," Janie said.

"Thank you so much for inviting me." Gabe held out the flowers and champagne. "I'm sorry it's not chilled."

Solo snatched it from her hand. "I'll stick it in the freezer for a half hour."

Janie arched her eyebrow, and Solo ducked her head slightly and smirked. "Normal rules for guests don't apply to Jacko; she's family."

Right on cue, something thudded into Gabe's calves, and she turned around to see a tiny human holding onto a technicolor zebra on wheels just as she backed up and thrust the plastic animal at Gabe again.

"Tia!"

At the sound of Janie's voice, Tia looked up with the perfect hand-in-the-cookie-jar expression before she burst into a fit of giggles. Bringing up her rear were her two identical sisters, though they had far less mischievous expressions. Gabe pegged Tia as the trio's ringleader, and she had to stifle a laugh as she rubbed her calves and made exaggerated noises of extreme pain.

"I'm sorry about that, Gabe," Janie said. "Tia, that wasn't a nice thing to do to your Auntie Gabe."

"Hidey boo," Tia said and giggled some more.

"That doesn't even make sense," Solo said as she scooped her up, though she had to tug a little to pry Tia's vice-like grip from the handles of her walker.

Gabe ran her hand over the top of her head, trying to get a handle on Janie calling her Auntie.

Solo used Tia like a guided missile and pushed her mini feet against Gabe's arm. "Auntie Gabe is made of iron, Tia. You can't hurt her."

Gabe threw her a warning look, but Solo simply laughed and used the kid to kick her again.

"What's wrong, Auntie Gabe? Is miniature me kicking your ass?"

"Hannah."

Gabe smirked at Solo's reaction to her wife's simple reprimand. Gabe didn't have the words to describe her expression, but Solo scuttled off to the kitchen with Tia cradled in one arm and the champagne in her other hand. "Wow, you've got her well trained. Our CO would be impressed; he tried for years to get her to follow orders without questioning them."

Janie looked mildly amused. "Which was probably why she never got promoted."

"Hey now, that's not true. I was a specialist." Solo returned with Tia on her shoulders, still giggling.

Janie pointed to the playpen under the window. "Gather your

troops, honey. I'll finish off the tortillas." She gestured to the table. "Please take a seat, Gabe," she said before she headed back to the kitchen.

"Thank you, ma'am." Gabe pulled out a chair and watched Solo corral each of her children into their little soft prison. "How are you supposed to tell them apart when they're all biological girls as well as being identical? Have you thought of little tattoos?"

"I heard that," Janie said from the kitchen. "Please don't put ideas like that in her head."

Solo's eyes widened, and she put her finger to her lips to shush Gabe. "She has the hearing of a vampire bat," she whispered.

"I heard that too."

Gabe glanced at the three captives. "Seriously though, how do you tell them apart?"

"What makes you think I can? Tattoos sound like a really good option." Solo laughed and wiggled her fingers like she was playing piano. "Janie paints the nails on both big toes. Tia is orange, Chloe is purple, and Luna is green."

Gabe shifted slightly to look at their feet. "They're wearing socks. Can't you paint their thumbs instead?"

"Definitely not." Janie came back into the room, placed a container of tortillas on the table, and took the seat at the head of the table. "The nail polish could be toxic if swallowed, and they're all constantly sticking their fingers into their mouths. But if you look at them again, you'll see they've all got something on in their color too."

"Ah." Now Gabe saw it: Tia's orange pants, Chloe's purple tee, and Luna's green onesie. "Ingenious."

"I can't claim credit, I'm afraid," Janie said. "I saw it on TikTok."

"So it's for more than just thirst traps and making an ass of yourself dancing then?" Gabe spooned some chicken onto her tortilla and inhaled the spicy scent. "This smells so good, by the way."

"Thanks."

Gabe snapped her attention to Solo. "*You* cooked these?"

Solo polished her nails on her shirt and looked smug. "You bet I did. Janie works crazy hours sometimes, especially when she's working a big case. There's only so much takeout you can eat, right?"

Janie ran her fingers across Solo's forearm and squeezed. "And it has nothing to do with you being an amazing wife *when* you put your mind to it?"

Gabe smiled at the gentle show of affection and the way Solo blushed.

"*You're* the amazing wife." Solo took Janie's hand and kissed her knuckles. "You gave birth to our three little miracles." She looked across to Gabe. "Then she went back to kicking ass at work after just four weeks."

"I don't know anything about this kind of stuff, but I'm guessing that the way you're saying it means that most moms take a lot longer?" Gabe took a giant bite of her fajita and nodded approvingly. "Tastes as good as it smells. I'm impressed."

"You got it. The average is twelve weeks—"

"But I'm quickly learning that your wife is anything but average," Gabe said.

"Han told me that you went to visit your old canine colleague at the Sanctuary." Janie smiled and smeared sour cream on her tortilla. "I had no idea that place existed."

So Janie was modest too. She was rapidly becoming one of Gabe's new favorite people. "Me neither until Toni floated it to the CO when he said Max would have to be put down." Gabe clenched her jaw at the memory.

"So how was it?" Solo asked.

Gabe relaxed her jaw and found herself grinning at a series of altogether different and far more pleasant memories. "It was really good."

Solo wagged her finger. "I know that look. It's the woman who runs it, right? Toni said she was pretty."

Gabe nodded. "Lori Turner. She's an interesting woman."

"You dog. You didn't even wait to start rescuing women in broke down cars."

"Explain," Janie said before she sipped her wine.

Solo took Janie's hand. "I told her that she'd find love here, just like I did."

"First, I'm not in love. And second, our meeting wasn't anywhere near as elaborate as the scenario you described." Gabe glanced at Janie, who still looked slightly confused. "Your wife has developed an overactive and unrealistic imagination since she left the Army; she's absolutely convinced that I'll meet the love of my life on a tow-truck job as soon as we open the garage."

Janie's expression changed from confusion to adoration as she nodded and looked at Solo. "She can be the most romantic person I've ever met, *but* that's developed over time, Gabe. Maybe the same thing will happen to you," she said and winked.

Gabe rolled her eyes. "Please, God, not you too."

"You're not open to falling in love?" Janie asked.

"I'm open to most things. I just don't believe in love at first sight or fated love or super-romantic ideals of love." Gabe shrugged. "Honestly, I have no idea if I'll ever find it, but I also can't say that I've been looking. The Army has been my everything almost all my adult life. I haven't had the time or inclination to even think about falling in love."

"If you weren't looking for forever, what were you looking for in the lingerie of all those women?" Solo asked before she shoved half a fajita into her mouth.

Janie sputtered wine back into her glass, and Gabe stifled a laugh. "You might've developed a romantic side, but that clearly hasn't drowned your crass side." She smiled at Janie, who looked marginally mortified. "It's okay, Janie. I'm used to Solo's directness, and it works just fine for me."

"Damn good job," Janie said and tapped Solo's forearm

anyway.

"I wasn't looking for anything at all, Solo," Gabe said. "All of that was a mutually beneficial way of passing time and letting off steam. No one ever took it seriously." She didn't emphasize that point with reference to Solo's similarly prolific performances with all the women she charmed into her bunk. Charmed was probably too strong a word for it. Everyone in the Army had needs, and it was no great hardship to find companionship.

A flash of understanding crossed Solo's expression as she likely realized that she'd led the conversation down a path she wouldn't want Janie to walk. "Okay, so you're not in love. Tell us how Max is."

Gabe pressed her lips together and shook her head. "Physically, he's fine, but his head? Not so good. Lori said he'd been doing well with their rehabilitation process to get him ready for a civilian home, but the Fourth of July celebrations did a number on him and set him back some." It had been like a knife to her heart the way he'd practically crawled out of his kennel and slunk his way closer to her. He'd always been such a confident dog, but it was like someone had reached inside him and pulled every ounce of that out.

"They make special canine ear defenders for exactly that reason. Surely they've got some," Janie said.

"Yep, and he was wearing them. But Max is a special dog—all his senses are superior to the average mutt—and they just didn't work well enough for him." Gabe wrapped another fajita. "They were expensive ones too. Lori said she didn't have enough for every dog so she's trying to get more donations before New Year comes around. She's got a TikTok channel to raise money, and the schools pay a little for their visits, but it sounds like she's got it tough trying to keep that place open."

"And what else?" Solo asked.

"I asked if she'd be okay with me visiting again while they helped him get better."

"And what else?"

"And nothing else. She said she was good with me coming back and thought that it would be a positive thing for Max as long as I committed to going regularly." Like that would be a hardship, seeing Max *and* spending some time with an interesting and intelligent woman. It hadn't been love at first sight—how could it be when she didn't believe in such a thing?—but the sparks could've set the Sanctuary's barns on fire.

"I don't know much about dogs, but that makes sense," Janie said. "If he starts to look forward to your visits and you don't make it, I imagine he'd be sad."

Gabe finished her mouthful of food and nodded. "Exactly. Lori said that would be harmful to his rehabilitation."

"Did you ask about adopting Max when he was ready?" Solo asked.

"Nah, I didn't want to say anything about that when I haven't made a solid decision." Gabe scooped up the last mouthful of guacamole with a tortilla chip.

Solo frowned. "I thought you said that was what you wanted?"

Gabe shook her head. "I said it was a nice idea, but I can't go in blind. It wouldn't be fair on me or Max...or Lori." She thought about all the upheaval and change in her life right now and sighed. If she let it, overwhelm could easily set in. "I just left the Army, I moved into a new home yesterday, and I'm starting a business. I've got a lot going on, and I don't see a dog fitting into that right now, you know?"

Before anyone responded, a blood-curdling scream came from one of the triplets. Gabe looked across to see Chloe, the purple one, throw herself on the soft ground of the playpen, clutching her face. Tia dropped onto her butt and grinned, adopting an angelic face that could've fooled the devil himself. Luna seemed unaffected by the chaos and continued stacking her over-sized building blocks. Janie and Solo were out of their chairs and at the playpen impressively fast.

"Tia. What have you done to your sister?" Janie lifted the screaming tot from the floor to inspect the damage.

"This is my fault." Solo picked Tia out of the playpen and turned to Gabe. "We should've put them to bed like normal, but I wanted you to meet them properly."

"Uh-huh." Gabe took a long drink of her beer because she had nothing else to say. Kids had never been, and likely never would be, that fascinating to her.

"Help me get them upstairs," Janie said, already heading out of the dining room. "I'll get them to sleep, and you can come back down."

"Right behind you." Solo threw Gabe an apologetic look. "Any chance you could grab the last one?"

Gabe laughed but then saw Solo wasn't joking. "Okay, sure." She pushed away from the table and picked Luna up gingerly.

"You don't have to hold her like she's an IED. She's not going to explode, Cracker Jack."

"Are you sure?" Gabe asked.

"Well, her butt might, but you've probably got another shirt in the truck, right?" Solo laughed and headed upstairs.

Gabe held Luna at arm's length; she'd bet money baby poop was a stubborn stink to get out, and she was wearing her last clean tee. Tomorrow was laundry day while she waited for her new bed to be delivered and for RB to arrive. Luna gurgled and bubbles of spit emerged from her mouth. "Don't even think about it. From either end."

She followed Solo to a huge bedroom with three large windows facing out to a lush yard edged with tall trees. The inside frames of each window and the cot beneath them had been painted to match the babies' color code, so it was easy for Gabe to figure out where she was supposed to dump Luna. She placed her down as quickly and gently as possible before backing away to avoid any projectile vomit the kid might aim her way.

"Are you okay there, Gabe?" Janie asked, smiling lightly.

"They don't break that easily, you know?"

"I don't want to find out," she said and moved farther away from the trio of trouble. What was Solo thinking, calling Gabe their auntie? She could be thankful that they hadn't asked her to be a godparent at least.

Janie laughed and shooed her away. "Go back downstairs, you two."

Solo clapped Gabe on the back. "Let's go. I'll show you the deck I built."

Gabe couldn't escape quick enough and happily followed Solo outside. She sat on a cushioned chair while Solo started a fire in the pit even though it was about seventy degrees. Solo regaled her with horror stories of the kids' early months and by their third beer, Gabe just had to ask. "Whose idea was Auntie Gabe?"

Solo chuckled. "I knew that got to you." She took another long pull of her beer. "We hadn't talked about it. I guess that Janie figures you're my family, so that makes you my kids' family too. And hers." She shrugged. "You want something more gender neutral? You wanna be Titi Gabe?"

Gabe shook her head. "It's not that, you idiot. It's just—"

"Just what? You don't want to be part of my family anymore?"

Solo glanced away, and Gabe wasn't sure if she was really hurt or just playing at it. They hadn't spent any solid time together for three years since Solo had left the Army, and Gabe was beginning to realize how much she'd changed, how much they'd both changed. They didn't really know each other anymore.

But Gabe was out now too, and they were starting a business together, so that would change. Their night out had proven how easy it was to slip into familiar patterns, and it had felt like old times. This, though...this was a different environment, and it was going to take some getting used to.

Solo shoved Gabe's shoulder. "Don't leave a bro hanging on a question like that."

"Don't be crazy; it's not that either." She hung her arm around Solo and pulled her into a half-body bro hug. "I think it's just going to take some time for me to adjust, that's all. I've been in the service for twenty years. I don't know why I was expecting to fit back into civilian life so easily." She looked back toward the house and shook her head. "Being here tonight has kind of brought that home."

"It'll be okay, Jackpot. It gets easier, I promise." Solo clinked her bottle to Gabe's. "And when we're all back together at the new garage, it's going to be perfect. All the fun and none of the danger."

"I'll drink to that." In response, the healed injuries on her back tingled and began to itch. She pressed her body into the firm cushioning of the chair and shifted from side to side.

"You're like a bear scratching its ass on a tree. Are you okay?"

Gabe nodded. "Sure. The scars sometimes feel like they're crawling around on my back, you know?"

Solo tilted her head. "Thankfully, I don't, but I can imagine. Everything's okay though, isn't it? You're fit and healthy?"

Gabe laughed. "You worried about your wife's investment?"

"Don't be an ass. I'm serious."

Gabe raised her bottle to the sky. "Thank the heavens, I'm in better shape now than I was in my twenties." She hoped that was going to make the stress of their new business easier to bear. "I was expecting Janie to ask more questions about the garage though. But she seems kind of Zen about the whole thing."

"She doesn't like to talk business at the dinner table," Solo said. "She's kind of old-fashioned that way. Plus, she's already asked all the questions she wanted to, otherwise she wouldn't have drawn up the agreement for us. She knows I want this really bad. The kids have grounded me a little, but I'd been floating since I got out." She shrugged and emptied the last of her beer. "I've had a few jobs, but nothing stuck. When you called to say you were getting out and asked if I was still up for our garage idea, I can't tell you how it made me feel." Solo smiled and looked up at the bright windows of the kids' bedroom. "Janie said I lit up, and she knew immediately that whatever it was, she wanted to help me make it happen."

"I don't know how you got that woman to agree to marry you." Gabe grabbed two more beers from the ice bucket Janie had brought out for them and handed one to Solo.

"I wore her down, I guess." Solo clinked her bottle to Gabe's. "Whatever it was, she's been the best thing that's ever happened to me."

Gabe raised her bottle. "I'll drink to that." As she took that celebratory drink in honor of Solo and Janie's happiness, her thoughts drifted to Lori Turner. A new life, a new business, and a new woman to get to know. Getting out of the Army and away from the only stability she'd known might not be so bad after all.

Chapter Five

LORI LOOKED UP AS Rosie came out of the bathroom stall and approached the sink. "Feeling better, honey?"

Rosie closed her eyes briefly and blew out a long breath. "It might be too soon to be sure, but I don't want to move far from this restroom for a little while longer."

"I don't think I've ever seen you move that fast." Lori pressed her lips together to prevent a childish giggle from emerging. There should be nothing funny about food poisoning, but the way Rosie had rushed to the bathroom as best she could with her knees clamped together was a visual it was impossible not to laugh at.

Rosie splashed water on her face and rinsed out her mouth. "I bet you're glad you changed your mind and had the grilled chicken."

Lori put her hand to her stomach. "So far, so good."

"Okay." Rosie straightened and dabbed at her face with a paper towel. "Let's go sit by the bar and pray that I'm done."

They left the restroom and took the last couple of seats at the end of the bar, close enough for Rosie to rush back should she need to. Lori ordered a mineral water with fresh lime for Rosie and a vodka tonic for herself.

"I'm sorry, Lori. This wasn't the night I had planned," Rosie said after she'd taken a tiny sip of her drink.

"Don't worry about it. I've had a nice time, and it was good to get out again."

"Have I done enough to have my friendship privileges restored?" She smiled, but the uncertainty was clear in her eyes.

Lori placed her hand over Rosie's. "They were never revoked."

Rosie tilted her head slightly. "Mm, then how come we haven't been out together in three months?"

"You know why." She was hoping to avoid this conversation. Up until the clam chowder had worked its evil magic on Rosie's digestive system, they had been having a good time, and Rosie hadn't mentioned fixing Lori up with anyone all night. "But that didn't mean we weren't friends, and it isn't like you haven't been visiting me at the Sanctuary. Have you really been concerned about that?"

"Of course I've been concerned. A few quick lunches while you're at work aren't conducive to a solid friendship." Rosie pouted. "I really thought I'd messed up."

Lori squeezed Rosie's hand. Solid friendships were based on honesty, and Lori hadn't been true to that aspect. "I was mad at you. I just need you to understand that I'm not ready to *think* about dating yet, let alone start doing it."

"I pushed too hard, didn't I?" Rosie asked. "I'm sorry. I hate what the lawyer has done to you, and I want to help you get her out of your system."

"Me too. But that's not something anyone can help me with." Lori finished her drink and ordered another. "I've got to work through this by myself, and I'll be ready when I'm ready. Everyone heals at different speeds, and there's no fixed timeline to mend a broken heart, you know?"

"I wish there was. I feel so helpless." Rosie rolled her eyes. "And I hate that the lawyer is parading around like the cat that got the cream."

With that comment, Lori resisted the desire to throw back her drink and just sipped it instead, though she was glad she'd ordered a double. She had no idea what the lawyer was up to, and honestly, she didn't want to know...unless it was something bad. But that made her feel immature and petty. At thirty-one, she was supposed to be beyond that behavior, wasn't she?

"I'm sorry, I shouldn't have said that," Rosie said. "I'm sure the last thing you want to hear about is her, and you've never been one for gossip."

Lori struggled to control the part of her that wanted to hear all about what the lawyer was up to and who she was up to it with. That self-destructive, masochistic part of her that would like nothing more than to convince her she was never worthy of the lawyer, that part that had always been waiting for the shoe to drop on their relationship—boy, she wished she could quiet that voice. She mostly knew it wasn't true. She mostly knew her own worth. But six years with a narcissistic partner whose self-important ambitions drove their every decision had worn away too many layers of Lori's resilience. And it was going to take time to grow them back.

"Let's talk about something else for a while," Lori said as the silence became awkward, despite the increase in volume as a DJ took to the decks.

"Are you sure we're okay?" Rosie asked. "If there's anything I can do to make up for being a pushy princess, you'd tell me, right?"

Lori smiled and nodded. "Of course I would. Your best friend status is in good shape." It wasn't like there were lots of other candidates lining up for the position anyway. With her time commitment to the Sanctuary, it was just as hard to cultivate and maintain friendships as it had been for a more intimate relationship. And maybe that's where she'd gone wrong with the lawyer; she hadn't given her the attention her ego required. "So how're you feeling? Ready to brave the ride home?"

Rosie took a deep breath and held her stomach. "I don't think so." She gestured toward the restroom. "I'm going to head back in there for a few minutes, and you don't have to follow me this time—unless I don't come back in fifteen minutes. Then you should check to make sure I haven't disappeared down the toilet with the rest of my insides."

"Ew, that's gross."

Rosie grinned. "Not as gross as that horse poop you were poking around in last week. I can't get that out of my mind," she said as she eased off her stool.

The restroom door had only just swung closed when the bartender leaned over the bar. She thumbed toward a tall woman a few stools down. "Casey would like to know if she could buy you a drink."

Lori looked away quickly when the woman raised her glass and gave her the butch nod. She was relatively attractive, but nowhere near Sergeant Gabriella Jackson's standard of cute. Not that Lori should be comparing anyone to Gabe anyway. She shouldn't even be thinking of her in her waking moments. It was enough that she'd been a constant companion in Lori's dreams since last Saturday. "No, thank you. We're leaving as soon as my friend comes back from the bathroom."

The bartender shrugged and left to relay the message. Lori slipped her phone from her clutch and opened TikTok so she had something to amuse herself with while Rosie was absent. She hoped it would serve the dual purpose of reinforcing her disinterest in the woman at the middle of the bar.

No such luck. She felt the woman's presence before she noisily pulled out the adjacent stool and settled beside Lori.

"Your friend can't hold her alcohol, I guess."

Lori closed her eyes briefly and sighed. "She had some bad clam chowder at the restaurant." She made swift and short eye contact to avoid being rude and then continued to flick through to her latest Max video to check the comments.

"Aren't you going to tell me which restaurant, so I know to avoid it?" She put her hand out between Lori's gaze and her phone screen. "My name's Casey. What's yours?"

Lori looked at the woman's hand for a moment, trying to decide what to do. She didn't like to be rude, but she also didn't want to take any steps into this dance. "Sorry, I don't shake hands.

Not with COVID still being around." She registered the woman's fleeting eyeroll. "I work with vulnerable animals, so I have to be extra careful." She sighed inwardly at her own pandering to someone else's issues. She shouldn't have to explain why she did or didn't do anything to a complete stranger. And yet...

Casey gave a throaty laugh and pulled her hand back. "I've heard of vulnerable adults but not animals. How's that work?"

Lori checked the restroom door in her peripheral vision, but it didn't move. Fifteen minutes could seem like a very long time when you were having a conversation you didn't want. "I work with horses and dogs, some of which have had surgery."

"So you're a vet?"

"No." Maybe if she kept her answers shorter, Casey would get the hint and go away. She laughed again, a sound that Lori already found irritating.

"This is like getting blood out of a stone. What do you do if you're not a vet?"

"I run a specialized shelter for ex-service animals." She scrolled down the comments, liking and responding to them, and prayed for Casey to leave her alone. With every question, she pushed a pungent mix of alcohol, stale cigarette smoke, and halitosis in Lori's direction. Casey's breath was looking like it might succeed where Lori's dinner had failed in making Lori nauseous.

"What? Like police dogs?" Casey asked, exhaling a noxious cloud in Lori's direction.

Lori nodded and took a long sip of her drink, inhaling deeply and hoping that the vodka might dull her sense of smell.

"Looks like your friend's gonna be a while. Are you sure I can't buy you a drink?"

"I'm sure. Like I told your bartender friend, we'll be leaving as soon as she comes back."

Casey blew out a long sigh, and Lori had to quell her gag reflex. Lori was tempted to give her gum but didn't want the offer to be misconstrued.

"Maybe your friend could go home, and you could stay."

Lori looked up, no longer able to maintain her polite rebuttal ploy. "My friend isn't feeling well, so I'll be going home with her because that's what good friends do. But even if we weren't leaving, I wouldn't accept a drink from you because I don't want to give you the wrong impression. I'm not interested, okay?"

Casey huffed and pushed off her stool. "No need to be a–"

"Don't," Lori said. "Please don't finish that sentence. I didn't ask you to come over here, and I tried not to be rude. I came out with my friend for a quiet night, and I wasn't looking to hook up with anyone. I'm not being anything other than straightforward with you. Okay?"

The bartender reached over the bar and tugged on Casey's shirt. "Come on, dude. Leave the lady alone. She said she's not interested."

Casey looked at the bartender. "Fine," she said and moved away.

"I'm sorry about that." The bartender wiped the bar around their drinks. "She's harmless enough until she has one too many knockbacks."

Lori raised her eyebrow. "So not harmless then?"

"I guess not." The bartender shrugged and walked away to serve another customer.

Lori rolled her shoulders and moved her head from side to side to relieve the tension that had crept in as that encounter had continued. It had been a while since she'd had to fend off unwanted attention, and she was rusty. She'd been blunt, and that didn't sit well, but neither did overconfident people who didn't take no for an answer. It was probably for the best that Rosie hadn't been there, or she might've gotten out her pepper spray and Casey would've ended up with bloodshot eyes as well as bad breath.

She refocused on her video's comments and saw one had

been posted a few hours ago by SoldierGabe: *I served with this #RealAmericanHero. Max located hundreds of explosive devices and saved thousands of lives.* The comment had garnered a ton of responses and hearts but more importantly, promises of donations. With the vague hope that at least some of those might be real promises and not just for the sake of social media appearances, she switched to the Sanctuary's PayPal account. Her jaw dropped when she saw the amount of money that had come in since she'd last checked early that morning. Their balance had risen by over twenty-five thousand dollars. She refreshed the screen, not quite believing her eyes, but there it was.

Time for a little light stalking. SoldierGabe's profile pic was of a beat-up old truck, but it was too small for Lori to see whether it was the vehicle Gabe had come to the Sanctuary in. And honestly, Lori couldn't remember the color of it, much less anything else. She'd been too focused on the woman who'd stepped out of it. She clicked on SoldierGabe's icon to go into her profile. The info was sparse and didn't give Lori anything of interest. But the posted videos did: Gabe in an Army camp doing bicep curls; Gabe under the hood of some kind of tanky-thing in just a tight T-shirt and her combat pants; Gabe bench-pressing another soldier; Gabe playing fetch with Max. Talk about a thirst trap. Even if Gabe hadn't posted them with that intention, they certainly had that effect on Lori. She *was* dehydrated, but she wouldn't be doing anything about it in the foreseeable future. Just like she'd told Rosie, she had no idea how long her heart would take to heal, and her mind needed plenty of work too.

Tomorrow afternoon, Gabe was making her first visit since Lori had agreed she could see Max regularly. She checked her watch to see how long Rosie had been in the bathroom and whether she should go rescue her. Now Lori wanted to get home so she could bake something more substantial than a few cookies to say thank you to Gabe for her comment. Obviously, she couldn't have known that it might get such an amazing reaction, but Lori still wanted to show her gratitude. That kind of money usually took months to raise, not hours.

She closed PayPal and flicked back to TikTok and saw there were some trolls too, mainly anti-Americans. She deleted them and blocked their accounts. She never engaged with the negative stuff on there. It was too mentally draining and a time suck she didn't need. But twenty-five thousand dollars? She and the Sanctuary definitely needed that.

Her phone vibrated with a message from Rosie.

Can you get us a ride home? I'll be out in a few minutes.

Lori laughed at the poop emoji that she'd once thought was chocolate ice cream before she ordered a Lyft, and then she watched more of Gabe's videos while she waited.

"Ooh, who's that hottie?"

Lori had been so engrossed in TikTok that she hadn't heard Rosie approach. "You remember I told you that Max's handler from the Army was visiting last week?"

"Oh, yeah, I forgot to ask how that went. Sorry." Rosie retook her seat and huddled alongside Lori for a closer look. "SoldierGabe? More like SoldierBabe. Wow, she's...really something."

Lori gave Rosie a sidelong glance. It was clear her friend was desperate to make the obvious comment, but she somehow managed to stay silent. "I know what you're thinking."

Rosie backed away a smidge and held up her hands. "I'm not thinking anything other than I can't wait to get home to put a hot water bottle on my stomach."

"I'm sorry, honey. Are you in a lot of pain?"

Rosie scrunched up her nose. "About as much as you might expect after you've expelled your entire insides. How long until our ride gets here?"

Lori checked her app and saw that the little car making its way to them was only a few blocks away. "Seven minutes. Do you want to wait outside and get some fresh air?"

"Yeah, that'd be great."

They took a final sip of their drinks and headed to the door slowly. Lori pointed to a bench on the sidewalk, and they sat down. Rosie drew in deep lungfuls of the warm night air and blew them out noisily. Lori could feel her practically vibrating with the effort of not saying anything about Gabe being exactly Lori's type and then some. The lawyer had been butch, but she was small fry compared to Gabe—literally. Gabe was about six inches taller and had a *lot* more muscle. Although that wasn't saying much since the lawyer had virtually none. Lori found herself *wanting* to talk to Rosie about Gabe, which wasn't a good idea because she'd get overexcited and want them to hook up.

"She's coming to the Sanctuary tomorrow to see Max again," Lori said as innocently as she could.

Rosie's head snapped up, and she looked like she might explode with all the questions she was holding in. "I thought she was just passing through."

"So did I." Lori ran her thumb across the screen of her phone as the videos she'd just watched played over and over in her mind. *Deep, deep sigh*.

"But?" Rosie said, her voice raising an octave.

"Turns out that she's settling in Chicago and opening her own garage with a few of her ex-Army friends. Auto repairs and custom spray jobs, that sort of thing."

Rosie turned slightly to face Lori. "And she wants to see Max..."

Or you, was Rosie's unvoiced question. They might have only been friends since Lori moved to Gary seven years ago, but she knew Rosie almost as well as she'd known any lover. "That's right," she said. Talking about how insanely attractive Gabe was seemed hypocritical after their earlier conversation, but it was only metaphorical. She had no intention of acting on it. She just couldn't. She was still gluing her heart back together and couldn't contemplate putting it in someone else's hands ever again.

"And you're letting her?"

"Why wouldn't I?" Lori asked, as much to convince herself that it was for Max as well as Rosie. "It'll be good for Max's rehabilitation. He perked up a lot after her visit last Saturday, and he stayed buoyant for a few days after too. I agreed that she could come as long as she came at least once a week and stayed for two hours minimum. Then he'll have something to really look forward to, you see?"

"I do see."

Lori would've had to be deaf not to hear the amusement in Rosie's voice. "And if she couldn't commit to that, then I wouldn't have agreed to her visiting at all."

"Of course not."

A car pulled up curbside with the ubiquitous Lyft sign in the bottom corner of its windshield, much to Lori's relief. It was killing her not to share her true feelings with Rosie, but she didn't want to encourage hope where there was none. She helped Rosie to her feet, and they got in the vehicle. "We'll get you settled at home first and then I'll get another ride."

"You're such a great friend," Rosie said. "I'm sorry again that I nearly messed that up with my match-making efforts."

She cuddled closer, and Lori put her arm around her. "I am a great friend, but you can stop saying sorry. I've accepted your apology, so let's just move on, okay?"

"I can say sorry again for tonight being such a bust though, right?"

Lori stroked Rosie's hair gently and shook her head. "Since it wasn't your fault, no, you can't."

"I'll make it up to you next time," Rosie said.

"There's no need, honestly." Lori hugged her gently. She knew where Rosie's concerns were coming from; childhood experiences could be incredibly difficult to shake as an adult. "I'm not going anywhere," she said, hoping that would be enough for Rosie to really hear her.

"Promise?" Rosie whispered.

"I promise." She continued to run her fingers through Rosie's hair, and she heard the change in her breathing as Rosie drifted to sleep. The exchange reminded Lori that she hadn't called her own family this week and that she needed to check in. She'd been lucky, a lot luckier than Rosie, with her upbringing. It had been far from normal, but there had never been any shortage of love. And since that was her only source of love right now, she couldn't afford to neglect it.

Chapter Six

MAX WALKED BESIDE GABE just as perfectly as he had when they'd been on the job together. When he was out like this, it was hard to reconcile him with the anxious dog who'd emerged from his kennel slowly again an hour ago. He'd come out a little quicker than he had last week, unless she was just imagining that because she wanted it to be true.

She glanced at Lori, who'd taken some convincing to accompany her. She was a beautiful woman, and Gabe wanted to get to know her better. Spending time with Solo and her family over the past week was beginning to show her that settling down after a lifetime of Army service really was possible, and really, what was the harm in trying now that she'd decided to put down roots in Chicago? Even if it didn't work out, a broken heart couldn't be as painful as the injuries and scars she'd gotten from the insider attack. Although RB, Woodchuck, and Lightning were doing their best to prove freedom was the perfect way of living with their constant drinking, gaming, and dogging around.

"This really is a beautiful place, Lori, but it's so big. How do you manage it all?"

Lori smiled brightly. "With a lot of help and a lot of passion."

"I've only seen Beth around. You've got more people, right?"

"Of course. But the weekends are quieter, especially Sundays, because we don't have the field trips," she glanced up at Gabe, "or any visitors...usually."

So she'd made an exception for Gabe. That had to be a good sign. "So I'm special?"

Lori laughed lightly. "*Max* is special, and you said you were going to be busy with your repair shop every other day. You didn't give me much choice, did you?"

Gabe smiled inwardly; she'd always been a big fan of feisty femmes.

"And since then, there's the not so small matter of you raising nearly $30,000 for this place."

"What?" Gabe stopped in her tracks, and Max immediately sat beside her, sinking to his haunches. "What do you mean?"

"You commented on one of Max's videos on our TikTok." Lori pulled out her phone and flicked around the screen for a moment before holding it up to Gabe. "Look at the likes and views; it's our most popular video ever, and we've gone viral a few times."

Gabe peered at the screen. "Is that over three *million* views? And two hundred thousand comments?"

Lori pocketed her phone and nodded. "That's not the best thing about it though. After you told everyone what Max had done for his country, a ton of people said they'd donate to the Sanctuary. After that, nearly $20,000 came in within a few hours with notes that referenced that video. It's closer to $30,000 today." She touched Gabe's arm briefly then began to walk again. "So I suppose you are special now."

A warm glow of pride bubbled up at the knowledge of how much she'd been able to help, and so easily. Being able to help Max felt pretty damn good too, and it must have scored some points—if Lori was keeping count. "That's great. Do I get a gold star?"

Lori wrinkled her brow. "No, but you do get a not fully decorated cake. I was going to finish icing it while you and Max were on this walk, but you kind of insisted that I come along."

"Homemade cake?" Gabe pressed her hand to her stomach. "If you make something every time I visit, I'm going to get soft real quick." She bit back a smile when Lori looked her up and down then blushed. Gabe could get on board with impure thoughts if that's what had just flashed through Lori's mind.

"Don't all beefcakes get cheat days? And I use a mix of sugar and sweetener, so they're not quite as bad for you."

Gabe laughed and flexed her bicep. "I don't think I've ever been called a beefcake before."

Lori prodded Gabe's upper arm. "With baseballs for biceps, I find that hard to believe."

"As long as you understand I've got some brains to go with the brawn, I won't be offended." Although Toni had told Gabe that Lori was gay, she hadn't gone into detail about the kind of women Lori liked. And while Lori seemed to be impressed with Gabe's appearance, Gabe had no idea whether that translated into a passing fling or something more substantial. She wanted to make it clear she was more than just a muscle head.

"I'm sure you do." Lori opened a gate between a long line of trees. "Otherwise you wouldn't be able to run a successful business."

Gabe led Max through the gate and closed it behind them. "It's not successful yet."

"But I'm sure it will be. An all-women auto repair garage will be a big draw for a lot of people, I think. Especially women."

"That's what we're hoping for." Gabe paused as they got to the end of the small walkway, and it opened up into another huge field with a large driveway joining the main road up to Lori's house. "What do you use that building for?"

Lori made a quiet noise that Gabe couldn't decipher.

"Nothing," she said and turned right to walk along the tree line away from the imposing structure.

"Seems like a waste. Can I take a look? If the garage does well, we might need a place to store cars before we work on them, and that place could be perfect." Gabe couldn't read Lori's expression, and she didn't respond immediately. Clearly, something bothered her about the place.

But then she smiled and gestured toward it. "Sure. I bet you can sniff the motor oil from here, can't you?"

Gabe fell in step with her again, and Max walked alongside them both. "What do you mean? Is it where your gardener keeps their ride-on and tractor?"

"Not exactly."

When they got to the building, Lori lifted the latch on the side door and tugged it, but it didn't budge.

"Can I help?" Gabe asked, cautious not to swoop in and assume Lori would want assistance.

"Please." Lori stepped aside and held out her hand. "Let me hold Max."

She gave Lori his lead and pulled open the door with relative ease. When she turned back, she caught Lori's gaze on her ass. Yep, Gabe was definitely right about a physical attraction.

"You could've made it look a little less easy," Lori said. She went in and flipped the light switch then stepped back outside. "There you go."

"You're not going in?"

Lori shook her head, and her jaw clenched slightly. "I don't need to; I know what's in there. I'll wait out here with Max."

"Okay." There was a story to go with the unloved building, but Lori obviously wasn't ready to share. Maybe she never would be. Gabe stepped inside and couldn't believe what she saw. Someone had clearly spent a lot of time and money setting it up as a garage, but it didn't look like it had been used at all. Along the length of one wall was a steel peg board with every tool anyone could need hung on it.

Her gaze moved to the center of the room, where a vehicle of some sort sat beneath a dusty cover. "Is it okay to look under the tarp?" she called out.

"If you want."

Gabe grabbed a handful of the tarp from the front and lifted it slowly, building the anticipation for herself. "Jesus Christ." She recognized the distinct shape of the bumper wings and folded back the tarp to get a better look. "No fucking way." She stepped back and shook her head. What the hell was the story here? Sure, it was in need of complete restoration, but a Ford Brewster town car? Sitting here, rusting and unloved. She pulled out her phone and took a photo of the front of the car's grill to show Lightning and the others.

Gabe let the tarp fall again and did a complete three-sixty to take in her surroundings. Someone had some serious plans, but they'd never followed through. She didn't want to make assumptions, but she didn't think this was Lori's abandoned project. But she could be very wrong about that.

God though, what a waste. Judging by the undisturbed dust, no one had been in here for ages. Maybe Lori would consider selling it, although all Gabe's capital was wrapped up in the garage. Then again, maybe she'd let Gabe buy it in a couple of years when she'd made some money. She wouldn't want to keep it—she'd always been a truck lover—but just working on it would be amazing. And when they'd finished the restoration, it'd be worth a lot of money. "That's it!"

Gabe rushed out of the building with an idea she was sure Lori would be interested in. "We could bring her back to life," she said when she got outside. "Restore the engine. Source some white wall tires. Give her a brand-new paint job—Solo is an artist with a spray can. We'd do all the labor for free, and we could get your TikTok people to fund all the parts. Then you could auction her off to raise money for the Sanctuary." Gabe stopped her rambling when she finally registered Lori looking less than enthusiastic.

"It's a wonderful offer, Gabe, it really is. But it's too much. I know how much work it would be, and I can't accept it because I can't offer you anything in return."

Gabe grabbed the bait and wiggled her eyebrows. "Are you sure about that?"

Lori bit her bottom lip and shook her head. "I definitely can't offer you *that*."

"Oh..." Damn it. She'd misread the signs somehow and

mistaken Lori's friendliness and interest as something more than just professional. She sidestepped slightly to put a little distance between them. "I'm sorry. I didn't mean to imply—"

Lori put her hand on Gabe's forearm, and her touch felt electric. Gabe didn't pull away, though the intensity of her reaction surprised her. Maybe it had just been too long since she'd blown off some sexual steam.

"It's okay." Lori removed her hand and ran it along the length of her ponytail. "It's my fault."

"Whoa, no, don't say that." Gabe resisted the temptation to reach out to her. "I'm to blame. You were just being friendly, and I got carried away because you're so damned cute. I'm sorry. I'm an ass. Can we hit reset and just ignore what I said? I need to keep visiting my guy, and I don't want to mess that up." She stopped rambling and waited for something—anything—from Lori.

"Take a breath." Lori put the latch across the door and offered Max's leash to Gabe. "Let's keep walking and talking. It's complicated."

"Okay." Gabe ruffled the fur on Max's head and avoided meeting Lori's eyes. It wasn't like she hadn't suffered her fair share of rejections, and they were still painful in their own way. And maybe it was for the best. With resettling in a new city, getting used to civilian life again, *and* starting a business, Gabe didn't need anything else to complicate her existence.

"Did Toni tell you much about my personal life?" Lori asked after they'd walked in silence for fifty yards or so.

"No, not really." She didn't want to cause friction between the two of them, and all Toni had told her was that Lori was a lesbian. Some people were protective of that kind of information and didn't want to be outed without their express permission. Looking the way Gabe did, it had never really been a consideration for her.

"I'm not usually one for sharing my private life with a virtual stranger. But I don't want you to get the wrong idea, so I'll give you some idea of what's going on with me right now." Lori tucked her hands under her armpits and led them around the field toward a small valley.

Gabe stayed silent and simply nodded. Her mouth had already gotten her into trouble, and she wasn't about to make the situation worse by adding anything else. If Lori had simply walked away, that might've been a better resolution. She looked down at Max and noticed his ears had gone down. So he was feeling the tension too, Gabe thought. She gave him a cuddle to reassure him everything was okay.

"I got divorced last year." Lori made the sentence sound like she'd committed murder.

"I don't need to hear any more. You're not ready to get back in the field, and that makes perfect sense," Gabe said.

Lori glanced at her and smiled, relief clear in her expression. "I appreciate that, thank you. But I still need to apologize for giving you signals that I shouldn't have." She tugged at her ponytail again then shoved her hands in her pockets.

Gabe relaxed a little, glad that her interpretation of Lori's behavior hadn't been completely wrong.

"I don't get away from the Sanctuary much, so I don't see many people other than my team and the vet if something's wrong. When you showed up last week, looking..." Lori pulled her hand from her pocket and waved it in Gabe's direction, "like that, I was knocked off my feet."

Gabe clenched her jaw tight to stop herself from grinning widely. Good to know that she could still attract a beautiful woman outside the service.

"My reaction caught me by surprise," Lori said, "and I couldn't seem to stop myself from flirting with you." She sighed deeply. "So you see, you're not to blame at all."

Gabe tilted her head slightly and smirked. "Well, I am to blame a little bit."

Lori frowned. "How so?"

Gabe ran her fingers through her hair. "Because I'm irresistible."

The invisible tension dissipated as they both laughed.

"Irresistible but not at all humble," Lori said.

"I guess not." Gabe noticed Max was panting hard, so she stopped for a moment under the shade of a silver maple tree. She unclipped the water bottle from her backpack and poured some into a collapsible bowl. Max sniffed at it but didn't drink.

Lori got to her knees and looked into Max's eyes. "He might be stressed rather than thirsty. We should probably head back."

"Why would he be stressed?" Gabe dropped down beside him and rubbed the back of his neck the way he used to like it.

"He hasn't been this far from his kennel base since he got here. We've been walking him a lot but always keep him relatively close to his new home. It's all about showing him he's in a stable environment, so he can relax." She looked at Gabe and shook her head. "I'm sorry. I thought he might be ready to go a little farther away with you by his side."

"Okay." Weight settled in Gabe's stomach as she looked at Max, with his ears fully down now and the whites of his eyes showing. In the back of her mind, the horror movie of the insider attack played without her permission, and she tried to blink away the images. She'd been injured in the same blast as Max and while she'd suffered no lasting effects, the fact that Max had tore Gabe apart. When she'd signed up for the Army, she'd known the risks, but her canine buddy didn't. He'd been bred especially for the job, and he'd had no choice.

"Are you okay?"

Gabe refocused, slowly becoming aware of Lori's soft touch on her forearm. "Yeah. I'm fine." She emptied Max's bowl and tucked it back in her pack before she stood.

"Bad memories?" Lori got to her feet and patted Max's head.

"We all have them," Gabe said. The way Lori took a step back made her regret her tone immediately.

"I'm sorry. I shouldn't have pushed."

Gabe smiled, appreciating Lori's emotional awareness. "We're apologizing to each other an awful lot today."

Lori's returning smile was stunning, and Gabe wondered what kind of an idiot let a woman like her get away. She didn't know the full story, but it was clear that Lori was on the receiving end of the hurting.

"I don't know if that's a good thing or a bad thing," Lori said.

Max jumped up and tugged on his leash in the direction of his kennel building.

"I think it's a good thing." Gabe followed Max's lead and didn't pull him back. "You wouldn't want to get to know someone better if they didn't give a damn about your feelings, would you?"

"I don't suppose I would."

"So it'd be okay if I wanted to get to know you better—with no pressure," Gabe said quickly. "As a friend."

"I could use a friend. I lost all but one in the divorce." Lori chuckled, and Gabe joined her. "Along with half of *everything* else."

Gabe gestured back toward the building with the old Brewster waiting in it, unloved and in need of attention. The parallel to Lori wasn't lost on her. "Except the amazing car and workshop."

Lori's expression darkened. "That's part of a much longer story."

"Is it one you'd tell a friend?" Gabe asked gently.

"A friend I know well, yes."

Gabe opened the gate they'd come through earlier and waited for Lori to go through before closing it behind them. "Then maybe you could walk with us every week and get to know me. I'd like to hear that story, and maybe I could change your mind about me and the guys restoring it for you to raise funds."

Lori opened her mouth, probably to protest.

"It's okay," Gabe said. "No pressure with that either. Just promise me you'll think about it. And I promise you I don't need anything in return."

Lori looked at Gabe and raised her eyebrows. "I think you're pushing our fledgling friendship by assuming we can make promises this early."

Gabe shrugged, recognizing Lori's playfulness. It was another thing to like about her. "Okay, you don't have to promise me anything. But I'm happy to promise my new friend that I'm being serious about the offer. It'd be a pleasure to restore a vehicle like that, and I *can* also promise you that the guys would feel the same way. We could make use of those tools too if you wanted to donate them to our cause." Gabe grinned, but she was only half-joking. Extra tools always came in handy.

Lori didn't look convinced, but she nodded anyway. Gabe didn't push, and they walked on in silence for a while. Lori clearly wasn't comfortable talking about her personal life and had probably shared more than she'd really wanted to considering that it was only the second time they'd met. Even so, Gabe knew that she wanted more. She couldn't honestly say that she'd ever spent time with someone she was attracted to without acting on it, so this friendship was going to be an interesting one that would test her self-control.

She glanced across at Lori, watched the way her long, wavy ponytail bounced down her back, the way the green hoody she was wearing made her eyes pop, saw how that same top molded around her breasts perfectly, and how the curves of her body flowed like the roll of a gentle wave, making Gabe desperate to run her hands along them, to hold her tight against her as they explored a friendship with very nice benefits.

She drew in a long breath and shook the thoughts away.

This friendship wasn't going to be *interesting*. It was going to be torture.

Chapter Seven

ELLERY PRESSED ON CASH'S abdominal area, and the horse groaned.

"I don't think I'll ever get used to how similar that sounds to a human," Lori said and continued to stroke his neck.

"If only they could talk like one. That would make my job a lot easier." Ellery moved around to Cash's other side and repeated the pressure, which elicited more moaning from the horse.

Lori smiled. "You're amazing with them. It's like you're speaking their language."

Ellery looked up at Lori. "That's kind of you to say, but Cash is being tight-lipped about what's bothering him. He's exhibiting signs of colic, but I'm not sure that's all there is to it. The antibiotics we gave him last week don't seem to have made much difference."

She went to her bag and came back with a stethoscope, then she pressed the acoustic cup just behind Cash's left elbow and listened intently. When Ellery shook her head, Lori's heart raced. She'd worked with animals all her life but losing one never got easier.

"What's going on, Ellery?" She was pretty sure she hadn't managed to keep the fear from her voice. Beth would be destroyed if there was anything seriously wrong with Cash.

Beth rounded the corner of the stable block before Ellery responded to Lori's question, and the concern in her expression was clear.

"You must've been early." Beth pressed her forehead to his muzzle, and Cash made a snorting snore. She stroked his forelock and whispered, "It's okay, boy. Everything's going to be okay."

Ellery returned the stethoscope to her bag and pulled on a pair of latex gloves. Lori concentrated on trying to stay calm and relaxed so she didn't spook Cash—or Beth—while Ellery performed a rectal exam. And it wasn't something she liked to watch anyway.

"His small intestine is distended." Ellery came back around and paused at Beth's side. "May I?" After Beth stepped aside, she stood in front of Cash, bending slightly to stare at his muzzle. "How has his temperament been lately?"

"I think he's been about the same, but Beth has been with him the most this week."

Beth's head snapped up, and she looked at Lori. "What?"

"Ellery asked how Cash has been all week. Have you noticed anything different about him?" She stepped closer to Beth and rubbed her arm gently. In the two years Beth had been working at the Sanctuary, they'd lost a few animals, and each one hit Beth harder than the one before. Lori sometimes wondered how many it might take before it became too much for Beth to handle.

Beth leaned into Lori's touch. "He's been a lot quieter than usual. And he didn't want to come out for any of the school tours."

"Mm." Ellery nodded. "You said you had a fresh stool sample?"

"Over there." Lori pointed to the Blue Bell ice cream tub on the tack table.

"Rocky Road? I'm hoping not," Ellery said and opened the container.

Lori pinched her nostrils when a waft of the poop's scent filled the air.

Ellery dipped her hand into the tub and messed around in there like she was mixing cake batter. "There's a lot of mucus... Is he eating well?"

Beth shook her head. "Maybe about half of what he normally puts away."

Lori noticed an escaped tear and offered Beth a tissue.

"What are we looking at, Ellery?" she asked again, hoping that the reason Ellery hadn't answered the first time was just because she needed more information.

"I think it might be proximal enteritis," she said, peeling off her latex gloves. "My next step will be nasogastric intubation to remove some fluid. Depending on what comes out, we'll have to do that every couple of hours. And I want to run some tests: blood count, chemistry profile, and an ultrasonography." Ellery closed her bag and looked at them both, her expression serious. "I'll need to get some fluids inside him too. Are you good to bring him to my clinic, or do you want me to call Mark?"

"I'll bring him," Beth said and put her arms around Cash's neck. "He'll be more relaxed that way."

Ellery looked to Lori for her confirmation, and she nodded. Drugs, tests, possible surgery... It was beginning to sound like it would warrant a funding drive, *but* Gabe Jackson had already inadvertently run one for them, which vastly reduced the ongoing pressure right now. She thought again about Gabe's offer to restore the lawyer's old project. There was no good reason not to let her do it. Lori was running a non-profit, and generous offers like that couldn't be declined. And it wasn't about being beholden to Gabe; they'd hardly spent any time together, but she seemed like good people. That said, the lawyer had seemed like good people too when she helped Lori secure this property. When she really thought about it, Lori was most concerned that it might mean she'd see Gabe even more, and that felt like self-flagellation.

"Lori?"

"Yes? Sorry, I was just thinking—"

"About how we're going to afford this?" Beth's eyes were wide, like a startled rabbit.

Of course. Beth hadn't been at work since Friday, so Lori hadn't had a chance to tell her about the money Gabe's comment had raised. "No. Not that."

Beth frowned. "We always have to think about that."

Lori smiled. "I have some news to share, but we'll talk later. Get the horse trailer so we can get Cash off to Ellery's." She tapped the radio on her belt. "And call Fran to help; I think she's over with the dogs at the moment."

Beth looked considerably brighter, and she scampered out of the stables, calling Fran as she moved.

"You have good news?" Ellery asked.

Lori turned back to her and grinned. "I have great news," she said and regaled the amazing story to Ellery as they prepared Cash for transport.

"That's wonderful, Lori. I don't suppose Gabe would be interested in somehow fixing my financial worries too, do you?"

Lori dropped onto a hay bale and patted the space beside her. "What's going on with you?"

Ellery sighed deeply and joined Lori. "My landlord is raising the rent on my building again. It seems that everyone is trying to scrape back every cent that they lost during COVID. He owns a lot of real estate, but over seventy percent of his tenants had to close down during the pandemic, and they've been unable to reopen. He's suing most of them for breach of contract, but I think they've all filed for bankruptcy, and he knows he probably won't get anything from them." She pulled out a piece of hay and began to twirl it. "So his next move is to squeeze the businesses he has left—"

"Until they're dry? But then he'll end with no rental income at all. Seems short-sighted."

"I'm not sure he has any other choice," Ellery said. "Which means I have no choice but to raise my fees too." She shook her head. "But like you usually are, all my clients are struggling to afford to keep their animals healthy. I'm worried that if I increase my prices too much, people will stop bringing their animals to me, and then they'll suffer. And lots of them might die too."

Lori put her arm around Ellery's shoulder and was about to

say something she hoped would be comforting when she was struck by an idea that might work out well for them both. "The building that you're in at the moment, is it too big, too small, or the perfect size?"

Ellery shrugged. "It works really well. I could always use more space, but it's been fine for over ten years."

"Do you want to stay where you are, or would you consider moving somewhere a little out of town?" Lori asked.

"You're being *very* cryptic." Ellery narrowed her eyes. "I like where I am because it *is* in town, and that makes it easy for people to get to me, but it's not so easy for clients like you. I don't know though; everyone is raising rents, and I don't have the capital to buy my own building, so I don't have much choice." She smiled ruefully. "Like I said, I need a Sergeant Gabe Jackson too."

"Well, Gabe might have inadvertently helped you by giving me a kick in the pants. I've got a large brick building on the far east side of the property, and nothing much has ever been made of its potential. Right now, I'm not using it for anything other than storage." She was storing more than just physical things; there were memories too. "And Gabe has offered to help with that particular problem. It's time I did something with it, and that something could be that you move in and make it your new place of business."

Ellery shifted to face Lori. "Are you talking about the large two-story brick building half a mile down the main road up to your house?"

"I am," she said, getting more excited with the idea as it continued to form in her mind. "It's around 3,000 square feet." The exact measurement eluded her for now. She'd put it out of her mind after all the arguments that building had caused. "I'm sure it's at least the same size as your current clinic. All the plumbing and utilities are already in place. You'd probably want to make different sized rooms, but that's just some drywalling work."

It was clear from Ellery's expression that she could see the potential too. "I pay my landlord $90,000 a year for 3,000 square feet, but I was only paying $78k before COVID hit. Would you be willing to split the difference and lease the building for $84,000?"

"How much would you say the Sanctuary paid you in fees and treatments last financial year?" Lori asked, though she was running through her own numbers in her head.

Ellery laughed. "I filed my taxes over four months ago, Lori. You can't honestly expect me to remember that."

"Fair enough, but I think it was easily fifty thousand."

Ellery cocked her head and wrinkled her nose. "That sounds feasible, but I honestly couldn't say."

"What if you took care of all the utilities and fees, paid $2,000 a month to lease the building, and treated our animals free of charge? And you could probably class your time as a charitable donation, which would be tax deductible. We could see how it balanced out at the end of the year and reassess if we need to shift anything either way."

"Wow," Ellery said. "How long have you been sitting on this?"

"I haven't. It's only just occurred to me." Lori held up her hands. "Gabe and I were walking the grounds with Max on Sunday, and she got very excited about the rusty old car in there." She swallowed, trying to push away all the building's underlying nonsense and focus on what good she could do in the here and now. She could parse out the bad stuff in the privacy of her house at night. And much later. "If I let Gabe undertake that project, then she'll pick up the car, and the building will be empty because she can take all the tools too."

Ellery shook her head slowly. "This is a lot to think about. And it's an incredibly generous and selfless offer—"

"Not totally selfless; my dogs and horses get a great deal too."

"Still," Ellery said, "it's hard to process. You could make a lot more money for the Sanctuary if you put the property on the commercial market. Why wouldn't you? I'm just your vet."

Lori took Ellery's hand. "You're not just my vet; you're my friend. And you've gone above and beyond for our animals for years, giving us extra time and cutting bills whenever you could. And I'll never forget that you gave me eight months grace on Cash's treatment when he first got here, *and* you built that amazing body sling and pool contraption so he could exercise without bearing weight or getting body sores."

Ellery's cheeks pinked, and she glanced away. "I don't think Beth would've let me back on the property if I hadn't done something drastic to help him."

"Exactly. You care deeply, as much as we do, and that matters more than a few extra dollars." Lori hoped her mom would agree when she talked to her about the plan later. "Look, I'll run it past my mom—she's the financial whizz—and you talk to your lawyer. Okay?"

The diesel engine of their horse trailer rumbled closer, and Lori stood. She went over to the storage box at the rear of the stable and pulled out some travel boots for Cash. "Beth won't be impressed that we've been chatting instead of getting him ready to go." She put the boots on the floor beside Cash and began strapping one on.

"I'll call Mark and tell him to get ready to receive him," Ellery said.

Lori had only gotten halfway through the process when she felt a hand on her shoulder.

"I can do this," Beth said.

Lori looked up and saw the distress in her eyes. "Okay, thank you," she said and rejoined Ellery on the hay bale.

Ellery hung up on her call and pocketed her phone. "He's getting prepared."

As caring as Ellery was, she was always careful not to give an early prognosis or indication of the outcome unless she was one hundred percent sure. Lori had read a recent article in *The Horse* about the survival rates and complications which could arise if the horse wasn't successfully treated. Right now, she didn't want to think about the worst-case scenario for Cash, so she kept the burning question off her lips and simmering in the background.

"Do you have to go?" Lori asked when Ellery checked the time.

"Not yet. I was just seeing if I had enough time for you to tell me about Gabe's project." Ellery tapped her watch. "I do."

Ellery, like most of Lori's close circle, knew about the lawyer and their acrimonious split, but Rosie was the only one with whom she'd shared details of their marriage during and after. The trouble with Gabe's project was that it involved a lot of personal stuff Lori wasn't ready to share with anyone else. She didn't like gossip, and she definitely didn't like being the subject of it. She figured that the less people she told about the whole mess, the quicker the overall story might fade from people's memories.

"An old rust bucket of a car came with the property, and I've never had the time or inclination to do anything about it," she said, deciding to stick with elements of the truth. "Gabe has settled in Chicago, and she's starting an auto repair and restoration garage with some Army friends. Like I said, she got very excited when she saw it, and she had the idea of restoring it and then auctioning it to raise funds for the Sanctuary."

"That does sound exciting," Ellery said. "I follow a grisly old trucker who goes around the country finding abandoned vehicles like that. How long will it take you to raise funds for all the parts and paint? And I bet it'll take them hundreds of hours to complete the restoration."

Hundreds of hours? Gabe's offer had blown Lori away even before she knew the actual time commitment. What had seemed generous was now almost unbelievably altruistic. She accepted charitable donations daily, but time was the most precious donation of all. "Really? It takes that long?" She'd had a feeling Gabe was good people, but this proved it beyond any doubt.

And Lori would get to be lucky enough to call her a friend. She decided to text her new friend to discuss the car project when she got back to the house.

"Close to a thousand for some restorations, but the finished project can sell for hundreds of thousands. There was an Aston Martin found in some woods in Massachusetts after forty years, and it sold for half a million dollars." Ellery nudged her gently. "It's not an Aston Martin, is it?"

"That doesn't sound familiar," she said. "Gabe did say, but she could've said blueberry marshmallow truck bike for all I know. She did seem unreasonably animated about it though." Lori thought about how adorable Gabe's excitement had been and smiled. "I'm only interested in cars that can get me from A to B, and they mostly look alike to me."

Ellery stood and pulled Lori to her feet. "Could you take me down so I can have a quick look?"

"Sure. I'll follow you on the ATV. I had no idea you were into this stuff."

"That's because when we talk, it's usually about your animals," Ellery said.

There was no judgment in her tone, but her expression said more than a few words could: Lori was married to her work, which left little time for anything else. It mirrored the lawyer's constant accusation, but Lori was sure it hadn't always been that way, and that she only buried herself in the Sanctuary when the lawyer's occasional late nights turned into every night and all weekend. She sighed deeply. One year on, and she still couldn't rid herself of self-doubt and recriminations.

Lori walked across to her horse. "Are you and Fran okay to handle Cash from here?"

Beth smiled and nodded, the sadness still clear in her eyes. "We've got him." She looked over Lori's shoulder to Ellery. "Will you be at the clinic when we get there?"

"I have a farm visit to make, but Mark knows you're coming,

and he'll get Cash on some intravenous fluids. As soon as I return, we'll begin the fluid removal and start some tests." She wandered over to the tack bench and retrieved the ice cream carton. "Starting with this."

Beth's jaw clenched repeatedly, and she looked up to the stable ceiling, blinking.

Ellery patted her on the shoulder. "I'll keep Lori apprised of the situation. You know I'll do everything I can."

Beth nodded. "I know," she managed to say before turning away abruptly to busy herself with Cash's preparations.

"Remember that horses are very attuned to the people they're close to, Beth." Ellery picked up her vet bag and slung it over her shoulder. "Don't give him anything else to cope with."

Lori leaned close to Cash's ear. "Don't forget you're a fighter."

The horse groaned quietly and pushed his head against her. She rubbed his neck and walked away, praying that it wouldn't be the last time she saw him.

Chapter Eight

GABE TOOK THE KEY from her pocket and offered it to Solo.

Solo stuffed her hands in her jeans and shook her head. "This is all you, Jack-in-a-box."

"Now that we're out of the Army, maybe you could just call me Gabe?"

Solo laughed. "And then you'll call me Hannah?"

"And I go back to being Carol," Woodchuck said and shook her head. "I would've preferred that in the service, but I'm sort of married to Woodchuck now."

"Even though it comes from a place of meanness?" Gabe gestured to Woodchuck's pronounced overbite.

"Even so." Woodchuck shrugged. "Our nicknames are a big part of who we are, who we've always been."

RB tapped her ever-present Ray-Bans. "I've always preferred it to my real name. I mean, do I look like a Felicity?"

Gabe and the rest of them chuckled. "It does go against your stereotype, I guess, although we could shorten it to Flick."

RB frowned. "That'd just be another nickname."

Lightning rubbed her shoulder. "I wasn't a fan of the way I got mine, but it makes a great story. *And* it has the added bonus of getting me laid most of the time."

"Okay, okay. I didn't mean to start a political debate." Gabe approached the door beside the shutters and stuck the key in the lock. "Are you ready?"

They responded with jeers of "get on with it" and expletives.

Gabe sighed and shrugged. "I thought it'd be nice to give the whole thing a bit of ceremony, you ungrateful bunch of—"

"You can have all the ceremony you want on the big opening day, Sergeant," Lightning said. "But for now, can we please get inside and out of this sun? You know I'm not a fan."

"Sure. Sorry, Lightning, I forgot." Gabe unlocked the door and pushed it open. "I'll get stocked up on SPF50 for you."

Lightning grumbled. "You better. This city gets a helluva lot more rays than Burlington."

"Ha. You were there for the ice cream, not the lack of sunshine."

Lightning rolled her eyes at Woodchuck. "If that were the case, Woody, how have I maintained my Nina Simone look?"

"Yoga?" Woody did a poor impression of a sun salutation.

Gabe grabbed hold of Woody's shirt and tugged her inside. "Get in and shut up."

Solo, RB, and Lightning followed. Gabe flicked the main breaker on, and the room was flooded with harsh light.

Solo shielded her eyes and lunged at the wall to flick the light switch off. "We're going to need some natural lighting bulbs and a dimmer installed."

"Sure. But this isn't your area, remember?" Gabe pointed to another door. "That is."

"I've only been here once, and I think I might've been a little buzzed from you plying me with alcohol," Solo said over her shoulder as she jogged toward the door.

"How did you even find this place?" Lightning asked.

"Hours and hours of googling." Gabe looked around. The place still took her breath away. Her dream—their dream—was finally a reality. It was concrete, and glass, and metal all around them, just waiting for customers to come driving into the main bays.

Gabe watched as the three of them wandered around the main space. RB raised one of the three inspection ramps to its full height and jumped into the pit below it.

Lightning ran her hand over the duck head on the tire

machine. "Everything in here still works?"

"Yep. It was a repair shop that went bust during COVID when no one was using their cars or bothering to get them serviced. That's why I was so eager to get this deal closed and had to rush you all into a decision."

"I thought it was a good decision just when I was looking at the video walk-through you sent us but being here now..." Lightning smiled widely and shook her head. "Well, it feels like an amazing decision."

Gabe stood beside Lightning and lightly grasped her shoulder. "And it feels like a dream too, right?"

For a second, Lightning didn't speak, and Gabe saw the sheen of tears in her eyes. The only traditionally feminine one in their tight-knit little group, Lightning had often held back any visible emotional reactions. Now that they were all out of the Army, maybe she'd decided she could give them free rein occasionally.

Lightning sniffed and looked at her. "Our dream come true," she said. "I really didn't think it would ever happen, Gabe. Did you?"

Gabe tilted her head slightly. "We all spent a helluva lot of time talking about it, so it would've been a damn shame not to even try."

Woody walked over. "I reckon we all thought you'd never leave the Army, Jacko. And you were the only one who would ever be able to get us all together again."

Gabe hung her arm over Woody's shoulder. She'd missed every single one of her group after they'd left, and she'd had no intention of letting their dream die when she eventually got out. "I say it was fate. This place belonged to a guy in his early sixties. Said he'd wanted to retire for a while, but he didn't want to sell to anyone who wasn't going to keep it open for the same purpose."

"That's weird," Woody said.

"Weird got us the bargain of the century." Gabe moved away from Woody and Lightning to check one of the Snap-on chests.

She slid open one of its drawers and caressed the selection of nickel chrome-plated wrenches. "Most everyone else wanted to strip it out, sell the fixtures and fittings, and use it for health supplies or IT manufacture. Once I'd told him about you guys, he only wanted to sell to us."

RB climbed out of the inspection pit. "Aw, that's a story to soften even the hardest heart, Jacko. Will you invite him to the grand opening?"

"Definitely," Gabe said. "And he'll be getting free oil changes for the rest of his life."

Solo emerged from the far door with a grin wider than Lake Michigan. "I can't fucking wait to get to work in this place. Anybody else?"

The shouts and yells in response gave Solo a definitive answer.

Gabe's phone vibrated in her pocket, and she pulled it out to check it.

Hi, Gabe. I've been thinking about your offer, and I'd like to talk to you about it properly. I could come to the city, and we could get dinner. Or lunch. Whichever you'd prefer.

Gabe grinned but didn't really know what she was happiest about: the opportunity to spend time with Lori away from the Sanctuary or the possible chance to restore a Ford Brewster.

"Message from Lori?" Solo hopped up onto the tire machine.

Gabe glared at her, but it was too late to stop the inevitable interrogation, and she couldn't actually make out any individual questions from the barrage of them.

"I'll get the cooler from the truck, and you can tell us all about it," Solo said.

"You asshole." They were thousands of miles away from the desert where they'd sat together countless days and nights, talking smack and making crazy plans, but nothing had really changed. Gabe headed to the closest inspection pit and sat on the edge with her feet dangling into it.

By the time everyone had joined her, Solo had returned with

the Yeti. She placed it behind Gabe and handed out ice-cold beers. "Spill the deets, Jackpot."

Gabe twisted the top from her bottle and tossed it back into the cooler. "How about we toast our dream garage first?"

"Later," RB said. "We want to know about Lori, right?"

Her motley crew clinked their bottles together to choruses of "hell, yeah."

"You're going to be disappointed. There's not much to tell." Gabe took a long pull on her beer, and they all leaned in like she was about to tell a cool ghost story around a campfire.

"I doubt that," said Lightning. "I might not have seen you for a couple of years, but I doubt you've lost your ability with the ladies."

"I can't be that charming; you never fell for it." Gabe ran her finger over the screen-printed label on her bottle, wishing it had the old-fashioned paper kind so she could peel it off. Someone had once told her that was a sign of sexual frustration, and in this case, they would've been one hundred percent right.

Lightning winked. "That's because you were already my ride or die. Stop stalling and tell us about Lori. We are talking about the same Lori who's looking after Max, right?"

Gabe nodded. "But there really is nothing to tell in that department." She opened the gallery on her phone, scrolled to the photo she'd taken on Sunday, and handed it to Lightning. "That's what she was messaging about. When we were walking Max, I saw that in one of her buildings."

"Oh. My. God." Lightning passed the phone to Solo.

"You're shitting me?" Solo handed the cell to RB, and it made the rounds back to Gabe. "What's the story, Jackpot? Does she want us to restore it? Man, the paint job I could do on that. The Brewster paint formula was like a state secret, you know? I'd have to do some research to see if we can get it made. It'd have to be black." Solo caught hold of Gabe's arm. "She doesn't want some pimp my ride drag car paint job, does she? I couldn't do that. Not for any amount of money."

"Cool your jets, Solo," Gabe said. "Like I said, that's what the text was about. She wants to set up a time to talk about it."

"You mean, like a date?" RB winked.

"No, I definitely don't mean that."

RB frowned. "*Have* you lost your touch? Or is she just straight?"

Gabe tsked. "Wow. Did you seriously just one-eighty the singularly most overused phrase in a deluded hetero guy's vocab?"

"Think of it as reclaiming language used against us," RB said. "Get on with your story and answer the question."

"No, she isn't straight, but I don't know any more than that. She's recently divorced and hasn't gotten over it yet. So she's not ready or willing to explore anything with me."

Solo tsked and clinked her bottle to Gabe's. "Bad luck, buddy. Good for you to put yourself out there for the rejection though. How'd it feel?"

"You make it sound like I've never been reject—"

"You haven't, to my knowledge," Solo said. "When we were on base, you didn't go home alone any time you needed a little something."

"Then you're misremembering." Gabe drained her beer then wiped her mouth with the back of her hand. "It sometimes took me two or three 'no, thank yous' to get to that."

"Then we're all misremembering." Woody raised her bottle, and everyone did the same. "You were our mentor on more than just the battlefield."

Gabe shook her head and accepted the adulation. If she had any charm, she hoped it might eventually work on Lori—when Lori was ready.

"Although I don't think any of us would've wanted to follow in your footsteps with the sergeant major's wife," Solo said.

"That was a mistake, I can admit that." One she wasn't proud of and was in no hurry to repeat or dwell on. "Anyway, I offered to restore the car for her if she could get all the parts so she could auction it and raise funds for the Sanctuary."

Lightning raised her perfectly trimmed eyebrows. "You did what?"

Gabe frowned. "There's a problem with that?"

"A restoration on a car like that would take three or four hundred hours." Lightning gestured around her. "You've got a new business to run. Where are you going to find the time to fit it in?"

Gabe tapped Solo's thigh. "I thought I'd get a little help from my friends."

Solo nodded. "I'm up for it. That's the kind of car I live to work on, and it's for a good cause, Lightning."

"Plus there's no hurry. From the looks of the dust on the tarp that covered it, the car hasn't been touched in a while." Gabe recalled Lori's reticence to talk about the vehicle and the story surrounding it, though it clearly had something to do with the ex. "And she wasn't that enthusiastic about the offer when I made it."

"She wasn't?" Solo looked bemused. "Why the hell not?"

Gabe shrugged. "I think it's complicated, and she wasn't about to share details about her private life with a relative stranger. But it's a good sign that she wants to talk about it now." She glanced at Lightning, who narrowed her eyes.

"She better not be taking advantage of your generosity," she said.

Gabe chuckled at her friend's protectiveness. "It's not like it was her idea, and she's not exactly pushing my arm up my back." She put her hand on Lightning's shoulder. "But thank you for looking out for me."

Lightning huffed. "Someone has to. Otherwise you'll be burning daylight working gratis for anyone and everyone."

Gabe smiled. "Only for the people in need."

"Look outside, Gabe," Lightning said. "Most everyone's in

need after COVID."

Gabe rolled her eyes. "Real need, then. Plus, I feel like I owe her. She saved Max's life, and she didn't have to. She did it because that's the kind of person she is; she likes helping people and animals, and I want to help her."

Lightning smirked slightly, and Gabe knew she'd revealed more than she'd wanted to.

"You like her, don't you?" Lightning asked to a chorus of whistles from the rest of the gang.

Gabe emptied her beer and grabbed another from the cooler. "Just for that, *you're* driving home." She shut out the resulting cries and calls from everyone, teasing her that she was in love. They knew it was nonsense as much as she did, but that kind of banter had always been part of their dynamic. She just hadn't been on the receiving end of it much before. "Have you guys been storing all of this up? Waiting for the day I was no longer your superior officer?"

Solo slapped her hard on the back. "Pretty much."

"Fine. Anyway, if I end up with the project, I'll do it after hours."

"Then so will we," said Lightning.

If Gabe had been the sentimental type, the solidarity of their friendship might've pushed a tear to the surface. But she'd only just come out of the Army and was way behind Lightning in that respect. It'd take a lot longer than a couple of weeks as a civilian to start getting in touch with her emotions, or whatever she was supposed to be able to do now that her life wasn't at risk every second of the day.

Solo nodded. "We could put it in the smaller workshop in the back, and we'd have her stripped down in a weekend if we all pitched in. That grill and the bumper looked like it was in decent condition though, so if the rest of it is as good, it might take less time to restore than Lightning thinks."

"I love the 'skirt in the air' look on the front fender," RB said.

Woody shook her head. "I'm not a fan. You shouldn't be able

to see all the front-end linkage. It's just not very modest."

"I thought you liked your cars like your women—upfront and open." RB laughed and gave Woody a shove so hard, she lost balance on the edge and had to jump into the inspection pit.

"Jesus, RB." Woody grabbed RB's ankle and tried to tug her in.

RB managed to squirm out of her grip. She shook her beer and sprayed it in Woody's direction.

"Beer fight," Solo yelled and sprayed her beer at Woody too, which encouraged them all to join in.

They only stopped when their bottles were empty. A beer-soaked Woody clambered out of the pit and shook like a wet dog all over RB and Solo, but Gabe managed to scramble out of the way.

"I've missed you guys," Gabe said, keeping the softness out of her voice, though the expressions on the rest of the gang's faces as she looked at them all made it clear they felt the same.

"But now we're all together, the mayhem can begin again." Solo handed out fresh beers. "The grill reminds me of a heart," she said.

"That's because you've turned into a soppy romantic," Gabe said. "I think it looks like the killer's mask from the *Scream* movies."

"Of course you would," Lightning said. "Did you know that mask was based on the Edvard Munch painting of the same name?"

Gabe didn't manage to suppress her laughter. "Trust the Yale graduate to elevate the conversation."

Lightning gave a bright smile. "The beautiful thing about being among lots of strong and self-assured women is that I don't have to dumb my intellect down. Correct?"

Gabe pressed her hands together and bowed her head. "One hundred and ten percent correct."

"So, are you going to text her back and meet her?" Lightning asked. "Just to discuss your very generous offer, of course."

Gabe didn't rise to Lightning's light sarcasm. "If everyone is onboard with it, yeah, I really want to do it. It's been a long time since I've had a project like this."

"I don't think you've ever had a project like this, have you?" Lightning did that tricky thing with her eyebrow.

"Have I told you lately that you can be like a sledgehammer?" Gabe asked.

"It's been a while." Lightning fluttered her eyelashes. "Go on then, text her. You have us all invested. We need to know if we're giving up our social life for the next six months for your charity woman."

"It's for Max too, not just... Never mind." Gabe pulled out her cell, opened the message, and reread it.

"There's that grin again," Solo said. "Buddy, you've got it bad."

"Shut up." Gabe thumbed a quick message. *That would be great. I told my team about it, and they're happy to help too. Are you free Saturday?*

"Wow," Solo said, hanging over her shoulder, "way to keep it formal, Jacko."

Gabe hovered her thumb over send. "It is kind of formal, isn't it?" She looked to Lightning for direction, but she just smiled knowingly. "Forget it. It'll do just fine." She sent the message, shoved the phone back in her pocket, and raised her beer bottle again. "A toast. To finally realizing our dream."

They all did the same and emptied their bottles. Everyone looked to Solo expectantly.

"It's all good," she said. "I've got more."

While Solo went back to the cooler and got beer for everyone, Gabe's phone vibrated in her pocket. She fought the instant desire to see if it was Lori, and she also dismissed the thought that Lori had been waiting for word from her. That kind of Pavlovian chain of thought would be warranted if there was any chance of a relationship between them, but Lori had made it clear that friendship was the only thing she was offering. Which was fine, wasn't it? Because it had to be. And friendship was better than nothing.

Gabe poured the next beer down her throat, hoping it would drown the flicker of hope for something more.

Chapter Nine

"What do you think?" Lori asked after she'd finished explaining her plans for the car and the old building.

On the video call, her mom nodded and smiled. "I think a couple of things," she said and held up her finger. "One, it's about time you did something about that vehicle. It feels like it's become a symbol of your old life, and I couldn't be happier that you're not only getting rid of it, but also that it has the potential to have a very positive outcome. But," she wagged her finger at the screen, "we'll get Bruce to draw up a contract and liaise with Ms. Jackson's attorney to ensure the particulars of your agreement are set in stone."

That lightened her burden considerably. The only lawyer she knew other than *the* lawyer was her divorce attorney. And Bruce had been the family attorney before Lori was even born; he was family in all but name. "Amazing, Mom, thank you. After everything that's happened over the past year or so, I want to make sure I have all the pieces in place and don't go into this blind."

"I understand, sweetheart. The lawyer seemed like a generous person too, didn't she?"

Lori took a deep breath and glanced away from the tablet for a brief moment. If her mom had been there in person, she would've gone in for a hug. But with over a thousand miles between them, she didn't want to take the lid off her emotions right now. Avoiding eye contact gave her a second to recompose herself. "It makes sense, doesn't it? I'm not being harsh?"

"You shouldn't second-guess yourself. After what the lawyer

did to you, it's little wonder that you'd be reluctant to trust anyone for a while, no matter how nice they might seem."

Lori smiled, appreciating her mom's willingness not to name her ex-wife.

"And it's a good lesson to learn: trust has to be earned. We should take the lead of most animals in this world. They get the lay of the land and sniff butts before they accept someone into their space."

"Animals are better than most people." Lori chuckled. "I'm not about to open negotiations by sniffing Gabe's butt, but I get what you mean." She'd been dreaming about doing other things to Gabe's butt *and* the rest of her, but in her waking hours, she could be far more civilized and detached. "Now I know that rust bucket could actually be valuable, I won't let anyone take advantage of me."

"That's my girl. Once bitten, twice shy."

Lori instinctively rubbed her forearm and shivered.

"Are you thinking about that giant centipede?" her mom asked.

"Yep. I still remember how much that hurt."

"It could've been worse, sweetheart. The Indo-Chinese spitting cobra could've paid you a visit instead," her mom said and winked.

Lori rolled her eyes but smiled at the memory. "That made me hate the place even more than I thought possible."

"That didn't last long once you met the baby elephants though, did it?"

Lori shook her head. That was the first time she'd fallen in love with something other than a Barbie doll. The grandfather clock chimed, and she looked across at it. "How is it noon already?"

"Tempus fugit, sweetheart, especially when we're chatting. Do you have somewhere to be?"

"I'm meeting Gabe at two for lunch in Chicago," Lori said, "to talk about how the restoration project might work and how long it could take. Logistics and things." With those *things* meaning the chance to get to know her better and work on that friendship she'd offered.

Her mom raised both eyebrows. "Chicago?"

"I thought it might be nice to drive to see her, since she's offering to do all the work."

"And that's a good idea, but that isn't what surprised me. You haven't been into Chicago for over a year, have you?"

"Not since the divorce, no." Lori knew what her mom was driving at. She'd become a relative recluse since the lawyer had abandoned her, only venturing away from the Sanctuary for emergencies.

"That's wonderful news. I'm so proud of you."

Her mom had never been one to interfere in her life, but she'd always been her number one fan, and Lori could see the relief in her eyes. "I've got an hour before I have to leave." She gestured to her face. "I've already gotten ready and put my mask on."

Her mom tilted her head slightly, the way she did when she registered Lori's subtext. "That's good, sweetheart."

"So you said you thought a couple of things about my plans," Lori said. "We've covered the car, and if the lunch goes well and the restoration project looks viable, I'll call Bruce to draw up a contract. What do you think about turning the building into a veterinary clinic?"

"I think it's a lovely idea, and it's so *you* to come to Ellery's rescue. You're like your father, that way."

Lori frowned. "You've both dedicated your lives to rescuing animals, which has often involved rescuing the people around them too. I think I get that from *both* of you."

"Correct, but I was also about to say that I love that you were able to put your emotions aside to think about the business benefits to the Sanctuary, and you definitely *don't* get that from your father."

Lori loved that her father could cry enough tears to provide a safe habitat for a clownfish after hearing a sob story. "Which is why I called to talk to you about this and not him."

Her mom smiled. "Exactly."

"So you think it's a good idea?"

"I think it's a great idea, but I wish you'd talked to me about figures before you made the offer. You've pitched yourself a little low."

Lori shrugged. "Which is where Dad comes back into it. Ellery has been with me since the beginning, and she's always gone the extra mile for me when I've needed it and more importantly, when I haven't known that I needed it. I know that I could make more income if I rented it to a commercial enterprise, but that could also be a huge headache with potential noise, and light pollution, and God knows what else.

Her mom smiled widely.

"What?"

"I love you, that's all. And I'm so proud of the woman you are."

"Mom..."

"Well, I am, and you should hear it. You've clearly thought through all the pros and cons, and you've come up with a plan that suits everyone. It's perfect. Is Ellery excited about it?"

"I don't think she knew how to feel about it," Lori said. "She said she was overwhelmed."

"That's not surprising. It's a very generous offer. Perhaps she wanted to talk it over with her mom too."

"That's okay though, isn't it? I don't think I'll ever get to an age when I won't seek your advice on things." And she didn't even want to contemplate the time when her mom simply wouldn't be around for her to ask.

Her mom waved the notion away like she was swatting a fly. "You'd better not!"

"Phew." Lori sighed and enjoyed the warmth that spread through her chest. She really missed her mom and loved talking to her, but they were both so busy, they didn't get to connect anywhere near as much as she liked. "Will you ask Bruce to draw up a contract and rental agreement for that too?"

"Not yet. I'll talk to him about it and get him to call you, but there's no point in us paying him for work that may not be needed. How long have you given Ellery to get back to you?"

Lori bit her lip. "I didn't give her a schedule. I didn't think there was any hurry."

"But she shouldn't keep you waiting indefinitely."

"She wouldn't do that."

Her mom wrinkled her nose. "I'm sure she wouldn't, sweetheart, but if she decides she doesn't want it, I bet there are plenty of non-profits in your area that you could look at. Now that you've made the decision to do something about that building, you should maintain your momentum. Remember, this isn't just about the bricks and mortar; that building represents a part of your life that you're getting away from."

Lori nodded. Her mom was right, of course, as she almost always was, which was only mildly frustrating. "How long should I give her to think about it?"

"No more than two weeks, for a principal decision anyway. You don't have to have all the answers and the particulars settled in that time, but she should be able to give a firm commitment that she wants to move forward with the idea." Her mom stopped to take a sip of iced tea. "Those lemons you sent me were beautiful, by the way. So tasty."

"Thanks, Mom. I'm glad they made it to you fully formed," she said. "So then Bruce will talk to Ellery's lawyer to hash out an agreement?"

"Exactly. And that might take a little more time than usual, given that you both need the flexibility to assess the picture at the end of each fiscal year and potentially change the figures."

Lori's enthusiasm for the idea had deepened as their conversation had progressed, and she couldn't wait to talk with Gabe and Ellery more. Although she had to admit that meeting

Gabe for lunch took precedence. It had been a while since someone new and exciting, and who didn't work for her, had come into her life, and she was looking forward to getting to know Gabe better. The restoration project itself held little interest, and it wouldn't until she could begin to plan the actual auction, but building a new friendship with a person as interesting as Gabe seemed to be was very appealing indeed.

***

Before Lori opened the large glass door to the restaurant, she waved at Gabe, who was sitting in a booth facing the window. Gabe's slightly crooked and awkward smile made it clear that she wasn't sure how to handle this lunch. That wasn't surprising given that Lori had all but dismissed Gabe's restoration project idea moments before shutting down any potential sexual relationship too.

She entered the burger joint, already fixed on establishing open communication. If they were going to have a business agreement, neither of them needed potential misinterpretation clouding the water, and Lori had never been someone who enjoyed playing power games with people, unlike the lawyer. She pushed that thought away for now and realized she had more processing to do; the lawyer had been on her mind a lot more since Gabe had come into her life two weeks ago. But that was for her and her therapist to sift through another time. Right now, she wanted to continue on this friendship path and not taint it with any comparisons to the lawyer.

"Hey." Gabe stood to greet her, still looking hesitant.

A hug? A handshake? A kiss on the cheek? Lori took all three options off the table by sliding into the booth opposite where Gabe had been sitting. "Hi, Gabe. How are you?"

"Really good, thanks. And you?"

"Great," Lori said. God, this wasn't even a date, and she was already reminded of why she hated dating. The best way to push through this phase was to dive right into the deeper stuff, wasn't it? That's what Rosie always purported anyway. And didn't it make sense that the same rules could be applied to friendships? In many ways, they were more or less the same as sexual relationships. There were just no physical benefits. "I chatted with my mom this morning, and that always brightens my day."

"Yeah?" Gabe smiled. "That must be nice."

Before Lori could dig into that response, the waiter came to the table to get their drinks order. She scanned the menu quickly. "Coke Zero, please."

"Do you mind if I have a beer?"

"Of course not," she said, wondering why Gabe would think she'd mind.

"I know it's early, but I'm a little nervous."

The shy grin that accompanied Gabe's confession was adorable, even though it seemed totally out of place. She'd seemed supremely self-confident in their previous two meetings. "Why are you nervous?"

"You're not?"

Lori narrowed her eyes. "Should I be?"

"I hope not." Gabe laughed and shook her head. "I'm nervous because I don't want to mess up like I did last time."

"As long as you don't start throwing out a bunch of cheesy lines, I'm sure you'll be fine." Lori was tempted to pat Gabe's arm to comfort her but thought better of it. She admired the intricate ink that covered almost all of the skin on her forearm now that she could see it up close. "Is that a Metatron cube?" she asked, pointing at the center of Gabe's tattoo sleeve.

Gabe tilted her head slightly. "You recognize it?"

"I do. Are you religious?"

"Much to my family's shame, not really. I believe in something, yeah, but not God, per se." Gabe ran her fingers over the design. "But that's not what this is about. I only had it done just before I came out of the Army."

Lori leaned back and settled against the soft leather of the booth's high back. "Is it symbolic in some way?"

Gabe nodded. "I like what it stands for: balance and harmony, and how everything's connected somehow. It's comforting, I think, to believe there's a point to it all."

Rosie was right. Going deep right off the bat seemed to have instantly relaxed Gabe. "How many tattoos do you have?" Lori had counted three on her arms and a fourth peeking out from her shirt collar, heading toward the nape of her neck.

"Mm..." Gabe said, then began to count them off with her fingers.

Lori was intrigued when Gabe needed her second hand but when she continued onto a third and then fourth round, Lori wondered if Gabe had any bare skin left at all.

"Eighteen." Gabe jutted her chin. "Do you have any?"

"Just one." And there was the specter of the lawyer again. "But I need to get it fixed."

"Bad artist?"

"Bad decision."

Gabe looked like she might push for further details, but thankfully the waiter returned with their drinks.

"Are you ready to order?" he asked.

"Sorry, we need another minute," Lori said and picked up a menu as he left them alone once again.

"You were about to tell me about your only tattoo and why it needs to be fixed," Gabe said.

"I don't believe I was," she said, more sharply than she'd intended. "It's a long story, for another time. I suppose it's the kind of thing I might talk about when we're in triple-digit friendship lunch territory."

"That's a lot of lunches." Gabe smiled. "But okay, no problem."

Lori wafted the thick menu book. "Any recommendations?"

Gabe shook her head. "I've never been here before, but my

buddy Solo said that we should just work our way through the menu over the next year or so."

"Solo?"

"Hannah Rodgers. Solo is her Army nickname, and it's not as easy as you'd think to let them go."

Lori frowned, not getting the connection. "So why Solo?"

"Are you being serious right now?"

She laughed at Gabe's suspicious expression and serious tone. "Yes?"

"*Star Wars*," Gabe said as if that explained everything.

"Peace planet!" Lori shook her head when Gabe looked even more befuddled. "Are we doing word association?"

"The movie, *Star Wars*. Han Solo was the hero. Her name is Hannah. Hence, Solo."

Lori pressed her lips together in an effort not to laugh. "So she's a movie geek or she was a hero?"

Gabe smiled. "I suppose she's both, but don't tell her I said that or her head won't fit through the door. We served together, and now we're in business together. She and her wife, Janie, live in Boystown with triplets."

Lori widened her eyes. "Triplets?"

"That was my reaction too. Three for the price of one. *And* they're identical. I had nightmares for a week after meeting them once. I think they're going to take over the world when they grow up. The oldest—Tia—is the ringleader. God help Solo and Janie now that they're walking."

"Do you like kids as much as you like dogs?"

Gabe grumbled. "We should maybe decide what we're eating before we go down that road."

"Okay," Lori said and tapped the menu. "But I still want your answer. I won't forget."

"I'm sure you won't."

Gabe held Lori's gaze long enough for Lori to appreciate the rich hues of green edged by chocolate brown in Gabe's eyes.

She pulled her focus down to the menu reluctantly and sighed.

"Is something wrong?" Gabe asked.

"Not at all. It's just...this is a lot of burgers." She flicked through the pages and pages of options.

"I know, right?" Gabe grinned.

She'd ducked that one. Her sigh had been nothing to do with the menu and everything to do with beauty in Gabe's eyes...but the lawyer had pretty eyes too, and Lori had failed to see the dark soul that lingered behind them until the very end.

When the waiter returned, Gabe ordered a triple-decker and Lori went with a simple burger with no cheese. Gabe raised her eyebrows slightly but didn't comment. "You're wondering about my choice when there are all these options, aren't you?"

Gabe shrugged. "Would you rather go somewhere else? I passed a sushi bar and a pie place just around the corner. Chicago's pizza is something else."

"No, this is fine. I love burgers." She gestured to her shirt. "I was severely tempted by the Tex-Mex one, but melted cheese, guacamole, and chili don't wash out of silk." Lori had overthought every aspect of this lunch, but she hadn't considered her outfit choice in relation to the food at all. Silk made her feel confident, and on her first sojourn into the city in so long, she'd needed that extra boost.

Gabe flicked out a napkin and tucked it into the open collar of her button-down shirt. "This always works for me."

Lori laughed. "I don't think it does."

Gabe straightened the napkin like it was a tie. "I think it gives me the professional look I'm going for. This is an important meeting, and I'm taking it very seriously," she said before grinning and pulling it off.

"Mm, nice segue." Lori clapped quietly. "Is that your way of avoiding my question about kids?"

"Wow, you really didn't forget. You're like an elephant."

"Hardly. It was only a few minutes ago, although I don't know how to feel about you comparing me to a nine-thousand-pound animal with tushes."

"Tushies? Don't all animals have tushies?"

Lori shook her head. "Tushes, not tushies. It's what female elephants have instead of tusks."

"Huh. So you don't just know about dogs and horses then?"

"I've worked with elephants too, yes. But that's another long story, and you're eager to get to business, so you should just answer my question about dogs and kids, and then we can talk about what you want to do with that rusty old thing on my property."

"Fine," Gabe said and gave Lori a crooked grin. "But you have to promise not to judge. My opinion on children has got nothing to do with my overall niceness, and it doesn't affect my qualities as a friend."

Lori arched her eyebrow. "Unless your friend has children and needs you to babysit."

"You don't have kids, do you?"

She laughed at the abject panic on Gabe's face. "Wow, you really don't like them."

"Whoa, hold on. I didn't say that. I'm just not a big fan, especially when they're young and don't really do anything useful."

Lori took a quick sip of her drink to prolong Gabe's agony. "You judge a child by how useful they are to you?"

"Oh my God, no! That's not what I meant at all. I—"

Lori put her hand on Gabe's wrist. "Relax. I'm just messing with you. I much prefer animals to children."

Gabe let out a huge breath then took a long pull on her beer. "I wanted one of these to help with my nervousness. Now I need a whole case to help me cope with your teasing."

"If we're going to be friends, you'll need to get used to my sense of humor," she said and released Gabe's wrist.

Gabe tipped her beer bottle to Lori's glass. "Here's to an interesting friendship."

Lori drank to the toast then said, "And a potential business relationship."

"You make it sound a lot more formal than a friend just helping a friend out."

"What you're offering is far more than that, Gabe. And I have to put certain things in place because it's for the Sanctuary."

"Oh, okay. Of course." Gabe nodded.

Lori noted Gabe's slight surprise but pressed on. "So should we talk about how this might work, and what you'll need from me first?" Lori opened her purse and took out her tablet. She started a new notes document and wrote *Rust Bucket Project* at the top of the screen.

Gabe pointed to the title. "You don't have much love for this car, do you?"

You have no idea. "I've never been a car person. As long as they're reliable and get me where I need to go, I don't really think about them. And this one has been taking up too much space in that building for way too long." And it had been taking up too much space in her heart and mind too. That damn vehicle had caused countless arguments, and she'd shed way too many tears for it. Thinking about it wasn't what she really wanted to be doing, but like her mom had said, the car was a symbol now, and dealing with it was part of her moving on.

But Gabe didn't need to know that to get this project off the ground.

"I bet when we've finished restoring it, you won't want to part with it," Gabe said. "I can imagine you behind the wheel—like a reverse Cruella de Ville, saving puppies instead of... Well, you know."

The metaphor made Lori smile, and she liked that Gabe saw her as chic and glamorous. But she was also very wrong. "I'll take that bet. What's the wager?"

"If I'm right, and you're even a *little bit* tempted to keep the Brewster, you tell me your tattoo story."

Lori resisted the extreme temptation to bargain for Gabe to strip naked and explain each and every one of her eighteen tattoos. "*When* I win, because I won't be even the tiniest bit tantalized to hang on to it, I'll figure out what I want from you."

"And you promise to be honest?"

"I promise, as long as you promise the same." She swallowed the bitter reminder of that part of her wedding vows and immediately decided to book an extra session with her therapist for next week.

"I do." Gabe held out her hand. "Deal."

They shook hands as the waiter arrived with their food. Lori pushed her tablet to the side and whistled at the sight of Gabe's giant burger. "*That* is a lot of meat."

When Gabe picked it up, it didn't look as big in her hands, and Lori stopped *that* train of thought before it even left the station of her mind.

"These muscles take a lot of fueling." Gabe took a huge bite and escaping mayo dribbled down her chin.

She wiped it away with her napkin before Lori could do anything she'd regret, *after* Lori had sneaked a glance at the way Gabe's biceps stretched the arms of her shirt to their limit. "I can relate," she said, gently patting her Buddha belly.

"You're perfect. What're you talking about?" Gabe said after she'd swallowed her food.

Lori's cheeks flushed, and she concentrated on counting the sesame seeds on her burger bun for the next minute.

"Sorry. Did that count as a cheesy line?" Gabe asked after a short silence. "I can compliment you as a friend, right?"

Lori nodded. "You can. I'm just not very good at knowing how to receive them."

"Hopefully you'll get better as our friendship grows."

"Hopefully." She smiled and continued to eat her burger. When she'd had enough, she pushed her plate aside and slid her tablet back into position. She looked up to see that Gabe had already finished, and her plate was impressively spotless.

Gabe gestured toward Lori's iPad. "Back to business without dessert?"

"I don't think we can say we're getting back to it when we haven't really started," Lori said.

"Are you in a rush to leave?"

"No. Beth's in charge at the Sanctuary, and I still have a few hours before I have to get back, but we haven't even started talking about the project yet."

"How about we have dessert and then go down the street to the Copper Pot coffee shop to talk business?" Gabe opened the menu to the sweets section, turned it to face Lori, and wiggled her eyebrows. "You can't tell me there's nothing on here to tempt you."

Lori sighed. It wasn't the desserts doing the tempting...

Chapter Ten

GABE'S GUILT AT PROLONGING lunch and adding a coffee stop was far outweighed by her pleasure at getting to spend more time with the enchanting Lori. She liked her confidence and sass, and Gabe would have to be a cold-blooded zombie to be immune to her physical charms, but mostly, she was simply enjoying Lori's company too much to let it end.

And she'd loved the way Lori had blushed when Gabe held the door open for her. Lori was obviously an accomplished and capable woman, but her reaction also indicated that she wasn't entirely against the occasional old-fashioned gesture. Which was a relief because Gabe wasn't sure she'd be able to rein it in. It didn't matter that she wasn't making an outright play for Lori's attentions beyond friendship; it was just the way she behaved around feminine women. But she'd had her fair share of lectures from women who *didn't* like it, so she should've checked first. She'd misinterpreted Lori's body language before. Maybe she blushed when she was irritated too. "Is it okay that I opened the door for you?" she asked before she made more of a fool of herself by pulling out Lori's chair.

"It was. I can open my own doors and I don't expect it, of course, but I do like it. I'd consider myself a feminist, but I don't think that precludes me from enjoying little things like that."

Gabe hurried around her to a table and pulled out a chair. "Then this would be one of those 'little things' too?"

Lori smoothed her skirt under her legs and sat down. "Most certainly."

Gabe grinned and took the chair opposite her. "My buddy

Lightning hates when I do it. It's not like I think any less of a woman's strength, mental or physical." She shrugged. "It's just the way I am."

"Well, I like the way you are."

Lori retrieved her tablet from her purse again and set it down on the table, making it clear she was ready to get down to the business they'd met to discuss. Gabe tried not to take it personally. Given the size of the Sanctuary and everything that was involved in running it, she probably had to be strict about her time. She could relate. Her time in the Army had been regimented down to the last second, and she'd been struggling to get out of those habits—until today, when she would've been ecstatic to have no plans so she could spend the rest of the weekend talking to Lori. It reminded her of the ridiculous rom-com movie Solo had forced her to watch where the two main characters stayed up all night chatting about anything and everything under the sun...and falling in love. Solo seemed far too invested in getting Gabe to settle down, like she needed her to couple up so they could go on double dates or some shit like that.

"Does your old-fashioned behavior extend to ordering us coffee?" Lori asked.

"Yes, miss."

"Then I'd love a double-shot latte with two sweeteners, please."

Gabe offered an informal salute as she stood and headed to the short line.

While she waited behind a short man whose dandruff situation made her take a step back, Gabe glanced at Lori. She had her back to her, so she wouldn't be able to see Gabe admiring her from afar, which seemed like the way it was destined to stay. When Lori had talked about her outfit, Gabe had wanted to tell her how amazing she looked in that silk shirt and skirt combo. Soft and sexy was Gabe's catnip. But instead, she'd acted goofy with a damn napkin. She shouldn't be giving herself a hard time for keeping her charm in check. She had to if she was going to make this friendship thing work. She'd already decided that she'd rather be Lori's friend than be nothing at all, and the last few hours had only reinforced that.

The barista took their order, and Gabe walked back to their table, where Lori had spread out some old-looking papers. "What are those?"

"This is the original vehicle title for the person who bought it new." Lori pushed the vintage sheet toward Gabe. "All the paperwork was in one of the glove compartments."

She picked it up gently, careful not to rip it, and noted the date of sale. "Wow, this piece of paper is nearly ninety years old. That's amazing. Miss Marie Zimmerman?" Gabe smiled widely. "That's got to be pretty rare in itself, right?"

"How so?"

"In the thirties? Women had only just gotten the vote a decade earlier," Gabe said. "It's hard to believe many unmarried women in the Great Depression had the kind of money and independence to buy a car like that."

Lori tapped the section where the owner's home address was typed out. "Isn't Gramercy Park one of New York's most famous neighborhoods? I think some of my family's most prolific donors live there. She was probably just a socialite or the daughter of a rich aristocrat." She wafted her hand. "But that doesn't matter. *I* own it now, and we're supposed to be talking about what you want to do with it."

Gabe frowned, not quite believing Lori's disinterest. "Of course it matters." And it also gave them more to talk about before they got to the nitty gritty of the restoration project. Because after they'd addressed that, Gabe knew Lori would be gone. She pulled out her cell, navigated to Google to type *Marie Zimmerman New York 1930s* and then hit search. "Ha, bingo. 'During the difficult economic times of the 1930s, Zimmermann was forced to limit her production of many luxury goods.'"

"So she was rich, whoopee. I'll see if the family is still monied and try to get them to help bankroll the project."

They were briefly interrupted by the barista bringing their drinks, giving Gabe time to scroll down some more of the search results. "Hey, she was an artist. A metalsmith, actually... She's pretty famous." She glanced up at Lori, who looked less than impressed at Gabe's distraction. "This is valuable research," she said and placed her phone sideways between them so Lori could see the screen too. "It could mean that the car will be worth more at auction if people want a piece of her history."

Lori leaned in. "Really?"

Gabe smiled. *That* got her attention. "Really."

Lori tapped the heading *The Marie Zimmerman Center for the Arts*. "She had her own art center. That *is* impressive."

The page opened, and a large black and white portrait of Marie Zimmerman caught Gabe's attention. "She looks quite masculine. Was short hair a thing for women in the thirties?"

Lori shrugged yet still managed to make it look elegant. "I have no idea, but you're right." She expanded the screen to increase the text size. "'A nationally acclaimed metal crafts artist with a half-dozen employees, coverage in national arts magazines, and exhibitions from coast to coast.' I'm starting to like this woman."

Lori was close enough for Gabe to smell—No. She stopped herself. How cliché to breathe in the scent of Lori's perfume...but damn, it was almost impossible to stop herself.

"What else can you find out?"

Gabe smiled at Lori's new enthusiasm for their impromptu dive into the woman's history. She went back to the original search page and scrolled down. "Can't beat Wikipedia," she said and hit the headline. A sepia portrait of Marie showed her with short hair again. It didn't take long for Gabe to find more evidence that she might be family. "'Calling herself "a craftsman" rather than an artist—'" she read out loud. "She's got to be gay."

Lori scrolled down the page until she got to the section

marked, *Later Life*. "Huh, you're right: 'Zimmermann was an avid fisher and hunter and lived for over forty years with her life partner Ruth Allen, a former actress and screenwriter.'"

Gabe winked. "My gaydar is never wrong. Let's look up Ruth Allen."

Lori hit the home button on Gabe's phone then turned it screen down. "You're incorrigible."

"I thought you said you weren't in a rush to leave."

"And I wasn't, but the clock keeps on ticking..." She gestured wildly toward Gabe. "It's like I'm with a time-swallowing black hole."

"Wow, I don't think I've ever been called a giant empty space before," Gabe said. "But isn't that a good thing? Don't they say time flies when you're having fun? Are you having fun? I'm having fun." She was having more fun than she could ever remember having outside a bedroom, but she'd been warned about the cheesy lines, so she didn't add that.

Lori laughed, shook her head, and blew out a long breath. "I *am* having fun, actually."

"Ugh, that word. *Actually*. Someone should ban it."

"Why? What's wrong with it?"

"It's like saying, I'm having fun, which I really wasn't expecting. In fact, I thought it was going to be a total bore, and I wouldn't be able to get away fast enough. But *actually*, you've turned out to be quite interesting. And against all odds, I'm *actually* enjoying myself."

"I don't even know how to respond to that *actually*," Lori said and laughed. "It's just an innocent little word. What's it ever done to you?"

"Plenty." Gabe crossed her arms and leaned back in her chair. "It's a bit of a bully *actually*." She picked up her cup and took a sip.

Lori held up her hands. "Stop! I'm enjoying this, of course I am, but I do need to get back to the Sanctuary soon, and I have to talk to my mom about our plans so she can activate our attorney."

Gabe chuckled at the strange phrasing before its meaning began to sink in. "'Activate our attorney?' Is he a robot?"

"Sorry, that's what my mom always says." Lori picked up a spoon and over-stirred her latte. "This is why I was eager to talk about the project you're proposing."

So Lori had clearly picked up on Gabe's discomfort, despite her joke. That had to mean she was expecting that reaction. "You like your alliteration," she said. "It's not so much of a proposal as a friendly offer, Lori."

Lori picked up her Apple pen again and drew a rudimentary car in the top corner of her notes. "I get that, I really do. Can I explain where we're coming from?"

"We?" Gabe asked then wished she hadn't. "You and the car are in on this together?"

Lori gave a small smile. "The Sanctuary isn't just me, Gabe. It's my baby, and I took it on when no one else would—"

"I'd like to hear that story."

"You would?"

Gabe nodded. She wanted to make it clear that whatever was happening here, it didn't affect their budding friendship.

Lori tapped her watch. "But not today."

"Not today, because I'm a time-swallowing black hole," she said and winked.

Lori turned her stylus over and over in her hand. "I don't know if you're still joking with me, or if you're genuinely upset."

"I'm not upset. I just don't know where you're going with this, but as long as you explain it to me, I'm sure it will be fine." *Hopefully...*

Lori visibly relaxed, and her smile seemed less anxious this time.

"That's wonderful. Okay, so the Sanctuary is part of the larger non-profit my family runs, Safe Haven. I can't make any large unilateral decisions without running them past the board. And though I totally acknowledge that your offer was made off the cuff, I can't just accept it and move forward without certain safeguards in place."

"You need safeguards because you think I might steal your car?" Gabe asked, not sure herself whether she was joking or not. She was beginning to struggle not to take all of this personally.

"*We* need safeguards. Think of it as a memorandum of understanding, one that works both ways. Like I can't take advantage of your extremely good nature and ask you to do more than you've already offered to do."

Gabe nodded and continued to sip her coffee, allowing Lori the space to continue.

She frowned and put her pen down. "I don't like when you're quiet. It's disconcerting."

"It's okay. I'm beginning to get it. Everyone involved needs to understand what's expected of them and what isn't, right?"

"Exactly." Lori grabbed her pen again.

Whatever she wrote was in capitals, but it was upside down so Gabe couldn't read it.

"You said you'd be happy to provide the labor for the project and that I could get donations from our followers for the parts and the paints and such, and I'd like you to have all the tools that are in the building too."

"Yeah," Gabe said when it became obvious Lori was waiting for her to agree.

"So we put things like that into the agreement, and then I can't say that you promised to pay for a new engine if I didn't manage to get it some other way."

"Okay." Gabe picked at a callus on her palm for a moment, then stopped herself, realizing it was a gross thing to do in public. "But if it *was* up to you, we would just go ahead, and you'd be happy with a handshake agreement?"

Lori's silence was more of an answer than her words could've been.

"You don't trust my word?" Gabe asked, trying to maintain

her calm.

"I don't *know* your word, Gabe. Or you. Not really." Lori sighed deeply. "And I've been badly burned by a handsome butch before."

Lori blinked rapidly and looked as though she'd said something she shouldn't have...or didn't want to. She was tarring Gabe with the same brush then. Jigsaw pieces of their previous conversations turned and twisted before beginning to form bits of a more solid picture. When Lori had first let Gabe see the car, it had been clear there was a story behind it. With that and the handsome butch comment, it made sense that it could be the ex-wife muddying the waters. "You think I'm a handsome butch?" she asked and wiggled her eyebrows.

Lori pressed her palm to her forehead. "I've got whiplash from you switching from serious to joker and back again."

"I know, I'm sorry." She shrugged. "It's just the way I deal with things like this. And I'm trying not to be offended when this all started with a genuine offer to do something charitable for your rescue center." Gabe held up a finger when Lori opened her mouth to speak. "But I understand what you're talking about with your family's company...and I'm also starting to get what's going on in the background with your ex." Gabe registered the slight panic in Lori's eyes. She reached across the table but stopped short of taking Lori's hand. "Look, I don't want to pry, but if we *are* going to be friends, I need you to know that you can trust me."

Lori stared at Gabe for a long moment before she clicked her iPad into standby and pushed it aside. Gabe could see the hesitation behind Lori's cool expression, and she had to quell the instinct to find this ex-wife and hammer her into the ground, because whatever she'd done to Lori, she was having trouble shaking it off.

"I do want us to be friends, Gabe. And I know that you can only earn my trust by me sharing a vulnerability with you and seeing what happens, seeing if you keep me safe. But that's harder for me to do...after what happened."

Gabe nodded, wishing that she hadn't stuck her finger in Lori's emotional wound and wiggled it around. "It's okay. You don't have to tell me any–"

"No, I do," Lori said. "My therapist says that I do, and I'm trying hard to take her advice."

Her smile was soft, betraying a weakness that Gabe regretted exposing. "Therapists don't always have all the answers." The therapy she got after the insider attack had done nothing but encourage her to have PTSD, which she really didn't have.

"Still. I want to." Lori took a long drink of her coffee. "If I'd known the conversation was going to go down this path, I might've suggested a bar instead."

Gabe thumbed over her shoulder. "We passed an Irish bar on the way here if you want to relocate."

Lori waved her hand. "No, no. I have to drive home in," she checked her watch, "less than an hour. I should do this without the aid of alcohol anyway. But I need to ease into it and give you the whole backstory, if that's okay."

"If you're sure," Gabe said.

Lori placed her hand over Gabe's briefly. "I'm sure. My family received a phone call from a lawyer nearly eight years ago about the Sanctuary. Except it wasn't called that. It was just a farm owned by an old guy who'd died. He had no relatives, and he didn't leave a will. But over the years, he'd collected a whole host of animals, some that were okay to own and some that he shouldn't have had. No one knew what to do with the place. The state was set to take the assets, and they were planning to euthanize or sell all the animals."

"That's harsh. What kind of animals did the old geezer have?"

"Cows, chickens, and horses–all fine if a little neglected. But also a pair of mountain lions, three snow leopards, and five bears."

Gabe shook her head. "That's unbelievable. What the hell was he doing with all of those? And where did he get them?"

"No one had any idea," Lori said. "Apparently, he was a virtual recluse and never allowed visitors." She smiled. "Thanks for asking questions. It's making it easier."

"It'd be hard not to. Do you have any photos or video?"

"I do, but I'll have to show you another time because it's all on my laptop at home."

"Awesome."

"Anyway, the lawyer reached out to us because we've done extensive work both here and outside the US, often handling exotic animals and endangered species. Mom and I had just done a piece with *National Geographic*, and the lawyer had read it."

Gabe whistled. "Wow, that's something. When Toni told me about you, I had no idea how impressive you were."

Lori shrugged and blushed slightly. "I wouldn't say that."

"You don't have to. I'll bet there are plenty of other people who'll say it for you."

"Anyway, I came over from New York to check it out, and I fell in love with the place. I'd just read a piece by Madison Ford in *Time* magazine about how many service horses and dogs were still being euthanized even after Robby's Law nearly two decades before, and that gave me the idea to start a whole new place, using the infrastructure already available."

"This is sounding like a great story so far," Gabe said. "But it has me rooting for a happy ending I already know doesn't exist."

Lori tapped her finger on the table. "That's not strictly true. We've rescued nearly two hundred animals since we opened, including Max."

The mention of her canine colleague made Gabe smile. "Good point. And I get to see him tomorrow. That's still okay, right?"

"Of course it is," Lori said. "He's looking forward to it."

"Me too." And not only to see Max but also to spend more time with Lori if Gabe could convince her to walk with them again. "So you were saying that you had an awesome idea."

"Right. So I put together a proposal, which the board promptly approved, and we bought the whole property, including everything in it—"

"Like the rust bucket? Or did that come later?"

"Including the rust bucket, yes." Lori sighed. "And the lawyer made sure everything went through as smoothly as possible."

"The lawyer who contacted you originally, not your family robot lawyer?"

"Yes. *That* lawyer."

Gabe sensed that this was where it got dark and complicated, though the sadness in Lori's eyes was a pretty obvious clue too.

"There was an instant attraction for both of us," Lori said. "And when we started spending so much time together working through the legalities and red tape for us to secure the property and handle all the animals etcetera, that exploded..." She stopped to empty her cup.

"Another latte?" Gabe headed to the counter after Lori nodded slowly, though she looked lost in her thoughts. There was only a small line, but it gave Gabe time to digest the story so far, and it explained a lot. Lori presented as a logical, thoughtful woman who liked to take her time to process every opportunity and decision, but she was also someone who seemed spontaneous and open, given her decision to take on the Sanctuary the way she had. Or at least that's who she'd been before this lawyer person. Whatever happened had caused Lori to shut down and withdraw—and made it hard for her to trust again.

When she returned to the table with the latte, Lori was dabbing her eyes with a tissue.

"Hey," Gabe said softly. "You don't have to keep talking about this." She tapped Lori's tablet. "I could tell you all about what I'm going to need to get the restoration project moving." Of course, that wasn't what Gabe really wanted. Now that Lori had cracked the door slightly, Gabe wanted to wedge her foot in and ease it open wider. She had the patience to do it slowly, sure, but she wanted the rest of this story too.

"It's okay." Lori tucked the tissue into her purse. "I suppose I'm not as far along in the process as I should be."

Gabe shook her head. "I don't think anyone can put a timeline on these things. It's different for everyone, isn't it?"

Lori smiled. Well, she looked like she tried to smile, but her grief was clearly having none of it.

"Have you had your heart broken too?" she asked.

Gabe rubbed the back of her neck and glanced away briefly. "Not in the way you might think."

Lori frowned. "What do you mean?"

Gabe squeezed her neck harder. This definitely wasn't the path she'd wanted this conversation to go down. Her own vulnerabilities weren't up for discussion here. "Family," she said. "It's complicated. A long story for another time." With any luck, that time would never come.

Lori arched her eyebrow. "You know I'm going to remember that. If this friendship is going to work, the trust has to go both ways."

"I get it."

"So is it fair to say you're the one who breaks other people's hearts then?"

"Nope, that would not be fair," Gabe said. "I've never had any serious relationships where hearts have gotten involved on either side. When I was on base, I was too caught up in the seriousness of my job to even think about love. And..." she paused, trying to decide how to put it in a way that wouldn't make her sound bad or that Lori would find distasteful, "the little time I had between postings, I spent traveling and didn't stay in one place for long." It was the nicest way she could think of describing multiple one-night stands in over thirty states.

"You didn't go home?"

"I didn't have one." She shrugged. "Like I said, it's complicated."

Lori glanced at her watch. "Time-swallowing–"

"Black hole, yep. We should talk about the car then," Gabe said.

"No, not yet. First, I'll quickly finish my sorry tale. We spent a huge amount of time together, fell in love, and got married as soon as I moved into the house here. Things were good for a while. She discovered the rust bucket in one of the old barns, moved it into the building you saw it in, and blew a huge amount of money on tools and such. But there it stayed for five years waiting for her to restore it."

"But she never did." Surely that couldn't be the root of the problem. People made plans then life got in the way all the time.

"Not exactly. Two years ago, she suddenly found her passion for it and began spending a lot of her nights and weekends in the 'cave,' as she called it. One night, I decided to check in on her and see how it was going. But it seems that she was working on a different kind of project, one on two legs instead of four wheels. All the time she'd said she was working on the car, she was actually working on another woman." Lori took a deep breath then blew it out slowly, as if preparing herself to say the words. "I walked in to find her chin deep between her paralegal's legs on the hood of that rust bucket."

Lori's body sagged, like telling the story had used up all her strength and she had none left to sit upright. Gabe experienced a similar effect but for a very different reason. That bombshell left her wishing she hadn't encouraged Lori to open her heart and share her vulnerabilities at all. Because *that* nugget of information slammed the door shut on the potential to them ever becoming anything other than friends. And even a friendship could be on wobbly ground if Lori found out about Gabe's indiscretion with the sergeant major's wife.

God damn it. She sighed deeply and knocked back the dregs of her first coffee, planning to wash it down with something harder as soon as she was alone again.

"Gabe?"

Lori's soft voice pulled her from her self-pity. "I'm so sorry that happened to you," Gabe said, the platitude falling from her lips easily. If Lori knew what she was holding back, she'd think Gabe was being insincere. And even though she wasn't, Gabe knew she represented everything Lori was running from, everything she'd suffered with the ex-wife. Even if Lori did learn to trust again, Gabe was certain that trust wouldn't extend to *her.*

"I've got a feeling that she cheated on me multiple times, probably with different people, but I suppose it doesn't matter. Once a cheater, always a cheater; isn't that what they say? And worse yet, the paralegal knew me. She'd even been to some of our fund-raising events for the Sanctuary. It takes a certain kind of person to smile and play nice with the person you're cuckolding."

Could a woman cuckhold another woman? "That's terrible. I can't imagine how painful that must've been." But Gabe had been the other woman too. She'd shaken hands with the husband. Saluted him. Played nice. Then she'd still bedded his wife. It hadn't been her finest moment, and she certainly wasn't proud of it. Even though the sergeant major was a gold-star misogynistic, homophobic asshole. Which was why Cynthia had chosen Gabe, of course: maximum damage. It wasn't a story that she could ever share with Lori. She was way too damaged to hear Gabe's excuses and justifications. Even though she did have a damn good reason for her actions, it wasn't one she expected anyone else to understand.

That realization sank into her consciousness with the weight of a thirty-ton truck. She couldn't outrun her past, and she couldn't keep it from affecting her future. If only she'd had the strength to resist the temptation, though it had been more than that.

She looked up at Lori, even more beautiful and now even more out of reach, and remembered a passage from the Bible: *He will not let you be tempted beyond what you can bear. But when you are tempted, He will also provide a way out so that you can endure it*.

Gabe didn't want a way out, but how the hell was she supposed to endure this temptation?

Chapter Eleven

LORI PULLED INTO THE parking lot of the strip mall and killed the engine. She took a moment to gather her thoughts and remind herself that going to therapy was okay. Rosie had convinced her to start going not long after the lawyer started divorce proceedings, and that had taken time and patience on her part. Up to that point in her life, Lori had been pretty self-sufficient and when she needed advice, she always went to her mom.

But the effect of seeing the woman she'd thought was the love of her life enjoying someone else with such vigor required professional help. And that's where Rae Trent came in. Marriage counselor extraordinaire. Except there was no marriage to counsel because the lawyer had been blunt about how miserable she was and that she had no interest in trying to salvage their relationship.

Still, Lori needed to work on her relationship with herself, and a visit here every two weeks had been helping with that. But this hadn't been on her Monday morning schedule until she'd called Rae on Saturday evening. Lori drifted back to the long afternoon she'd spent with Gabe, and a lunch that had turned into her dumping her baggage at Gabe's feet. The fact that Gabe had asked her to didn't matter. What mattered was how emotionally wrung out she'd been during and especially after her confession.

Clearly, she still had a lot of work to do.

She took one of those deep, cleansing breaths Rae had taught her and blew it out slowly. Apparently, some people could draw air into their lungs for over two minutes, but even on her best attempt, Lori hadn't made it beyond forty-five seconds. Maybe if she could get to the two-minute mark, she'd finally be able to release all of the toxic waste inside her along with the out breath.

She could hope.

Lori grabbed her purse and to-go mug, pre-loaded with her strongest home brew, and headed into Rae's office. The receptionist directed her to go straight in, so she knocked and entered when Rae called out.

"Hi, Lori," she said, in her evergreen breezy tone.

"Good morning, Rae." She hadn't registered that she had her bag clutched to her chest until Rae raised both her eyebrows and directed her gaze at Lori's torso. "Oh." She dropped her arms and hung the purse on the arm of the chair she never sat in before she lowered herself gently into the plush armchair she always preferred and placed her mug on a coaster on the table beside her.

Rae gestured to the coffee. "Leaded or unleaded?"

"Leaded. Heavy, heavy lead," Lori said and smiled.

"It's one of those days?"

Lori nodded. "Thank you for squeezing me in today on such short notice."

Rae waved her hand. "Let's not waste our precious time on unnecessary pleasantries, Lori. I told you I'd always make time if you were having difficulty between sessions." She picked up her writing pad and smiled. "What's brought you to me today?"

"Is there supposed to be a timeline on this?" Lori asked, not quite ready to get into the meat of her issue.

Rae's mouth twitched slightly, and she narrowed her eyes. "You think you're moving too fast or too slow?"

Lori pressed herself into the back of the chair. "I thought I was moving along just fine."

"Until?"

"How long do you spend with your average client? A year? Two? Do you think I'll have to see you for the rest of my life?" She blinked away the unexpected presence of tears and tried to distract herself with happy thoughts. Elephants in Koh Samui. White sand and turquoise sea water. Papaya salad... But Rae hadn't answered her question. "What do you think?"

"I have patients who've been with me for years and others for a few months. And I think you'll come to see me as long as you want to, Lori. You're an intelligent woman; you know your own mind and what you need."

Lori shook her head. "That used to be me. Now I'm an emotional time bomb who could go off any given second. I'd been doing really well, hadn't I? I thought I was doing fine." She rolled her eyes, realizing she'd repeated herself, and she knew what would follow.

"Until?" Rae asked again.

They'd been doing this dance for a year, and yet Lori was ever hopeful that Rae would move differently, that she might simply give Lori the answers instead of having her root around the dark of her own insides with a match that kept burning down to her fingers. How she longed for a frigging Maglite. "Until about a week ago. And even then, I'd been managing to keep a lid on it in front of everyone. If you ask Rosie or Beth or Fran, I bet they'd say I was fine. Or as fine as I've been since the lawyer left me."

"I'm not interested in their opinions, Lori. You know that."

Yes, she knew that. Rae was only interested in getting Lori to spill her thoughts and feelings, her terrors and fears. Which was only right, of course, since Lori was paying for the privilege. But God, sometimes...

"What happened a week ago, Lori?"

"I was vaguely tempted to swing into the adjacent nail salon instead of keeping our appointment today." She stretched out her hands and inspected her non-existent manicure. God, she'd been letting so many things go that she used to take pride in.

"And what do you think about that temptation now?" Rae asked, pen poised over her legal pad.

Lori considered that for a moment. Seconds ago, she'd

thought it was avoidance, but it wasn't. "It seems like it might be a kind of progress in itself."

"How so?"

"I can't really remember the last time I had my nails done." She held her hands closer for Rae's inspection. "I don't even paint them myself. I suspect that'd be a disaster though, so it's probably for the best that I don't try."

"So in what way is it progress?" Rae asked.

"I might be starting to think about taking better care of my appearance, more so than just the basics, I think." Lori picked up her coffee and took a far longer sip than she should have, and she coughed. She glanced at her watch; her time was ticking away, and she had to get back for Gabe to pick up that fricking car. She looked up at Rae, who waited patiently, as she always did, never filling the silences that were all Lori's. That space was reserved, awaiting only her words and feelings. "A week ago, I went back to *that* building for the first time since, well, since the last time. *The* time. When my world imploded."

"And why did you choose to do that?"

Lori huffed. "I didn't *choose* to do it. I was with someone who wanted to see what was inside."

"And you chose to let them?"

Yes, she knew what Rae was getting at; she always had a choice. She could choose how to act, how to react, what to say, what *not* to say. "She asked nicely," Lori said, instantly aware of the petulance in her voice. You're thirty years old, she told herself.

"Were you worried what they might think if you said no?"

She paused before snapping out a rote response and gave Rae's question the time it deserved. "I didn't think about that. I wanted her to be happy, and it seemed like going into the workshop would do that."

"Is there a reason her feelings mattered more to you than your own, Lori?"

"I wasn't thinking about my feelings, really. I didn't want to go in, so I didn't. But Gabe did, and I thought I'd be okay if I let her."

"But it wasn't okay?"

"She got very excited about the stupid car. And that started a whole chain of events I hadn't anticipated." She clasped her hands together then rested them on her lap, trying to keep them relaxed. Then she relayed the story about the restoration project, the possible repurposing of the workshop to a veterinary clinic, and the damn contract Bruce had drawn up in an impossibly speedy time.

"You seem most upset about the contract," Rae said.

And waited.

"It's not the contract, per se. It's what it represents." A flash of the confusion and disappointment on Gabe's face came into her mind. Lori had ached to take it away, but she couldn't. And she'd hid behind the requirements of her family's non-profit. All of which were true, of course, but there was so much more behind her motivation to wrangle Gabe into a legally binding document.

"What does it represent, Lori?"

She bit her lip. Trust was earned, her mom had always said. But equally, wasn't a modicum of it automatically afforded in order to build on for any kind of relationship? The lawyer had taken a wrecking ball to Lori's trust foundations.

"Lori, I can see you processing internally. Saying those things out loud can often breathe life into them. And once they're really alive, you can choose whether to nurture them or begin to systematically deconstruct them."

Or kill them off completely. That would be Lori's preference. "Apparently, the contract represents my inability to trust anyone new in my life. Even if our board hadn't required it, I would've insisted on one anyway. I kind of told her that too."

"How did she react?"

"She was incredibly understanding, actually." She stifled a small giggle, remembering Gabe's rather vociferous objection to that word. Lori would never have expected a soldier to care that much about language. But Gabe was no ordinary soldier, and Lori was fast realizing that.

"Gabe is an ex-soldier you're allowing to visit her old bomb dog who's one of your rescues, is that right?"

Lori nodded. "Yes, my friend Toni arranged for Max—the dog—to be sent to the Sanctuary because he was no longer able to do his job following a bombing. I said yes to Gabe visiting, but then it turned out she was settling in Chicago, and she asked if she could visit him weekly."

"And how did you feel about that?"

Lori focused on her to-go mug again and took another overly long drink. The caffeine hit the back of her throat and sent a jolt through her entire system. Maybe she'd put in one scoop too many. "How did I feel about that?" she asked as though it wasn't the same phrase she'd heard from Rae a hundred times over the past year. Therapy only worked if she was honest... "She's a character from one of those war-duty-blow-up video games. Six feet tall. Carved from marble. Beautiful eyes that you could stare into for days." Lori sighed deeply. She hadn't had that kind of visceral reaction to a woman for a long, long time.

"And that was...what?"

"Terrifying," Lori said. "For a nanosecond, the thought of a one-night stand crossed my mind. The attraction was mutual, and better yet, she was just supposed to be passing through, so there wouldn't be any awkwardness in the afterglow." She shook her head. "Thankfully, that thought didn't manifest into action, because I think I would've had to move back to New York."

"Why?"

"Isn't it obvious? I couldn't have faced her again. One-night stands are fantasies for me. I wouldn't have been able to take the shame of seeing her every week."

"Shame?"

"Embarrassment then, if shame is too strong a word for you."

"This isn't about what I think about words though, is it?"

Lori rested her head in her hand and tried to summon the strength and patience to continue. This was why people didn't want to go to therapy; it was too much hard work. *What's hard is also worthwhile.* She didn't need a peppy fridge magnet quote; she could always rely on her mom's voice in her head. "I'm not a one-night stand person. I don't judge anyone who is, but I'd find it mortifying to bare everything to someone and then have to keep seeing that person at the coffee shop or the bank. Sex is more than just sex to me, and that's not going to change just because my heart has been stomped on."

"So has the attraction faded now that Gabe is part of your everyday life?"

Lori snorted. "The opposite. I'm even having dreams about her. And before you ask: yes, they're sexual."

"And how are you handling all those feelings?"

"I'm not handling them. That's part of the problem." Lori closed her eyes and pushed her head against the back of the chair. Rae knew everything; she knew all about the far-reaching effects of the lawyer's infidelity and the emotional abuse that followed.

"Do you know how you would like to handle them?"

"How I want to handle them is nothing like how I should handle them, and how I should handle them bears no resemblance to how I'm currently able to handle them." *But, God, how I'd like to handle Gabe.*

"Okay. Well, let's talk through what's going on and, just for now, put aside how you think you should be handling it."

Lori nodded. "I'll try."

Rae gave an encouraging smile. "That's all we can ever do."

Break it down into bite-size pieces. That strategy usually worked for her. "If I'm honest, I think that I've been avoiding dealing with the workshop and the car without really being conscious of it."

"They are elements that you've never mentioned before," Rae said.

Lori was about to protest but stopped herself. She remembered telling Rae about finding the lawyer in flagrante delicto—a phrase a little too on the nose—but not *where*. "The location didn't seem important at the time. I was more concerned with what she was doing, not where she was doing it."

"Understandably."

"I've been focused on my emotions surrounding the betrayal and the aftermath, on everything she said to me and accused me of. I've wanted to get back to my old self, the me that she destroyed, and away from the person I'd become as a result of that relationship and its failure."

Lori's mom had been the one to illuminate that issue in a particularly frank conversation post-divorce. *I'm afraid I'm losing you*. Her mom's words had been the final push to acquiesce to therapy.

"And that's been going well, hasn't it? You've been working on rebuilding your self-confidence and your social life. You told me that the night with Rosie went better than expected, even if it was cut short with food poisoning."

Lori laughed but shouldn't have. It took poor Rosie a week to get back to some semblance of normality. "It has, you're right. And Rosie is respecting my wishes and has stopped trying to set me up with someone else. Meeting Gabe was a good thing, even though my physical response to her was a little overwhelming. I've never had that kind of...overtly sexual reaction to a person. It was feral and animalistic, like a bonobo ape." Even now, she had to squeeze her thighs together when she thought of those dreams. "I've always been more of a panda when it comes to sex."

Rae noted something on her pad for the first time. "I like that you give me something to research almost every time we meet. You're better than the *Discovery Channel*."

"You'll appreciate them; they're a matriarchal society."

Rae smiled and glanced at her books on the extensive floor-to-ceiling shelves covering the largest wall of her office. Lori knew very little about Rae, as she'd come to discover was key to a successful therapist-client relationship, and most of what she knew came from paying careful attention to what was on those shelves. While therapy books were the most prominent, second place went to feminist texts aplenty.

"Anyway," Lori said, aware of the ever-ticking clock and her session time dwindling, "Gabe's presence triggered the next step in me putting the lawyer in my rearview. I just didn't know there was another step, so I guess I stumbled and fell flat on my face."

"And the next step is?"

"Dealing with the workshop and unpacking the emotions connected to it."

Rae nodded and looked impressed. Or that's how Lori interpreted her expression. Rae had said from the very beginning that Lori had all the answers she needed and that she could work everything out for herself. Only now was she beginning to believe that. And boy, it felt pretty damn good. "So my feelings around Gabe are complicated. She made it clear that she'd be interested in dating me, and I shut her down immediately. We've agreed to be friends, which is especially good now that we're kind of working together in addition to her visiting Max..."

"Now that you've said all that out loud, how do you think you're handling all those feelings?"

Lori smiled and allowed herself a certain smugness. "Not so bad, I guess. I've communicated my feelings, my past, and my reservations to Gabe, and she's accepted all of it without... Huh," she muttered when the penny dropped. "Without judgment. And I can't remember the last time I didn't feel judged about the failure of my marriage and my reaction to it. Apart from you, of course."

"That's great, Lori. Usually you like to identify a new goal to work toward at the end of each session, but this wasn't a scheduled one, so what are your thoughts on that?"

Lori nibbled the inside of her lip while she considered Rae's question. Gabe was the source of her conflict, but she could also be part of the solution, especially for Lori to overcome the workshop obstacle she hadn't even realized was on her path to healing. "My goal is repurposing the building for something positive."

"A physical, achievable goal. Wonderful. And you have a plan that's already in motion with both the car renovation and the veterinary clinic," Rae said. "Do you want to set an emotional goal?"

Lori sighed deeply. This was the big one, the emotion at the root of her inability to move beyond the lawyer and the key for her to consider embarking on a new relationship. "Trust. I have to be able to trust again."

"And do you have a plan that will help you work toward that goal?"

"I think so. And it revolves around Gabe," Lori said. "I've agreed to be her friend, but I have to make the time and space for that to evolve. In spending more time with her, I can begin to share myself again. The real me behind the walls and the hurt. And hopefully, Gabe will be someone who can hold that vulnerability, which will mean that I can keep sharing. Eventually, that turns into trust." And after that, who knew? Maybe it could turn into something deeper. Maybe she *could* share her heart again.

Chapter Twelve

GABE BACKED THE TOW truck out of the driveway, barely missing the trash cans on the sidewalk.

Lightning leaned out of the passenger side window and chuckled. "You sure you don't want me to drive?"

"Nope."

"Seems like your mind might be elsewhere," Lightning said. "Anything you want to share with me before I put my life in your hands on the interstate?"

Gabe put the truck in park. "If you don't feel safe, you're welcome to swap out. You know Solo wanted to ride shotgun. I could give her a call and see if she's free."

Lightning gestured for Gabe to move on. "Solo *always* wants to ride shotgun alongside you. I thought that marrying Janie might've curbed that hero worship thing she's got going on with you, but so far, I've been disappointed."

"It's not hero worship, it's just respect," she said and glanced sideways. "Like everyone apart from you gives me."

Lightning winked. "You wouldn't want me any other way."

"I guess not." Gabe shrugged and headed up the street. Lightning wasn't wrong, and that's what had made her Gabe's best friend for nearly twenty years. She'd always kept Gabe's ego in check, especially early on, when Gabe thought she was invincible. One tour in Afghanistan had disabused her of that notion, and she wouldn't have made it through if it hadn't been for Lightning.

"No GPS?" Lightning asked after they'd grabbed coffee from a drive-thru and gotten back on the road. "You've already memorized the route?"

"It's signposted off the I-90. Even Woodchuck would be able to find it." Gabe didn't need to take her eyes off the road to know that Lightning had arched her brow high enough to touch her braids. She'd been gently probing since Saturday when Gabe had come home late after a night out alone. Gabe had been too drunk to know what she'd said to Lightning, but Lightning's interest had been piqued, and she wasn't about to give it up, apparently. In hindsight, Gabe should've brought Solo if she didn't want to be interrogated.

Maybe she did want to talk it through.

"Okay," Lightning said in the tone she used when she was done pussyfooting around. "You've been off since Saturday night, and it got worse when you came home from visiting Max on Sunday. What's going on?"

Gabe took the on-ramp to the freeway and gunned the truck to the speed limit before she answered. "Cynthia's come back to haunt me."

"What? I thought you said she was still in Germany with Nelson?"

"She's not here physically. I mean the situation is a problem again."

Lightning shifted and sat sideways in her seat to face Gabe. "How can it be? You got your punishment for that, and you're out. Nelson can't touch you now that you're a civilian."

Gabe twitched at the return of that unwanted memory. For a relatively small guy, he packed a vicious right hook. And every other boxing strike there was. "It's about Lori."

"She knows the Nelsons? You're not making any sense."

Gabe gripped the steering wheel hard. "If you'll let me get it out without all the questions, maybe it will make sense."

Lightning sucked her teeth. "Easy, sergeant. Remember who the real enemy is."

"I'm sorry. I'm just tense." Gabe had often used that phrase to calm Lightning when they were serving, and its repetition did its job. She stretched out her hands and tried to relax.

"I know that," Lightning said. "That's why we're having this conversation. Spill, and don't leave out any details if you don't want me to ask questions."

"I told you that Lori had just gotten a divorce and that she wasn't ready to start dating," Gabe said. "And you know that we'd agreed to be friends." She picked at a stray thread on the leather wrap around the steering wheel and kept her eyes on the road. "What I didn't say, but I think you probably knew, was that I hadn't given up on the possibility that she might change her mind as time passed and her pain faded."

Gabe briefly looked at Lightning, who simply nodded. Of course she'd know Gabe was still interested. She was the only other person on the planet who'd known her longer than her parents, and they'd never really wanted to know her.

"When we met on Saturday to talk about the restoration project, we also talked about friendship and trust. And that ended up with Lori telling me the whole story about the ex-wife." Gabe shared a shortened version then said, "So, that's it. I've been so cranky because I've fucked it up before it even had the chance to start."

"You don't know that for sure unless you tell her about Cynthia."

Gabe frowned and shook her head. "You're kidding, right? I already know she won't be able to trust me as a lover, but if I tell her about what I did, she won't want me even as a friend."

"The circumstances around what happened with Cynthia and you were totally different," Lightning said. "She mounted a consistent and frankly very impressive campaign to get you into bed. I'm surprised you held out as long as you did. And there were other issues at play."

Gabe gave a rueful laugh; neither of them wanted to revisit those issues. "I don't remember you saying you were impressed when it was happening."

"I wasn't impressed with *you*, no. But you have to give Cynthia props for persistence. She knew you were the way to get back at the sergeant major, and she didn't give up until she got what she wanted. You're not the first hot woman to succumb to the wiles of a femme fatale, even if it was for revenge."

Gabe half-smiled at the "hot woman" reference, but now wasn't the time for their usual banter. It was the no bullshit aspect of their friendship she needed now. "I shouldn't have let her use me as a pawn in her scheme."

"No, you shouldn't have. But it worked both ways, and you owned it. And with three cracked ribs, for damn certain, you paid for it."

"And now I'm paying for it again."

"That's not clear though, is it?"

Gabe shook her head. "If I can't be her lover, I want to be her friend, and I can't risk losing that."

"How long have you known her, Gabe?"

"Just over two weeks. Why?"

When Lightning didn't answer, Gabe glanced at her questioningly.

"And how much time have you spent together?"

"I don't know exac—"

"Try to work it out."

Gabe bumped her head back against the headrest and clenched her jaw. "I've seen her three times... I guess, maybe ten or twelve hours."

"You've talked on the phone? Texted each other?"

"Sure, yeah. Why?"

"I'm trying to figure out how she's become so important to you in such a short space of time," Lightning said. "Do you know? Because it's not like you've got a track record for letting new people into your life, is it? You were in the Army twenty years, and you've got *four* friends. And let's be honest, I'm the only one you've told everything about yourself and your history."

She swallowed her instinct to rage at Lightning, knowing it would be useless. No matter how many times Gabe had done that in the past, it had never discouraged her. Mainly, it'd had the opposite effect. "What're you saying?"

"I'm not saying anything. I'm asking if you know what's going on. What's so special about this woman that you haven't seen in the hundreds before her?"

Gabe tsked. "It hasn't been hundreds."

"The exact number that preceded Lori isn't important, though I'm sure my estimate is dead on. It's the *why* and the *what* I'm asking about."

Lightning didn't press any further, and Gabe didn't give an instant answer. It didn't escape her attention that she *felt* different when she thought about Lori, and that there was more than a physical attraction. To be honest, she'd never much thought about her previous encounters beyond the immediate connection. But here, emotions had gotten involved. Emotions Gabe didn't have a basis to understand nor the language to express. But she did know that she wanted more of all of it, and she wasn't prepared to have that opportunity taken away from her by her past.

Like Lightning had bluntly pointed out, Gabe didn't make connections easily and she didn't have a lot of friends, let alone people close to her. She was a hundred percent certain there was no chance of a sexual relationship, but Lori had offered her friendship and maybe that was better. Gabe had real intimacy with Lightning; they'd never muddied the waters with sex, and their friendship was solid. In reality, it was the most real, honest, and long-lasting relationship she'd ever had. Gabe had room for more of that. And she could get the sex in the city whenever she needed it. Compartmentalizing the whole thing seemed like a no-risk win-win, and she liked her odds.

"I guess I've connected to her on a similar level to the way you and I connected," Gabe said. "And now that I'm out of the service, I've got more time for that."

"Okay, but our friendship has never been sexual."

Gabe grinned. "Maybe not from your side because you're into the same kind of women as me, but I thought you were hot when we first met."

"I'm still hot, and I know that, but that disappeared almost instantly, right?"

Gabe shrugged. "More or less."

"And why was that?"

"Because we hit it off as friends."

"Maybe the same thing will happen here, and you have nothing to worry about then."

"I'm not worried about the sex stuff," Gabe said. "I can handle that. I'm worried that she won't even want to be friends if she finds out about what went down with Nelson and his wife."

"So don't tell her. As far as you know, she has no connection to anyone in the Army, does she?"

"She's friends with Toni James."

Lightning waved her hand. "Toni is a civilian, and she hasn't been embedded with the British Army for over a year. She wasn't even in the same country as you for longer than a week, was she? Nelson kept it very quiet, and when they moved him to the Dagger Complex because of what happened, they kept it hush-hush, so there's no way she could find anything out to pass on to Lori."

"I don't know much about relationships, but I know that a friendship based on lies isn't a solid one."

Lightning shook her head. "You're not lying. You're simply holding back something that you think, but don't *know*, would hurt her. And friends do things like that. How many times do you think I've withheld my opinion on your choice of women?"

"Probably not as many times as you've wished it was you taking them back to your barracks." Gabe laughed, and the tension ebbed away a little.

"Fair. You certainly had a lot more opportunities than I ever did."

"Maybe you need to start looking at younger women. They don't seem as caught up in the whole butch/femme dynamic as us Gen-Xers."

Lightning looked like she was about to slap Gabe with a pithy comeback when she tapped on the windshield repeatedly and bounced on her seat. "That's an Aston Martin DBS Superleggera convertible!"

"God damn, she's beautiful." Gabe opened her window. "Listen to that V12 engine," she said as it roared past them and zoomed out of sight. "You know, they only made—"

"Less than two hundred of the convertibles and only three hundred coupes. Yeah, I know. Who do you suppose is behind the wheel? A movie star or a football player?"

"Damn sure not an average Jo like us." Gabe whistled then returned her focus to their conversation. "You really think it's okay not to tell Lori about the affair? I trust your judgment, you know that. I just don't want to screw this up."

"Look, Gabe, it's clear this woman is important to you, and that you want to be in her life. With Max *and* the restoration project, you've pretty much got that wrapped up, so don't rock the boat. You've decided not to push things beyond a friendship, so I think that your past is irrelevant. Who you are as a friend is different from who you are when sex gets involved, and since she's not going down that road, it really shouldn't matter."

Gabe nodded. "Okay, that makes sense."

"Of course it does," Lightning said. "Besides, I *do* know how you are with women, and I still want to be your friend."

She glanced at Lightning and smiled. "Yeah? Why's that?"

"Seriously? You're fishing for compliments right now?"

"Uh-huh. Like you said, you know my history; you know my ego needs plenty of love—friend love," she added quickly.

Lightning rolled her eyes and tsked loudly. "Because you're

a lot of fun, and we get each other. That's all I'm giving you; don't be so needy."

Gabe grinned as she took exit 17 onto East 15th and pointed to the brown sign for the Sanctuary. "See? I don't need to memorize it."

"Don't need to, but you have anyway."

Gabe sighed. "One of the worst things about our friendship is the way you always have to have the last word."

"*One* of the worst things?" Lightning asked, clasping her hand over her chest. "There can't be more than one."

Gabe shook her head and continued to navigate to Lori's place. The low-level hum in her stomach became more pronounced the closer they got, and she realized she was eager to get there. In fact, she could hardly wait. She'd become aware of the feeling the second time she'd visited Max and had attributed it to getting to see him. But it had been there again while she'd waited to meet Lori for lunch on Saturday and again the next day when she was visiting Max. Whatever it was, it was a good thing. The cut grass smelled sweeter, the sun shone brighter, and—

Gabe stopped before she made herself nauseous with sickly sweet sentiments and concentrated on counting the number of green cars instead. That game was one of her few good childhood memories. The remainder of the journey zipped by fast enough, and she turned at the final signpost to the Sanctuary. She headed up the long driveway and pointed to the workshop on her left. "That's where the Brewster is, but the main buildings are still a half-mile away."

"I feel like a little kid at Christmas," Lightning said. "I can't wait to pull the tarp back and see exactly what we're dealing with."

"Me too," she said, glad that Lightning already shared her enthusiasm for the project. Gabe had hoped she would since they'd talked about restoring cars on so many long patrols back in Syria. She'd wondered if that would just turn out to be idle chatter when she eventually left the Army, but Lightning had been her first call and the first one to get on board with actually making it happen.

As they approached the rambling house that dominated the landscape, the door opened, and Lori stepped out.

Lightning took one look at her and punched Gabe's arm. "Since you've decided you're not going there, what's your policy on letting your best friend date your new best friend?" She pulled the scrunchie from her ebony hair and shook out her braids.

"Don't even think about it."

"Too late," Lightning said and popped a button on her shirt to reveal her cleavage.

"Put those away, or I'm not even stopping the truck. I'll pull straight out and dump you up the road so you can go visit Janet Jackson's house."

Lightning arched her eyebrow. "You assume I'd want to go there because I'm Black?"

Gabe nodded as she pulled up. "Of course. Or it could be that I assumed you'd want to go there because you're always singing her songs, and because you said you'd be going to Vegas as soon as she launched her new residency."

Lightning laughed. "All right then," she said and hopped out of the truck.

"Hey, wait." Gabe's seatbelt locked in her hurry to yank it off. "God damn it." She looked up to see Lightning was already meeting Lori. "Shit." When the thing wouldn't budge after multiple attempts, Gabe considered slicing it off with the emergency escape tool.

"What's keeping you?" Lightning shouted and wiggled her eyebrows.

Gabe gave the belt one last try, and it released as if it hadn't just been a total bastard. She caught her foot in her hurry to get out of the cab and stumbled out, smacking her head on the door's window.

"Oh, goodness," Lori said and was by her side within seconds.

"Are you okay?"

Gabe touched her head and detected a tiny bump, but there was no blood on her fingers. "I'm fine. No sense, no feeling," she said and grinned.

Lori touched her cool fingers to Gabe's forehead and sucked in a breath. "There's a lump there already. Let's go inside and get an ice pack on it. Are you sure you're okay?" She hooked her arm into Gabe's and led her into the house. "You don't feel dizzy or lightheaded?"

"No, ma'am." Gabe registered Lightning shaking her head and laughing.

"Extreme measures," Lightning muttered as Gabe walked past her.

Gabe glanced at her and winked then flicked her gaze to Lightning's unbuttoned shirt. "Gotta use what God gave you," she whispered.

"Did you say something, Gabe?" Lori asked.

"Uh, no. I don't think so. Did I?" Gabe gave Lori a goofy smile. "Maybe I hit my head harder than I thought."

"You sneeze harder than that," Lightning said.

"Best to be safe," Lori said to Lightning. "It's lovely to meet you, by the way. I didn't get the chance to say that before Gabe fell out of her truck."

"And I'm *very* pleased to meet you too, Lori. I've heard such a lot about you."

Gabe recognized the difference in Lightning's voice and rolled her eyes.

"Oh...really?"

Gabe liked Lori's surprise. "Really," she said. "I hope that's okay."

Lori's shy smile was wildly cute. "I hope it was all good."

"I haven't experienced anything other than good. Great, as a matter of fact. You're great." Gabe squeezed her eyes shut briefly. Maybe she *had* hit her head harder than she'd thought.

Lori took Gabe to the dining room table, where cookies, brownies, and fresh lemonade were laid out along with two piles of legal paper about a half-inch thick.

She pulled out a chair and guided Gabe into it. "Wait there while I get a cold compress from the kitchen."

When Lori had left the room, Lightning smacked Gabe upside the head.

"Hey, don't make my concussion worse." Gabe pushed Lightning's hand away then held the back of her head as if she'd been battered with a rifle butt. "And, ow."

Lightning narrowed her eyes and somehow managed to frown at the same time. "You haven't been out long enough to go that soft." She sat in the chair beside Gabe and leaned in. "She is beautiful."

"She's out of bounds."

Lightning clapped Gabe on the shoulder. "I know that, you idiot. I was just messing with you, like I have a thousand times before. Interesting that you took me seriously this time..."

Gabe glanced toward the hallway to make sure Lori wasn't coming back. "I was messing too," she said, sounding as false as her claim.

"Yeah, okay, Captain Panic Pants." Lightning tapped her short, manicured fingernail on one of the stacks of paper. "Is this the contract?"

"I think so. I read an electronic version, so I don't know how many pages it was. I *do* know that it took me half a day to read it and barely any of it made sense."

"Knucklehead. It's good that we've got a lawyer in the family then, huh?"

"Janie was a sweetheart to go through it all so quickly."

"Janie as in Hannah's wife?" Lori asked as she came back into the room. "Sorry, I just can't call her Solo."

"That's right," Lightning said. "And Janie would thank you for not calling her Solo."

Gabe hadn't responded because she was too busy being impressed that Lori had remembered her friends' names and one of their nicknames. "Uh, yeah. Janie is a lawyer for one of the top firms in the city." She saw the instant but brief change in Lori's expression. "She's one of the few good attorneys out there," she said, hoping to rescue the mood.

Lori looked like she'd stopped herself from asking a follow-up question or maybe from saying something mean. Although being mean would seem out of character from what Gabe knew of Lori, she also knew that broken relationships were complicated things that made people do and say things that they usually wouldn't. She'd learned that useful life nugget firsthand from Cynthia and the sergeant major.

Lori approached Gabe and gently placed the ice pack on her forehead. "I've wrapped it in a dish towel so it doesn't burn your skin."

She held it there for a moment longer than was necessary while her other hand rested on Gabe's shoulder. Gabe didn't miss the quiet sound that escaped Lori's mouth when she touched her, and she tensed her muscles in response.

Lori pulled her hand away instantly and didn't make eye contact. "Help yourself to something sweet," she said.

Gabe couldn't look at Lightning or she'd almost certainly laugh. Both of them would've liked to help themselves to the sweetness of Lori, and Gabe knew Lightning would have that mischievous expression she got when she was on the hunt.

Instead, she snagged one of the gooey-looking brownies and took a bite before she moaned appreciatively. "These would tempt Amenadiel to this earthly plain," she said after swallowing the delicious treat.

Lightning gave her signature WTF expression but didn't say anything.

"I thought you said you didn't believe in God?" Lori handed her a glass of lemonade.

"I don't. I just grew up in a very religious environment, and it's kind of stayed with me." Gabe clenched her jaw, and she saw the flash of concern in Lightning's expression. "Do you have one of those special photographic memories?" she asked, steering the conversation onto a safer track.

"An eidetic memory, no. Hyperthymesia syndrome? Yep. I remember absolutely *everything.*"

"So I was dead on when I said that you had a memory like an elephant?" Gabe asked.

"In essence, yes. But I really can't forget anything even if I tried."

Gabe caught the sadness in Lori's words and wanted to reach out and hold her. Because friends were allowed to hug, weren't they? Maybe she and Lightning didn't do it all that often, but they were Army, and that kind of emotional expression wasn't encouraged. She looked at Lightning and wondered if it'd be weird to embrace her.

"Would it be okay to say hi to Max?" Lightning asked just before the silence became awkward.

Gabe took the ice pack from her forehead and placed it on the table. "Not unless you're going to visit him every week."

"Actually—and I'm using the word in a good way," Lori said, "I think it would be great for Max to see another familiar face."

"Oh, I get it." Gabe tsked though she smiled at yet another impressive recall from Lori. "I looked like an Army mutt, and you couldn't risk Max being exposed to me, but she's got pretty long hair and looks like a model, so she gets preferential treatment." She held up her hand and shook her head when Lori opened her mouth to protest. "It's okay. No need to come up with any half-ass excuses. I'm used to it."

Lori laughed. "*Actually*, I was going to say that your visits seem to be making a big difference to Max's progress, so seeing someone else from a time when he was happy might be helpful." She checked her watch. "Beth will be over there preparing lunches, then she'll be taking each of them out for walks. Do you have time to take him out? Or are you in a rush to get out of here?"

The question was directed at Lightning, but Lori looked at Gabe, who could've sworn that Lori's expression was hopeful, like she *wanted* them to stay longer. Lightning eyeballed Gabe too, though her expression was one of wry amusement.

"We've got all day," Lightning said. "Picking up the Brewster is the only thing I have on my schedule for today. What about you, Gabriella?"

Gabe cocked her head and glared at Lightning. "I'd cleared my day too, *Shanae*."

Lori looked between them, clearly not quite understanding what was happening. "That's a beautiful name. Is that your Army nickname or your real one?"

"My Army nickname is Lightning." She put her hand to her shoulder, like she always did whenever she was reminded of how she got that moniker. "That's a story for another time. Right now, I want to go see Gabe's other best friend."

Lori's eyebrow quirked almost imperceptibly. Maybe she'd thought there was something else between them.

She unclipped the radio from her belt and hit the talk button. "Beth. Can you head to the house? I'm sending..." She depressed the button and looked across at Lightning. "What should I call you?"

"My non-Army friends call me Shay."

Lori smiled widely as if she liked the idea of being Lightning's friend. She pressed the talk button again. "I'm sending Shay your way. She'd like to come with you when you take Max for a walk, okay?"

"Sure thing, boss. I've just finished chowtime, so I'll head over right now."

"Thanks, Beth." Lori replaced the radio back on her hip and headed toward the front door. "Shay?" she said, beckoning her to follow.

Lightning got up from her chair and gripped Gabe's shoulder as she passed by. "You're welcome. Have fun."

"We're just friends," Gabe whispered.

"Then have fun getting to know your new friend without me in the way," Lightning said and wandered away.

Lori opened the door and stepped out. "Head straight up that way toward those big buildings on the right."

"Excellent. Thanks, Lori."

"My pleasure, Shay," she said and smiled again. "She's lovely," Lori said after she'd closed the door and was walking back to rejoin Gabe. "Is it okay to say she wasn't what I expected when you told me you were in business with a group of Army friends?"

"That depends on what you mean," Gabe said, hoping that Lori didn't hold any racial bias.

"I imagined a whole band of big, butch Army types," Lori said. "But Shay...isn't that. God, I just assumed she was gay. Is she straight? Lucky I didn't say anything to her. You won't tell her, will you?"

"Whoa, relax." Gabe laughed lightly at Lori's sudden verbal outburst; she was more than a little relieved that Lori's focus was on Lightning's perceived gayness. "Shay gets pretty pissed when people assume she's straight, so she'll be happy to find out that you assumed the opposite." She poured herself another glass of lemonade to busy her hands, which wanted to reach out for Lori. This friend thing was going to take some serious self-control and self-talk. "And of course I'll tell her about your cute little meltdown because she's my best friend, and I *actually* do tell her everything."

Lightning's reminder that she was the *only* person Gabe told everything to poked her brain and prompted her to think about opening up to Lori now.

"Have you always been just friends?"

"God, yeah. She likes the same type of women I do," Gabe

said. Women like you, she thought, though why Lori had asked that question was interesting. Unless she was interested in Lightning and working up to asking Gabe about going on a date with her.

"Good to know people still have types." Lori sat in the chair Lightning had vacated and dragged it closer to the table to snag a cookie. "I feel like we're a dying breed."

"What do you mean?" Gabe kept her eyes fixed firmly on Lori and willed her gaze not to drift to Lori's legs.

"Young people seem so much more fluid with their sexualities these days," Lori said. "And there are a lot more gay women with long hair than there ever used to be."

Gabe smiled and nodded. "I used to have long hair."

Lori tapped Gabe's leg. "You did not!"

"I really did." Her hair style seemed like a good place to gently work her way into a deeper conversation.

Lori narrowed her eyes, her expression disbelieving. "I can't imagine you with long hair. Do you have photographic proof?"

Gabe laughed. "Why don't you believe me?"

"Someone with your confidence? Feels like you were the kind of kid who knew exactly who they were from a young age and didn't let anyone hold you back."

She sighed at the description, but it was exactly the persona Gabe had cultivated to disguise the truth. "I like that you think that, but I have to disappoint you and tell you that I was *not* that kid. I wasn't even that adult until a few years after joining the Army."

"When I told you that I'd talked to my mom and how it always brightened my day, you said, 'That must be nice.' Does that have anything to do with the kind of kid you were?"

Gabe took a long swallow of lemonade, hoping it would give her the time to steel herself to open the door Lori was knocking on. "You remember that too?"

"Word for word." Lori pressed her lips together and looked

rueful. "It can be as much of a curse as a blessing. I really can't forget anything...even the unpleasant things. And I can recall every detail: the phrasing, the words, the time, the place. All of it."

She seemed to shake it off as she tapped the tabletop with her fingernail, and Gabe thought about dust storms in Syria instead of imagining Lori's nails raking across her back.

"But I won't be put off a second time," Lori said. "Are you going to quid pro quo me on my emotional info dump last Saturday? Or are you keeping your family trauma to yourself?"

"You're assuming trauma?" Gabe pointed to the plates of goodies. "Is that why you always break out the sugary treats? Comfort food for world-weary guests?"

"As a matter of fact, those brownies are made with protein powder and almond butter, so they're quite good for you." Lori waved her hand in Gabe's general area. "I figured that I should find some recipes to suit your eating plan given everything that you're doing for me."

Gabe grinned. "That's sweet of you, thanks. Because I couldn't keep eating your real treats and keep these." She flexed her arms and caught the flash of appreciation in Lori's gaze. Maybe they could have one of those safe flirty friendships where both parties knew it would go nowhere. That might be easier and more fun than keeping her own appreciation of Lori's charms quiet.

"So, for the third time," Lori said, with a knowing look, "I've shared some of my suffering, and the laws of friendship dictate reciprocation in order to maintain a relationship that's balanced and equal."

Gabe frowned. "Am I going to need a copy of those laws to make sure I don't fail in my duties as your friend?"

Lori raised both her eyebrows, indicating an unwillingness to respond without something from Gabe.

She held up her hands. "Okay, I'll try sharing. You should know that talking about my past isn't something that comes naturally. Shay had to use a crowbar and a case of Jack D." Gabe took a big bite from a brownie. "I guess this will have to do."

Lori placed her hand on Gabe's forearm. "If talking about your family is too much, maybe you can tell me something else. Like why you joined the Army. I don't want to push if it's too painful."

"Thank you, But you're right; the trust has to go both ways." Gabe looked at Lori's small hand resting on the center of her Metatron cube tattoo. Balance, harmony, and connection. Maybe she'd find all those things in this friendship. "And why I joined the Army is kind of caught up with my family shit."

Lori squeezed Gabe's arm, then she released her and sat back in her chair. "If you're sure."

Gabe remembered saying those same words to Lori when she was about to share part of her story. She had to show Lori the same trust that Lori had given her. But God damn, she wished she had three fingers of Jack in a glass instead of homemade lemonade.

"I guess your family life wasn't a Disney movie then."

Gabe looked up following Lori's prompt. She must've drifted off into her not-so-happy place. "I don't know about that. Don't all Disney movies begin with a family tragedy? Although my parents didn't die; I think they just wished that I would."

"Oh, Gabe, is that really true?"

Gabe shrugged. "They certainly made me feel like that's what they wanted. You said that I was probably the kid who was confident and didn't let anyone stop me. I was the complete opposite. I figured out that I liked girls when I was about eight, but I didn't know anything about being gay. For a while I thought that I should be a boy. As I got older, I wanted to be like all the heroes in the TV shows. When I used to play with my friends, I'd always get the role of the good guy, and I always took my shirt off. I never did need a bra, even back then." She motioned to her chest and flexed it, making her pec muscles bounce.

Lori giggled. "That's just like the Rock does it."

The adorable sound made Gabe do it again to get the same

reaction, and she was rewarded with an even bigger giggle, which served to relieve her tension a little.

"Sorry," Lori said. "Please keep going."

"It wasn't until I started watching *Buffy* when I was ten, and things started falling into—"

"Is it okay to interrupt and say that Amber Benson was amazing?" Lori asked.

"Of course."

"They made history being the first same-sex couple on TV," she said, as if Gabe wouldn't know *everything* there was to know about the series. "When I realized who *I* was and I found out about that show, I bought every season on DVD and watched each episode ten times. I went on a total stalky internet search too. I discovered the stuff about how she'd kicked ass when she'd been trolled because Willow chose her instead of the guy, and that was so inspiring to me as a young kid. She said, 'being a beautiful, heavy, lesbian witch rocks,' and that made me feel good about my weight and size. I loved that."

"You didn't watch them when they first came out?" Gabe asked. Any little lesbian with access to a TV made sure they soaked up every episode as soon as it came out. She took the opportunity to finish the brownie, which *did* taste pretty damn good.

"I was four. So no."

Gabe half-choked on the brownie and had to sputter some of it out onto a napkin. "Sorry," she said when she'd washed down the rest with a mouthful of lemonade. "I didn't know you were... what does that make you? Thirty?"

Lori nodded. "Thirty-one next month. You thought I was older?"

That was a trick question, and she wasn't falling for it. "I guess I hadn't really thought about it." Which was true. She'd just assumed Lori was in her mid-thirties because of the way she came across, educated and full of life experience from traveling the world.

"Do you have a reverse ageist thing going on? Don't you want to be my friend now that you know how young I am?"

Gabe shrugged. "Doesn't matter to me. You're old enough to go drinking with, and that's all I have to worry about." She smiled as she thought about their difference in age; seven years wasn't that much. Hell, it didn't even qualify as an official age-gap. And since they weren't ever going to date, it was really a non-issue.

Lori made a dramatic show of wiping her brow. "Phew. I thought you might use it as a reason to stop telling me your story just as I was getting used to the idea of having a super soldier as a friend."

Gabe grinned widely. "You think of me as a super soldier?"

She nodded. "I do, *actually*. I've been doing my research. The Medal of Honor *and* a Purple Heart. You've been blazing quite the trail for women in the forces."

Gabe narrowed her eyes. "You've been stalking me?"

Lori fluttered her eyelashes. "No," she said firmly. "I've been googling you. There's a difference. But one day, I'd like your version of events if you wouldn't mind telling me."

"We're going to have to spend a lot more time together if you want all my war stories."

Lori smiled. "That wouldn't be so bad, would it? That's what friends do."

"So Shay tells me."

"Well, we're together now, so maybe you could finish this story."

Gabe laughed and shook her head. "I haven't finished because you keep interrupting me."

"You're right. I'm sorry," Lori said and pretended to zip her lips closed.

"Anyway, it took a couple of years until I realized that I didn't have to be a guy to kiss a girl." She gestured to herself once again. "But the way I present is often wrongly judged as *wanting* to be a guy, and my parents were very traditional *and* super religious in a very narrow-minded way. They wanted me to wear dresses and little heels, wear pink and play tennis. They wanted me to be everything I wasn't, and everything I could never be."

Lori had pressed her lips tightly together and looked fit to burst with either questions or comments.

Gabe laughed and shook her head. "I don't have photos of any of those things, no." It seemed strange though because, for the first time, she was able to see how her past might be amusing to someone who only knew her as she was now.

"That's not what I was going to say," Lori said then covered her mouth.

"Then what do you want to say?"

Lori dropped her hand. "That I'm sorry. And that I've got an unusual anger building inside me at the thought of your parents trying to mold you into their idea of a perfect daughter instead of letting you define and discover yourself. It's just...it's incredibly sad, and I'm sorry."

Lori's emotional reaction to her story and the invisible connection of solidarity and support surprised Gabe. And it was also strangely comforting to be understood without condition and judgment. "I'm guessing that's not behavior you recognize in your parents."

"I consider myself very lucky when I say definitely not," Lori said. "But that's a topic for another day."

"With everything we want to talk about, I feel like we're not going to have time for anything else."

Lori crossed her legs and leaned back in her chair. "There's no rush though, is there?"

"Nope," she said but thought the opposite. She had a desire to know all there was to know about Lori and to know it yesterday, though she had a feeling that the more she found out, the more her attraction would deepen. *Let the chips fall.* The only way to stop that freight train now would be for one of them to move away, and that clearly wasn't going to happen. But she was an adult, and she could handle those feelings. It couldn't be that hard, especially when physical connections with other women would take the edge off. "Back to *this* story. I kept trying to be the daughter they wanted, but nothing was ever good enough. So when I was seventeen and a girl named Liliana came into my life on a foreign exchange trip and gave me my first lesbian kiss, I realized that I'd never be able to make them happy, so I'd try to be happy instead."

"You came out?"

Gabe nodded. "And predictably, they kicked me out. School had never really been my thing, and I had no job prospects and no other family members who would go against my parents and take me in. There'd been a career day the week before, and the Army seemed like the only place to go to keep me off the streets. The last thing, and the best thing, my dad did for me was give his consent for me to join early. I never looked back."

"Have you seen them since?" Lori asked.

"No. No, I haven't." She swallowed around the unexpected ball of...something as she thought about not having seen a single member of her family for twenty years.

"They didn't even reach out when you were awarded your medals?"

Whatever Lori's childhood had been like, it was obviously a far cry from Gabe's, because her look of complete shock and disbelief was undiluted. "No, but I never told them either."

"No, please don't do that." Lori pulled her chair even closer to Gabe and took her hands. "Don't make excuses for them or lay any blame at your own feet. They failed you, Gabe, and now they're missing out because they don't get to see the amazingly kind and generous person you've become."

The cold rush from the A/C vent almost directly above Gabe did nothing to cool the fire rising up her spine and into her face. Shay was a great friend. She was her ride or die and had been for nearly two decades, but this felt like a completely different kind of friendship, one that Gabe was almost too embarrassed to accept.

Lori was so close now that Gabe became aware of the subtle, citrusy-fresh scent of her perfume, and of the soft bounce of her curls, and most distracting of all, how full her lips were. So damned kissable. Gabe wanted to crush her mouth against Lori's and not come up for air. She wanted to wrap her hand in Lori's hair and press their bodies together, to feel the sexy softness of Lori's curves against the hardness of her own. Everything else in her peripheral vision faded out of focus, and all Gabe could imagine was taking Lori in her arms and carrying her to the couch so she could drag her fingers along Lori's thighs and make her way, slow and hard, inside her.

And then there was nothing but cold air between them as Lori pulled back and jerked her chair away.

"Thank you for sharing that with me, Gabe," Lori said. "I can't imagine how hard it was."

That's not the only thing that's hard. Gabe squeezed her thighs together in an effort to stave off the swelling in her boxers. She drew in a deep breath and finished her second glass of lemonade, hoping the ice-cold liquid would work against the incessant heat in every cell of her body. She pulled on the memory of Cynthia and Sergeant Major Nelson to remind her why she and Lori could never be. Gabe was beginning to let Lori in, to let her see who she was, but she'd never be able to show or share everything. The kind and generous Gabe that Lori was so quick to praise had to be all Gabe ever revealed. Because if she told Lori what she'd done, the trust they were building as friends would be destroyed faster than a missile could turn a mountain range to rubble.

And she couldn't risk that happening because this friendship was already turning into something too precious to lose.

Gabe tapped one of the paper piles on the table and noted all the colored tabs sticking out. "These are the contracts for me to sign?" She glanced at her watch. "I told the rest of the gang we'd probably get to the garage around four, and I don't know how long it's going to take to get the Brewster out of the building and safely onto the flatbed without damaging the wheels."

Lori nodded, though she obviously hadn't forgotten that Gabe had said she'd cleared her schedule and was in no rush. With that memory thing she had, she *couldn't* forget.

"Of course, and don't forget all the tools." Lori unclipped her radio and checked in on Shay and Max.

"Shay says to tell Gabe she'll meet her at the workshop. I'm taking her there now, and then I'll walk Max and Junker back," Beth said. "It's okay to leave her there, right?"

"Yes, of course," Lori said. "We'll—Gabe will be over in about ten minutes when we've completed all the paperwork."

"Ten-four, boss," Beth said and clicked off the line.

"You're not coming to oversee the operation?" Gabe asked, wanting every minute she could get with Lori. And she didn't want that awkward moment to be what they parted on.

Lori huffed and shook her head. "If I didn't have to see that car again, I would be a very happy woman." She was silent for a moment before she glanced at Gabe and sighed. "But I've told my therapist that this whole project is symbolic of me getting the final piece of the lawyer out of my life, so I suppose I should come with you."

Gabe smiled, her mood brightened considerably by the small concession. "Well, if you've told your therapist, then it has to happen, right? Accountability or something, I think."

"Indeed." Lori pulled one of the paper stacks toward her and flipped it open to the first colored tab. "And you're definitely happy with everything in the contract?"

Gabe laughed. "Honestly, I only skimmed it. But Janie has read it, and that's good enough for me. The gist of it is that we're both promising not to screw each other over, right?"

Lori nodded. "That's a great way of condensing about

fifty-thousand words of legal language, yeah."

Gabe picked up one of the pens on the table. "Then let's get this out of the way because I can't wait to get that car back to the garage to show the team."

"And I can't wait to get it off my property."

Gabe put her squiggle alongside the first tab. "Here's to the beginning of a great partnership."

Lori's hand moved elegantly across the paper, caressing it with the pen to create a beautifully flowing signature. What Gabe would give to be underneath Lori's hand instead of that damn contract.

She grabbed another brownie to distract herself from the unhelpful train of thought. Maybe with more exposure to Lori, Gabe could become immune to her unassuming charms.

Yeah, and maybe tomorrow we'll have world peace.

Chapter Thirteen

"Just to be clear and to make sure I understand the current parameters of our friendship," Rosie said as she put her car in park and turned off the engine, "I'm not allowed to set you up because you're working through your baggage. And that's going to take as long as it takes, but *you're* allowed to introduce me to women you think I might like." She turned in her seat and faced Lori. "Do I have that about right?"

"You have it exactly right." Lori gave Rosie a sweet smile and stepped out to wait for her. "Did you have to take a spot so far away from the elevators?"

Rosie hooked her arm through Lori's as they began the trek toward the elevators. "I told you: I'm minimizing the potential damage to my paintwork by parking far from the madding crowd."

"I wish you told me before I chose these shoes."

Rosie whistled. "They are killer heels, and they look spectacular. Your TikTok followers will love them, I'm sure."

"That's the idea. I'm happy to exploit any angle if it means I can attract more donations." That hadn't been the reason for her choice in footwear, of course. She wanted to feel confident when she saw Gabe again, and heels did that for her. They also made her feel sexy, which was something she hadn't even thought about *wanting* to feel for a long time. "But anyway, you don't have to worry about your car now that your best friend has connections. I hear Hannah is a whizz with a spray can."

"This is the very first time I've been able to afford to buy a car that *no one* has ever sat in, or spilled coffee on the dash, or flicked a bitten-off nail into the backseat. I don't want anyone with halitosis in this ride, so I really don't want someone to ding the door yet. And you said that Hannah was married too, so she's not going to give me any preferential treatment, is she?"

Lori shook her head. "You wouldn't have been interested even if she wasn't married to a—" Nope, she couldn't quite bring herself to say that word in a good way anymore. "If she wasn't married to a woman she's just had triplets with. Trust me when I say that Hannah is definitely not your type. And you have to let your Toni fantasy go, because she's busy living her happily ever after with her own soldier girl. I'm doing you a favor, like the good friend I am."

Rosie hit the button on the wall of a bank of elevators. "I'm not sure there really are any happily ever after stories. Everyone around me is either miserable and single or miserable and married. I thought *you* were the exception."

They stepped into an empty elevator, and Lori leaned back against the mirrored interior. "You're not the only one who thought that. But don't give up. A new love could be just around the corner."

"Which brings you nicely to the woman I'm about to meet by accident," Rosie said.

"Exactly. Her name is Shanae, but her civilian friends call her Shay." Lori waved her hands in the air as if Shay's name were up in lights.

"Mm." Rosie looked up into the same space. "That's a good start. I can hear myself calling out her name in the throes of passion."

Lori scoffed. "Pillow queen."

"It's just my fingers I can't use, Lori. I have plenty of other methods to please my partner." Rosie extended her hands to display her perfectly manicured nails.

Lori admired them. Each nail was a deep, almost-black, maroon and every alternate nail was adorned with a delicately painted rose. "They're exquisite." Lori clasped her hands together to hide her own nails, which were desperately dull in comparison.

"When was the last time you treated your nails to some love?" Rosie asked.

"The trouble with someone knowing me so well is that I can barely do anything without my words or actions being interpreted."

"And the good thing about someone knowing you so well is that you can barely do anything without someone caring about it," Rosie said and smiled gently.

"That *is* a good thing, and I'm grateful for you." She pulled Rosie into a hug.

The elevator reached the ground floor, and they exited directly onto the street.

Rosie stopped and held Lori at arm's length, looking at her with a serious expression. "When we're done here, we're heading to the closest nail salon. My treat."

Lori hooked her arm into Rosie's again and headed toward Gabe's garage. "That's not necessary. It's not that I can't afford it, it's more that I haven't *wanted* to get them done."

"Don't you think I know that? But if I want to treat my bestie to a manicure, I think I should be allowed. *Especially* if you're about to introduce me to my soulmate."

"Okay, let's do it." She'd always liked having her nails polished and neat, and it was another thing that she'd neglected over the past year.

Rosie glanced at Lori briefly, and it was clear that she wanted to say something else but wasn't quite sure if she should.

"Go ahead," Lori said.

Rosie laughed. "Premonition: another good thing about us knowing each other so well," she said. "I hope I'm allowed to say that it's good to see you in heels *and* being okay with me dragging you to have your nails done. It's progress, isn't it?"

"I'd like to think it is, yes." Lori pointed toward Bonnie's Brew just ahead of Gabe's auto shop. "Do you want a caffeine fix? I think I need one before I go on-screen."

Rosie's sideways glance made it clear she wasn't fooled by the feeble excuse. Lori had been neglecting their friendship as much as she'd been neglecting herself, and it was time to change that too. Spending a few extra moments alone with Rosie would be good.

Lori snagged a couple of high barstools by the window while Rosie went to place their order. She also wanted a little bathroom pitstop to fix her makeup and prepare herself to see Gabe again. It had only been a day since Gabe had picked up the car, and although Lori was glad for it to be gone, she was also grateful for the ongoing excuse to see Gabe more regularly than her weekly Max visit.

Rosie returned quickly with their matching lattes and scooted onto the seat beside her. "This is starting to feel like old times."

Lori caught the hint of melancholy in Rosie's voice, and guilt tugged firmly on her conscience. She placed her hand over Rosie's and squeezed. "I'm sorry I disappeared on you."

"Hey, no, you don't have to apologize," Rosie said. "You did what you had to do, and I'm here for you. I'll always be here for you."

Lori sighed deeply. "Still, I froze you out, and you stuck around. Thank you for that."

"It's what friends do. How many times have you been there to pick up the pieces with me?"

Lori began to count. "I don't have enough fingers," she said and laughed.

"Point made. My love life has been a total mess the whole time we've known each other, and there's no sign of an uptick in my future, so I wasn't about to duck out on you when you needed me." Rosie shrugged then winked. "Besides, it's only a matter of time before I'll need you to dig me out of another emotional black hole."

"That's not the kind of positive thinking I know and love you for."

Rosie sipped her coffee then dabbed at her resulting foam mustache with a napkin. "Which is why I need you and why I stuck around." She gestured toward Lori's tall glass mug. "Anyway, you've got your caffeine fix, so why don't you tell me why we really stopped here?"

"To continue my metaphor, I guess that I'm finally beginning to melt the ice walls I constructed after the lawyer left."

"Okay, that's good, and I'm relieved to hear it," Rosie said. "But you seem to have shifted into a higher gear than you've been in for over a year. Want to share what's kickstarted that?"

"I do," Lori said. "You already know about Gabe and Max."

Rosie grinned and wiggled her eyebrows. "Of course I do. She was super-hot in that overtly strong way you're a big fan of, and she helped raise a chunk of cash for the Sanctuary. I may have been a little out of it because I was chucking my guts up, but I wasn't about to forget that."

Lori clasped her hand over her mouth in a futile effort to stop a giggle emerging. "I'm sorry, I shouldn't laugh."

"No. You shouldn't," Rosie said then laughed herself. "But I'll let you if you continue the story."

"Okay. And you know about the lawyer's workshop and the car she never fixed?"

Rosie harrumphed so loudly that an old couple at a nearby table looked their way, distinctly unimpressed. "I remember how much money she spent on getting ready to fix it too."

"All of it wasted," she said. That had been an issue because they had shared finances, and Lori had never been a spendthrift, while the lawyer let money slip through her fingers like water. Lori didn't get a large salary from the Sanctuary, but the lawyer still managed to blow through that as well as her own salary. She had to admit to liking Rosie's indignation, but just as she hadn't told her therapist about where *exactly* she'd found the lawyer and her clerk, she'd neglected to give that detail to Rosie too. There were some things she just didn't want to share... She ignored the voice that chided her for sharing with Gabe and not her best friend, justifying it as the quid pro quo they'd agreed on.

"I get all that," Rosie said. "And it's led to Gabe's offer to fix up the car, which is why we're here. Are you saying that Gabe is the catalyst for the sudden change in pace of your healing?"

"It's all inextricably linked." Lori took a moment to have a long drink of her latte before it cooled too much. "Gabe's second visit set off a chain of events that prompted me to address what's probably the final piece of my life with the lawyer."

"The car," Rosie said, nodding. "When the car is sold for auction, it will close the book for you."

"That's a big part of it, yes. And so is my friendship with Gabe."

Rosie wrinkled her nose. "Just a friendship?"

"Yes. For now. I've come to realize that I dived in too soon with the lawyer. We had an instant attraction, and we based a whole relationship on it. But after the sex faded, which wasn't long after we'd gotten married, we didn't have all that much to talk about, and we had no common interests."

"Lesbian bed death. It's a curse."

Lori shrugged. "I don't think it was that. Sex has just never been that important to me."

"Really?" Rosie looked baffled.

"Really. It's not that big a thing for more people than you might think," Lori said. "The problem was, without a lot of sex, which was a big thing for the lawyer, there was nothing to keep us together."

"It sounds like you're taking the blame for her cheating on you."

Lori shook her head. "No, I'm definitely not saying that. She should've told me that she wasn't happy, and we could've separated without all the acrimony of infidelity."

"Or you could've stayed together and agreed to have an open relationship."

"I've thought about that, but I know now that I wasn't getting anything from the marriage. She didn't support me, she wasn't interested in what I was doing at work or in my limited spare time, and we had no shared hobbies. If any of that had been different, I might've considered the option of her sleeping with other people."

"I couldn't do that," Rosie said. "I couldn't share someone. I want to be all things to one person and for that person to be all things to me. Maybe that's why I'm still single; maybe I've got unrealistic expectations."

"No, I don't think so. To be honest, I'm not sure why you're single, but it's not because of your expectations, which you're entitled to and should stick to. I think all relationships are different, and people have to find the right balance for themselves. And that's easy to say and hard to achieve." She used a spoon to push the foam down the glass and into the last half of her coffee before she stirred it. "But you should stick to your standards and keep looking."

"So you're saying you have new standards now, and Gabe isn't anywhere near them?"

Lori shook her head, perhaps a little too vehemently. "I'm saying it's different with Gabe. I want to build a friendship and find out what common interests we've got."

"But you're attracted to her, aren't you?"

Lori pictured Gabe getting out of her truck the first time they'd met, and she blew out a long breath. "Like a north to south pole magnet."

"The same way you were attracted to the lawyer?" Rosie asked.

She thought about that for a second longer than she'd needed to, because the answer in her head had been instantaneous. "Gabe is like a neodymium magnet. The lawyer's was ferrite."

"I have no idea what that means or how you do. Is that a no?"

"Neodymium magnets are up to seven times stronger than

ferrite, so no, it's not the same level of attraction at all. I had to do some research for the strongest magnets for doors to our elephant enclosures in Koh Samui."

"Ah, of course, and you can't forget it."

Lori shrugged. "Even if I wanted to. And I can tell you I was an eight-year-old using screechy dial-up internet on a Power Mac G4 500 cube, eating imported Cap'n Crunch's peanut butter cereal."

"God, I remember that stuff. It was like eating caramelized razor-blade sugar."

"Yep. It ripped the roof of your mouth off, didn't it?" Lori laughed at the memory, grateful that it was one of the good ones given the subject of their conversation. "But it was so addictive, like the cereal version of cocaine. I used to eat it dry by the handful."

"Ha! Me too! And that weird film it left on your teeth... Jeez, I have no idea why I ate it."

"It was my mom and dad's one concession to junk food."

Rosie shook her head and motioned to the huge clock on the wall. "We're going to be late if you don't get back on topic."

"Right. Gabe. I was saying that I want to build strong foundations of a friendship with her, slowly, and if that works out, and I'm still attracted to her too, then I'll see what the future holds."

"What if that takes so long that Gabe has been snapped up by someone else?"

"Then I'll wait, or I'll move on." Lori swallowed the last of her coffee and smiled inwardly. If she didn't put pressure on her friendship with Gabe, it would be so much easier and so much more enjoyable to get to know her. "The process I've got to go through to get to the other side of this is for myself, not for someone else. Gabe can't be the light at the end of the tunnel. That light has to be finding myself again, discovering what I really want from a relationship. If Gabe's not still around, or if she's with someone else, then we aren't meant to be. And maybe things will change later. But I've spent seven years of my life trying to make someone else happy when they didn't even want to be with me. I won't do that again. I need to know that there's more than just a physical attraction that will fade as my boobs sag, my skin wrinkles, and my Buddha belly gets bigger."

Rosie got up from her stool, wrapped her arms around Lori, and hugged her so tight that it almost constricted her breathing.

"I've missed you. I've missed this *so* much."

"I've missed you too, babe."

Rosie let her go and hopped back up on her chair to finish her coffee. "Okay, now that we're back on track, I think you were just about to describe Shay-Shanae in detail."

Lori laughed and shook her head. "It's just Shay. She didn't tell me her last name, and I don't think her Army moniker is any help in that department."

"Which is what?"

"Lightning. She said that was a story for another time, and she touched her shoulder, but I don't know if that was significant or she just had an itch."

"Mm. Could be that lightning only strikes once, meaning she only has one-night stands."

Lori frowned. "That's what you get from that nickname? Not that she might be a fast runner, or that she was super-fast at fixing tanks in the field?"

"You know me: the first place my mind goes is sex," Rosie said. "So maybe you're not introducing me to the love of my life but to the best sex of my life. Either way, I'm still taking you to have that manicure when we're done, okay?"

"Okay." Lori got up and gathered her purse. "I need a few minutes in the ladies' room to make sure I'm camera-ready, and then we can go."

Rosie grinned. "Of course. All for the camera."

Lori didn't respond to Rosie's implication, even though she

was exactly right, and headed to the restroom bouncing with a kind of newly found freedom in her step. Unlike Rosie, she'd released all expectations of a new relationship and was starting with a blank page...

A page she couldn't wait to fill with her discovery of everything Gabe.

Chapter Fourteen

"SEEMS TO ME THAT sex just complicates things unnecessarily." Gabe searched the pile of tools Lori had donated and selected a shiny half-inch, open-end wrench for the bolts connecting the right side of the hood to the chassis. "Me and Shay have—"

"Whoa, hold up." RB patted the wing of the Brewster. "What's with *Shay*? Are you embracing the civilian life so much that you've discarded our hard-earned nicknames?"

"It's my preference." Shay waved Gabe away and sprayed WD-40 onto the rusted hinge bolts that weren't budging without chemical assistance. "I don't want to have to keep explaining my Army name to everyone I meet; it's like I have to come out as a scarred woman as well as a gay woman. I met a couple of people at the Sanctuary who used my given name, and it made me remember that I really like it."

Solo grumbled then repeated Shay's words in an annoying mimicky way. "You can all forget it if you think I'm okay with losing my Army name. Only my wife uses my real name, and she mostly shortens it to Han—"

"Unless you're in trouble," Gabe said, remembering Janie curbing Solo's nonsense with a curt use of her full name.

Solo rolled her eyes. "Yeah, but only then. Just because you've both made friends with a load of civilians doesn't mean I have to suffer."

Gabe frowned at Solo's reaction, and Shay raised her eyebrows as if she'd expected the outburst. Maybe Shay had been right about Solo feeling left out when Gabe had taken Shay to pick up the Brewster. If this was her way of expressing her feelings, she had a lot of growing up to do to raise her triplets.

"Anyway, I was saying that me and Shay have a great friendship, and that's due to not complicating it with sex, right?" Gabe directed her question at Shay, who nodded. "I can do the same with Lori: build a great friendship and not have sex. I can get all the sex I need from the women I meet in bars."

RB jutted her chin and grinned. "Just like last night."

Gabe shrugged and returned the grin. She wasn't about to admit that her one-night stand had been less than mind-blowing. She would've described it as functional, at best. The woman had been more than satisfied if her very vocal encouragements and blasphemy were anything to go by, but it hadn't had its usual effect on Gabe. There'd been no Zen moment of relaxation and peace after the woman had fallen asleep, exhausted in her arms, and she couldn't get out of there fast enough.

"Ah, Cracker Jack, you have no idea what you're talking about. I'm sorry to contradict you but there's nothing better than having sex with your best friend, with the person who knows everything about you. That level of honesty and connection... It's sublime. I mean, not everyone is as lucky as me. Plenty of people don't class their partner, or their wife, or whatever as their best friend. And they like spending time apart. It works for them. But the strongest, happiest relationships are the ones like me and Janie, where you get to share *every* part of you. I had no idea what I was missing until I met Janie, and she made me the luckiest woman alive when she agreed to marry me."

Woodchuck shook her head. "What the hell happened to you, Solo? Gabe was the one in the bomb attack, not you. You're like a whole 'nother person now. Like someone cracked you upside the head, disturbed all your neurons and whatnot, and turned you into someone else."

Solo shrugged. "That's what love is. A wake-up call. I'm not someone else; love just made me the person I was always supposed to be."

Gabe couldn't help but be slightly impressed at Solo's sudden show of emotional maturity in contrast to her earlier behavior, but Shay gagged loudly.

"That's great for you, Solo, but Gabe and I'll *never* have sex. Ever."

Solo waved her away. "I'm not talking about you; I'm talking about Lori, the friend Gabe *does* want to have sex with."

Gabe leaned under the hood and worked at one of the hinge bolts Shay had treated. "I think you're missing the point, buddy. Lori doesn't want to have sex with me, so I've made peace with that, and I'm accepting what she is offering. Which is friendship." The bolt didn't move so she popped back up and nodded for Shay to spray some more lubricant.

Solo shook her head. "So you've given up already?"

Gabe shared a look with Shay and clenched her jaw slightly. If she hadn't been okay with the nickname, her second option had been Bulldog because when she locked onto something, she wouldn't let go. Usually, Gabe could handle Solo's persistence, encouraged it even, but today her irritation prickled under her skin. "It's not about giving up. It's about respecting Lori's decision that she's not interested in me romantically. It's called taking no for an answer, Solo."

"She'll probably change her mind the more she gets to know you," Solo said. "Will you let her have a second chance when she does?"

"There's been no first chance." Gabe twirled the ratchet in her hand, inwardly cursing the rusted bolts and wishing she could just get on with the job and be done with this conversation. "And she won't change her mind." She didn't know that for sure, but it really didn't matter if Lori did address her trust issues over the coming months as their friendship developed. Because if she ever found out about Gabe's past with the Nelsons, she would never trust Gabe. And *that* she was sure of. Lori had said it herself: once a cheater, always a cheater. Gabe assumed that meant cheating from every angle, but she wasn't about to ask.

"I bet she will," Solo said. "Then it'll be her bad luck, and she'll be kicking herself."

Gabe caught Shay's eye, and Shay shook her head slightly.

"I could do with coffee," Shay said. "Anyone else needing caffeine?"

RB made a show of checking her watch. "It's two p.m. on a Saturday afternoon. Isn't it beer time?"

"Coffee sounds great," Gabe said, grateful for Shay's artful interception before she blew a gasket at Solo. She still didn't know why she was so irritated today though. Maybe it was the combination of too much alcohol, too little sleep, and mediocre sex that had ramped up her rage level. Shay had shown her the meditation she did every morning and suggested Gabe join her. Gabe had declined but figured she might well accept the invitation tomorrow morning before she headed out to see Max and Lori, who didn't need a rage monster showing up at her place.

"Solo, can you grab an order from Bonnie's just down the street?" Shay picked up her phone and tapped away on an app. "What does everyone want?" She looked at RB. "They've got a liquor license if you want beer."

While Shay ordered, Gabe dipped back under the hood to attack the hinge bolts for some peace. The one she was working shifted a quarter turn, so she persisted with a slow and steady hand. "Hey, Woodchuck, RB, can you come over and take the weight? The bolts are coming off."

"Sure thing, boss," Woodchuck said and got into position on the opposite side.

RB slid into the driver's side and reached through the hole where they'd already removed the delaminated windshield to help take the strain.

"I'll be back in five," Solo said.

"No rush," Shay said.

Gabe chuckled quietly at her masterful redirection of Solo's energies and continued to tug away with the wrench. After getting six of the bolts free, sweat began to seep into her eyes so she stood and pulled up her tank to wipe it away.

"You might want to put those away. We've got visitors," Shay said.

Gabe dropped her top to cover her stomach and looked up to see Lori with an attractive friend beside her, both of them wide-eyed and immaculately dressed. And did Lori just bite her bottom lip? She couldn't quite see because she hadn't managed to wipe away all the sweat. She looked around for the giant roll of paper towels and ripped some off to finish the job.

Shay wiggled her eyebrows and smiled, making it clear she shared Gabe's opinion on the friend.

Lori smiled brightly. "Hi, Gabe."

"Hey, Lori, how are you?" Gabe glanced at the wall clock made from a truck tire. "I'm sorry, I didn't realize the time, or I would've cleaned up." She pulled a ReadyClean wipe from the tub next to the paper towel and rubbed at the grease all over her hands.

Shay did jazz hands to show off her black latex gloves. "I keep telling you to use these."

"I don't have pretty nails to protect." Gabe tossed the wipe into the trash and rubbed her hands on her jeans, but it was no use. She was in a mess only a hot bath and a damn good scrub could deal with, and that was just the way she liked it.

"This is my best friend, Rosie," Lori said.

"It's great to meet you, but I don't expect you to shake hands." Gabe saw the look of horror on Rosie's face at that possibility and tried not to laugh. "And this is *my* best friend, Shay." She gestured to Woodchuck and RB, still wrangling the hood, and introduced them. "Could you just give me a second to get these last few bolts out so we can take the hood off?"

Lori nodded. "Of course. Do you mind if I film you doing that?"

"Sure, no problem."

After Lori had told her about the response to her TikTok comment, Gabe was happy to come on board with any and all coverage of their restoration project. That enthusiasm had only increased when she and Shay had pulled back the tarp on the Brewster back at Lori's Sanctuary, and it became immediately clear that they were going to need all the financial help they could get to strip down and rebuild the car Shay had dubbed Cruella.

She waited for the few seconds it took Lori to retrieve her phone from her bag and set up a fancy gadgety little tripod. When she went back to work with the final few bolts, she made sure her flexing biceps were in clear view of Lori's lens. Maybe Gabe could get the garage some business from the lusty women who lurked around TikTok, drinking up all the thirst traps on offer.

She removed the final bolt, and Woodchuck took the weight of the hood while RB scooted out of the driver's side to help. Shay went around the car and indicated where they should lower it onto the large soft tarp that she'd laid out for all the pieces they'd be removing. Gabe watched while Lori moved around the car to follow the action.

Rosie cleared her throat beside her.

"It's beautiful, isn't it?" Gabe asked, hoping to cover the fact that she'd been staring at Lori's sweet form as she filmed.

"Beautiful but incredibly fragile," Rosie said.

Gabe bit her tongue softly to stop from grinning. So this was going to be the "Hurt my friend, and I'll hurt you" spiel from a woman eight inches shorter and about sixty pounds lighter. But Gabe knew better than to underestimate the power of a feminine woman, particularly one with such lengthy, weapon-like nails. "It's okay, Rosie, you don't have to give me this speech. Lori and I are just friends."

"Friends can be the ones who have the ability to hurt us the most," Rosie said.

Gabe motioned to Shay. "Should I get my bestie to have the

same conversation with Lori?" she asked and laughed lightly.

Rosie tilted her head slightly and arched her eyebrow, clearly not amused. She looked Gabe up and down slowly, and not in the appreciative way she was used to by ultra-feminine women but more like the way someone would when they were sizing her up to try to knock her down.

"You don't look like the kind of person who needs extra care from her bestie."

Gabe tried to stifle her amusement by biting harder on her tongue. She had to get Rosie on her side to have any chance of keeping Lori as a friend. They were obviously tight, and Gabe didn't want to alienate Rosie by laughing in her face. "Looks can be deceiving," she said, struggling for anything other than a cliché, then she decided to just try being upfront. "Seriously, I understand your concern, but you don't need to worry. Lori's told me about the breakup of her marriage, and she's made it clear that she just wants a friend. And honestly, I'm good with that because I could use more friends now that I've left the Army, and I'm trying to settle into civilian life." She gave Rosie her most genuine smile. "And then there's Max. I don't want to do anything that might jeopardize my access to him."

Rosie nodded and looked like she might believe her. Obviously, Gabe wasn't about to share the reason why she was no longer in a position to make a move even if she wanted to. That kind of information would give Rosie the power over her friendship with Lori, and she didn't want to give her anything else to be suspicious of.

"Okay," she said slowly, perhaps not yet fully convinced. "I'm going to cut you some slack for now, but—"

"I know; if I do anything to hurt her, I'll have to answer to you." *Mom*, she wanted to add but was sure it wouldn't land in the way she intended.

"What are you two deep in conversation about?" Lori asked as she approached with her camera still attached to its tripod.

"We were just discussing your TikTok channel and how great the response has been to this joint project of yours," Rosie said without missing a beat.

Gabe smiled, as much in admiration as agreement. There was no way anyone could've suspected that she'd just pulled the protective mama bear act.

"Spoilsport." Lori pursed her lips briefly and frowned. "I wanted to tell Gabe about that."

"She didn't get to the details," Gabe said. "She was just warming up the crowd for you to swoop in with the big news. So what's been happening? Are we good to progress with the schedule I sent you yesterday?" Gabe saw the miniscule twitch of Rosie's eyebrow, and she took that as a nod to her playing it cool.

Lori clasped her hands together and smiled widely. "Yes! And I *love* that schedule, by the way, thank you."

Gabe shrugged. "Who doesn't love a good spreadsheet?"

Shay stopped short of a full guffaw. "*You* don't, for starters. You should've seen her tapping out each line one finger at a time while I dictated it."

Rosie's laugh was genuine, and Gabe saw her lightning-fast appraisal of Shay's body from tip to toe. She wasn't sure if Shay had caught it too, but she'd be sure to tell her as soon as their well-heeled guests left.

"Is that true?" Lori asked, arching her eyebrow.

"Busted," Gabe said. "I figured that you'd like that kind of detail to go with the contract."

"Oh."

"Hey, no, I didn't mean anything by that," Gabe said, hearing a hint of disappointment and possibly even hurt in Lori's tone. "I'm just learning that you like things to be organized, and Shay said you'd appreciate it." Gabe raised her eyes to the ceiling. "Though the color-coding thing took forever." She smiled at Lori, and the grip around her heart released a little when she smiled back.

"Ah, that's okay then," Lori said. "For a moment there, I thought you were still annoyed by the whole contract thing."

Gabe touched Lori's arm gently. "Definitely not. I totally get that, and I'm glad it's in place."

"Me too." Shay nudged Lori's shoulder. "We wouldn't want you taking advantage of us poor mechanics, would we?"

"You're sure you wouldn't like that?" Rosie asked.

Shay's attention snapped to Rosie, and she gave her a trademark full-on flirtatious look. If she hadn't seen Rosie's appreciation earlier, Rosie had certainly made it blatantly obvious now.

"Only in the right circumstances," Shay said and winked.

Lori cleared her throat. She took her phone off the tripod and thrust it under Gabe's nose. "These are all the email strings from companies and individuals who have responded to our campaign so far."

Gabe chuckled at Lori's clumsy shift back to the original conversation. She looked at the list and nodded. "That's a lot of interest."

Lori pulled her phone back and opened an email. "Not just interest, Gabe. These are bona fide pledges from people who want to see the car restored. But that's not even the best thing. Based on the estimates you sent over with your carefully crafted spreadsheet yesterday, I don't think we're going to need them all."

"No way. You think you've secured all the funding already? That's amazing."

"And *that's* why *I* wanted to be the one to tell you."

Lori shot a pointed look toward Rosie, but Gabe noted she was too busy gazing at Shay to acknowledge her friend's displeasure. "That's got to be a record for you," Gabe said, wanting to bring all of Lori's attention back to her while Rottweiler Rosie was otherwise distracted.

"It is." Lori refocused on Gabe and sighed deeply. "It's amazing. We've gotten quite a few offers from parts manufacturers, but the Garrison family have offered to underwrite the whole thing… on one condition."

Gabe's stomach sank. Conditions equaled strings, which often meant someone else wanted to be in control. She steeled herself for bad news while trying to figure out how to let Lori down easy. Gabe had offered her team's services, but only if they maintained project management. She really didn't want to have a conversation with Solo to convince her she had to paint the Brewster in wild pink for some trust fund kid. She cursed herself for not putting *that* in the contract when Janie had asked if she wanted to add any conditions.

"Who are the Garrisons? And what's the condition?" She expected the worst from an uber-rich family, who likely had too much money and too little taste.

"They're regular supporters of my family's work," Lori said.

"Yeah?" Damn, this was getting more dire by the second. A long history between the two families was sure to mean no compromise, and Lori was about to get very defensive when Gabe put her foot down. She wasn't about to risk her team's reputation when they were only just starting out in the business.

"Yep. They donate a very tidy sum on an annual basis, but this offer is in addition to their usual support."

Gabe looked over Lori's head to see Woodchuck and RB glaring at her with their arms crossed. So they were listening in too. She held up a finger to Lori. "'Scuse me one second," she said then spoke around her. "Why don't you check out the other side of the hood? I'll bet those bolts have soaked up the WD-40 and are ready to pop."

They grumbled and gave her unimpressed looks before getting to it.

"Sorry, Lori. You were saying?"

"Coffee and beer delivery," Solo shouted as she ducked under the front metal shutter. She held up the tray of drinks and an overstuffed paper bag. "Do I need to go back for wine?"

"That's okay," Lori said. "We just had coffee. We're fine."

"Great," Solo said with a little too much enthusiasm before she introduced herself.

She gave Gabe her flat white and distributed the rest of the drinks. Gabe heard the hiss of air being released from beer bottles by the side of the car where RB and Woodchuck were and wondered how much work she'd get out of them now that they'd cracked open their first of the day. "Sorry again," she said to Lori.

"No problem. You're busy, and we're interrupting." Lori motioned toward the door they'd come in by. "We should probably get going and leave you alone."

"No, no," she said far too quick and loud. "I mean, it's okay. You wanted to get some more video for your TikTok, right?" And Gabe needed to know what this damn condition might be.

Lori nodded. "Absolutely. I mean, we don't need it to raise funds for this now, thanks to the Garrisons, but I still want to pump up interest for the eventual auction which, thanks to your amazing scheduling," she said and winked, "we can set a date for now."

"Can you tell me what the Garrison family condition is?" Gabe asked as vaguely as she could muster, even though the knot in her stomach had tightened with every second since Lori had so casually mentioned it.

Lori narrowed her eyes. "You don't have to worry, Gabe. It's nothing you'll have to deal with."

Given that Lori had seen through Gabe's veil of disinterest so easily, she was going to have to get better at keeping her simmering attraction under wraps. "Okay, cool...but what is it?"

Lori raised her eyebrow in possible amusement, and Gabe squirmed a little under her intense gaze. That was new; she was used to maintaining eye contact in difficult situations. What the hell was going on?

"They've got a racehorse with some sort of leg defect,"

Lori said, "and they want me to take it in rather than having it euthanized. Are we good? Or do you want to run an ethical background check on the Garrisons?"

"Nah. I'm good. We're good." In stark contrast to the ease with which Lori had read her, Gabe was unable to decide whether Lori was serious or not. She was able to register Shay's delight at her stuttered behavior though and wanted to throw something at her head. She motioned to the Brewster instead. "Maybe you can film us removing the engine?"

Lori gave her a knowing smile. "Sure. That'd be great," she said, set her phone on its tripod again, and moved into position.

As she and Shay worked to get the engine loose, Gabe had trouble concentrating on what she was doing and tried to forget that Lori's lens was focused on her every move. But that didn't work, and she found herself tensing and over-straining her muscles for effect—not for the thirst trap but for Lori's benefit. She didn't rise to Shay's occasional smart-ass, whispered comments, but she did quietly promise Shay that she'd get her own back soon enough.

Solo operated the winch to lift the engine out once they'd gotten it free, and Gabe guided it safely over the Brewster's chassis and mounted it onto the engine stand where they'd strip it down and rebuild it piece by piece.

Lori packed her movie kit into her purse, and Gabe was careful not to stare now that Rosie's attention was no longer focused on Shay, who'd headed to the restroom.

"And I'll see you tomorrow...when you come to see Max?" Lori asked.

Gabe liked the sound of hopefulness in Lori's voice, like she was genuinely looking forward to seeing her again. "Absolutely."

Woodchuck tapped Gabe on the shoulder. "Did you tell her about that?" she asked and jutted her chin upward.

"Damn, I totally forgot. Sorry, bud." Gabe clapped her on the back and pointed to the camera that Woodchuck had wall-mounted. "Woody set that up so you'd have a time lapse recording of the whole restoration. She's set up a second one in the back room where she and RB will do the spray job."

Lori inspected it from where she was and shook her head. "That's wonderful...Woody?"

"You can call me Woody," she said. "It's preferable to my real name."

"Thank you, and thank you for that." Lori gestured to the camera. "I didn't even think about something so clever. What a great idea."

Woody grinned, clearly pleased with herself. But a cold sweat crept over Gabe's shoulders—that thing would be recording everything, including what they'd been saying, and then Lori would watch it and listen to it. She glanced at Shay, and if her expression was anything to go by, she seemed to be having the same lightbulb moment. "It's just video though, right? I think you'll have to put a voiceover or music on it to make it more interesting."

Woody looked offended. "Audio and visual. I thought it might be good to give a commentary on some of the work as it was done."

Shit. Gabe was sure Woody hadn't mentioned that when she told her about the idea. Or maybe Gabe just hadn't thought to ask. "We could do that after, couldn't we? In post-production, or whatever they call it. There's always a lot of cursing when we work, and TikTok closes down accounts for that sort of thing. I got a community violation notice for captioning a photo of us in the garage with *Kick-ass mechanics*."

Lori pressed her lips together and wrinkled her nose. "Ah, that's right. But the video will be perfect anyway. I can do voiceovers, like Gabe said, and maybe we could do a live TikTok at some point, and you could talk the audience through a particular part of the restoration."

"We better go if we're going to catch the salon before it closes," Rosie said.

Gabe stopped herself from commenting for fear Lori would think she was making moves again.

"What do either of you need? No salon could improve on perfection," Shay said, ripping the words from Gabe's mind.

Her brazen comment was met with giggles and blushes from both Lori and Rosie, leaving Gabe wishing that she'd just had the guts to say it. Friends could compliment each other, couldn't they?

Lori touched Gabe's bicep, and when she instinctively flexed it, Lori exhaled a short breath. Of desire? Gabe kicked herself; she shouldn't be trying to elicit that kind of response. She had to keep telling herself Lori was out of bounds. Maybe she should have a new tattoo to that effect etched in her palm. God damn Cynthia Nelson, and God damn herself for the path she chose.

"Tomorrow then," Lori said and walked away.

She hooked her arm into Rosie's, and they went out the front entrance. Gabe tried to keep her jaw from hitting the floor as she watched them sashay out with the style of catwalk models, then she turned and grabbed a beer from the bag Solo had brought in.

Shay came to her side and leaned in close. "God help you, Gabe, because I'd be powerless if either one of them set their sights on me. Screw the past."

Gabe smiled but didn't feel the emotion she put behind it. She'd love to screw the past, but that's what had messed everything up, and now the past was screwing her.

Chapter Fifteen

"We're going to delay the opening of the garage while we get the Brewster finished," Gabe said. "We thought we'd have to do it piecemeal while you gathered the funding, but now that you have the Garrison money in place, there's no reason to wait."

Lori pulled the horse trailer into the parking lot of Ellery's clinic and cut the engine, not quite able to believe what she was hearing. "Are you sure you want to do that? Don't you need to open so you can start earning money?"

"Honestly, it's what we all want. Then we can fully concentrate on the grand opening and getting new business through the doors. This is a great way for us to get used to working together again."

She looked at her phone screen and the sneaky picture of Gabe and Max that she'd taken on Sunday when they were walking together. She wished they were FaceTiming so she could see Gabe's face to make sure she was telling the truth and that she hadn't just strong-armed her team into it for Lori's benefit. She did like that she was somehow able to read Gabe so easily but wasn't sure how that had developed so quickly. The lawyer had held herself behind shutters of iron, and Lori had never been able to melt them down. She was trying hard not to compare them, but this was another positive difference she couldn't ignore. "There's really no rush, Gabe. Mom and I are less than a week into planning the auction. The earliest we could pull that together is two months from now, and that would be pushing it. The calendars of the high society type we want to attract fill up months in advance."

"I don't think you'll have to worry about that. The people with money for this kind of thing are likely a different crowd from the ones you're used to schmoozing."

Lori huffed lightly. "Schmoozing? Is that what you think I do?"

"I do, yes. Schmoozing. Lori the Super Schmoozer. That's you."

Lori giggled then caught herself. Since when did she *giggle*? Was she a fourteen-year-old girl again? "What does that make you? Gabe the Garage Go–" She stopped herself short, not wanting to offend her.

"Were you just about to call me a gorilla?"

Too late. "No?" she said.

"That sounds like you're asking me."

"No," she said with more conviction. "Gopher. I was going to say, Gabe the Garage Gopher."

"No, you weren't."

Lori giggled. Again. "No, I wasn't. I'm so sorry!"

"I don't know what to say to that. I'm wounded. That's more hurtful than any bullet I've ever taken."

Lori gasped. "How many times have you been shot?"

"Too many to count."

Lori drew in another short breath. She was lucky Gabe was still alive. No. Well, yes, but *Gabe* was lucky she was still alive.

"I'm just kidding," Gabe said. "I've actually never caught a bullet–just a bomb."

"Because that's so much better?"

"I don't know. I don't have a bullet wound to compare it to... Just the wounds from your words."

"Stop it. I have to go," Lori said, remembering she was here to pick Cash up and finally take him home. "But seriously, are you sure about the car work?"

"We're positive, honestly," Gabe said. "Besides, I'm not their superior officer anymore; I can't make them do anything they don't want to."

The comment made Lori wonder if Gabe still had her uniform...and what she looked like taking it off. *Stop it.* Now that she'd opened the floodgates to Possibility River, she couldn't seem to stem its flow. But with Gabe already proving herself to be as wonderful and trustworthy as Lori had hoped, she was becoming more at ease with her own progress and happy that Gabe was in the picture as motivation, even if she wasn't the end game.

"And you're still good to help me babysit the Trouble Town Triplets?" Gabe laughed. "Maybe that's not how I should describe them when I'm trying to enlist your help. Think of it as saving first responders work, because if I do this on my own, it'll be worse than an earthquake."

"Of course. You don't have to convince me. I love babies," she said. "I've always dreamed of having my own someday, so this will be good practice."

"Oh." Gabe sounded surprised. "This'll be good for you then. I can relax on the couch and watch the game."

Lori felt herself begin to slide into unpleasant memories of conversations with the lawyer about making a family, and she pulled the brakes. "Hey now, don't think that me coming means you get to abdicate responsibility for the little humans."

"Are you *sure*?"

"I'm positive. I'll see you on Wednesday. I'm looking forward to it. Bye." She ended the call. She couldn't wait to meet Solo's triplets, and of course, she was looking forward to spending more time with Gabe in yet another environment. This friend thing was going well so far, although Rosie didn't seem impressed with Gabe. She suspected there might be a little jealousy brewing. Lori had disappeared on her for months and now that she was back, Gabe was around too. By her own admission, Rosie never had been good at sharing, which was a residue of her childhood.

She got out of the truck and headed into the clinic's reception area, putting Gabe and Rosie to the back of her mind and focusing on why she was here.

"Hi, Lori," Mark said as he emerged from a treatment room, followed by an older man with a cat box.

She waved and approached the front desk.

"Thank you so much, Mark," the old guy said. "You've saved both our lives."

Mark smiled and put his hand on the man's shoulder. "That little one did all the work, Mr. Johnson."

Mr. Johnson walked past Lori with a grin as wide as the cat from Alice's adventures and left the clinic. She'd seen that same look many times when she'd helped out at a veterinary clinic for a year after college.

"Ellery's in the back with Cash," Mark said. "Follow me."

He'd already turned and was walking away before she answered, so Lori followed him along the corridor and out of the building to their makeshift stabling area. She quickened her pace when she saw Cash standing proud and looking like his usual magnificent self. A young intern was brushing him down, and Cash was clearly enjoying the attention.

Ellery came around from his hind quarters and smiled broadly. "Lori, it's good to see you. I thought Beth might be the one to pick him up."

"She wanted to, believe me. But I thought I'd come so we could talk about that business opportunity." Lori didn't want to specify the building offer in case Ellery hadn't discussed it with Mark.

"I think it's wonderful," he said before retreating back into the clinic.

"You've talked it through with Mark?" Lori took that as a good sign. She put her head against Cash's and wrapped her arms around his neck. "It's good to see you, boy." His answering whinny was a welcome relief, and she hugged him tighter. "It's been too long since I heard you sound so happy."

"I did," Ellery said. "He's not my partner, but my decision affects him. I've consulted everyone who works here for their input."

Lori nodded though she was slightly surprised. She'd always thought of Ellery as a one-woman band who didn't seek or need anyone's opinion. "And what's the general consensus?"

After pinning down the restoration project contract, this was the next step in her plan to upcycle the building and move on from what had happened within its walls, and she'd given Ellery about as much space and time as she could. Like her mom had said, there were easily ten more local NPOs who would love to relocate, so if it was a no from Ellery, she could get on with finding a different tenant.

"It's a resounding yes," Ellery said and then directed the intern to dress Cash for transport. "So perhaps I can give my lawyer's contact info to yours, and we can move forward?"

"That's fantastic news." Lori released Cash and held out her hand to shake on the deal. "Bruce has already drafted an agreement that he can send to you and your attorney. I explained it would need to be flexible and that it would need an annual review, making sure we're both happy with the financials."

Ellery laughed. "You move fast when you want something done, don't you?"

"It's been a long time coming, so I'm eager to get it moving," Lori said. "But yes, I do, especially when I've got my mom in my ear, pushing me forward."

"The indomitable Karen Turner. She'll be over to visit for your birthday soon, right?"

"Yep. She's coming a week early this year now that there's so much going on with the car auction and the building development." Lori was looking forward to this visit even more than usual. She wanted to know what her mom thought of Gabe, without the weight of the "meet the parents" label. She liked her mom to meet all the important people in her life, whether they were colleagues, potential business partners, friends...or more. Her mom could get a good sense of people pretty quickly, though even she had been fooled by the lawyer on their first meeting.

"And how's the car thing going?"

Lori brought her up to speed, including this morning's revelation to postpone the garage opening.

Ellery raised both eyebrows. "Sounds like Gabe has quite the philanthropic heart for an ex-soldier."

Lori frowned at Ellery's inferred disconnect between the two but didn't feel the need to rush to Gabe's defense. "She's assembled quite the team. I think the garage will be a great success. I know that's where I'll be taking all my vehicles, and I'll be recommending them to everyone else."

"After we'd talked last, I checked out the TikTok video that you said Gabe had commented on."

"You always look at them eventually," she said, sensing an impending interest in her love life, as it seemed to be the sport for everyone around her. "You're a busy woman."

"All ready to go, Ellery," the intern said.

Lori smiled widely, grateful for the perfectly timed interruption. "Wonderful." She took Cash's reins and began to lead him around the building to where she'd parked. "Beth is desperate to have him back. We can't thank you enough for getting him healthy again."

Ellery's emailed report, as thorough as always, had taken Lori almost thirty minutes to digest. All Beth was interested in was the executive summary—was Cash coming home? And now all Lori was interested in was getting away from this potential inquisition into her personal life. That job was Rosie's privilege, and Lori only allowed it begrudgingly.

"Tess, come with us and help get Cash loaded into Ms. Turner's horse trailer."

"Thank you, Tess." Lori handed the keys to Tess so she could run on ahead and get the ramp down. "Don't forget to send me your attorney's contact info so I can put them in touch with Bruce. And let me know when you and your contractor want to come around to figure out the alterations you'd like to make so the building is perfect for you." That couldn't happen soon enough. Bruce had been particularly efficient with the contract for the restoration project, and she expected a similar turnaround for this. Her mom would've explained the need to expedite them both; she was almost as invested as Lori in this final chapter of her old life being closed.

"Can you recommend someone?" Ellery asked.

"Anderson Construction has done all the work we've ever needed at the Sanctuary for the past seven years. Do you want me to text you their number?"

"That'd be great."

As they continued around to the parking lot, Ellery made no attempt to revisit her earlier foray into Lori's personal life, for which she was grateful. She needed some time to get her own head around the sudden changes that were happening in that department, and she wasn't ready to share that with anyone but Rosie. Heck, she hadn't even talked to Gabe about it, and she was part of the equation.

They loaded Cash into the back with ease, helped by his apparent eagerness, and Lori headed back to the Sanctuary, filled with thoughts of seeing Gabe and the triplets later that week.

She'd barely gone three miles when the truck began to sputter and jerk. Seconds later, the damn thing stalled altogether, and Lori had to cruise over to the emergency lane with her hazards on. Cash gave a little squeal to indicate his annoyance at the bumpy ride.

"It's okay, Cash. Just relax," she called behind her, feeling far from relaxed herself. She put the truck back into park and turned the engine over. Nothing but the sound of it trying to start. "Come on." Still nothing. She looked at her phone mounted on the dash. She *did* know a mechanic who might be able to help. Lori hit call. "Gabe, I'm on my way back from the vet, and I've broken down in the horse trailer with Cash in the back. Is there any chance you could talk me through some checks I could do and try to get started again?"

"Oh, okay. Hi, by the way."

"Sorry. Hi. I'm just a bit freaked out."

"No problem," Gabe said. "How has the engine been sounding lately?"

"Fine, I think. There's been a bit of a ticking sound, but the check engine light wasn't on, so I didn't pay it much attention. It's due for service next month, and I thought it could wait until then; I was going to bring it to you."

"That'd be our first confirmed booking," Gabe said. "Except it sounds like your timing belt might've just broken so you're not going to have an engine for me to service."

Lori groaned. "Tell me that's your brand of mechanic humor."

"Sorry, nope. But I could be wrong. Do you have a tow service close to you?"

"I don't know," she said, crossing her heart and silently asking God to forgive her the mistruth. She didn't want a stranger coming to her rescue... She wanted Gabe. "I've been lucky enough not to break down in all the time I've lived here."

"Okay, I'll come and get you," Gabe said. "Do you know where you are?"

"I'm on route six heading back to the Sanctuary."

"And are you safe? Did you manage to get into the emergency lane?"

Lori checked her side mirror and watched the cars thundering past. "I did."

"Good. Stay put, and don't get out of the truck, okay?"

"I won't."

"Promise me. No matter what noise the horse makes. No matter how distressed it sounds, you stay in the cab."

Even though the situation sounded serious, Lori allowed herself a small smile at Gabe's protectiveness. She liked the idea of someone caring so much. And as if Cash understood what Gabe was saying, he gave a small nicker. "I promise. I can send you my location. Would that help?"

"That'd be perfect. Do that now, and then I'll text you to let you know how long it's going to take me to get to you. And remember: stay inside the cab. Don't get out for anything or anyone."

"Not even for the police?"

"If the cops see you, they'll stop to check on you, but they won't ask you to get out," Gabe said. "They might stay with you because of the horse, or they might just check to make sure the trailer is secure and the horse can't get out. That's going to depend on how diligent the officer is."

"Thank you, Gabe, you're a lifesaver."

"So they say."

With the call over, Lori dropped a pin of her location to Gabe and then sent Beth a message to let her know what was happening. Seconds later, her cell vibrated with an incoming call.

"Is Cash okay?"

"I'm fine, Beth. Thanks for asking."

"Of course you are. You're always fine. That's why I didn't ask."

Lori couldn't argue given that was her stock answer when anyone asked how she was. "Cash is fine too. He made his irritation known when we stopped, but he's been quiet since."

"How quiet?" Beth asked. "Could he have collapsed? Can you check on him?"

"I haven't heard anything to suggest a twelve-hundred-pound horse hit the trailer floor. The earth would literally have moved beneath me."

Beth grumbled. "Still...can't you just take a peek?"

"I've been told not to get out of the truck, so I really can't, Beth," Lori said. "But I'm certain he's all right."

"How long will it be before Gabe gets to you?"

Lori checked to see that Gabe had sent her a message estimating her arrival time and quickly did the math. "Just over thirty minutes."

"Should I come and keep Cash and you company?"

Lori saw flashing lights in her mirrors as a patrol car pulled in behind her. "No need. It looks like a police officer is about to do that. I'll text you when we're on our way so you can be ready to unload Cash. I'm sure he'll be very pleased to see you."

"Okay," Beth said slowly, clearly unconvinced.

Lori ended the call and wound her window down as the officer approached her. Just as Gabe had predicted, the policewoman checked the security of the horse trailer and said she'd wait until her tow arrived. Lori thanked her, feeling much safer for both her and Cash when she saw the passing traffic move over into the fast lane due to the police officer's presence. She dropped the passenger side window to encourage a light breeze through the car, then settled back into her seat to wait for Gabe to ride to her rescue in her shiny tow truck chariot.

Chapter Sixteen

GABE SLOWED THE TRUCK to a gentle stop in the driveway of the Sanctuary, not wanting to freak out the horse in the back. She recognized Beth as she came running to the horse trailer. Beth gave them a short wave but didn't stop and headed around the back of the vehicle. "More worried about the horse than you?"

Lori laughed. "She *is* devoted. Anyway, you seemed worried enough about me for all of us."

Gabe cut the engine. "You wouldn't believe the number of people who die in roadside crashes," she said. "Couldn't have that happen on my watch. I think that would be an official 'bad friend' stamp, wouldn't it?"

"It definitely would," Lori said, "but thank you for being concerned about me anyway. It felt good."

"Glad to be of service." Gabe hopped out of the cab and went around the back to see how Beth was doing before she fell any deeper into Lori's soft gaze and said something she really shouldn't.

Beth had already unlocked the trailer and was at Cash's side. "He seems calm; you must've driven pretty steady."

"I always do when I have precious cargo," Gabe said.

Lori smiled brightly as she rounded the horse trailer to stand opposite Gabe, having obviously heard what she'd said. And there was that soft look she could get lost in again.

"Did Ellery say anything else about his recovery plan?" Beth asked.

"You know Ellery—everything was detailed in the report she emailed."

Beth uncoupled Cash and began to back him out. "I printed out the diet sheet and gave everyone a copy as well as pinning it to the wall in the feed house."

Gabe nodded toward Lori; she appreciated anyone that dedicated to their work.

"I'll get these shoes off him, saddle him up, and take him for a gentle ride," Beth said. "I bet he's desperate to feel the wind in his mane after being cooped up at the clinic for nearly two weeks." She patted Cash's neck and looked at Lori. "Diesel and Madonna need some exercise too. Why don't you and Gabe join us?"

Gabe held up her hands and shook her head. "Horseback riding is one skill I've never mastered." And if the horses Beth just mentioned were anything like the size of Cash, she didn't think she should try.

Lori narrowed her eyes. "Never mastered or never tried?"

Gabe frowned. How did Lori reach into her mind like that? "The closest I've gotten to having something that powerful between my legs is when I've ridden those crazy mechanical bulls, and that never worked out so good."

Lori raised her hand to her mouth as if she was covering a laugh. "I imagine you're used to being the powerful one."

Gabe wanted the earth to open up and swallow her whole. If this was how Lori talked to her as a friend, it was going to make sticking to her guns a damn sight harder.

"So do you want to try, or are you too scared?"

Gabe rolled her neck. *Gauntlet thrown*. "Are you calling me chicken?"

Lori gave her a wicked grin. "That'll depend on your answer, won't it?"

"Whoa, whoa, whoa," Beth said and guided Cash between them. "I need to get Cash away from this combustible situation."

Lori laughed and patted Cash's rear end as he passed her. "We're just kidding around, Beth. There's no fire."

Gabe clenched her jaw and *other* parts of her. They'd have to agree to disagree on that one.

"So what do you think?" Lori asked as they watched Cash and Beth head toward the stables. "If you haven't got any plans, I'd like to make you dinner to say thank you for the tow." She glanced at her watch. "But it's still a little early for that, and I need to exercise the horses."

Lori's little show of hot minx had all but disappeared, and she seemed to be her usual controlled self again. Gabe let out a relieved breath, knowing she'd be powerless to resist that kind of game. "Dinner sounds great. Shay and Woody are taking turns on cooking duty, and neither one of them are Dominique Crenn."

"You're a foodie?" Lori hit the button to raise the trailer ramp.

"Nah, I just like to read about powerful and influential women," Gabe said and winked, immediately regretting it. Maybe dinner wasn't such a good idea. But she was never going to become immune to Lori's charms without temptation and exposure.

"And beautiful women..."

Gabe forced herself *not* to interpret either Lori's words or her tone. "That never hurts."

"Sometimes it does."

Lori's playfulness disappeared entirely, and the sparkle in her eyes dulled.

"Yeah, I guess it can." Gabe shrugged.

"Ah, of course, you've 'never had any serious relationships where hearts have gotten involved on either side.'"

"Something like that," Gabe said, "but given your curse-gift, it was probably exactly like that."

Lori's expression was answer enough. Gabe gestured to the truck. "How about you exercise your animals while I inspect the truck's engine?"

"You really don't want to give the horseback riding a try?"

"Another day, for sure," Gabe said.

Lori arched her eyebrow. "You know I won't forget you said that."

"It really *never* fails?" Gabe asked. "How big must your brain be to hold all that information?"

Lori smiled. "Big enough or too big, depending on my perspective at the time." She thumbed toward the stable. "If you're sure, I'll catch up with Beth, and I'll be done in an hour."

"Perfect."

When Lori returned just over an hour later, Gabe was under the hood of the tow truck removing the final spark plug to clean it up. She hadn't had much chance to check its engine since they'd bought it as part of the garage. And it hadn't taken long to discover the source of Lori's troubles, so she tinkered under the hood for something to focus on other than the thought of Lori's lips and the way they'd quirked when she was teasing Gabe.

"Is it a good or a bad thing for me that you're not still working on my trailer?" Lori asked.

Gabe glanced across as Lori got closer and pulled in a breath. Dressed in cowboy boots, jeans, a snap button shirt, and a cowboy hat, Lori looked like she was about to model for one of the calendars Gabe always had pinned up in her tent on base. She swallowed and pushed away the desire to press Lori against the truck, pull open that shirt, and bury her face between Lori's breasts. "Er, I'm sorry to report it's a bad thing." She replaced the plug without tending to it and slammed the hood shut. Gabe was about to continue but Lori held her hand up.

"Stop. Please don't say anymore. I don't want to hear bad news on an empty stomach or without a glass of red wine in my hand." Lori hooked her arm into Gabe's and tugged her toward the house. "Do you like lasagna?"

"I *love* lasagna."

"Excellent. I baked a couple fresh last night, so it just needs to be warmed while I rustle up some fresh garlic bread." Lori opened the door, and Gabe followed her in. "The bathroom is the door at the far end of the corridor if you want to freshen up."

"Thanks." Gabe closed the door behind her and stared at

herself in the mirror before turning on the faucet. She pumped the soap a couple of times and lathered it up over the grease spots, working it in as she continued to study her own face. How was this thing going to turn out? Gabe wasn't an animal; she could control her urges around Lori, but how healthy was it to keep torturing herself? Surely there were other women out there she could be friends with and not have an inescapable sexual attraction to.

She rinsed and dried her hands. The dispenser adjacent to the soap was moisturizer in a matching lemongrass and coconut scent, so she applied some, aware that her knuckles were looking a bit dry from the de-greaser at the garage. In fact, her hands were looking rough but not in a rugged way that some women liked. That shouldn't matter right now though, since she was with a friend and didn't need to worry about things like that.

Gabe pulled her phone from the thigh pocket of her cargo pants and fired off a quick text to Shay to let her know she wouldn't be back for whatever faux-gourmet meal she'd be burning.

Cozy dinner for two doesn't sound like the friend zone. I hope you know what you're doing.

Gabe sat on the edge of the tub. *I'm playing it by ear. Friends can have dinner together. How many times have we done this?*

I don't think us eating slop out of tin dishes in the middle of the desert is comparable. Ask her to invite Rosie, and then I'll come over to chaperone you. I'll borrow your truck.

Gabe grinned. *You know better than to touch my truck. And if Rosie was here, you wouldn't notice if Lori and I started making out next to you. I'll think about you all while I'm eating homemade lasagna.*

Asshole.

Gabe smiled and slipped her phone back in her pocket before she headed to the kitchen. Lori pressed a chilled-to-perfection bottle of beer into her hand with practiced ease, making it impossible not to imagine the same scenario each night after a hard day's work at the garage.

"I figured one beer would be okay with a heavy meal since you're driving," Lori said and pushed a dish of olives and cheese bites on the kitchen counter toward Gabe. "I've had a snack and now I have alcohol; lay the bad news on me."

Gabe touched her bottle to Lori's wine glass then took a long pull and savored its flavor for a moment before answering. "Am I easing you into this? Or–"

"Rip the Band-Aid off, Gabe. I have a feeling a spoonful of sugar won't help one iota."

"The cam belt snapped, and your engine is toast," Gabe said. "The truck itself is sound though, so I'd recommend a new engine rather than a whole new trailer. I checked a few of our suppliers, and we could source one for just over three thousand."

Lori didn't seem to be affected by the news or the price, but Gabe supposed these kinds of hits came all the time running a large business like the Sanctuary.

"Okay." Lori took a deep breath. "What about the labor? How long would it take you to fit the new engine?"

Gabe hadn't made assumptions, so it made her seriously happy for Lori to want her to do the work. "It should take us about five hours if we don't hit any snags. Ten at most."

"And what's your hourly rate?"

"One ten, but–"

"No." Lori shook her head. "No buts. You're doing enough for me and the Sanctuary with the rust bucket and the money your TikTok intervention raised."

The look that Lori shot Gabe made it clear she wouldn't be convinced to change her mind, and the team would appreciate the work, so she didn't press. "It won't be so much of a rust bucket by the end of the week. RB and Solo will have it stripped down by the end of this week. There won't be an oxidized metal spot in sight."

"While I was waiting for you to pick me up, I called Mom to

let her know that we could make the auction a little earlier than planned," Lori said. "She just texted to say she's booked the Regina Park for September 14; is that too early?"

Gabe shook her head. "We think we'll be finished by the end of next month."

Lori smiled widely. "That'll be a wonderful birthday gift, and there's a nice symmetry to it. I get to start my life again on the day I was born."

"When's your birthday?"

"August 21."

Gabe nibbled the inside of her lip, deciding whether or not to ask the question that prompted.

"Did you want to ask something?"

Gabe frowned and leaned back against the kitchen island. "How are you doing that? It's like you can read my thoughts." Which would be a bad, bad thing.

Lori shrugged. "It seems like you're an open book. Are you not?"

"Not to anyone else. Except Shay, but she's known me for nearly twenty years."

Lori raised her eyebrows. "You served together all that time?"

"Yeah. We met when she saved my life."

"Color me intrigued," Lori said. "Shay saved *your* life, not the other way around?"

"Don't worry, I've restored my butch credentials by repaying the favor a couple of times since then, including resuscitating her after she was struck by lightning."

"That's how she got her Army nickname?"

"Yep. We're not a particularly imaginative bunch." Gabe sniffed the air. "That smells amazing."

Lori smiled. "I'm glad you think so. If you like it, you can take the second one home for the rest of your team– Is it okay to call them your team?"

"Sure. It's easier than naming them all, and they're used to being called that. I'm not sure how I feel about sharing though." Gabe peered through the glass front of the oven to avoid Lori's questioning gaze. "How did you make the garlic bread so quickly?"

"I had fresh dough in the fridge from last night too."

"Wow. I didn't leave until six. Were you at it all night?"

"Kind of. I bake when I'm... I bake to distract myself."

Gabe wasn't sure whether to push or not, so she left the silence for Lori to fill if she wanted to explain. She didn't, leaving Gabe to wonder what she needed distraction from. Gabe glanced at Lori's hand wrapped around her glass and spotted white swirls on peach-colored polish. "You and Rosie managed to find an open nail salon on Saturday?" Gabe briefly touched Lori's fingers. "I can remember stuff too," she added when Lori looked impressed.

Lori stretched out her hands and smiled. "It was a nice thing to do. I've been a little neglectful of my femme armor recently."

Gabe resisted the urge to run her fingers over Lori's nails, but she was unable to stop the thought of Lori raking her nails down Gabe's back. "You think of your nails as armor?"

"I suppose that sounds ridiculous to a soldier," Lori said, blushing slightly.

"No, not at all. I've just never thought of them that way." The only way Gabe had ever thought about the nails of any woman she was attracted to was in direct connection to her core.

"I suppose it's even more ridiculous that I neglected them when I needed them so much."

Gabe hated the profound sadness that radiated from Lori, and once again wished she could meet the ex-wife in a dark alley to extract some revenge for all the hurt and pain she'd caused Lori. Though she realized that was more about alleviating her feelings rather than Lori's. "But you're coming out the other side of that?"

Lori nodded slowly. "I am. Getting the rust bucket out of my life and repurposing that building are the last physical actions I need to take to finally move on." She gave a soft smile. "At least that's the conclusion my therapist and I have come to."

Great. Lori was moving on, which would mean that eventually she'd be back on the scene, and Gabe would have to listen to her tales of disaster dates and fabulous fucks. She almost physically recoiled at the unwanted images that popped into her head of Lori with other women. The only way Gabe would be able to cope with that would be mindless sex of her own immediately after any conversation with Lori so that she could distance herself from her own actual feelings.

"That must feel good," Gabe said, the sentiment genuine even if the consequences were likely going to be painful for her.

"It really is. Especially now that Ellery is on board with the development."

Gabe listened intently as Lori lit up while talking about her plans for the veterinary clinic. She tried to focus on the words rather than the way Lori's mouth moved and wondering how her full lips would feel between Gabe's legs. As she squeezed away the throbbing in her center, she reminded herself this torture was essential so she could control her lust and concentrate on their friendship. "Seems like a great match," she said when Lori finished talking.

"We should save a lot of money, which we can use elsewhere," Lori said. "Like on a new engine for that damn vehicle outside."

"Speaking of, I left it hooked up so I could take it straight to your local garage." Gabe grinned. "Which is us, obviously. Did you want me to do that? Or did you have a different plan?"

The timer on the oven beeped. "Hold that thought." Lori pulled out the steaming lasagna and golden-brown garlic bread. She placed a plate in front of Gabe and gave her a large, flat metal spatula. "Would you serve for both of us?"

Serve. Worship. Cherish. Yes to all of them.

Gabe carved up two pieces of lasagna and followed Lori to

the dining table, where Lori placed their drinks before going back for the piping hot bread. Gabe scooped a forkful of food into her mouth and sighed. When she'd swallowed it down, she asked, "How did you get to be such an amazing cook?"

"When your parents are busy rescuing elephants from abandoned wells and would-be poachers, it behooves you to learn some culinary skills."

"Be-what?" Gabe laughed around another mouthful of edible heaven.

"Traveling expands your vocabulary too," Lori said and wiggled her eyebrows. "You have a year in England to thank for that particular word. But back to your earlier question; it would be great if you could take the Oakley tonight and fix it as soon as possible. Fran was supposed to be driving to Louisville on Friday to pick up Camden Market, the racehorse I told you about."

"The condition for their support to restore the Brewster?"

Lori nodded. "It's really no imposition. We've just rehomed Cannonball, and we had a free stall. Ellery is looking forward to treating her too." She nudged Gabe's shoulder. "Maybe she can be the horse you learn to ride."

"I thought you said it had some sort of leg injury. I doubt putting one-hundred-and-sixty pounds of me on her back would help that. And learning on a race horse doesn't sound optimal."

Lori glanced at her briefly as if she might say something, but then she pressed her lips together and looked at her plate.

"It's mostly muscle," Gabe said, in case Lori had been surprised by her weight, which, unlike too many women, she was proud of.

This time, Lori's gaze lingered on her arms. "It looks like it's *all* muscle."

Gabe grinned. "Nice of you to notice, friend."

"I'm healing from heartbreak; I'm not blind."

Gabe didn't even try to maintain eye contact; that kind of behavior would likely lead to a misplaced kiss. She tore off a chunk of bread, dipped it in the meat sauce that had gathered on her plate, and occupied her mouth with chewing instead. She vaguely wished she'd taken the seat opposite Lori to put some much-needed distance between them. This close...this close, it would be too easy to slip and do something she'd regret—something she was damned sure they'd both enjoy—but definitely something they'd both regret too.

Several moments of blissful silence followed, and Gabe took the time to savor the delicious food.

"I'm glad you mentioned Rosie earlier," Lori said. "Has Shay said anything about her?"

Gabe put down her fork and shifted on her seat slightly to face Lori. "Has Rosie said something about Shay?"

Lori prodded Gabe's forearm with her fork. "I asked first. You can't answer a question with another question."

"You saw the sparks too then?" Gabe finished the last of her beer and poured a glass of water from the jug on the table.

"I think the NASA space station would've seen those sparks if they'd been looking."

Gabe laughed and nodded. "Shay is Rosie's type?"

"Oh God, yes," Lori said.

"And yours too?" Gabe didn't hold back her surprise at Lori's enthusiastic response.

"Oh God, no." She frowned then widened her eyes. "I didn't mean that to be as offensive as it sounded. She *is* stunning, but she's not for me, no."

"I wasn't offended," Gabe said. *Relieved, yes. Offended, no.* "Although you're very much her type, as is Rosie."

Lori blushed again. "Did she say that?"

"Why wouldn't she? You're a beautiful woman."

Lori seemed to shrink back into her chair a little. "That's something I haven't heard for a long time."

"Not even when you were married?"

She shook her head and slipped back under that cloak of sadness again, making Gabe wish she hadn't asked.

"I'm not sure the lawyer ever thought I was beautiful. Exotic and well-traveled, someone to parade in front of her friends and make her seem more sophisticated, perhaps. But no, after the first few months, the compliments were as dry as our sex life—sorry, you probably didn't want that level of detail."

Gabe placed her hand over Lori's. "Then she was a moron. Someone as beautiful as you are, inside and out, shouldn't settle for anything less than total adoration."

And there it was... That moment where the line between friends and lovers was illuminated, flashing bulbs neon-bright and unmissable. Lori's lips were so close. Gabe could wrap her hand around the back of her neck and softly pull her in, press them together, meld their intentions into hot, sensual action. Lori's breasts rose and fell with her deep, long breaths, inviting Gabe to touch them, to discover exactly how Lori wanted to be held and explored and discovered. And God, if Gabe didn't long to blast through their ban on anything beyond friendship, then she longed for nothing at all.

Gabe wet her lips and stared at Lori's, just a breath away from finding out how she tasted.

Then in her head, she uttered her safe words: *Cynthia Nelson*. And she pulled back from the brink of abandoning all logic and restraint. Friendship was what she needed from Lori, and it was what Lori needed from her. This was just the heat of Lori's vulnerability, and anything she did in this moment would spoil everything.

Gabe cleared her throat and reached for the lemonade, hoping the sour taste would destroy all thoughts of the anticipated sweetness of Lori's kiss. "I should go," she whispered then said it again in her regular voice. "Shay's waiting at the shop to help me unload your trailer."

Lori blinked as if she were clearing the same fog of desire, then she nodded. "Of course. Yes, it's getting late. I'm sorry for keeping you."

Gabe smiled. "You never have to apologize to me," she said and stood. "Thanks again for dinner; this is the best food I've had in ages, maybe ever."

Lori remained seated and pointed toward the kitchen. "Don't forget to take the second one home with you. It's on the middle shelf in the fridge."

"Are you sure?"

"I'm sure. I can always make more."

Lori shrugged and smiled, but it lacked her usual glow, and Gabe ached to take her in her arms and rock away all the pain.

"I'll see you Wednesday, okay?" Gabe asked, though forty-eight hours seemed like too far away. "Do you want me to come pick you up?"

"No, don't be crazy. I'll pick you up on the way through."

"That'd be great if you don't mind. I'll send you the address." Gabe could only face the thought of babysitting for Solo and Janie because Lori had agreed to help.

"And I'll bring the ingredients for pad Thai, so make sure you don't eat."

Gabe nodded. "If I'd known friendship came with these kinds of benefits, I would've widened my circle a long time ago."

"Me too. It works both ways; you're really helping me out getting the truck fixed quickly."

"Of course. I'll order the engine when I get back to the garage, and we should have it ready to pick up by Thursday. No need to change Fran's plans." Gabe waited for a moment too long before she went to the kitchen for the lasagna. "They're gonna love this. Thanks again."

"Absolutely my pleasure," Lori said.

Gabe hovered in the hallway, trying to decide whether or not to go in for a hug. She decided against it when Lori didn't move. "Cool. I'll see you Wednesday at six," she said and walked out into a hot July evening. She closed the door behind her and hesitated, every fiber of her being desperate to go back inside so she could hold Lori tight.

She looked up at the sky and saw it was a full moon. Weren't people supposed to do crazy things on a night like this? *Cynthia Nelson*. That was the last crazy thing she'd done, and that had turned into a shitstorm of epic proportions. And she was still feeling its tremors.

Gabe crunched across the gravel driveway to her tow truck and jumped in the cab. A cold shower and a double whiskey would have to chase the crazy away tonight.

Chapter Seventeen

"YOU SHOULD'VE GONE WITH a stony-puke color. Rookie mistake."

Gabe straightened the shoulders of her T-shirt. "I look better in black."

Shay arched her eyebrow. "And why would that matter? I don't think the triplets will care what color shirt they barf on."

Gabe ignored the question and wrinkled her nose. "They'd better not, or Solo will be buying me a new one. And they'll be asleep, won't they?"

"I'm not the encyclopedia of babies; how would I know what their sleeping habits are?"

"Because you've got nine hundred younger siblings, and you raised most of them." Gabe ran back upstairs to her room and opened her T-shirt drawer. She ignored Shay's advice and selected a dark gray marl instead. She did choose a slightly looser fit than the one she had on; they weren't going on a date, after all.

Shay stood at the base of the stairs with her arms crossed. "I don't have nine hundred siblings, asshole."

Gabe sighed, recognizing she'd overstepped. "Sorry, Shay, that was an asshole thing to say; I'm just nervous."

"Thanks. I should be used to it by now." Shay smiled. "You really think desensitization therapy is going to work on a person?"

Gabe took her denim jacket from the coat hook and put it on. "I don't have any other choice. And I don't see why it wouldn't. I've never been interested in a woman for much longer than a week."

"You're already passed that milestone. How's that working out for you?"

Gabe shrugged. "I haven't slept with her," she said, knowing it didn't answer the question.

"Maybe you *should* just sleep together and get her out of your system. Maybe a one-night stand is exactly what Lori needs to move on from the ex. You'd be doing her a favor as well as curing your own fascination."

Gabe looked at her phone and rolled her eyes. It was still another fifteen minutes before Lori was due to pick her up. She dropped down to sit on the stairs, figuring she may as well get comfortable for another fifteen minutes of interrogation. "I'm not *fascinated*."

"What would you call it?"

"Interest," Gabe said. "I think she's an interesting woman. And you told me I should let more people in, so that's what I'm trying to do."

"I did, and I stand by that, but maybe you could've picked a straight person or a gay guy. Someone interesting you couldn't or didn't want to sleep with."

A horn sounded outside, and Gabe jumped up. She scooted past Shay and opened the door to see Lori waving from inside her Chevy Bolt. "She's early." Gabe took a set of house keys from the bowl on the sideboard and glanced back at Shay. "See you later."

"When we'll pick up this conversation," Shay said.

"Can't wait." Gabe closed the door and jogged down the path to Lori. She tossed her spare shirt into the back, then folded herself into the passenger seat, her knees practically hitting her chest.

Lori looked like she was suppressing laughter. "Maybe we should take your truck?"

"Why? Because your car is one step up from a kid's toy?"

Lori shoved Gabe's shoulder. "It is not."

Gabe waved her on. "It's fine. We don't have far to go." And

Gabe didn't want to go back into the house to face more questions from Shay. The longer she could delay that conversation, the happier she'd be.

There seemed to be no residual awkwardness from Monday night during the short drive to Solo's house. They'd exchanged a couple of messages on Tuesday, mostly about the repairs to the Oakley, and a part of Gabe had wanted to address the almost-kiss. But she decided to put it down to the combination of wine and vulnerability rather than an active attraction on Lori's side. She had to remind herself that she was the one who didn't want to act on *any* attraction.

"So we'll definitely have the truck finished for you by noon on Thursday," Gabe said. "Do you want us to drop it off?"

"Oh, no, I can't ask you to do that. Fran will pick it up." Lori pulled to a stop at the lights alongside Millennium Park. "What's your take on the Bean?"

"Huh?" Gabe followed the direction of Lori's pointed finger to a sculpture.

"The Bean," she said again. "Do you like it?"

The light changed to green, and Gabe studied the mirrored lump as Lori cruised past it. "I like the reflections of the skyline, I guess. Are you looking for a critique? Because I'm no art buff."

"You don't have to be an art expert to know whether or not something artistic appeals to you."

Gabe shrugged. "Then no, I don't like it. I don't see the point of it."

"Does art have to have a point?" Lori asked. "Isn't the point of all art simply to exist?"

Gabe frowned. "Like I said, I'm not an art person. I didn't realize you were." She called up images of Lori's kitchen and dining room in her mind and couldn't remember seeing anything particularly arty on the walls or surfaces. But then Gabe wouldn't know art if it smacked her in the face with a picture frame.

"I'm not," Lori said brightly. "But I like sculptures."

"Thank God. I thought you were working up to asking me to go to an art gallery with you because none of your other friends would."

Lori gave her a sideways glance. "You don't have to worry about that, ever. I've never been interested in paintings. I like the kind of art that you find in parks and on the streets. Art that's accessible and for everyone, not just pseudo-intellectuals and snobs."

"That's not judgmental at all," Gabe said.

"Sorry. I'm sure that's not the case overall. I've just met a lot of those kinds of people through the lawyer's family and friends plus all the funding drives we've done."

"Super-rich people?"

Lori nodded. "Yeah. Their lives are so...unreal. Can you imagine being able to spend $30 million on a boat and not miss it?"

Gabe laughed. "I miss the thirty dollars I spend on burgers at StopAlong. But their generosity keeps you going, doesn't it?"

"Absolutely, and I'm not being ungrateful or jealous or any other negative emotion. It's just that sometimes it reminds me of the inequality in the world, and I wonder if I'm doing enough to help."

"Of course you are. The work you're doing at the Sanctuary is amazing, and it's making a difference to the animals you rescue and for the kids who get the chance to interact with them." Gabe turned toward Lori as much as she could in the cramped space. "Has something happened?"

Lori glanced at Gabe and half-smiled. "Yeah. I was talking to Mom earlier today, and she told me that one of our major donors has pulled their support. Post-COVID slump and all that."

"Is the Sanctuary going to be okay?" Gabe didn't need to analyze why her first thought went there rather than concern for the whole family company.

"I don't know yet. Getting the clinic set up and running will help. Our accountant has to work on new projections, and Mom and Dad will have to go on the hunt for a new donor. It's a mess we don't need."

Gabe picked at the seam of her jacket, knowing she had nothing to say that would improve the situation. "I'm sorry. You should've let me know and canceled."

Lori huffed. "And subject the triplets to just you?" She smiled and shook her head. "Nope. And I need the distraction. There's very little I can do from here. Mom's visiting next week for my birthday, so she should know more by then." She put her hand on Gabe's knee briefly. "And you're helping with the rust bucket. I googled auction sales after I'd talked to Mom; hopefully, ours will be nearer the $200k mark."

Gabe's mood lifted. They had to make the Brewster ultra-desirable to bring in the top car collectors from all over the world. At least she had the ability to do that for Lori. "Have you started putting together the information booklet yet?"

"Bruce is handling that, but yes, I think it's in motion. Why?"

"The first owner, the artist—I can't remember her name, but that should be front and center. People go wild for the possessions of dead celebrities." Gabe shifted in her seat and smacked her head on the roof.

"I hope you haven't left a mark," Lori said and chuckled.

"Your concern for me is overwhelming, thank you." Gabe rubbed the top of her head for effect.

"I feel like I'd only need to be concerned if a whole building fell on you. Anything less, and you'd just shrug it off. Am I wrong?"

Gabe grinned. She liked being thought of as indestructible. "Anyway, I'll bet there are collectors out there who'd love to own the Brewster just because she used to own it. What was her name again?" she asked.

"Marie Zimmerman." Lori took the off ramp and turned left onto West Belmont. "That's a great idea, Gabe. When we get to the house, I'll send a quick email to Bruce for him to follow up."

"Woody's been busy setting up our website and social media presence," Gabe said. "She's planning a whole section of the site to be dedicated to our restoration projects because that's going to be a big part of the business. Once she has it up and running, the Brewster will be all over it. If you could get Bruce to send us anything he finds, Woody can feature it, and we can help build interest."

"Perfect." Lori touched Gabe's knee again. "Thank you for everything you're doing." Lori followed the next couple of instructions on her GPS and pulled up outside Solo's house. "Wow. This is a nice neighborhood. Do they have a boat at the yacht club across the street too?"

"Actually, yeah. Solo's got a forty-foot sailing boat, but I'm pretty sure they didn't pay $30 million for it."

"That's a shame. They might've wanted to support our work." Lori got out of the car and pulled an overstuffed grocery bag from the back.

Gabe joined Lori on the street and took the bag from her. She opened the gate and gestured for Lori to go in first.

At the top of the stone steps, Janie stood in the doorway. "Please do something with your friend before I do something I can't defend myself from in court." She hugged Gabe then stepped aside for them to enter and offered her hand to Lori. "You must be the Sanctuary angel I've heard all about."

"Really?" Lori blushed. "Most people just call me Lori, but I like that title much better."

"You look stunning, Janie," Gabe said, taking in Janie's elegant scarlet dress and heels.

"Thank you. I'm glad someone noticed." She smoothed the dress at her hips. "I wasn't sure I'd still fit in this after the triplets."

"You're not so much fitting it as rocking it. Solo is a lug-head if she hasn't fallen to your feet already. Are you sure she's *seen* you?"

Janie looked exasperated. "Probably not. She's far too

preoccupied."

"What's she doing now? Having trouble with her bow tie?" Gabe asked.

"She's in the playroom with the babies. See for yourself." Janie hooked her arm into Lori's and took the bag of food from Gabe with the other one. "I'll show Lori to the kitchen."

Gabe looked at Lori to check she was okay, and Lori waved her away. "Go. Fix your friend. We'll be fine."

"Okay." Gabe headed to the back of the house where she found Solo in a black tux, pacing around their playpens. "You're looking sharp."

Solo turned around briefly before focusing back on the babies. "You're early. Still on Army time?"

"Nope, this is all Lori," Gabe said. "What're you doing in here? Your wife is dressed to kill, and you haven't told her how amazing she looks. Is a divorce really what you want?"

"Huh?" Solo spun around. "Is that what she said? Fuck." She looked to the door and then back to the babies and then back to the door.

Gabe grabbed Solo's shoulder. "Hey, I was just kidding. What's going on?"

"Are you sure you're going to be all right?" Solo's eyes darted from Gabe to the triplets. "Should we just stay in and order takeout?"

"Lori's here to help me, and she's already in the kitchen getting ready to cook. So, yes, we're going to be fine, and you need to take your beautiful wife to the theater. What are you going to watch?"

"*Medea: Priestess, Princess, Witch*. You know what that's about? A mother who kills her kids."

"Well, maybe she doesn't in this version, and I promise you I won't either. Your girls are going to be fine." Gabe gave Solo a firm shake. "Come on, buddy. What's the problem? You've been leaving the babies every day for a few hours. This is no different."

"This will be the first time I haven't put them to bed." Solo stuffed her hands in her pockets. "I like that I'm the last thing they see before they go to sleep."

"What about when you went out with me? You were out all night."

"Yeah, but I'd put them to bed and read their favorite stories before I came out."

"Is this why you've been in a hurry to leave the shop every day?" Gabe asked as Solo's recent behavior and this new information formed the full picture. She'd assumed Solo was in a hurry to get home to her gorgeous wife, which she could understand. She hadn't even considered the possibility that Solo had been missing her kids.

Solo shrugged and didn't meet Gabe's eyes. "I know, I'm a sap. Sorry."

Gabe shook her head. "Sorry for what? Loving your kids? I'm pretty sure you shouldn't apologize for that." She was powerless not to draw the comparison to her own parents and their *lack* of love. "I think it's kind of sweet to see you like this."

Solo snapped her head up and frowned. "You're fudging with me."

Gabe laughed. "Fudging?"

"If a curse is one of their first words, Janie will kill me. Seriously though, since when do you think anything is sweet?"

Gabe held up her hands. "What can I say? What worked for me in the Army doesn't work out here in the real world. I'm learning to be a different person, I guess. Like you did. You've changed so much since coming out of the service that it's sometimes hard to recognize you."

Solo finally smiled. "And I suppose your changes are nothing to do with your *friend* in our kitchen?"

"Lori is part of it, yeah, but so are you and Janie...and the girls," she said, gesturing to the relatively cute-looking triplets, though they'd probably transform to gremlins the moment their moms left the house. "The business is a big part of it too. It's everything, not just one thing. You should know that; you've been through it and come out great on the other side." The thought of other Army buddies who hadn't navigated the change dropped like an engine block in her gut. "Not everyone does."

Solo nodded and cast her eyes downward again, but this time in respect. It didn't need to be said out loud. Every veteran felt it. Every soldier who survived their tours *and* civilian life never forgot the thousands who didn't.

Gabe grasped Solo's shoulder again. "Say goodbye to your girls, go to the kitchen and *look* at your wife, then go out and have a great time. Okay?"

Solo slung her arm around Gabe's shoulder and pulled her into a bro hug. "Thanks, Gabe."

She jutted her chin in acknowledgment of Solo's use of her actual name instead of yet another play on her last name. "I could get used to that."

Solo tilted her head. "I guess I could too as long as it doesn't have to go both ways."

"It doesn't." After Solo had kissed each of her kids goodnight, Gabe shoved Solo out the door.

Back in the kitchen, it looked like Janie had just finished going through a long list of dos and don'ts and was showing Lori a video monitor.

"It's linked to every room, so you just cycle through to the playroom or the babies' bedroom, and you can keep an eye on them from wherever you are," Janie said.

"Wife, you look fantastic." Solo wrapped her arms around Janie's waist and kissed her briefly.

"You're all set?" Janie asked.

"We are," Lori said. "Go and enjoy yourselves."

"We will if Solo isn't checking the nanny cam every five seconds." Janie rolled her eyes. "And we should be back around eleven."

After they left, Lori grabbed Gabe's arm. "Take me to the babies!"

Gabe laughed and led Lori to the playroom. "You have to watch out for that one." Gabe pointed to Tia, who grinned at her like butter wouldn't melt. "That smile doesn't fool me, devil child."

Lori whacked her shoulder. "What are you talking about? She looks like a little angel. They all do."

Gabe nodded her head slowly. "You'll change your mind by the end of the night. I promise."

Lori scooped Tia into her arms. "Let's put them all in the playpen in the kitchen to keep us company."

Gabe picked up the purple-clothed one—Chloe, if memory served—and held her at arm's length to follow Lori back into the kitchen.

After Lori had gently placed Tia into the play area, she turned and gasped. "You don't have to hold them like one of your bombs, Gabe." She took Chloe from Gabe's grasp and placed her down beside the ringleader.

"Are you sure? Because I've seen them explode in much the same way a couple of times now."

Lori chuckled and went back to get the third baby. "They have beautiful names," she said, putting Luna alongside her sisters. "And the color-coding is genius." She dropped down onto the sofa and stared at them for a while. "Although you can see tiny differences if you look hard enough."

"Then it's good that you have such a great memory," Gabe said. "If we do this more often, we might end up bathing them, and if their nail polish wears off, I'll definitely mix them up."

Tia tossed a soft building brick in Gabe's direction, almost like she was proving her individuality, and it bounced off the rails and struck Luna in the face. Her eyes went wide as she opened her mouth and let out a blood-curdling scream that lasted about five seconds before she went silent and picked up the brick to play with it.

"Except that one." Gabe pointed at Tia. "I could pick that little troublemaker out even if they'd had sextuplets."

"She can probably sense your apathy," Lori said.

"Hey now, it's not apathy. It's self-preservation."

Lori shifted on the couch to face her. "What do you mean?"

Gabe gestured to the kitchen island. She'd done enough soul-searching for tonight with Solo, and she was hungry because she hadn't eaten after the gym. "Weren't you about to rustle up another tasty dish for me to try? My muscles need protein."

Lori flicked her gaze to Gabe's arms then rose from the sofa and went to sift through the ingredients she'd assembled on the countertop. "I can cook and talk. Get over here."

Gabe raised her eyebrows at the instruction but didn't say anything because the only thing that came to mind was sexual. Solo's countertop was ice-cool marble, and Gabe thought it wouldn't take long for them to set it on fire. Dutifully, she followed the order and sat on one of the stools opposite Lori.

"Janie made us a fresh pot of decaf. Would you like one?"

"I'll get it," Gabe said and began to move.

"Nope. You stay right there."

Gabe watched Lori move elegantly around the kitchen as if it were her own. Her movements were graceful and precise, like she was dancing around the space in her own little musical performance.

Lori located honey in the fourth cupboard she'd opened and added the perfect amount. It shouldn't surprise Gabe that Lori remembered exactly how she took her coffee, but she took it as a sign of her thoughtfulness anyway. She placed the mug in front of Gabe and didn't let go until Gabe met her eyes.

"Talk to me about self-preservation," she said and released the handle.

"Or we could talk more about the restoration project. Did you get a chance to send an email to Bruce between all the instructions you were given?" Gabe picked up the long, handwritten list Janie had left them and studied it.

"No, I thought it would be rude if I tapped away on my phone while Janie was talking." Lori slid her phone from her pocket. "I'll do it now, and then I can put it out of my mind."

Janie's list was extensive. She should've probably typed it so she could reprint it for the next suckers they got to babysit their tiny terrors. Gabe glanced over her shoulder at the playpen where the girls looked innocent enough, gurgling and talking away—maybe not so much talking as making sounds that only they could understand. Would she have wanted a sibling? To speak a language that was just theirs, to hate and support each other in equal measure. Would they have stuck by her when her parents threw her out on the street?

"I don't think we should talk about the rust bucket," Lori said and drew Gabe's attention back to her. "That's work. I don't want our friendship to revolve around work." She tilted her head to catch Gabe's gaze when she looked back down at the piece of paper. "I'm really enjoying getting to know you, Gabe, and I want to learn your thoughts about everything. Is that okay?"

Gabe sighed deeply. "Why?"

"Because that's how strong relationships are built. I want to understand you and how you navigate the world." Lori shrugged. "I think that's fascinating."

Gabe smiled at the same word that Shay had used as a jab earlier than evening, but Lori's intention was far kinder. "Okay, but can you not gaze at me like you're about to drag me into a world-record comfort hug?"

Lori laughed and wielded her chef's knife. "Fine. I won't look at you," she said and began slicing the chicken breast.

"I suppose it goes back to my family," Gabe said.

"My therapist tells me that's where most things are rooted, good or bad."

"That makes sense." Gabe folded the edge of Janie's list and ran her finger along the crease. "You're so put-together because you had a wonderful, loving family."

Lori tossed the meat into the nearby frying pan. "Mostly, yes. I think it gave me a solid platform to launch myself into adult life. But it isn't perfect armor; it didn't stop me from getting hurt by the lawyer."

"Can I ask why you never use your ex's name?"

Lori narrowed her eyes then nodded slowly. "That's a fair question. I can't expect you to lay yourself open if I won't, can I?"

"Exactly." And Gabe would use anything to delay this inspection of her soul.

"Names have power. People choose whether to use your first or last name, or they purposefully get your name wrong to play a psychological game, or they use a nickname that's been made just for them, like you do with your Army buddies." Lori rinsed her knife then began to dice fresh ginger. "Using a name is personal, and I no longer want to think of her in that way, close and personal. Referring to her by profession, as *the lawyer*, distances me from the painful, emotional baggage that's attached to that relationship." She looked up, her eyes tearful. "Does that make sense?"

"It makes perfect sense." Gabe was glad of the five feet of marble countertop between them, because her reaction to Lori's vulnerability was as predictable as the sunrise, and she wasn't certain she had the *friend hug* down yet. And she'd definitely struggle not to react to the feel of Lori's body pressing against hers.

"Good." She wafted the knife point in Gabe's direction. "Back to family," she said.

Gabe was beginning to see that there were disadvantages to this memory thing; Lori was always able to bring a distracted conversation back from the tangent they'd disappeared along, never allowing Gabe off the hook. "I've told you about my family. Even before they completely disowned me, things weren't good. I wasn't nurtured, or loved, or even held when I hurt myself."

She looked back down at the piece of paper and continued to fold and crease another edge. "Family doesn't have any positive meaning for me."

"What about your chosen family?" Lori asked. "You've got four sisters, and now," she motioned to the playpen, "you've got Janie and three little ones. She told me they're calling you Auntie Gabe."

"That's different. We're adults, and I never agreed to be anyone's auntie."

"You really don't like children?"

"I don't like the responsibility," Gabe said, catching Lori's edge of disappointment. "What do I know about babies, and growing up, and teaching a kid life skills? I know about survival, and pain, and abandonment. They're not things I want to share with anyone." She rolled her eyes. "Except you, apparently. Because you don't want to talk about the dire state of our country's liberties or the latest episode of *True Detective*."

"I'll happily talk about any of those things between deep getting-to-know-you conversations like these."

Lori's bright smile comforted Gabe and dragged her out of her self-pitying hole. "So what do you think of Jodie Foster's Chief Danvers?"

Lori waved her knife from side to side. "I said *between* the deep conversations, and we're not done with this one yet."

"Are you sure? I think we could be done. We could just move on to the next topic, and we'd be done. Easy."

"We're nearly done, I promise," Lori said. "And then we talk about whatever you want. Okay?"

Gabe grumbled and rolled her shoulders. "Fine. What else?"

"How do you feel when you see Solo with her kids?"

"Oh, come on." Gabe pushed the paper away. "I thought we were having a conversation, not a therapy session."

"Humor me. Please," she said quietly.

Gabe shook her head. Lori could ask her for anything in that way, and she'd happily give it. "I'm happy for them, and I like the way Solo is around them. She's always been immature and kind of shallow. She's got depth now, and I like that about her. But I'm not sure how I'm supposed to be a positive part of that."

"I think you're short-changing yourself and those babies. It sounds like you think that you can't be part of a family because yours was so bad."

"That sounds about right," Gabe said. "And it sounds logical too."

"You've learned through experience what a bad family is, so you know the mistakes you have to avoid making in any family you allow yourself to be part of. *Because* you had an awful family, your own will be full of love. You're a wonderful, kind, and generous person, Gabe. You should open yourself up to sharing that, and you could start right here with those three gorgeous babies."

"God damn it, woman." Gabe turned her stool around and looked at the triplets with fresh eyes, trying to see them as the person Lori had just described Gabe to be. She made a lot of sense, of course she did, but that didn't take away the very real fear of repeating the mistakes her parents made. Though she really wanted to be the person Lori seemed to think she was. The more time she spent with Lori, the more she could feel herself wanting to be that person. She wanted to be open and yes, even emotional. Her childhood and twenty years in the Army had beaten those things down, but they weren't gone. They weren't irretrievable.

For Lori, and for this friendship, Gabe would pull those characteristics back from the depths of her psyche and embrace them as strongly as she wanted to embrace Lori. And maybe they would overwhelm and dilute her sexual attraction, making a truly platonic friendship possible.

Yeah, and maybe we'll finally get a Black, female president elected...

Chapter Eighteen

"Do you think I'm inflexible and lack spontaneity?"

"Is this more of the lawyer's nonsense surfacing?" Rosie pushed a shot of tequila closer to Lori. "I thought you'd completed this stage?" She narrowed her eyes and leaned in. "Or is this something your new friend has leveled at you? I'll kick her ass. I don't care how big she is; I'll gnaw on her kneecaps."

Lori laughed at the visual. "It's neither, and also, I'm not sure when that stage ever finishes. But part of me wishes I could see you have a go at Gabe though, jealous heart."

Rosie knocked back her first shot from the rack of ten and slammed the glass back on the bar, upside down. "I'm not jealous. That's an ugly emotion. I'm envious and protective. You're just starting to come back around after the lawyer, and I wouldn't want my best friend disappearing again if Gabe breaks your heart." She poured salt on her hand, licked it, and munched on a fresh lime segment. "Although she told me you were just friends, and she wouldn't do anything that could mess with her access to Max, so I suppose I really don't have anything to worry about." Rosie pushed the glass closer to Lori's hand. "I can be envious of the amount of time you're spending together though, can't I? If I didn't care, what kind of best friend would I really be?"

"She said we were just friends?"

Rosie arched her eyebrow and gave her *the look*. "*That's* what you got from all that? Now you can see why I'm envious; even when we're together, you're more concerned about what Gabe's thinking." She tapped the glass in front of Lori. "Drink. Or I'm grabbing the first hot woman who comes through that door and taking her home, leaving you to the rest of these shots and your preoccupation with Sergeant Gabriella Jackson."

Lori grasped the glass and went through the ritual, wincing when she bit down on the particularly sour lime. "Isn't it good that you're the one I want to talk to about her?"

"I suppose that depends on the context," Rosie said. "How did the babysitting go the other night? Has it made you all broody and hormonal?"

"So what if it has?" Lori took two glasses from the rack. They downed them, and Lori sucked on the same lime piece, foregoing the salt. "If you ever settle down, do you want children?"

Rosie shrugged. "I haven't really thought about it. It feels like I'm so far from finding my princess that it doesn't seem fair to tease myself about the life we might lead together."

"Maybe you're not that far." Lori wiggled her eyebrows, the effect of the tequila already releasing her playful side. "Shay would make a pretty princess."

Rosie clutched her heart and fake-swooned. "Shay is a goddess, and she's out of my league. And I get the impression that she's too busy playing the field to sit on the bench. But we're not talking about me, we're talking about you and your hormones." She nudged Lori lightly. "Obviously, I don't need to ask you the same question; you've got a whole ranch full of surrogate children. Have you thought about in-vitro or adopting?"

Lori shook her head. "I want children, but I want them *with* someone. I want to share in the joys and heartaches of raising little humans." She pulled out her phone, flicked to one of the many, *many* photographs she'd taken of the triplets on Wednesday, and showed it to Rosie. "Aren't they the most adorable thing you've ever seen?"

"Wow." Rosie pinched the screen to enlarge the picture. "They really are identical. I hope they don't dress them all the same as they get older. I think that suffocates their potential for individuation."

Lori grinned. "I do love your psycho-babble."

"She says, while disparaging it as babble."

"Lovingly disparaging."

Rosie lined up another two drinks, and they dispatched them quickly. "I don't know how you've managed to stay in therapy so long when you hold it in such low regard."

Lori shrugged. She wasn't sure how she'd managed it either, though she had a feeling. "Desperation," she said, loud enough that the bartender looked over and winked.

"Ooh, hottie at two o'clock," Rosie said.

"Where does your inner feminist go when you get drunk?" Lori stacked a little tower with her empty glasses.

"She doesn't go anywhere. She just makes a little room for my vamp." Rosie prepared their fourth shots. "Anyway, back to adventures in babysitting. What does the big, bad, super-strong soldier think of helpless babies?"

"That's complicated." Lori didn't want to betray Gabe's confidence, since it was clear she was reluctant to share her story. "She was a little distant from them, and she doesn't seem to be embracing Hannah and Janie's desire to involve her in their family."

"Sounds like she might need help with some deep-seated childhood issues. But I'll bet she's even less interested in therapy than you."

Lori nodded. "Strong, silent types, huh? But I still had a great night. I'm so comfortable around her. I don't have to pretend to be anything. She has zero expectations, and I really like that."

"That's how all good friendships start, isn't it?"

Lori chewed on her bottom lip and didn't respond fast enough not to raise Rosie's suspicions.

She narrowed her eyes and sighed deeply. "That's where you're at, isn't it?" Rosie asked. "It was less than a week ago when you told me that you wanted to find yourself before you rushed into anything new. I believe you said you wanted to build a friendship first, and if Gabe was still around when you were ready, great. But if she wasn't, never mind."

"I've had another therapy session since then," Lori said and winked. "Seriously though, I'm wondering if there's any real reason to wait longer. Everything feels so good, and I don't think I want to risk losing Gabe to someone else. I know she's out tonight with the rest of her team; it's only a matter of time before someone realizes she's golden and snaps her up."

Rosie wagged her finger. "You think jumping into something you said you weren't ready for six days ago because you're worried Gabe won't be around is a good basis for a relationship?"

Lori downed the final shot. She bit down on a fresh piece of lime, and its tang zinged down her throat. "I don't need you as a therapist right now; I need you to talk to me as a friend."

"Okay... Are you sure you want to go down this road with her even though you've only known her a month?"

"I am, and I'm not. But I don't need to be a hundred percent sure. There are no certainties in life, and isn't that the beauty of it? I'd lost sight of that. So what will I know until I see where it goes? We enjoy spending time together. She makes me laugh, and we have great conversations. She's been there when I needed help. She dropped everything to rescue me from the freeway and to fix the Oakley. And she's delayed the opening of her garage to spend more time on the rust bucket—a project she's getting no money for." Lori flicked through her phone to the photo she'd secretly snapped of Gabe with Max. "She's better with dogs than kids, and she's been vulnerable and open enough to share why that is."

The bartender came over and asked if they wanted another rack of shots.

"No," they said together.

"We know our limits," Rosie said and smiled. "We'll take two mojitos, please."

Lori waited until she'd gone before she resumed her

explanation, which she needed to hear out loud to make sure it made as much sense as she thought it did. "Gabe does things for me because she wants to, not because there's any obligation. And that feels amazing."

Rosie's acceptance was clear in her smile. "So when are you going to tell her all that?"

"My birthday dinner. Mom will have already met her and told me what she thinks. I guess her opinion is the last part of the puzzle for me. And then, this is where you come in, I need you to make sure Mom gets home so I can take Gabe to a fancy hotel. We'll have mind-blowing sex, the likes of which I've never experienced."

Rosie stroked her chin like a pessimistic detective. "You've never really been that into sex though, have you?"

"Right! But it's all I can do to stop myself from pushing Gabe against a wall and running my mouth all over those slabs of muscle I keep getting peeks of. I mean, did you *see* her six-pack at the garage? And she was all hot and sweaty... Mm."

Rosie nodded. "I did. It almost made me entertain the thought of going butch for once."

"Exactly. The thought of sex with her is driving me insane. And she's been so understanding." She thought back to Monday night, and the almost drowsy look of desire in Gabe's eyes. "We were on the brink of kissing the night she towed the horse trailer, but she pulled back. She's respecting my rules and being a wonderful friend. But I'm sure she still wants me. I don't think that's changed from the first day we met. She's just doing a fantastic job of controlling herself."

The bartender returned with their drinks, and Lori took a long gulp like it might douse the fire of her craving.

"But I don't want her to hold back. Not anymore. I want to be more than just friends. I know that's not enough for me. I want all of her, and I'm going to tell her. And I'll be giving myself the best birthday gift ever: permission to please myself."

Rosie clinked her glass to Lori's. "We should toast then. Because it sounds like you've given this a lot of thought."

"Yes and no," she said and took a sip to celebrate. "I don't want to overthink it. That's why I asked if you thought I was inflexible and not spontaneous. I used to be flexible, and I'd act on the spur of the moment all the time. I used to believe in myself and be free, just like my parents encouraged me to be. But I lost that while I was with the lawyer, and I'm not letting her continue to influence my life or who I am. That's what I was doing though, holding back and not trusting myself and my feelings. And I'm done with that."

Rosie smiled widely. "Welcome back, Lori Turner. I've missed you," she said and drew Lori into a bone-crushing hug.

"Are you two celebrating something special?"

Rosie came up for breath to see Ellery and her on/off girlfriend at the bar beside them. Ellery smiled, but Lennie's lips were a fixed line as if someone had superglued them together. God, she was the most sullen person Lori had ever had the displeasure of meeting. Why Ellery kept taking her back was baffling.

"We weren't," Rosie said, "but I hear you've got something to celebrate. Congratulations on your new clinic."

Ellery's expression fell, and it became clear from Lennie's comedy-like eyebrow raise that Ellery hadn't yet shared that news with her.

"New clinic?" Lennie asked, enunciating each word like she was talking to an academically challenged six-year-old.

Lori prodded Rosie's arm and offered an apologetic look. "Sorry for putting our foot in it and spoiling tonight's surprise."

Lennie's face relaxed a little—well, Lori thought it had, but it was hard to tell under all the Botox—and Ellery mouthed a silent thank you out of Lennie's eyeline.

"We're celebrating?"

Ellery kissed Lennie on the cheek. "Surprise. I was going to tell you over a bottle of Veuve Clicquot."

"Veuve Clicquot?"

Lori glanced at Rosie and tried not to laugh, sure she must be thinking the same thing: that Lennie had injected so much Botox that it had limited her speech to two-word questions. Maybe if she said much more, her face might crack.

"You'd prefer something else?" Ellery asked.

Lori bit the inside of her cheek. That question was going to cost Ellery dearly.

Lennie pointed to the selection of champagnes under cool lightning at the back of the bar. "Not Krug?"

Rosie coughed her drink back into her glass. "Sorry. Escapee mint leaf went down the back of my throat."

"I read that Veuve Clicquot is America's favorite champagne," Lori said, though she knew her attempt to help would probably be futile.

"I'm sure it is," Lennie said, raising her nose in the air, "for people who can't afford the more superior Champagne house."

Ellery's forehead creased like she was in pain, which was unsurprising given the cost of a bottle of Krug. Lori hadn't seen a single bottle sold in this bar before, and she was sure their stock had been there since they opened in 1976.

Ellery waved for the bartender's attention. "Can I get a bottle of Krug, please?"

The bartender looked taken aback by Ellery's request and leaned in closer as if she hadn't heard correctly, then she backed up to the champagne display and pointed to the bottle of Krug, still not looking convinced that she'd understood Ellery's order.

Ellery nodded. "That's what I want?"

Lori would've laughed if she hadn't felt so sorry for her; Ellery was way too soft for her own good, and Lennie had been taking advantage of that for far too long.

The bartender pulled a chilled bottle from the lower fridge and arranged it in a Krug-branded ice bucket that looked unused too. "How many glasses would you like?"

Lori put her hand on Ellery's forearm and squeezed gently.

"We don't want to mix our drinks, Ellery." She shot Rosie a look when she frowned in obvious disagreement.

Ellery's sigh of relief was audible even over the mid-level music thumping in the background. "Are you sure?"

Lennie put her hand above Lori's on Ellery's forearm. "They're sure."

Lori wondered just how much of the over-priced grape juice Ellery would actually get to drink. She was surprised Lennie hadn't just asked the bartender to fix a teat to the bottle so she could keep it all to herself.

"Two glasses, please," Ellery said and held her card to the payment terminal when the bartender indicated it was ready. She glanced at Lori and gave her a tight smile before tearing off the gold neck wrapping and popping the cork.

"You should keep that and write the date on it," Rosie said. "It'll be a nice reminder."

Once again, Lori had to stop herself from laughing and lightly tapped her foot to Rosie's shin. "Troublemaker," she whispered, and Rosie grinned.

"When will you be moving in?" Rosie asked.

"Soon, hopefully." Ellery finished pouring a half glass and offered it to Lennie.

She raised her eyebrows and didn't take it, so Ellery filled it to the brim and tried again. Lennie nodded as if she were the queen of everything and accepted it this time.

Ellery smiled, but she still looked pained. "The building is in great condition, and I just need a couple of walls put in to create treatment rooms and a reception area." She poured herself a full glass and took a long, slow drink like it was the nectar of the gods.

It would damn well have to be at that price. But at least she looked like she was enjoying it. "Jen's confident she can get it done in four days," Lori said, "and she got a cancelation, so she's starting on Monday. With any luck, you could be officially moving in by the middle of August."

"That's fast," Rosie said to Ellery. "Your landlord must be nice."

Ellery nodded. "I've paid up until the end of the month, but we were in contract negotiations, and he's been kind enough not to insist on any notice."

"Should we take a table," Lennie said in a way that clearly wasn't a question.

"You're right; we've kept you long enough," Lori said when Ellery didn't respond. "Have a lovely evening. And I'll see you next week, Ellery."

Ellery seemed to force a smile. "I arranged to come over mid-week and see how Jen's doing. Is that okay with you?"

"Absolutely." Lori got up from her stool to hug Ellery; she looked like she needed one. "We've got a few youth groups coming in, but I've got some new college volunteers, and I'll be able to step away for a while. And Mom will be there too. She's looking forward to seeing you again."

"Great. I'll combine it with a follow-up on Cash." Ellery picked up her ice bucket. "I'm assuming he's doing well?"

"No boring work talk." Lennie placed her hand on Ellery's shoulder then gave a smile that looked more like a grimace. "It's a rule." Then she literally pulled Ellery away.

Rosie clutched Lori's arm. "If I *ever* get involved with someone like that and for some reason can't see how toxic they are, promise me that you'll tell me."

"You wouldn't listen."

"I would. I definitely would," Rosie said.

Lori shook her head. "It's like she's got her claws dug in so deep, Ellery can't get them out. You've known her for longer than I have; why doesn't she dump the leech?"

Rosie whistled. "Ooh, it's not like you to gossip or cast judgment."

Lori put her hand over her mouth. "I know, I'm sorry."

"Don't be. You're right, and I don't have the answer."

"She looks so unhappy," Lori said. "Is that what I looked like all those years?"

Rosie swirled the stick in her drink, which Lori took as an affirmative answer.

"But it's not what you look like now." Rosie clinked her glass to Lori's and took a drink.

Lori blew out a long breath, and regret flooded her soul. "I never thought that I'd be someone who wasted years of my life in an unhappy relationship."

"You always have such a lot happening in your life. Sometimes it's hard to see what's going on when you're so deeply enmeshed in it."

"Mm. I won't be making that mistake again. Spending time with Gabe has made me see what a good relationship could look like, and that's what I want. That's what I deserve."

Rosie raised her glass. "Hell, yeah, I'll drink to that."

Lori drank the last of her mojito and ordered another round. Her phone vibrated, and she checked the message.

We're having a few beers after the game. If u and Rosie are still out, do u want to join us? Or we could join u?

She slid her cell over to Rosie for her to read the message. "Shall we? Shay will be with her."

Rosie grinned wickedly. "You don't need to ask me twice," she said then held up her finger. "But if Shay's with someone or she starts putting the moves on someone, we're out of there, right? I don't want to see that."

"Definitely." As she fired off a response to Gabe, she thought about what Rosie had just said. What if someone came on to Gabe? Or worse, if Gabe spotted someone she liked, and she took her home. Maybe joining them wasn't such a great idea after all.

Chapter Nineteen

SHAY TOSSED GABE'S PHONE back to her after reading the message she'd just sent to Lori. "You see, I *thought* we'd had a good conversation the other night. And I *thought* I understood what you were doing. And it kind of made sense, in a Gabe-logic way. And I'm here for you, to support your self-imposed exposure therapy. *But*, and this is a big *but*, Saturday nights are supposed to be your night to blow off the steam you've built up over the week. It's your time to release the sexual tension you're feeling from being around Lori and playing happy family with Solo's babies. And I've got to point out, in case you've already drunk too much, and you've lost track of what time, or day, or even what year it is, that it's Saturday. We've watched some baseball, and we've had some beer. Solo's gone home to her wife, and now the four of us are supposed to be looking for the rest of the evening's entertainment." She tapped Gabe's forehead three times. "Is any of this ringing a bell? Do you remember telling me all about your plan to *not* drive yourself insane from lust?"

Gabe shoved Shay's finger away. "Please don't poke me. You know I hate that."

"Explain yourself then."

"I can go one week without meaningless sex," Gabe said. "I'm not an animal who can't control their urges."

Shay raised her eyebrows. "You've never had to control this particular urge before."

Gabe took a long pull on her beer and watched RB break at a nearby pool table. "What's your point?"

"My point is I'm worried that you won't be able to control

yourself tonight, and that you might do something you'll regret. You've already got plenty of beer in you, and now we're in a club. It's dark, the music's pumping, bodies are pressed together on the dance floor. You think you can resist all that and not make a move on Lori when she gets here?"

Gabe nodded. "That's exactly what I think. I told you already: she's important to me, and I won't do anything to ruin the friendship. We've had the near-miss, and I didn't succumb. I promise I won't tonight either."

"What're you going to do when someone hits on you?" Shay asked.

"Nothing."

Shay rubbed her forehead. "Why not?"

"Because I'm not here for that tonight." Gabe didn't say that she probably wouldn't be here for a pickup in the near future either. Her last encounter had been empty and lacking connection, and she could give herself better orgasms. And then there was the tiny issue of feeling like she was cheating on Lori, like she'd rather have no sex at all and feel good about herself than stick to her original plan of satisfying that side of her with transient women.

Shay let out an exasperated sigh. "How long is this going to last?" she asked gently. "I've never seen you like this, and I'm worried about you."

"You don't need to worry. I'm having fun, and I'm happy. Would I be happier if Lori and I were having sex? I don't know, because for the first time ever, sex doesn't seem that important to me." Gabe held up her hand when Shay opened her mouth to comment. "That's not the same as not *wanting* it. But it isn't on the table, so I'm trying hard not to think about it. And maybe you were right all along. Maybe eventually I'll be able to tell Lori about what happened with the Nelsons, and she'll understand. But I'm enjoying myself too much to risk what we have right now, even though it's not the whole package."

"Don't you want the whole package?"

"I've never had the whole package, so I don't know what I'm missing." She looked at RB and Woody as they chest-bumped, and she smiled. "Coming out of the Army terrified me, Shay."

Shay frowned. "*You* were terrified?"

Gabe nodded slowly. "I didn't know for sure that the team would still be interested in the garage idea, I had nowhere to live, and I had no family to lean on. We all know veterans like me have ended up on the streets for the rest of their lives."

"I never knew that's how you felt," Shay said. "I'm your best friend, Gabe. How could I not know that?"

"Because I didn't tell you, and you're not psychic. But everything worked out, and now I've got this," she motioned to Woody and RB and then to Shay, "and we're opening the garage next week. I get to visit Max every week, and I've got someone new in my life who I really care for in a way that I didn't know I was capable of. I'm the most content I've ever been in my life, Shay, so there really is nothing for you to worry about. Okay?"

"You're *sure* you're okay?"

"I'm sure." She stood and pulled Shay to her feet. "Let's go shoot some pool and show those lug-heads how it's done."

Gabe and Shay had won three games by the time Lori and Rosie arrived, both looking stunning in blouse and skirt combos matched with heels that Gabe couldn't imagine them trying to dance in. But she'd learned long ago that there was very little a femme *couldn't* do in heels.

Everyone greeted and hugged them, and Woody and RB headed to the bar for drinks while Shay began to chat with Rosie.

Lori hooked her arm into Gabe's and pulled her aside. "One thing about work, and then the rest of the night is for play. Is that okay?"

"You're setting the rules," Gabe said and grinned. "We can talk about whatever you want to."

"I just wanted to thank you again for getting the Oakley fixed,"

Lori said. "Fran's staying in Louisville overnight, and she said it was running like a dream."

"That's great news. How's the horse?"

"Nope." Lori put her finger to Gabe's lips. "I've said my one thing. Now you're going to teach me how to play pool."

Gabe groaned internally, and Shay just shook her head slowly, mouthing, "Good luck," silently. She followed Lori back to the pool table they'd commandeered and didn't stop herself from enjoying the way Lori swayed her hips or the soft curves of her calves. She snapped her eyes up when Lori spun around.

"Before we start, I need to ask you one thing, and it might sound strange."

Gabe shrugged, more concerned with proving to Shay that she could keep her eyes and hands off Lori while she draped herself all over a pool table. "Ask away."

"Are you on the prowl tonight?"

Gabe laughed and leaned against the table. "Am I what?"

"You know... Are you hoping to hook up with someone?" Lori blushed slightly and glanced away.

"No," she said though every bit of her wanted to ask if Lori would be irritated if that was her intention.

"What about Shay?" she asked, though this time, she glanced across at Rosie.

"It's not very often Shay goes home alone on a night like this. Why?" Gabe thought she knew the answer, but she wanted it confirmed before she said anything to Shay.

Lori looked like she was stopping herself from saying something. "No reason. Will RB and Woody be looking for someone to go home with?"

Gabe racked up the balls and tucked the triangle back under the table. "You'd have to ask them. Are *you* hoping to hook up with someone?" she asked, half-joking and then wished she hadn't opened her mouth at all. What if Lori said yes? What if she'd gotten super-comfortable in the friend zone and wasn't even considering Gabe even if she had decided she was ready to get back into dating?

She took a breath and rolled the cue ball up the table. If and when Lori was ready, would that be the time for Gabe to tell her story and give Lori the chance to make her own mind up about culpability? And would she be able to continue to trust Gabe? That was the main issue here. The thought of losing Lori was just too much to contemplate. Would seeing her with some other woman be any more or less painful?

Lori joined her at the head of the table after picking up a cue from the rack on the wall. "I'm definitely not interested in hooking up with anyone," she whispered. "Rosie and I just don't want to be playing third wheels."

"Ah, okay. That makes total sense," she said, strangely relieved that Lori still wasn't ready to jump back into the dating pool. That gave their friendship more time. "Do you want me to find out and let you know?"

"No, that's okay." Lori chalked her cue and gestured to the table. "You should probably break. I almost always sink the white ball when I do it."

"Do you know how to hold this?" Gabe got into position and slid the cue slowly and deliberately between the thumb and forefinger of her left hand.

"Not properly, no," Lori said and watched intently.

"Your left hand is just the guide. Hold it with your right hand about here but don't grip it too tightly."

"Got it."

"Line the cue up to the center of the white ball but then look down the table at where you want it to hit. If you're going to hit it hard and split everything, go for the very center of the first ball, yeah?"

Lori nodded. "But don't look at the white ball again?"

"Nope. Think eye to target, like when you drive," Gabe said, maintaining eye contact. "Once you know where the steering wheel is, you don't keep looking at it, do you?"

"Huh, I guess not. I hadn't thought of driving that way before."

Lori's smile held such a genuine openness that Gabe's knees went weak, and she eased up so that she could lean against the table. Over Lori's shoulder, Gabe could see Shay continuing to watch the unfolding scene with the interest of a nature photographer watching a safari hunt play out.

"Do you want to try?" Gabe asked.

"Sure."

Lori approached the table, looking hesitant, and Gabe stepped to the side so she could concentrate on how Lori held the cue and see where she was looking. If she'd stayed where she was, her view would've been of Lori bending over the table, and she was pretty certain her resolve wasn't strong enough for that temptation.

"That looks great," Gabe said. "Now just relax, keep your eye on where you want to strike, and then shoot."

The cue ball ricocheted off the pack, splitting them and sending balls all over the table...including the second ball into a middle pocket.

Lori jumped up and did a little happy dance. "Yay for me!"

Woody whistled as she approached with their drinks. "Looks like she's hustling you, Gabe," she said, giving her a beer and a mojito.

Gabe narrowed her eyes and passed Lori's drink to her. "Is that what's going on?" she asked and grinned, hoping that wasn't the case; she needed her turn at the table to breathe between watching Lori take her shots.

Lori put her hand to her chest and batted her eyelashes. "Beginner's luck."

Woody clapped Gabe's shoulder. "She's hustling you," she said, "and I'm going to sit and watch it happen."

Great. Another spectator. Although maybe that was a good thing: another person to keep her from doing something she'd regret in the morning.

"What did I sink?" Lori sipped her mojito.

"You're stripes, and I'm solids." Gabe watched Lori bend over the table again and had to take a long pull on her beer to keep from staring. Lori didn't sink anything, so Gabe stepped up and lined up her shot. She pocketed two balls in a row and could see the path to another three, but she didn't want the game to end that quickly in case Lori didn't want to play again. So she caught the edge of the fourteen and sunk the cue ball instead. She stood and shrugged. "Foul."

"What does that mean?"

"You get two shots, and you can place the white ball anywhere on the table."

Lori frowned and ran her finger over the head string. "It doesn't have to go behind here, like when you break?"

"Nope," Gabe said and collected the cue ball from the top pocket.

"Doesn't that make it too easy?"

Lori's fingers grazed Gabe's palm as she took the ball from her hand, and Gabe rubbed her hands together. "That tickled," she said, though she wasn't ticklish at all. Lori's touch had just traveled straight to her core, and she needed to get rid of the sensation.

Lori laughed and looked pleased with herself. "The super soldier is ticklish? Surely not?"

"Anyway," Gabe said, not wanting to compound the white lie, "it's supposed to make it easier. If you had to shoot from behind the line, hustlers like yourself might foul on purpose to put the other player at a disadvantage."

Lori arched her eyebrow. "If I was hustling you, wouldn't we have something riding on the game?"

Gabe crossed her arms and took a step back from the table. "Are you suggesting we make a bet?"

Lori placed the ball on the table and rolled it back and forth.

The inanimate object had no idea how lucky it was.

"You seem reluctant," Lori said.

"You seem eager," Gabe said, unable to resist playing along. "Is five dollars a game too rich for you?"

Lori shook her head. "Not rich enough. How about ten dollars? But the pot stays on the table. We could play best of five, and if we're tied after four games, let's make it interesting and bet fifty dollars."

Gabe didn't know if Lori was already a little buzzed, or if this was just how she was when she was out. Whatever it was, Gabe was enjoying this side of her. "For someone who wanted me to teach her how to play, you sound pretty confident that we'll get to five games."

"Are you worried your reputation will suffer if you lose to a novice?"

Lori turned her attention to the table again and positioned the ball where there was no clear shot for her. She was either clueless or Woody had her pegged.

"I'm beginning to think I might not be playing a novice," Gabe said.

Lori walked away to Rosie and returned with a crisp ten-dollar bill from her purse. She placed it on the edge of the pool table and weighed it down with the chalk. "Rosie thinks you won't take the bet, but Shay said it'd be like taking candy from a baby." She motioned to their little group a few feet away. "They're actually taking their own bets."

Gabe grinned. Yeah, she liked this side of Lori *a lot*. "I'll take your money, no problem." She withdrew her wallet and put ninety dollars on the table. "I'll even put it all down now."

Rosie hurried over with Lori's purse, and she swapped out the ten for two fifty-dollar bills.

"That's too much," Gabe said.

"It doesn't matter since it'll all be going back in this purse in less than an hour anyway," Rosie said and winked. Then she strutted back to a chorus of banter and catcalls.

Gabe laughed and shook her head. "She seems strangely confident too."

"Besties are supposed to have your back, aren't they?" Lori asked.

"If it turns out that you're some sort of pool-savant and you *are* hustling me, I'll never look at you the same again."

"Maybe that's what I want." Lori winked and bent over the table to reposition the cue ball and take her shot.

Ah, hell, what was she supposed to make of that statement? Gabe simply watched, drawn into Lori's orbit, and relaxed into the magnetic inevitability of her feelings. Friendships lasted beyond most sexual relationships, and maybe the idea of exploring that with Lori would be better than the reality, which might not last beyond a few fantastic weeks.

"Which ball do you think I should go for?" Lori asked.

Gabe circled the table to keep from staring at Lori's ass, but the front view was no less appealing. Her low-cut blouse dropped away from her body to reveal a black lacy bra. Of course it would have to be lace...and it'd be a matching set, no doubt. "You still want me to give you tips even when there's money on the table?"

"Seems like that would be the chivalrous thing to do." Lori looked up at Gabe and bit her lip as she struck the cue ball. It nudged the side of the number twelve, which eased into its intended pocket.

"Are you supposed to be so blasé about the hustle?" Gabe asked. "That kind of behavior could get you into trouble." She took a long pull on her beer just to tear her gaze away.

Lori caressed the edge of the table as she walked around it to her next shot. "Is that a promise?"

Gabe choked on the beer and covered her mouth while Lori laughed, clearly reveling in her femme power. "Do you always flirt this mercilessly with gay friends?"

"I don't have many gay friends, so I can't answer that question,"

Lori said. "Is it a problem? I'll stop if it is."

"Nah, it's fine. You said it'd been a long time since you'd been out on the town properly, so I figure you're just letting your hair down and enjoying the fact that you can do that without the risk of any expectations from me. Am I right?"

Lori shrugged elegantly and glanced away. "Sure. Let's say it's that."

That was an explanation that didn't explain anything at all. Gabe blew out an exasperated breath and looked to Shay, but she was too busy in an intense-looking conversation with Rosie, paying no attention to Gabe's distress, and Woody and RB had drifted to an empty table for their own game.

"Looking for moral support?" Lori leaned over the table to take her next shot, which she missed narrowly.

"Sure. Let's say it's that."

Lori chuckled and gestured to the table. "Now we're having fun."

Gabe put her beer down and cleared the table of solids. She paused to empty her beer before switching the cue to her other hand to pocket the black. "*Now* we're having fun."

The two of them emptied the pockets and rolled the balls to the far side of the table. Lori did a neat little balancing trick with the top ball, clicking the rack downward for the ball to fall into place.

Gabe chalked her cue and tapped the stack of bills. "You're going to need more than that fancy move to take my money."

Lori sashayed around the table and took the chalk from Gabe's hand. Her touch had exactly the same effect as the first time, but Gabe couldn't bring herself to lie again. Instead, she simply locked Lori's gaze and held her breath. She could play this game too, couldn't she?

Lori chalked the end of her own cue, drawing it back and forth slowly, and once again, Gabe cursed the luck of the inanimate objects getting all the attention.

Lori returned the chalk to the pile of dollars and went to the head of the pool table. "Loser breaks, correct?"

Gabe shook her head. "I suppose you know that because you read it somewhere back in 1998 as opposed to you being a pool shark who actually knows *all* the rules—and how to break them."

Lori positioned herself once again, and Gabe imagined being beneath her, looking up as Lori straddled her hips. Lori looked at her as if she knew exactly what Gabe was thinking, and she smiled wickedly before driving the cue ball into the pack and sinking two off the break.

"I'll take stripes since that worked so well for you," Lori said.

Gabe nodded and enjoyed the show as Lori almost danced around the table and cleared it with her next seven shots. She had no idea what the hell was happening but decided to relax into it. Lori was having fun and flirting harmlessly. Nothing was going to happen tonight or any other night.

Was it?

Chapter Twenty

LORI PRESSED GABE AGAINST the wall of the corridor beyond the restrooms. The shirt Gabe was wearing stretched against the movement, and two snaps opened, revealing the deep line between Gabe's pecs. Lori ran her tongue along the gorgeous groove, loving how granite-hard Gabe felt against the softness of her lips. Gabe's responding moan was hoarse and throaty, and she somehow softened against Lori's hand, despite the firmness of her muscles. The thrill of having a woman this immense, this formidable under her hand pulsed through Lori like a natural high. No alcohol or drugs could compare, she was sure of that.

"I like this side of you," Gabe whispered.

"I like *all* of you." *Lori* popped another button open, and her breath caught at the sight of a huge tattoo under the line of Gabe's chest. "Is this an angel?"

Gabe shook her head lightly. "It's Alectho, one of the Greek fury sisters."

Lori traced the delicate feather detail, and her nail grazed Gabe's breast. She sucked in a breath at Gabe's half-lidded eyes. She looked helpless, almost weak and desperate for Lori's touch, but in the most fantastically seductive way possible, and the control it gave Lori ran through her like an electrical charge. She wanted to tear Gabe's shirt off to fully appreciate the artwork, not caring that they were in a bar where anyone might walk this way and catch them.

Gabe wrapped her hand around Lori's neck and pulled her in closer. "Kiss me."

Lori put her finger against Gabe's lips. "We shouldn't. Not

here."

"Where then?" Gabe twirled Lori's hair between her fingertips. She tilted her head toward the emergency exit. "In the alley?"

The thought sent a thrill surging through Lori's body, ending with a fierce throbbing at her very core. She'd never been the kind of woman to indulge in spontaneous sex in public places. Even spontaneous private sex had been rare. But, *God*, Gabe made her feel things she'd only ever read about in erotic novels. Could she be that kind of woman? Even if it was just for one night?

Gabe stroked Lori's cheek. "Let me take you to a hotel close by. I've wanted you since I first saw you—I can't wait any longer."

Lori ran her finger along the defined line of muscle under Gabe's collarbone. *She* couldn't wait any longer either. Maybe she'd always been this way, just waiting for a woman like Gabe to come along and untether her from self-imposed disinterest. "That's the kind of woman you think I am?"

"I'm hoping," Gabe said breathlessly. "I'm really hoping."

Lori glanced down at the onyx black wings on Gabe's skin. She didn't want to deny herself an exploration of Gabe's body, and to discover where she imagined the fury sister's toes disappeared under the waist of Gabe's jeans. She didn't want to deny herself anything about Gabe anymore. She crushed her lips to Gabe's and savored a kiss that gave passion and lust a physical taste, igniting a craving so all-consuming that Lori could never imagine it fading.

Lori's phone buzzed insistently in her pocket.

"Ignore it," Gabe whispered and kissed her neck lightly. "Come with me."

The phone though. The phone just kept ringing, but it wasn't in her pocket.

"Come with me...please. I need you."

I need you too, but the words wouldn't come out of her mouth.

And that damn phone.

Lori's eyes snapped open and slowly adjusted to the bright afternoon sunshine piercing the window. Disappointment blanketed her awareness and dulled her still pulsing core. So now Gabe had made her way into Lori's daydreams too.

And her phone was still ringing. She picked it up and shot out of her chair when she saw it was her mom calling. "Is everything okay?" A quick check of the time told her that her mom should still be in the air.

"Of course it is, sweetheart. You sound breathless. Are *you* okay?"

"Did you miss your flight?"

"No, I'm calling you from the plane," her mom said. "I wanted to surprise you."

"You certainly did that." Though she was more surprised by the increasing intensity and regularity of her Gabe-themed fantasies. She didn't need to check to know that she'd have to change her underwear before she left the house. That was another thing she'd never experienced before meeting Gabe. They hadn't even slept together yet, and Lori was beginning to feel like her libido was a long-sleeping chrysalis finally metamorphosing and spreading its wings.

Wings. Did Gabe really have a tattoo of a Greek fury? Lori's brief view of her abs indicated it couldn't be real. All she'd seen there were perfectly symmetrical bumps of muscle.

"Lori? Are you still there?"

"Sorry, Mom. I just woke up."

"Really?" her mom asked.

Her family didn't waste time on naps; they always had too much to do. "I've been up a while... I had a late night, that's all. I'm a little tired."

Her mom cooed. "Really? I look forward to hearing all about that when I get there. Although we'll have to send your dad to do some chores while you do."

"Dad's with you?" she asked. This visit would be even better for his presence.

"I just told you that," her mom said. "You must've drifted off. That's what the surprise was, but I couldn't wait until I got off the plane, so I called you."

"Oh, wow. That's wonderful." Unbidden worry kicked in when she thought of their donor recently pulling out. "Dad never comes with you; he's always too busy. Are you sure everything's all right?"

"Everything's fine. We'll talk when we're all settled in with you. See you very soon."

Lori wasn't convinced. *Everything's fine* and *We'll talk* didn't go together. "Okay, Mom. I'll be there when you land."

They said their goodbyes, and Lori hung up. The feeling that something was wrong persisted, and she stood to shake it off. Her mom never lied to her, so if she said everything was fine, then everything was fine. She looked at her phone screen again to see she had messages and missed calls—eight of them, a mix from Gabe and Rosie—and she realized she hadn't looked at her phone since she'd woken. Care of her epic hangover had required her full attention. She read the messages then listened to the voicemails; Gabe was worried about her because she hadn't heard from her since they parted last night, and Rosie wanted a full debrief of her behavior. *God, what did I do?* She drank a hell of a lot more than she had in a long time, probably since college.

And played pool.

She remembered hustling Gabe and having far too much fun for it to be legal. That explained the nature of the daydream; she'd spent all night thinking about doing all those things and a whole lot more to Gabe in that bar. And in the hotel: a hotel that would've needed thick, soundproof walls.

Stop it. Gabe would be here in a few hours; she was coming to see Max later than usual because Lori had to pick up her mom, and now her dad too, from Midway. She sent a reassuring text to

Gabe and video-called Rosie, deciding it would be easier and faster to face the inevitable inquisition.

"Who are you and what have you done with my friend?"

Lori sank back onto her chair and stared at Rosie. "What did I do?"

"It might be easier to tell you what you didn't do," Rosie said. "You *didn't* act like the Lori Turner I've known for the past six years. You *didn't* stop drinking even when I advised you that it might be worthwhile to slow down a little. You *didn't* act like Gabe was your friend, and you—"

"Whoa, stop there. How *did* I act toward Gabe?"

Rosie shook her head slowly like a disappointed nun. "The word for it is 'vampy,' I think."

Lori clasped her hand over her mouth. "Was I that bad?"

Rosie grinned. "You were *that* good."

"But you just said—"

"I was kidding. You were awesome." Rosie was literally vibrating through the screen. "I've never seen you like that, and it was something to watch, I tell you. Don't you remember any of it?"

Lori rolled her eyes to the ceiling and searched for recollection. "I played pool with her?"

"You played *with* her, and yes, there were a few games of pool too. Where did you learn to play like that?"

"It's all angles and math; it's not complicated." She waved off the compliment to return focus to her main concern. "Did Gabe seem okay? Did she seem mad?"

Rosie raised her eyebrows. "Mad? Why would she be mad?"

"I don't know. Maybe because I told her that we could only be friends and then acted like a clit-tease."

Rosie shrugged. "Are you a clit-tease when you have every intention of following through in a few days?"

"But *she* doesn't know that."

"Maybe she does now."

Lori covered her face with one hand. "What have I done?"

"Nothing to be embarrassed of, that's for sure," Rosie said firmly. "Never be ashamed of your sexuality."

Lori looked up. Pieces of the night were coming together in her mind; Gabe certainly seemed to have enjoyed their interaction. And she would've surely stopped it or walked away if she'd been uncomfortable. All Lori could remember was her beautiful laugh and the joy lighting up her face. "Did we go home before them? Did Gabe stay at the club? We took a cab home, didn't we?"

Rosie narrowed her eyes. "Did you fall out of bed and bang your head last night? We all took a cab. Gabe insisted on dropping you home first."

Something passed over Rosie's eyes, and her lips quirked into a smile, but it was gone in a millisecond.

"And then what?" Lori asked.

"Gabe walked you to your door, you went in, and we left."

Rosie glanced off screen, and Lori saw a look she never wanted to see on her best friend's face. She was clearly with someone from last night, and she hadn't finished with them yet.

"I have to go. I'll see you later in the week for lunch with your mom," she said.

Rosie ended the call before Lori could ask who she'd—*Shay?* No wonder she looked like the cat who'd gotten the proverbial cream.

Lori's phone pinged with a message.

Is it still okay for me 2 visit Max today or aren't u up for visitors? I bet ur hangover is epic.

Lori's fingers hovered over the keyboard, trying to decide on the tone of her response. She was desperate to know what Gabe thought of her after her "vampy" act. *So I should be an adult and ask her.*

Pain pills took care of that. I'm not quite as bulletproof as I was in my twenties. And yes, of course you should still come over. We have to stick to Max's schedule, or he'll get grumpy with us. I have a question I need to ask you though...

She didn't have to wait long before *Gabe is typing* appeared below her name as Lori stared at her phone.

Cool thank u What's ur question? U can ask me anything

Lori closed her eyes for a moment, hoping that might help her figure out how to word it. She decided she was overthinking the whole thing and should just get it out. Gabe had been straightforward with her to this point; why would she change now?

Did I do anything to make you feel uncomfortable last night? I don't want to ruin our friendship. Please tell me if I messed up.

There. It was said, and she wouldn't pull it back. While *Gabe is typing* flicked on and off the top of the screen repeatedly, Lori's stomach churned with the notion that she *had* acted inappropriately. It didn't matter that she'd never done anything like that before; she had to be responsible for her own behavior, and she definitely couldn't blame Gabe for being so unbelievably sexy and apparently, utterly irresistible, like some kind of lesbian catnip driving her wild.

U haven't messed anything up. U were funny drunk & it was great 2 c u having such a gr8 time. U were more relaxed than I've ever seen u. I loved it. Trust me u couldn't ruin our friendship. I think only I could do that.

Gabe was right; she'd had the best night she could remember having in a long time. And Gabe had been the catalyst. From the moment she'd entered Lori's orbit, her world had begun to spin on a different axis, and she'd been able to see her life from a new perspective. And once she'd said the words out loud last night, the moment her intentions toward Gabe were out in the Universe, Lori had felt like she'd released herself from a self-imposed prison. Sure, the lawyer had helped weld the bars shut, but Lori had forged the iron herself.

Thank God for that. I don't want to think of losing or hurting you. I have to go. See you at 3 x

She deleted and reinstated the kiss three times before sticking with it. She wasn't a text kisser, not even with Rosie, but she was finding that she was changing in all sorts of ways and embracing it was feeling more and more like the most natural thing in the world. Satisfied that was settled and she could still forge ahead with her birthday and hotel plans, Lori went to the bathroom to put on makeup and get ready to pick up her parents. She smiled and touched her fingers to her lips. She hadn't smiled like that in a while either. She couldn't wait to see her mom, as usual, but a visit from her dad made it even more special. *Everything's fine. We'll talk when we're all settled in with you.* Lori hoped there was nothing sinister going on, and everything really was fine.

***

Lori went faster than she ought to up the gravel drive back home. She hated being late for anything at the best of times, but she definitely didn't want to keep Gabe waiting.

"Careful, honey," her dad said and chuckled. "I don't think these cars are built for cornering at this speed."

"Where's the fire, sweetheart?" her mom asked, clinging to the dashboard and the door handle.

She rounded the corner and saw Gabe leaning against her truck with her hands in her pockets. God, why did she always have to look like she'd stepped directly out of Lori's fantasy world? Was the Almighty tormenting her just for kicks?

"Ah, there's the fire, Hank."

"Mom..." She could say little else. Her mom knew her too well for her to protest too much.

Gabe waved and pushed off her truck as Lori pulled up beside her. "Sorry, I'm a little early." She opened the passenger door for Lori and held out her hand.

Without thinking—or maybe it was just without caring—Lori

accepted Gabe's offer. She still stumbled slightly in her heels on the uneven ground and had to catch herself against Gabe's chest...Gabe's incredibly hard chest.

"Have you thought about getting a section of this paved?" Gabe winked and held Lori's weight like she was a feather. "I'd hate for you to sprain an ankle or worse in your cute shoes."

Lori laughed. "Is that the first time you've ever used that word? Did it feel strange as you said it? Like you were speaking a foreign language?"

Gabe shook her head. "I'm learning a whole new language being in your company, hustler."

Lori stayed in Gabe's arms for a moment longer than she needed to but nowhere near as long as she wanted to. She'd all but forgotten her parents were in the car until they threw open their doors and emerged, all greetings and big smiles. Her mom pulled Gabe into a hug, and Lori laughed at Gabe's look of total surprise and awkward body language.

"Don't mind Karen; she's always been a hugger." Her dad came around the car and offered Gabe a more traditional greeting, which she looked far more comfortable with. "Lori tells us that you're a highly decorated soldier, Gabe. I won't bust your eardrums with the usual meaningless platitudes. We're people of action; we're currently negotiating a state-wide pilot to tackle food poverty among veterans. We figure that's more help than an empty thank you, however heartfelt."

Lori had watched Gabe's expression turn from wariness as her dad began to speak to a look that said she was even more astonished than she had been at Lori's mom's hug. Lori's parents had a long history of making her proud to be their daughter.

"That's exactly what we need, Mr. Turner. Thank *you* for recognizing that."

"Wow, Dad." Lori wrapped her arms around his waist and hugged him tight. "I didn't know that you'd finally gotten that project off the ground."

Her mother grumbled. "Off the ground? It's nearly put him in the ground. That's why I made him come with me. He needs a break."

"Hey now, you never have to force me to come see my beautiful, accomplished daughter." He rolled his eyes. "But she is right, as usual. A little time away from the fray is exactly what the doctor ordered."

Panic flared in Lori's chest. "The doctor? Why are you seeing a doctor?"

"Oh, honey." Her dad cupped her face and kissed her forehead. "It was a figure of speech. I'm fitter than I've ever been. Your mom has me on a new diet."

"It's not a diet. It's a healthy eating plan. You're not dieting." Her mom looked at Gabe. "He doesn't need to diet, does he?"

"No, ma'am, he does not," Gabe said.

"Goodness, my mother is a ma'am. Please call me Karen."

"And I'm Hank, not Mr. Turner."

"Okay, Hank and Karen, can I help you with your luggage?"

Her dad widened his eyes. "God, yes. Karen's brought her whole wardrobe with her."

"We'll leave you to it," her mom said and took Lori's arm. "I have a thirst for your homemade lemonade."

Lori looked back over her shoulder as her mom pulled her away. She didn't expect Gabe to be their valet, but Gabe waved her away.

"It's okay," Gabe said. "We've got this."

"Thank you," Lori said, once again marveling at Gabe's generous spirit and easygoing nature. Could she be any more perfect? *I'm going to find out on Saturday night*. She couldn't help but give Gabe a wicked grin, but she looked away before she could see Gabe's response. It was one thing to flirt shamelessly fueled by alcohol but quite another to do it stone-cold sober.

When she and her mom were inside, Lori closed the door and took hold of her mom's hands. "What do you think? Do you like her?"

Her mom twirled a strand of Lori's hair between her fingertips and smiled. "*You* like her. It shouldn't matter what I think."

Lori's heart made a resounding thud as it metaphorically dropped to the wooden floor. "You don't like her? Why don't you like her?"

Her mom pressed her lips together and shook her head. "I didn't say that at all. I do like her. She seems lovely, so far. I've known her for nearly two whole minutes."

"You don't want to jump to conclusions because you were so wrong about the lawyer, do you?"

Her mom turned up her nose and muttered something Lori wouldn't repeat.

"I might be a little cautious after that, yes." She pulled Lori toward the kitchen. "Come on, I'm parched."

Lori went without complaint and didn't push any further. Gabe would prove herself to Lori's mom easily, especially when she saw how great the rust bucket was looking, and how she was with Max, and just...just how she was period. She'd only just gotten the jug of lemonade from the fridge when Gabe and her dad came in with her parents' baggage of two suitcases, a carry-on bag, a duffel bag, and a suit bag.

"I only travel light when it's absolutely necessary," her mom called after Gabe as she followed Lori's dad upstairs as if pre-empting any comment.

Lori poured four glasses, all with ice except for Gabe's, who she'd noticed never seem to have it. When they came back down, Gabe's lips twitched into a crooked smile as she clearly registered the lack of ice in her drink.

"Thank you," Gabe said and emptied the glass in one quick burst. She nodded toward the door. "I should go see Max. He's gotten pretty good at telling the time."

"I'll come with you." Lori placed her glass on the kitchen counter. "I won't be long."

"No problem, sweetheart. We know you have work to do."

Gabe wasn't work at all. Gabe was play, or she very much would be if Saturday went according to plan. But she'd let her mom know that later in the week. They had a lot of planning to do for the auction before Lori could let herself drift into birthday celebrations.

"It was wonderful to meet you both," Gabe said. "Lori said she was going to bring you to the garage to see the Brewster during the week, so I guess I'll see you then. My team would love to hear more about your vet plans, Hank."

"Absolutely, Gabe. And if any of you have any buddies in New York who would benefit from being part of it, write me a list of their names and where to find them, and I'll make sure they're some of the first people to be part of the project."

"Thank you, Hank. We'll give it some serious thought."

Lori followed Gabe out of the house. Gabe's biceps strained at the cuffs of her T-shirt, still pumped from hefting all her parents' bags upstairs. Lori bit her lip as she thought about Gabe's arms straining for other, more fun, reasons. "Thank you for playing valet for my parents. Dad doesn't look like his usual energetic self. I think that might be the first time I've ever heard him accept help like that."

Gabe shrugged. "It was no problem, really. Luckily it was chest and shoulders day at the gym this morning, so my arms could cope."

Lori laughed and tapped Gabe's shoulder. "Like those few bags were a strain." She looked away from Gabe's inquisitive glance. She had to tone it down, or she'd never make it to Saturday. And she *really* wanted to make Saturday special. She wanted their first time to be on Egyptian cotton sheets in a room with a view of Lake Michigan, and their second round to be in a steamy, marbled wet room. And their third round over the back of a suede sofa with that same view, city lights and moonlight sparkling off the water's surface.

She pulled herself together and unlocked Max's gate. "Max is doing so well," she said. He was already waiting at the end of his run for Gabe to arrive. Lori put him on a leash and handed it to Gabe. "I think it's time to start thinking about getting him a forever home."

"Oh, really?" Gabe ran her hand across the back of her head and nibbled on her bottom lip. "What does that entail? How long does it take?"

"It's not complicated. Although potential adopters have to fill in an application form, and we do a couple of house visits to make sure they're a good fit and the family home is stable. But it's impossible to say how long that might take."

"House visits?" Gabe didn't look at Lori and stroked Max's ears. "Do you only allow locals to adopt?"

Lori shook her head. "Our adoption program covers the whole country. That's one of the reasons we can attract the funding we do."

"You make it sound as serious as fostering kids. Do they have a checklist that they have to score a minimum percentage on?"

"It is serious, Gabe." Lori thought Gabe understood that. "We have to make sure that people aren't adopting our pups just to put them to work—or worse. There are some horror stories out there, you know? People might think our checks are excessive, but we don't care. Our primary concern is for our dogs' welfare." She eased up, realizing that she'd gone into placard-waving defensive mode. "So yes, we have a comprehensive checklist and a pass percentage."

Gabe cleared her throat and looked up at Lori. "Do you think I'd pass?"

Lori sighed. That's what was going on. How had she missed it? "That depends on your answers to the questions and your home situation. Dogs are social animals, and a lot of what we've been doing with Max over the past couple of months has been on recultivating that instinct. If you're out at work all day, every day, then—"

"I'd take him with me to the shop," Gabe said. "I wouldn't leave him at home all day alone. I know that's not good for a dog."

"Has this been your plan all along?" Lori asked, not yet certain if she'd be angry if it had been. She didn't want to think that Gabe had just gotten closer to her so that she'd have a better chance of adopting Max.

Gabe wrapped her arm around Max's neck and pulled him closer to kiss his snout. "Actually, no. I wasn't sure I'd be up to it until I got settled. I won't lie and say that I hadn't thought about it though, but I didn't know if it would be possible, if he would ever go back to the Max I knew before the insider attack."

"And has he?"

Gabe's wide grin was a far more genuine answer to Lori's question than any words she could utter. "You've got to admit that he's a different dog from how he was even when I first showed up, right?"

Lori nodded. "I can't argue that. He advanced more in the first two weeks of you being around than he had in the previous ten months."

Gabe's eyes lit up with a joy Lori thought could illuminate the darkest recesses of her fears and put the shadows to rest.

"Exactly," Gabe said. "So who else do I have to convince that he'd be more than okay if he came to live with me?"

Lori looked toward the house. She had to get back to her parents. They had a lot to discuss, but she also didn't want to leave this conversation, didn't want to leave Gabe. "No one else. Whoever the dog or horse takes a shine to more than the other staff gets to do the interview process. Max has always been more comfortable with me, as much as he was comfortable with anyone until you came along, so I'll be the one assessing anyone who wants to adopt Max."

Gabe frowned. "Woody showed me the adoptee page on your website. Would Max have to go on there, and I'd have to compete with other people?"

Lori wanted to tease her and say that yes, that was the process, but Gabe seemed so vulnerable and emotional right now that Lori just couldn't do it. "That's how it usually works, but when the animal's old handler shows an interest, they jump the line."

"Oh my God, really?" Gabe half-moved toward Lori then stopped. She gave Max's hind quarters a firm pat instead. "Just say the word. I'll jump through whatever hoops you need me to, but I'm serious about this. I want Max to come live with me."

Lori squeezed Gabe's arm and smiled. "We'll talk about it next week when my parents have gone. My focus is the auction while they're—"

"And your birthday," Gabe said. "That's the main reason your mom's here, isn't it?"

"Yes. Yes, it is," Lori said. "And I really, *really* can't wait until Saturday night. I've got a feeling it's going to be the best birthday I've ever had."

"Yeah?"

"Yeah." She drew in a deep breath of fresh country air. "Life is so good right now. The rust bucket is almost out of my life, Ellery is moving into the clinic soon, and I have a very special new friend." She gazed up into Gabe's eyes and swallowed. How easy it would be to step up onto her tiptoes and press her lips against Gabe's right now. She'd bet the reality would smash her fantasies out of the park.

Lori took a step back and motioned to the house. "I have to start dinner. If you're okay to settle Max and lock his gate when you're done, maybe you could stay for some food."

"No, that's okay. I don't want to intrude on family time, so I'll just honk when I leave."

Lori almost pursued the matter but didn't. Gabe was always honest with her answers, so Lori knew she wouldn't feel comfortable having dinner with them tonight. What Lori didn't know was whether it was yet another sign of Gabe's sensitivity to the needs of others or whether their happy family was too painful a reminder of her own childhood. She nodded. "Perfect."

"And then I'll look forward to seeing you on Tuesday at the garage," Gabe said.

"Okay." *And I'll look forward to seeing all of you on Saturday night...*

Chapter Twenty-One

GABE PUSHED THE KNOTTED material upward and shifted her tie to sit just lower than the open top button of her shirt. There; smart but casual. She glanced at the matching vest lying on the bed, trying to decide if it might be too much.

"If you're trying to impress her parents, I think you're wasting your time," Shay said from the doorway of Gabe's bedroom. "If they don't like you after their Tuesday visit to the garage, they never will."

"You don't think they like me?" She could've said that she wasn't *trying* to impress Lori's parents, but Shay would've seen through the lie before she'd finished the sentence.

Shay arched her eyebrow. "I think they're two steps away from adopting you, or maybe even all of us. Since they're branching out into human care now, you'd be a good starting point."

"What did you think about that?" Gabe shoved the vest back in her closet. "I think it sounds too good to be true."

Shay entered Gabe's bedroom and eased herself onto the armchair, her slinky dress and heels clearly making it difficult to go that low. "You don't think he's going to pull it off?"

"I didn't say that. I'm just not convinced that it will go any further after his pilot project. You know what governments are like with fresh initiatives; they grow tired of them and move onto the next shiny object that will keep their presidential approval ratings high."

"I don't know about that. If he secures the backing of that billionaire tech woman, he can almost do what he wants, where he wants to. He won't need government approval. RB seemed really excited by it." Shay eyeballed Gabe through her reflection in the mirror. "Or don't you *want* it to work in case Lori gets pulled into it?"

"Do you think she'd leave the Sanctuary?" Gabe turned around to face Shay. "I mean, of course I want it to work. It's a fantastic idea, and anything that helps us all when we leave the service is great. Obviously."

"But you don't want to lose your new...*friend*."

Gabe sat on the edge of her bed. "Friend, yeah."

"So last Saturday was just drunk, harmless flirting and nothing more?"

It'd been beautiful torture but knowing nothing could come of it also had her feeling a little melancholy about it still. "Yep. Thankfully."

Shay laughed. "Rather you than me. She brought her A-game out. If I'd been you, I would've taken her to the nearest hotel before we even finished the first game of pool."

"Lucky it wasn't you then, but you did end up with her best friend, so it wasn't exactly a bad night for you either."

Shay wiggled her eyebrows. "I'm aiming for a repeat performance tonight."

"Be careful, Shay. If you mess Rosie around, it'll make things awkward with Lori."

"Relax, you don't need to worry about that. No-strings sex, like always."

"Which is fun till it unravels, right?"

"No one's unraveling, Gabe. We're just having fun, and we both know it. Anyway," Shay tapped the arm of the chair, "we were talking about you, Lori, and her family."

Gabe huffed and shook her head. "I thought parents like that were fictional. Have you ever seen anything like them outside of the movies?"

"You *know* I haven't experienced it, just like you. It was a bit tough to watch if you want my honest opinion."

Gabe pulled her shoes on and began to tie the laces. "Wasn't it? Don't get me wrong; I'm happy that Lori has great parents but seeing that kind of love in action just made me wonder how the hell my mom and dad managed to fuck me up."

"You didn't turn out so bad," Shay said and winked.

"No thanks to them."

Shay sighed. "You molded yourself and became a hero despite their influence, Gabe."

"Yeah, I know that. But coming out of the Army has made me realize that I've still got some big hang-ups because of them." And talking out her childhood stuff with Lori had furthered that realization.

"Like what?"

"When Lori and I babysat Solo's triplets, we talked about having kids—"

"Whoa. Rewind. You talked about having kids with your *friend*?"

"No, of course not. Not together." Gabe buffed the toe of her shoes with a cloth and then sat back on the bed. "But Lori said she couldn't wait to have kids, whereas I couldn't think of anything worse than having to be responsible for raising little human beings."

"Because she's had great parents, but you think you'd mess it up?"

"Exactly." Gabe stood and went into her en suite for some cologne. "I could just repeat the same mistakes, or I could be a great parent *because* mine weren't."

RB rapped on Gabe's open bedroom door. "Our ride's here. Are you guys ready?"

"Yeah." Gabe grabbed her leather jacket and slipped her wallet and phone into the pockets.

When Shay got to her feet and smoothed her dress, RB leaned against the doorjamb and shook her head. "Man, you clean up good."

"Sorry I can't return the compliment," Shay said and sashayed out into the corridor.

Gabe grasped RB's shoulder. "Do you own anything other than jeans, sweats, and T-shirts?" she asked, taking in RB's outfit.

"Nope. What's your problem? These are my best jeans, *and* I'm wearing a new shirt."

"Might've been nice if you'd hung the creases out, buddy," Gabe said.

"I'm going out for dinner, not for a job interview." RB shoved Gabe out of the bedroom. "Let's go. You don't want to be late for the birthday girl, Romeo."

"Fuck off with that. And don't say girl; it's sexist." Gabe jogged downstairs and waited for everyone to leave, then she locked the door and squeezed into the backseat with RB and Woody, trying to ignore the squad of butterflies assembled in her stomach.

After the quick cab ride to the restaurant, Woody and RB went for drinks while Gabe and Shay took a booth in the bar to wait for everyone else to arrive. Gabe was savoring a sip of her whiskey as it warmly snaked down her throat when the restaurant door opened, and Lori walked in.

Or maybe she floated in, because she cast a magic spell the moment her high heel stepped over the threshold. Gabe had never seen any woman look that spectacular. Her cabernet-colored, floor-length dress brushed over her hips but clung to her breasts. Gabe could barely keep from staring at Lori's plunging neckline. As she took another step, the dress parted in a slit that revealed Lori's leg—was she wearing black opaque stockings? Jesus Christ, they were the Devil's own work. Even from this distance, Gabe could see her nails and heels matched perfectly. And her hair... Tumbling curls cascaded onto her shoulders, forcing Gabe to imagine wrapping her fingers into the ringlets as she pressed Lori against the wall and kissed her the way she'd wanted to from the first moment she saw her.

"Oh. My. God," Shay whispered. "The spirit is willing, but the flesh is weak."

Everything had gone weak. Gabe placed her drink on the table to avoid dropping the glass. "Are you seriously quoting the Bible at me right now?"

"I am. You're going to need Her help if Lori puts the moves on you looking like that."

"Truth."

Angie Davis. Elodie Fontaine. Rachel Harari. All the beautiful movie stars in the world could've walked in behind Lori, and Gabe wouldn't have seen them. It was like she suddenly had tunnel vision as everything else in the restaurant went into a soft-focus vignette, while Lori went into sharp, high-res HD.

Gabe locked eyes with her and gave her a weak-ass wave, as if all her power had drained out of her and her bones lacked the strength to hold her up. How the hell could one woman possess that kind of dominance over her faculties?

"Pull it together, Gabe. Her parents are right behind her, and you're being more than a little obvious."

Gabe blinked, breaking the connection. For now.

"Looks like Rosie only has eyes for you," Gabe said when she saw the obvious desire in Rosie's gaze, which was fixed on Shay. Rosie had come dressed to kill too.

"As it should be," Shay said.

Cocky words aside, Shay looked nonplussed as she looked at Rosie in her black sheath dress. Gabe stood as Rosie, Lori, and her parents were led over by the maître d' holding a stack of menus. They all said their hellos as they followed him to their table toward the quieter part of the restaurant. Lori's hand brushed Gabe's, and though she wanted to grab hold and never let go, she stuffed her hand in her pocket instead. If she had any chance of surviving tonight without doing something she'd promised not to do, there was no way she could lean into Lori's flirtatiousness. And *especially* not in front of her parents, whom she did want to impress in spite of herself.

She inhaled deeply when she became aware of Lori's signature citrusy scent. Then she prayed that Lori's parents would insist on sandwiching Lori between them so Gabe could have some much-needed distance.

"Gabe, why don't you sit at the head of the table with Lori?" Hank asked.

He couldn't have read Gabe's mind because if he had, he would never have put his daughter anywhere near her. "Er, no, that's okay. You should both sit with her."

Hank patted Gabe on the shoulder. "Absolutely not. This is a double celebration: Lori's birthday and the restoration project, which never would've happened without you."

He gently pushed her closer to Lori, who slipped her hand around Gabe's forearm and squeezed.

"Lucky me," Lori whispered.

God help me if she's already buzzed. RB and Woody threw her amused glances and sat at the opposite end of the table.

"Hey, everyone. Sorry we're late."

Gabe looked up to see Solo and Janie, dressed to kill but looking flustered.

"Let me guess: Tia?" Lori asked and laughed lightly.

"Got it in one," Solo said as she pulled out Janie's chair, scraping it loudly across the floor.

"She's gotten into the habit of pulling Luna's hair until Luna starts to sob," Janie said. "When Luna cries, Chloe starts for no reason." She shook her head and looked at Lori's mom. "Karen, I'm beginning to see the wisdom of just having one, like you and Hank did."

Karen chuckled. "Oh, I don't know. I think Lori would've liked a sibling, even one that yanked her hair."

Lori nodded. "Didn't I spend two years nagging you for a sister when we first moved to Thailand?"

"You did, that's right," Hank said. "But your sole reason was that you wanted someone to speak English to. You were scared that you were going to forget the language while you were at school all day."

Lori placed her hand over Gabe's. "In my defense, I was only eight..."

The touch of Lori's hand sent a wave of heat through Gabe's body, but she managed to stay in place. "Then you're forgiven," she said, sure that she'd forgive Lori anything anytime.

"Should we look at the menu?" Karen asked. "I'm hungry after all the riding we did today."

Hank ordered some champagne, then everyone settled into small talk while they checked out the food.

Gabe edged toward Lori. "Are you sure you're okay with sharing your birthday like this?"

"Already asked and answered on Tuesday, Gabe," Lori said. "I love that my dad wanted to thank you for what you've done." She leaned in close so that her breath whispered against Gabe's ear. "You and your team have been so wonderful, I'd share anything with you."

Gabe gulped. She wanted Lori to clarify that last part—anything with her or anything with all of them?—but said nothing. She'd been getting a better handle on this friendship thing until Lori's hustler performance last weekend. Now it was like she was back to the beginning, struggling to control herself.

She felt the warmth of Lori's thigh against hers.

"I should be more specific," Lori whispered. "I meant I'd share anything with you, and you alone."

Lori opened her menu and ran her finger along the entrees as if she hadn't just busted open Gabe's head.

Shay caught Gabe's eye. "They've got a 24oz porterhouse. Want to go 70/30 on it?"

"Sure," Gabe said, though food had suddenly become unimportant. She felt Lori's foot against her shin, and then Lori's hand on her thigh. Was this really happening? The air in the restaurant thickened, and the heat became stifling. Gabe wanted to rush out of there into the cool summer air—after grabbing Lori, of course.

But she couldn't, could she? Because Gabe still hadn't summoned the courage to tell Lori about her past and what had happened with the Nelsons. As they'd gotten closer, the omission had begun to feel more and more like a lie, invading their intimacy like an aggressive cancer, threatening to eat away their relationship. And if she just had the chance to calmly explain the circumstances, maybe Lori wouldn't equate the situation to her own experience.

Gabe barely noticed that a waiter had arrived and was halfway around the table taking orders, and their glasses were already full of champagne. After he'd gotten their preferences, Hank stood on the other side of Lori and tapped his knife on the champagne bottle in a bucket beside him. Lori withdrew her hand and gave all her attention to her dad, allowing Gabe to breathe easy again.

"I want to propose a toast," he said and looked at Lori. "First, I want to say thank you to the God Almighty for blessing us with a beautiful, talented, and driven daughter. A daughter who has shown us time and time again that she has an infinite pool of kindness from which she waters all the animals and people in her life and watches them grow in her care. A daughter who has suffered emotional torment at the hands of another human being and yet hasn't let it diminish her capacity to love and care for everyone around her. Lori, you made us proud from the moment you entered this world, and that pride has grown with every single thing you've done, every achievement you've made, and every animal you've saved." He took Karen and Lori's hands and smiled brightly at each of them. "When we started our first care program with hack towers for bald eagles, we imagined building an NPO to help animals worldwide, and you've helped us make that dream come true. Thank you for giving us more joy than we ever imagined possible. You're the most amazing human being we've ever known."

Hank picked up his glass and toasted Lori, and everyone did the same. Gabe concentrated on the elaborate lighting rig snaking across the ceiling and blinked her eyes repeatedly. His speech had been incredible; the only other time Gabe had been overcome with emotion like this had been at her Army graduation ceremony. When she refocused on the people at the table, she could see his words had had the same effect on every one of them, including her team, and the soft lights of the restaurant were reflected in the tears pooling in their eyes. She was glad no one would be asking her to say anything because she couldn't follow that, *and* she was sure she wouldn't be able croak anything past the ball of emotion in her throat.

"Thank you, Daddy," Lori said after the clink of glasses and explosion of applause had died down. "I could never have been any of those things or done a fraction of what I have in this world if I hadn't had the most wonderful parents a daughter could ever hope for. You've supported me in everything I've ever wanted to do, even when it was a little crazy—like when we were in Koh Samui, and I wanted us to fly to New Orleans to help rescue people's abandoned pets after the hurricane—"

"And did you go?" Gabe asked, astonished.

"We couldn't stop her," Karen said, her pride shining from her face like a lighthouse beacon. "We were there for six weeks."

Gabe shook her head, and her admiration for Lori grew even more. She looked back at Lori's parents, whose love for her was so clear that it was almost a physical presence on the table. What would it be like to be loved *that* much? She glanced at Shay, who seemed to have the same kind of wonder in her eyes. They shared a look and a rueful smile. It was impossible not to be envious of the relationship Lori had with her parents.

"*Anyway*," Lori said and gave Gabe a light shove, "if I could continue? I wouldn't be the person I am today without the parents that you are." She raised her glass. "To Mom and Dad."

Another round of shouts and applause erupted.

Hank raised his glass again. "And my second toast goes to the five ex-soldiers of Company E, 2nd Battalion, 5th Special Forces Group, who have generously given their time and considerable expertise to the restoration of what has turned out to be a very special car indeed. And because of its provenance and connection to the world-renowned and widely celebrated craftsman, Marie Zimmerman, I've been told that the Brewster will probably sell for upward of half a million dollars."

Solo whistled loudly. "No fucking way!"

Gabe frowned, a little stunned by the outburst and the fact that Solo already sounded buzzed. She saw Janie place her hand on Solo's forearm, but she shrugged her off and emptied her glass before refilling it again. There was definitely more to their story than Tia acting up. She shared another look with Shay, who rolled her eyes as if she'd expected it. Solo had always been the baby of the team, but she'd seemed to mature with Janie.

Lori's hand on her thigh, dangerously close to her crotch, slammed her attention away from Solo's issues and back to her own, while, to Hank's credit, he largely seemed to ignore Solo's interruption and laughed.

"So thank you to Gabe, Shay, Woody, RB, and Solo for your fantastic hard work. Having looked at Woody's photographs and seeing what you've already done, I can't wait to see the finished product in a couple of days. And I really can't wait to see Lori put a huge check in the Sanctuary's bank account after the auction!"

Hank sat down to another sea of cheering, and though Gabe had been touched by his words, she was on fire from the touch of his daughter. Gabe slipped her hand under the table and placed it over Lori's. "What're you doing?" she whispered.

Lori wiggled her eyebrows. "If you have to ask, I can't be doing it right."

"Oh, you're doing it right. Too right for a *friend*."

Lori didn't answer and took a sip of her champagne. Gabe

watched the way her mouth held the lip of her glass as the alcohol swirled into her mouth. Damn, Gabe longed to be that glass. But she couldn't...could she? But, but, but—fuck the buts.

"I don't just want to be your friend anymore, Gabe." Lori placed the glass on the table. "I want more than that," she said as she slipped her hand all the way up onto Gabe's crotch and squeezed. "So much more."

Gabe tensed every muscle in her body to stem the insane reaction to the feel of Lori's hand cupping her sex through the soft cotton of her trousers.

"You're so hot down there," Lori whispered.

Hot didn't even begin to cover it. Gabe was on fire, and she had to fight against the desire to make an excuse that could take her and Lori away from this dinner celebration and straight to bed. She couldn't think of anything feasible— Hell, she could barely think at all.

Several waiters circled the table to serve their food, and everyone's attention was on them while Lori behaved like a woman possessed. What had brought this on? And did Gabe even care to ask in case Lori came to her senses and simply stopped?

The waiter placed the porterhouse and two plates of roasted vegetables and baked potatoes with all the trimmings between Gabe and Shay. It smelled amazing, but it had no chance of taking her attention from Lori and her gently probing fingers running up and down her thigh.

Lori removed her hand to begin eating her salmon, and Gabe didn't know whether to sigh in relief at the respite or shout in frustration at the loss of her touch. Lori cut off some pieces of her fish, speared one with her fork, and popped it into her mouth. Gabe had barely had the time to figure out what she was supposed to be feeling, let alone think about eating the steak Shay was slicing into before Lori's hand returned to her thigh.

She rubbed her finger along the seam of Gabe's crotch. "I've wanted to touch you like this since the moment you stepped out of your truck the first time you came to the Sanctuary," she whispered then put another piece of salmon into her mouth as innocently as if they were discussing the weather.

Gabe closed her eyes briefly, remembering that same moment she'd laid eyes on Lori and thought exactly the same thing.

"It was like you'd walked right out of my wet dream."

Lori's whispered words triggered a flood of sensations, driving all her attention to the feeling between her legs. How had Lori's ex been stupid enough to let her go? Gabe shoved away the intrusive and unwelcome thought. *Her loss, my gain*. Could it really be her gain though?

"Gabe, I don't feel well." Lori grasped her wrist. "I'm a little shaky. Would you take me to the restroom?" She turned to Hank after Gabe had nodded weakly. "Dad, I feel a little queasy. Gabe's taking me to the bathroom, okay?"

"Honey, what's wrong? It can't be the food, surely?"

Lori shook her head. "It's just the time of the month," she whispered. "I'll be fine."

Gabe placed her napkin on the table and stood to help Lori up, who produced an Oscar-worthy performance, almost stumbling into Gabe's arms. Shay arched her eyebrow and shook her head almost imperceptibly. The look in her eyes told Gabe that she knew exactly what was going on. Gabe chose to avoid her gaze and headed away from the table.

But they didn't make it to the restroom. Lori dragged Gabe beyond it and pushed her up against the hallway wall with more strength than her stature implied she should have.

"You're driving me insane, Gabe Jackson." Lori ran her hands across Gabe's chest and tugged on her tie. "I *have* to have you tonight."

Before Gabe knew what was happening, Lori got onto her tiptoes and pressed her lips to Gabe's. Stars collided, fireworks exploded, and the little control Gabe was clutching onto disappeared like sand between her fingers. She wrapped her hands around Lori's waist and lifted her from the ground as their kiss deepened, and their surroundings fell away into white noise.

Lori grasped the back of Gabe's neck and pulled her in harder then broke away. "I have a room booked at a hotel around the block. When the meal is over, will you take me there?"

Gabe claimed Lori's mouth again. Now that she was in this position, she didn't want to waste a moment of it. "Can't we just go now?"

Lori dragged the nail of her index finger across Gabe's lip. "We're the guests of honor; we can't really disappear on everyone, can we?"

Gabe groaned, the rush of desire overtaking all her logic and sense. "Can't we?"

Lori sucked Gabe's lower lip between her teeth and nibbled on it. "No."

The noise of the restaurant crept back into her consciousness, and she tried to get a grasp on her sensible self. "Are you sure this is what you want?" Gabe asked. "What happened to just being friends?"

Lori ran her hand along the back of Gabe's neck and gave a low growl. "We've both known that was never going to last. I just needed a little time to put the past firmly *in* the past."

Lori's choice of words dragged her back to earth with a painful thud. Maybe now Gabe could do the same. "I have to tell you something."

"No." Lori pressed her finger over Gabe's lips. "Not tonight. All I want to think about right now are the things we're going to do to each other all night long."

Gabe swallowed hard and didn't resist another insistent kiss.

"You do want this too, don't you?" Lori asked.

For a fleeting second, Lori's dominant display dissipated, and Gabe saw a flicker of vulnerability in her eyes. Gabe lowered

Lori to her feet slowly and cupped her cheek. "More than I've ever wanted anything in my life."

The fear disappeared as quickly as it had intruded, and Lori ran her hands down Gabe's chest and to her belt. "Good. And in the breaks between the mind-blowing sex we're about to have, I want to know the story behind every tattoo you have, including Alectho."

Gabe frowned. "Alectho?"

Lori shook her head. "Never mind. I had a dream where you had a winged fury on your abdomen."

Gabe grinned and trailed her finger down the plunging neckline of Lori's dress. "You've been having dirty dreams about me?"

"Incessantly." Lori rolled her eyes and hooked her fingers in Gabe's belt. "Day and night."

"I like that. I like that a *lot*."

"Mm," Lori said. "They've given me plenty of ideas, that's for sure."

"I can hardly wait." Gabe leaned down for another kiss, each one tasting better than the last, fueling her desire like oxygen to fire.

Lori put her hands against Gabe's chest and pushed her back against the wall. "You'll have to. We should get back to the table before my dad sends my mom to see how I'm doing."

Gabe blew out a petulant breath. How was she supposed to go back to that table and eat anything when she only had an appetite for Lori? And the last thing she wanted to do was prolong the time between now and when they hit the sheets.

Lori straightened Gabe's tie then smoothed down her dress. "Ready?"

Gabe closed her eyes and tried to cool her raging passion. It was finally happening, and she could see a way beyond the past that had tried to mar her future. Lori was a wonderfully kind human being; Gabe would explain everything about her incident with the sergeant major and his wife, and Lori would understand. And then every night could be like the one they were about to have. She opened her eyes and nodded. "Ready," she said and followed Lori back to their table.

The conversation seemed to be in full flow, with Solo seemingly holding court, loudly, and Gabe noticed she was slurring her words a little. Janie looked uncomfortable and strangely focused on the plate in front of her instead of listening to her wife.

"Solo was just telling us that you're the first woman to receive a Purple Heart and a Medal of Honor," Hank said as she and Lori took their seats.

Gabe glanced at Solo and shrugged as she sat down. "Captain Parker Snow received a Medal of Honor in 2020 for pulling several of her colleagues out of a helicopter that had been shot down over enemy territory. So I was the first for that medal, but now I'm not the only one. Solo's right that I'm the only woman with both though."

"It seems surprising that you didn't go further up the ranks after receiving those honors," Hank said.

"Gabe could've become the US Army's first female five-star general. Our very own superhero who could do no wrong," Solo said, loud enough for the whole section of the restaurant to hear. She laughed and waved her steak knife in Gabe's direction. "But then she screwed the sergeant major's wife, which got her blackballed."

Gabe made a slashing motion across her neck as ice-cold panic swept up her spine.

"That's enough, Solo," Shay said.

But it was too late. Gabe should've told Solo and the rest of them about Lori's ex-wife cheating on her, should've told them never to say anything. But that would've dragged them all into this and made Gabe even more deceitful.

"What?" Solo raised her glass, looking confused at the tense looks being shot her way. "He was a prick, and he deserved it."

Shay grasped Solo's arm and slammed it on the table. "Shut your mouth, Solo, or I'll shut it for you."

Gabe braved a sideways glance at Lori. She looked stunned, and tears edged her eyes. Gabe reached out, but Lori swatted her hand away.

"Don't."

Her ice-cold tone was like a punch to Gabe's heart, like Lori had frozen her emotions and shut down everything they'd just shared in the hallway, and every conversation and intimate moment they'd had disappeared in the tornado of Solo's declaration.

Lori tossed her napkin on the table and pushed out her chair. "Mom...would you–"

"Honey, what's going on?" Hank asked.

"I have to leave, Daddy," she said, her voice trembling just a little.

Gabe sagged in her chair, like gravity was pulling down extra hard and iron chains had wrapped around her to hold her in place. *Say something*.

Hank frowned. "Solo has just had one drink too many, honey. She didn't mean anything by it, I'm sure."

Lori shook her head. "It's not her, Daddy." She squeezed his shoulder and stood. "I'll explain later, but right now, I have to get out of here."

Hank moved to get up. "I'll get the bill. Wait for me?"

Gabe became aware of Rosie's presence between her and Lori.

"Let's go, Lori," Rosie said and glared daggers at Gabe. "I *knew* you were too good to be true. You nearly had us all fooled. Great acting: you missed your vocation."

"Lori, please. Hear me out," Gabe finally managed to say, but Lori didn't look back. The four of them headed out of the restaurant, leaving the celebrations behind. Gabe fought against the imaginary shackles and began to stand, but Shay put her hand on her forearm.

"Let her go," Shay said. "Let her go for now. She'll calm down, and you can explain everything."

Gabe sank back into her chair and turned to Shay. "What if you're wrong?" Tears misted over her eyes, and she looked away from the glances of the rest of her team, the question of what the hell had just happened clear in their expressions. She couldn't make eye contact with Solo right now either because she might just knock her out.

Shay stood and pulled her up then guided her over to the bar. Gabe didn't resist. All her strength and resolve had withered away when she'd seen the look of complete disappointment and hurt in Lori's expression.

"Stay here," Shay said. "I'll make our excuses, and we'll go find a bar."

Gabe nodded. "I've fucked everything up, Shay."

"She just needs some time, Gabe. You're not the person you were when all that happened. She'll understand that, and she'll forgive you."

"I hope you're right." Gabe wiped an escaping tear with the back of her hand. She had to get Lori's forgiveness. All the time they'd spent together, all the intimate non-sexual moments they'd shared, all the laughs they'd had... Gabe didn't want to lose that. She *couldn't* lose that. She liked the person that she'd so naturally become around Lori. She liked how Lori made her feel. She...*loved* her. The emotion she'd never thought she was capable of flooded through her. When she was around Lori, it had filled her with a warmth she couldn't explain, but the loss of her now chilled Gabe to the core. She'd spent so much of her life essentially alone. Maybe that was what she deserved.

Chapter Twenty-Two

LORI CLOSED HER EYES, sore from all the tears she'd sobbed in the cab on the way home and from the past hour she'd spent lying on her couch with her head on her mom's lap. In the cab, no one had pressed her to talk or asked what was going on. They knew her well enough to know the answer. But Lori hadn't wanted an audience for this breakdown, and she'd been glad when her mom had suggested that they drop Rosie at home on their way back to the Sanctuary. Rosie had left quietly with a promise to check on her tomorrow.

She didn't look up when she heard the stairs creak. "Mom," she said and trusted her to understand what she needed.

"I know, sweetheart." Her mom continued to stroke her hair from the top of her head all the way down to its end, just the way she had when she was a child.

"Karen, is everything okay?"

"Not right now, but it will be," her mom said. "You go back to bed and get some sleep."

Lori felt her father come closer and heard their gentle kiss before his footsteps retreated along the hallway and up the stairs. "Tell me again how you and Dad met," she said, desperate for a distraction from the devastating ache in the deepest, most hidden part of her soul.

Her mom sighed. "My boyfriend at the time wanted me to watch him play basketball, and I agreed, even though it was my least favorite sport. I figured I could sit in the back of the bleachers and read *The Great Gatsby* for my literature class." She drew in a long breath and let out another sound of contentment. "All the players came onto the court, and I looked up to feign interest as he waved at me. I smiled and waved back, thinking that he'd forget I was there as soon as they tipped off." Her chuckle rocked Lori's head gently. "I hadn't counted on his gorgeous teammate, who, it turned out, also happened to be his new best friend."

Lori allowed herself to concentrate on their love story. "Tut tut, Mom, for not respecting the bro code."

"Oh, those curls, and his gorgeous blue eyes, and he was so tall." Her mom squeezed Lori's shoulder. "I was powerless to resist."

Lori smiled and sat up. She never tired of hearing that story. "Did you know that you loved him from the start? And that you were meant to be together?"

Her mom shook her head. "I knew I lusted after him from the start, but I had no idea we were meant to be together. Ryan and I had been high school sweethearts, together for six years. I thought I loved him." She shrugged. "But I soon realized I had no idea what love really was until your dad and I fell into it."

"Do you think you can love someone and hate them at the same time?"

"Yes," her mom said. "You can love someone and hate what they've done. Definitely."

Lori settled down on the other side of the sofa so she could face her mom, who had clearly realized where she was going with this conversation.

"I bet she and her buddies had a good laugh after I'd told Gabe what the lawyer had done with her paralegal. 'That's terrible, and I can't imagine how painful that must've been,' she said. She looked me in the eye, Mom, and pretended that she cared."

"Hey, you don't know that she doesn't. From what I can see, I don't think any of what you've told me has been pretend."

Lori scoffed. "Are you serious? *All* of it is. She's been pretending to be such a kind and generous person when all the time she's the kind of woman who can happily break up marriages."

"Mm. I saw all the work that's gone into your rust bucket when we visited the garage on Tuesday. None of that is pretend."

"She can do all those things and be a cheater." Lori frowned. "Exactly whose side are you on, Mom?"

"Yours, sweetheart. Always yours. But that doesn't mean that seeing the other side of the argument isn't in your best interest."

"What do you mean by that?" She wrapped her arms around her knees and prepared for some Mom-wisdom.

"For years now, you've been existing, not living. Even before you found that woman cheating on you, you'd become a ghost of yourself."

"Why didn't you say anything?"

Her mom shook her head. "As much as I love you and want to protect you, I can't live your life for you. You have to make your own mistakes, and you have to find your own way out of the situations you find yourself in." She shrugged. "To be honest though, we see a lot less of you since you moved here to run the Sanctuary, so it was hard to know whether you were changing because of those responsibilities, or if it was the lawyer. And she had your father and me fooled for a long time too. She put on a hell of a show whenever we visited; she made it look like you were the center of her world."

Lori didn't say anything for a moment and thought about what her mom had said. "Why did it take *me* so long to realize that? I was the one living with her."

"I imagine it's because you were so focused on making this place viable. And maybe you blamed yourself for the cracks, so you didn't see she was the one slamming an axe into the foundations of your marriage."

Lori sighed deeply. "I don't want to talk about her anymore. The auction will mark the end of that for me, once and for all. It's Gabe I'm angry with now."

Her mom smiled. "I brought it up because it's important to

see how much you've changed since Gabe came into your life—maybe not so much changed as recaptured your spirit. It's like she's switched the light on so that you can see the beauty of your life again. Your dad and I saw it when you picked us up at the airport." She reached over and squeezed Lori's hand. "I can't tell you how wonderful that was. And your soul practically levitates when you're around her or talking about her. Your dad says that you look like he felt when we first met—and every day since." Her mom looked off into the distance, like she was watching old memories play out on the walls. "It's all we've ever hoped for: for you to find the kind of love that we share. It's a luckier discovery than any hidden treasures found at the bottom of the sea."

Lori placed her hand over her mom's, finding the solidness she needed. Could she dare to hope that she and Gabe could be as symbiotic as her parents? Maybe she could have before tonight's big reveal. "You and Dad aren't cheaters though, Mom."

"Well, that's not strictly true..."

Lori narrowed her eyes. "What's that supposed to mean?"

Her mom looked away and inspected her nails.

"Mom?" She'd heard this story a hundred times, and there'd never been any hint of impropriety.

"I wasn't sure your father was serious. I mean, he was a hunk, and I was smitten—"

"Ew, Mom."

Her mom shook her head. "I swear children are programmed to believe that they really are delivered to parents by storks."

"I don't think that," Lori said. "I just don't want to think about it *at all*."

Her mom waved her protestations away. "Well, anyway, I had a lot to lose. Ryan and I were engaged to be married, and my parents thought the sun shone out of his butt. His parents were rich and influential, and they were grooming him for a career in politics."

"Which worked, didn't it? Isn't he a New York senator?"

Her mom nodded. "Indeed he is. Which is why my parents were so set on us marrying. But your dad was less...conventional, *and* he had a bit of a love 'em and leave 'em reputation. I wasn't sure I wanted to risk the stability of the life that had been planned for me just for...well, just for something you don't want to hear me talk about."

Lori rolled her eyes. "Then maybe you could skip that part and get to the rest of the story that you've never told me before."

Her mom gave Lori's knees a light shove. "I'm giving you context, sweetheart. These things don't happen in a vacuum. Circumstances are very important."

Lori tucked a pillow between her head and the sofa and settled against it. "Okay. Please continue."

"So we saw each other while I was still seeing Ry–"

Lori bolted upright and stared at her mom, open-mouthed. "You cheated on Ryan with Dad?"

Her mom nodded. "I had to be sure. I didn't want to throw my future away for something that was only powered by lust and something that burned bright but wouldn't burn long. We're not proud of how we started, but we accept that it simply was what it had to be."

"How long?"

"How long what?"

"How long did you cheat on Ryan before you made your decision?"

"Six months. Before me, the longest your father had been with anyone was..." She flicked her hand in the air. "Well, let's just say that he hadn't proven himself to be a keeper."

Lori squeezed her eyes shut. Once she had the detail, she could never let it go, but the curious child within her was desperate to know *almost* everything. "I may as well have the full picture since you're ruining my fairytale."

Her mom chuckled. "I do love your dramatic side. Are you sure?"

Lori nodded, and her mom gave a naughty grin, something Lori had never seen before and wasn't sure she'd want to again.

"Forty-eight hours. The weekend was all anyone else ever had. Until me."

So the grin was pride. "You're pleased with yourself because you changed the leopard's spots, aren't you?"

"In a way, I suppose I am. But your father, by his own admission, was untethered and floating through life. I became his anchor, something to ground him but also someone to fly with him too." Her mom chuckled and winked conspiratorially. "And what brought us together hasn't faded yet."

"I didn't need to know that." What her parents got up to in the privacy of their own house was something Lori really didn't want to ever think about. "Were you never worried that he'd get bored and cheat on you because of the way you started out?"

"No. We both knew what we'd found, and there was no way either of us were ever going to risk letting it go," her mom said. "And besides, you don't go out for a hamburger when you've got steak at home."

Lori sighed. She'd been briefly distracted by her mom's story but now remembered why she was hearing it at all. "So you're telling me that I shouldn't be mad at Gabe for whatever she's gotten up to with the sergeant major's wife? For being involved in a cheating scenario."

"I've never told you how to feel, sweetheart, and I'm not going to start now. But you owe it to yourself to give her the chance to explain. You have no idea how long ago it was or what the circumstances were. What she's done in the past doesn't necessarily define what she'll do in the future. Look at how you railed against helping the elephants in Koh Samui. We were beginning to think that you wouldn't become part of the family business, and that you'd end up in some corporate, money-grabbing, greed-fest for a job. Now look at you, running this place all by yourself."

She gave a half-smile. "But that's not the same thing, is it?"

"It shows how people can change. Your father changed when he met me. Pieces slotted into place, and everything made sense in the world."

Lori's phone pinged with a message, and she glanced at it on the coffee table where it peeked out of her clutch.

"Don't you want to check if that's Gabe?"

She shook her head. "It'll probably be Rosie."

"Is that who you want it to be?"

"I'm not sure what I want at the moment, Mom. This isn't just about the cheating, it's about Gabe not *telling* me about it. She knew what I'd been through, but she still didn't tell me that she'd done the exact same thing to someone else." Lori reached for her phone then thought better of it.

"Perhaps she kept it to herself because she knew how you'd react and didn't want to hurt you," her mom said. "Until you know all the facts, I don't see how you can make an informed opinion or decision. As far as Gabe knew, you were just supposed to be friends; *you're* the one who changed the parameters of your relationship without talking to her about it. Maybe if you'd talked to her about it instead of hatching your little hotel plan, she might've told you all about her past indiscretion."

I have to tell you something. She'd been the one to stop Gabe from saying anything. But that could've been something else completely unrelated to a potential confession. She grabbed her phone and checked her messages. Sure enough, there was one from Rosie, and her view of the situation was predictably angry on Lori's behalf and best friend-like in its solidarity. She'd known she wouldn't get the same response from her mom, which was why she'd sent Rosie home... She needed her mom's level head and relative objectivity.

If and when u're ready, can we talk so I can tell u everything?

"Well? What does Gabe have to say?"

"She wants to talk." Lori placed her cell face down on the

couch.

"Tomorrow's Sunday," her mom said. "She'll be coming to see Max, won't she? Or are you going to tell her that she can't?"

"Of course not." But the thought of seeing Gabe tomorrow turned her heart inside out. She thought she'd been doing the right thing by getting to know Gabe and making sure she was safe before she let her heart enter the equation. None of it had worked. Beating beneath her ribs, it was already a traitor. It already belonged to Gabe. "Beth is covering my work tomorrow..." *Because I was supposed to be up all night having mind-bending sex with Gabe.* "So Gabe can still see Max. I don't have to be around." Lori had promised that they could talk about Max's possible adoption, but there was no way she could face that right now.

"You're going to avoid her?"

"Clearly you don't think that's a good plan," Lori said, "but it's the only one I have right now. I felt like I was almost healed after the lawyer, but this has knocked me on my ass, Mom. I've got a therapy session on Monday. I'll talk to Rae and try to straighten everything out in my head."

"Okay, sweetheart." Her mom shifted so that she could pull Lori into a hug. "Would you like me to stay? I can cancel tomorrow's flight."

Lori relaxed into her mom's arms and rested her head on her mom's shoulder. "No, I don't need you to do that. You'll be back next week for the auction anyway. And Dad needs to get back to his new project. I haven't seen him this excited about something since the time he got back from that orca rescue."

"I don't mind." Her mom kissed the top of Lori's head. "I'll take any excuse to be with my baby. You'll always be more important than any project we've got going on. You do know that, don't you?"

Lori smiled. Her mom's love seemed to be easing the headache that had formed after all her crying. "I do, Mom. I've always known that. I'll be okay. I just need some time."

"Good, but you can't ignore her forever. At the very least, you're bound by the restoration project until the auction."

"I know." *We're bound by a lot more than that. I'm just not sure I want to be*.

Chapter Twenty-Three

GABE FILLED ANOTHER HELIUM balloon, and this one expanded into the shape of a wrench. She should've appreciated its novelty, but her mind was too occupied with thoughts of Lori to be here, where it should be. She plugged the end of the balloon and wandered over to the reception area to tie it around the scaffolding desk RB had made by hand. It was another thing she should be appreciating. RB had been excited to show it to her, but Gabe couldn't quite muster the enthusiasm needed.

"Still no response to your text?" Shay asked as she climbed down from hanging the *Opening Day* banner.

Gabe shook her head. "I haven't heard from her all weekend. I want to send more. I want to call her. But I'm not being that stalky asshole."

Shay hoisted herself on top of the desk. "That's a good decision. You don't want to blow up her phone when it's obvious that she needs time to process."

Gabe tightened the knot in the balloon ribbon, let it go, and watched it float toward the ceiling. "But I can't just let her go, Shay." She pulled her phone from the pocket of her cargo pants and stared at a screen void of messages.

Shay gently took the phone from Gabe's grasp and placed it on the varnished wooden surface. "You've got to let Lori have the power, buddy. I get that this emotion shit is all new to you, but you have to let it be and let it hurt. She won't ignore you forever." She gestured to the Brewster in the back with the new tarp covering it. "The auction isn't far away, and then there's Max."

Gabe blew out a short breath. "I hope I haven't fucked that

up too. She wasn't there when I saw Max yesterday. The last time we talked, she said she'd start the adoption process with me and that they wouldn't go advertise that Max was available. What if she changes her mind?"

Shay wrinkled her nose. "Nah, she's not that kind of woman. She knows Max is going to be better off living with you, and she wouldn't sabotage that just to punish you."

Gabe frowned. "You think she wants to punish me?"

Shay grasped Gabe's shoulder and squeezed. "I have no idea what Lori wants, but I'm pretty sure she's not a vindictive woman scorned. She'll talk to you eventually, and you've got to wait patiently—because she's worth waiting for, right?"

"God, yes."

"And you're prepared to wait as long as it takes, right?"

Gabe nodded. "That had been my plan until I found out about the cheating ex. I told you Lori wouldn't react well to my history with the Nelsons."

"Maybe it's that, or maybe she's so pissed because you *didn't* tell her after she'd spilled her guts about the ex-wife. If you remember correctly, I *told* you to tell her about Cynthia."

"You also said that I didn't need to." Gabe shrugged. She didn't have Lori's memory for detail, but she did remember that. "I was too worried that it would ruin the friendship."

"So it's out in the open now, and you have to figure a way forward, hopefully together."

"I guess... For someone who's never had a serious relationship, you're pretty good at navigating them."

"You have to be when you've got as many brothers and sisters coming to you for advice as I do."

Gabe gave a rueful smile. Shay had so many family responsibilities, but she handled them quietly and never made a big deal of any of it. "How is the family?" she asked though Shay often didn't want to talk about them either.

"Which one?" Shay waved her hand as if flicking the inquiry

away. "They're all...still there. You know what they're like; they're still asking for advice and then doing the exact opposite."

Gabe shook her head. "I don't know how you keep your patience with them all."

"Who said I did?" Shay jumped down from the desk. "But what am I going to do? They're family. For better or for worse, they're mine." She motioned across to the back entrance. "Speaking of which, Solo just arrived."

Gabe clenched her jaw and her fists. She hadn't heard from Solo after she and Shay had left the restaurant, and Gabe had written and deleted several texts before sending nothing after deciding she'd rather confront her face-to-face.

Shay stepped in front of her. "Solo was a jackass on Saturday, but she was drunk, and she didn't know anything about Lori's past or that you hadn't told Lori about Cynthia." She took Gabe's fists and unfurled them. "In her head, it was a compliment."

Gabe raised her eyebrow. "How was telling everyone that I fucked up my career by fucking the sergeant major's wife a compliment?"

"Not that bit," Shay said. "The bit about you being a five-star general. You know she hero-worships you. But we're a family, Gabe, and every family has at least one mouthy brat. Solo is ours. But she is *ours*, and we chose her. Remember that."

Gabe rolled her eyes and nodded. "And every family has a wise woman," she said and pulled Shay into a full hug. Over her shoulder, Gabe saw Solo offer a weak wave. She released Shay and jutted her chin toward Solo. "I'll go clear the air then."

"Good idea. Maybe consider telling her what's going on with you and find out what's happening with her too. I think there's trouble in paradise."

"You do?" Gabe asked.

Shay laughed gently. "It was obvious, but you were otherwise occupied with Lori and pretty oblivious to everything else going on around you. Which is as it should be when you're in love." She patted Gabe's bicep and headed into the office.

"Wait—what?" How did Shay know Gabe was in love when she'd only just realized that herself? But Shay didn't turn around or respond. Of course Shay would know; she knew Gabe better than anyone, even herself sometimes. She looked back across the garage to where Solo was still apparently waiting for permission to enter. "Hey."

"Morning." Solo shifted from foot to foot and looked at the ground. "I was expecting a less friendly greeting."

"Oh, yeah? What were you expecting?"

"A broken nose, maybe? Minimum, a busted lip. Possibly a broken rib or two."

"I'll leave that to Tia. I don't want to be the one setting a bad example for your kids."

"I'm sorry for shooting my mouth off, Gabe." Solo ran her hand through her hair and looked up. "I upset everyone and ruined the celebrations."

Gabe tilted her head slightly. "You definitely did that. I should've told you that I hadn't shared that part of my past with Lori, but you shouldn't have shared something like that over dinner either."

Solo frowned. "Why hadn't you? Told Lori, I mean." She shrugged. "I know your go-to is Shay, not me."

Solo sounded more resigned than petulant, so Gabe decided to leave that be. "Lori's past with her ex is complicated, and I thought that if I told her about Cynthia, she wouldn't want to be friends, let alone more." It wasn't for Gabe to share the details of Lori's story without her permission. She'd only told Shay because she knew Shay could be discreet, and Gabe needed her advice.

Solo nodded. "Still, I was a drunken asshole, and I'm sorry. Are we good?"

Gabe pulled Solo into a brief bro hug. "*We're* good, but what was happening with you that night?"

Solo shook her head and pointed toward the rest of the

balloons that needed filling. "That's not important. Today's opening day."

She was clearly aiming for uplifting but missed the mark by a half-mile. Gabe followed her, and they were silent for a while as they worked through the remaining balloons and fixed them up outside.

"Is Janie dropping by today?" Gabe asked. Instead of Solo's eyes lighting up, they seemed to darken with a tangible sadness, a marked difference to her usual reaction to the mention of her wife.

Solo stuffed her hands in her coveralls and sighed. "I don't think so. She's busy with a big case right now. She's supposed to be in court most of the day." She tapped her watch. "I haven't seen RB and Woody. Didn't they come in with you and Shay?"

"Woody's upstairs doing some socials, and RB's gone to Bonnie's for coffee and bagels," Gabe said. "Everything's in place, so you can stop avoiding the issue and save us some time by just telling me what's going on with you and Janie."

"She's..." Solo swallowed hard and turned away. She picked up the helium cannister and put it under the desk then came back around and sat on one of the leather couches in the waiting area.

Gabe joined her and sat beside her. "What's going on, Solo? Are the kids okay?" She almost laughed at her instant concern for Solo's family. She was actually beginning to take her auntie role seriously.

"The kids are fine. They're with the new nanny... But apparently they're part of the problem." Solo glanced at her watch as RB came in the side door with a tray of coffees. "We're opening in five minutes. Let's put a pin in this and maybe chat at lunch, okay? I'll be fine." She stood and headed toward RB with a false grin and a too-cheery greeting.

Gabe rubbed the back of her neck to ease the building tightness. Solo and Janie were supposed to be a paragon of what a good family could look like. If they were floundering, did Gabe really have any hope of building anything with Lori after her own breach of trust? Or maybe it was just that families and relationships were hard, and required work, and could be incredibly difficult to navigate.

Shay emerged from the office holding up the key for the front shutters. "It's time, my friends," she said and looked around. "Where's Woody?"

"Right here." Woody jogged down the stairs and jumped the last few to hit the ground with a thud. "Free oil changes are live on our socials. Let the mayhem commence."

Shay unlocked the shutters and hit the button to open them, then stepped back to stand alongside Gabe. The line of cars snaked around the block. Gabe pushed all thoughts of Lori to the back of her mind and grinned, but where Solo's had been forced, her own was genuine. This was still her dream, and she wasn't about to ruin it for herself.

***

The metal shutters rattled noisily against the ground, and Gabe dropped onto one of their waiting room couches, exhausted but elated. Their five bays hadn't been empty from the moment they opened the shutters to forty-five minutes before closing time, when they'd had to start turning people away. It'd been a great opening day, and it was nice to see Mr. Jones, the old owner, drop by too.

She wiped her greased-up hands on her cargo pants before accepting the ice-cold beer Shay offered her. Woody, RB, and Solo flopped down, and all of them sighed heavily.

"I think I'd forgotten how to work that hard," RB said. "Pushing paper in an office has made me soft."

Gabe grinned. Of the five of them, she'd been the only one still used to hard physical work. "But it was mentally tough, wasn't it?"

RB shrugged. "Only when the applications weren't successful."

Woody twisted the cap from her bottle and raised it in the air. "Cheers to us having a successful launch day."

Their bottles met mid-air, and beer spilled all over the glass-topped engine block table. Solo dropped to her knees and pretended to suck it up.

"That's so gross," Woody said. "Aren't you worried you'll catch something and give it to the girls?"

Solo got up and sat back on a couch. "I didn't do it for real, Woody."

Woody laughed. "You say that like you haven't done the exact same thing a hundred times before."

Solo shrugged. "That was before I had kids to keep safe." She took a long pull on her beer and sighed.

Gabe shared a worried glance with Shay. They'd been too busy to have lunch together, so she hadn't gotten the chance to pull the pin out and chat with Solo.

RB tapped the screen of her iPad. "D'you want the stats?"

"Sure." Gabe relaxed back into the sofa, not sure if she'd be able to get up again. Maybe she could just sleep here tonight.

"We did 102 oil changes and used 597 liters of oil."

"Jesus," Shay said. "That's $5,060.22 worth of work. Thank God Janie bankrolled that initiative."

Gabe didn't miss Solo's jaw tighten at the mention of her wife again. What the hell was going on there? "You did that math quick."

Shay held up her bottle. "A couple more of these, and it might've taken me a few seconds longer."

Gabe and the rest of them laughed.

"So, fifty-four percent of clients today came in with the QR code from our social posts," RB said, "thirty-five percent were from Mr. Jones' client base, and the rest were passing drive-ins."

"That's pretty damn good, right?" Gabe asked and put her feet up on the table, avoiding the pool of beer.

"It's better than that," RB said. "Even if we only retain twenty percent of those clients for the first six months of business, we'd be doing great."

"I'd like to propose a toast," Gabe said. "I want to say thanks. RB, Woody, and Shay—you pulled up your lives on a dime to relocate here for this, and Solo, you convinced your wife to put in the lion's share of financial backing. We used to sit around an oil drum in the desert, drinking beer and dreaming about this day, and I can't believe it's finally here." She fiddled with the label on her beer to give her bubbling emotions time to settle. "Not only did we make it happen, but we also made it a huge success, according to our stats guru *and* our aching bodies." She glanced beyond her gathered friends to the Brewster in the far corner of the garage. "And then there's that little project in the back..."

"I'm nearly finished editing the video of the whole restoration." Woody shook her head. "It's going to be better than I thought it was, even after I take out all the conversations that shouldn't go beyond this shop. When it's ready, I'll put it on a flash drive for Lori, and I'll put snippets up on the website to create more interest for the auction." She looked at Gabe. "Should I send it to her? Or will you take it personally?"

Gabe's elation drained out of her work boots. "I can't answer that right now," she said and sighed deeply.

"Yes, you can."

Gabe snapped her head around so fast that she almost wrenched her neck. "Lori?" She jumped up from the sofa and half-jogged toward the side entrance where Lori was waiting awkwardly in the door jamb. "Come in."

Lori shook her head. "You come out."

Gabe glanced over her shoulder, and Shay shooed her away, mouthing, "Go."

Lori turned, and Gabe followed her outside. A hundred things ran through her mind, all competing to get out of her mouth first. In the end, she remembered what Shay had said about letting

Lori have the power, so she said none of them.

Lori had parked her car in the alleyway, and she sat on the hood.

Gabe waited for her to say something, to yell at her for betraying her trust, or to calmly tell her to stop texting and that they were no longer friends. But Lori simply stared at her, saying nothing at all.

"You should bring your car around front so I can check it. The Bolts had a run of bad axles, and they can catch fire," Gabe said after the silence had become unbearable.

"You should get in my car so I can take you somewhere to talk." Lori pushed off the car and got in.

Gabe bit the inside of her lip. Lori was even sexier when she was angry, and her command pushed buttons Gabe didn't know she had. She took a step forward obediently then remembered she'd spent the day under twenty or so dirty cars. She motioned toward her greased-up pants. "I probably shouldn't sit in your car like this."

"I've covered the seat with an old blanket," Lori said. "Just get in and shut up before I change my mind and drive away alone."

Gabe rushed around the snub-nose hood and jumped in the passenger side without having to be told a third time. She didn't question where they were going; it didn't matter. All that mattered was that Lori wasn't ignoring her anymore. The atmosphere was about as ominous as she imagined a court-martial would be, but she also had a sense of hope. She was sure that the way Lori had looked her over was sexually loaded; there'd been a glint in her eye, and her lips had twitched slightly. Under the intense scrutiny, Gabe had twitched in an entirely different place.

Lori drove in silence through the evening traffic and swung into the underground parking lot of the Hotel Quantum. "Don't get any ideas," she said as she switched off the engine. "I just want somewhere private to talk, and somewhere I can walk away from at any time."

"Okay." It made sense, of course, but the explanation didn't keep Gabe's hope from kicking into overdrive. If Lori would just hear her out, if she could explain what she'd done, and if Lori could be open-minded enough, maybe Gabe would be able to convince Lori that she could trust her, that she would hold her heart as tenderly as if it were her own.

An unwelcome saying from her father slipped into her mind. *If ifs and buts were candy and nuts, then we'd never go hungry...*

Chapter Twenty-Four

LORI PAUSED OUTSIDE THE elevator in the hotel lobby. "Wait here," she said without looking at Gabe then headed toward the bank of iPads which served as the hotel's AI reception desk. She needed some distance to cool down. Seeing Gabe standing in the alley in her dirty white T-shirt, scruffy combat pants, and work boots had almost exploded her resolve there and then. A super short and super sexy movie of Gabe taking her on the hood of the car with a strap-on had played in her head as she swept her gaze over Gabe's insanely hot body.

A little time and a lot of anger had done nothing to reduce Lori's sexual attraction, that much was clear.

She confirmed her reservation with the friendly machine, shamefully grateful that she hadn't had to deal with a real person who would surely have spotted Gabe hovering in the hallway and made assumptions about Lori's less than honorable intentions—even though Lori hadn't decided on her intentions yet herself.

She activated only one keycard, made a mental note of her room number, and headed back toward Gabe. Either they'd be staying together, or she'd be leaving alone. Whatever happened, they didn't need two keys. Gabe caught her eye, and Lori motioned for her to call the elevator. When she got there, she hit their floor number and then pressed the close button repeatedly as a well-dressed couple advanced toward them. The doors slid shut before they got there. Just as Lori hadn't wanted the judgment of a hotel employee, she didn't want loaded glances from other hotel guests either.

She didn't speak as the elevator glided up to the thirtieth floor.

In the small box, the musky scent of Gabe after a hard day's work only served to ramp up her irritatingly active hormones, and she didn't trust herself to say anything that wouldn't indicate this was a booty call.

Even though that was exactly what this might turn out to be.

The elevator pinged to indicate its arrival, and Gabe motioned for Lori to exit first. She sashayed, one hundred percent on purpose, in the direction of the exact same hotel room they were supposed to have been in on Saturday night under very different circumstances. In the mirrored hallway, she could see that Gabe remained a few steps behind her, also very clearly one hundred percent on purpose. Her gaze was directed at Lori's butt, so she exaggerated the swing of her hips just a little more.

When she got to the room, she handed Gabe the keycard. Gabe took it without a word, flashed it across the pad, and held open the door for Lori to cross the threshold first. Without looking back, Lori headed straight to the mini bar. Whatever it was she was about to hear, she was pretty sure a little kicker wouldn't go amiss. She grabbed the ice bucket from the sideboard and turned around to hand it to Gabe. She'd stopped just inside the room and rushed over to take it from her.

"I don't want to wait for room service," Lori said. "Can you get that filled?"

"Sure," Gabe said and left the room.

Conscious of the void that created, Lori took a deep breath and stopped questioning herself. Her session with Rae this morning had solidified what she already knew deep down: she was ready for whatever came next. She was ready to hear what Gabe had to say, and she could trust herself to make the right decision after listening to the sordid tale. Okay, so she was still feeling a little judgy right now, but she was being as open-minded as she could be under the circumstances and given her own experience.

And that was exactly what it was—*her* experience, but she

wasn't about to let that get in the way of what she was feeling for Gabe. Well, she was going to try damn hard not to anyway.

Lori took two heavy tumblers from the shelf and set them down before selecting the large bottle of Absolut from the fridge. Not so mini after all, thankfully. She cut a couple of slices of lemon and tossed them in the glasses then wandered over to the window, drawn by its view of Lake Michigan. The cloudy sky created a gorgeous palette of fire as the sun set, and Lori imagined Gabe's arms around her waist as the light faded, and darkness settled around the city. Would they get to share romantic moments like that? Or had that ship sailed, and they would no longer even be friends?

She heard the click of the door, and Gabe returned with an overflowing ice bucket.

"Vodka?" Gabe asked, still standing at the edge of the hallway as if waiting to be fully invited in.

"Absolut," Lori said. "Did you know that they've supported our cause since the eighties? They've donated tens of millions of dollars to LGBT centers. The one in LA got $2 million after the lesbian director Rix Reardon approached them for support."

"I didn't know any of that," Gabe said.

Of course she wouldn't know any of that. Lori only knew it because she'd read about it six years ago, and it had lodged in her brain, as everything was wont to do. Gabe looked lost and unsure of herself in a way that Lori had never seen before. She had to admit that she liked it a little bit; it made her feel powerful and in control, again in a way she'd never felt before. Gabe was over six feet tall and made of brick wall muscle, but right now, she was waiting on Lori's cue. "I've put lemon in the glasses. Maybe you could add ice and pour."

Lori took a seat in the huge armchair by the window. There was a couch, but she couldn't risk being too close to Gabe. Not yet. Not until she'd heard and processed her story. She kicked off her shoes and tucked her feet under her. She watched Gabe cross the room, watched her open the bottle with ease and pour very generous measures for them both, watched the way her muscles shifted and flowed beneath the thin material of her shirt.

Gabe placed the glasses on coasters on the coffee table. She gestured to the pale cream sofa and then to herself. "I should've brought your blanket up from the car."

"You could use a towel." *Or you could get naked and give me all the power.* Lori bit her lip and tried to control her rampant sex drive. How had Gabe awakened something so base and almost uncontrollable within her where previous partners had failed? She'd never thought of them as failing though; she'd always just thought herself as not very good at it.

Gabe nodded and strode away to the bathroom. She returned with a graphite-colored bath sheet and draped it over the center of the couch, and then she sat on it carefully.

Lori picked up her glass and swirled the transparent liquid around, enjoying the hiss and crack of the ice cubes and the way they'd already begun to melt, a little like Gabe seemed to be doing as she waited in silence. "You wanted to tell me everything," Lori said, focusing on the primary reason for being here.

"Thank you for giving me the opportunity to do that. I know you're probably going to find it hard to hear."

"Is that why you didn't tell me sooner? Because you thought I was too fragile to hear whatever you have to say?" She partially regretted her combative approach, but if she'd learned anything over the past year of therapy, it was that she should give her emotions the oxygen they needed. Squishing them down into the bottom of her heart and mind was as unhealthy as feeding a dog chocolate.

"No, that wasn't it." Gabe reached for her own glass and took a long drink. "*I* was too fragile to tell you, because I didn't want to risk losing your friendship."

Lori hadn't expected that. Nor had she anticipated complete honesty and a total lack of ego. And the softness in Gabe's gaze made Lori glad she was sitting down, or her knees would surely have given way beneath her. A butch carved from marble and filled with marshmallow...was that even legal?

"It was obvious from our first couple of meetings that you were a special person, Lori, and when you declined my advances, I just figured that I'd wait until you were ready." Gabe glanced away, and she blushed. "I knew you were worth waiting for. But then you told me about your ex-wife cheating on you, and I was bummed. Not just for what you'd been through, but for what that signaled."

"Which was?"

"That you'd never go out with someone like me, someone who'd been part of a cheating thing, just like your ex." Gabe rolled her glass between her hands. "But I also thought that I couldn't tell you about my past in case that meant you didn't even want to be my friend." She shook her head. "I couldn't face that. Shay is my best friend, and I'm close to the other guys, but not in the same way. I've only ever shared my past with Shay...and then you. Because it felt so easy, so natural to talk to you."

Lori gripped her glass tight. "But they all knew about you and the sergeant major's wife, didn't they?"

"Everyone on our base knew about that eventually, and that wasn't because I was bragging about it. It's not something I was ever proud of doing."

"So why did you do it? Surely there were enough single women on base that you didn't have to pursue a married woman. Don't those vows mean anything to you?"

Gabe ran her hand through her hair and leaned forward. "I didn't pursue her at all. I resisted her advances for—"

"For how long, Gabe? How long was it before you hit *fuck it* and fucked her?" Lori pushed back in her chair, surprised by her colorful outburst. From Gabe's expression, it was clear she shared her reaction. "Well, how long?" she asked when Gabe didn't answer.

"About six weeks." She paused, perhaps expecting another

indignant interruption. "Every night, Cynthia sneaked into my tent, sometimes when I was already asleep, and tried to...y'know."

"Seduce you?" Lori laughed at the images Gabe's story was manifesting in her head. "A big tough soldier like yourself was intimidated into sex with the older woman? I assume she was older, just to be that little bit extra cliché."

Gabe shook her head. "I wasn't intimidated, no. She was a beautiful woman, and yes, she was a decade or so older than—"

"How old were you?" Lori asked, remembering that details like that mattered. She should probably have made a checklist, but it wasn't like she would actually forget any questions.

"It was seven years ago," Gabe said. "I'd just turned thirty."

"Have you done it to anyone else since?"

"No."

"Had you done it to anyone else before?"

"No."

She thought about asking Gabe how many women she'd been with but decided she probably didn't want to know, not really, and that didn't have anything to do with the cheating aspect anyway. Lori took another sip of the neat vodka and wished that she'd asked Gabe to add some of the Coke Zero which was sitting on the top shelf. Everything that Gabe had said so far indicated that she wasn't a serial cheat or homewrecker. She recalled her mom's words, *"I'm giving you context, sweetheart. These things don't happen in a vacuum. Circumstances are very important."*

"Why did you eventually do it after six weeks?"

"The sergeant major was a piece of work. Sexist. Homophobic. Racist. He was a good ol' boy from Birmingham, Alabama. He'd been messing with all of us for one reason or another—"

"All of you?"

"Shay, Solo, Woody, and RB. But especially Shay. Being a Black, gay woman, she represented everything he hated." Gabe put her drink on the table. When she sat back, her fists were balled so tight her knuckles went white, and her jaw clenched and unclenched repeatedly.

"You couldn't report him?"

Gabe gave a small laugh. "Not really. Not if we didn't want to be shipped off to shit duty in BFE. But we supported each other, and we were handling it."

"But?" Lori edged forward on her seat, gripped by Gabe's tale and torn between wanting to hear it and dreading what Gabe was about to say.

"He went too far with Shay." Gabe glanced over at Lori. "I'd rather not share the details. It's not my story to tell. Suffice to say, it was bad."

Lori held up her hand. "Of course not." She'd seen far too much cruelty over the years, and all of it stayed with her in vivid technicolor; selfishly, she didn't want Shay's experience forever in her mind.

"I didn't hold any power to do anything about it outright. None of us did. So I did the only thing that I could to hurt him. That night, and every night for three months, when Cynthia came into my tent, I gave her exactly what she asked for."

"Why did she choose you?"

Gabe shrugged. "I never asked her."

"And he found out somehow?"

Gabe shook her head. "He was too self-absorbed to have suspected, and he'd probably never have found out. Which was no good to Cynthia, who was doing it for the same reason I was in the end. To hurt him. So she told him. Everything. How often. How long. How many. How good. All of it."

Lori gasped. If he'd been an asshole to Gabe before, she shuddered to imagine how he treated her afterward.

"His CO got wind of his subsequent actions, which had put me in a medic tent, and he was transferred off the base." Gabe put her hand to her ribs and smiled. "So I'm not proud of what I did, but it was worth it to get rid of him and to get a little of our own back." She gazed across at Lori. "At least, it was until now."

Lori's heart caught in her throat. If ever there was a justifiable reason for having sex with a married woman, twisted and unhealthy though it might be, that was definitely it. "I wish you'd trusted me with the truth earlier."

Gabe pressed her lips together and looked at the floor. "It's not a nice story to tell, and it's a part of my past I'd rather forget. Even with the situation, it still seemed like it would be too much to expect you to ignore."

So her mom was right. Circumstances *were* important. Lori emptied the remnants of the vodka and took a deep breath. "I can't say that was the story I was expecting."

Gabe nodded and stood up. "I understand. Thanks for letting me tell you what happened. I know that's hard when you remember everything *forever*." She gestured to her half-empty glass on the table. "And thanks for the drink. I'll let myself out," she said and headed for the door.

Lori pushed herself up from the chair. "No," she half-shouted, and Gabe turned. "You don't have to go."

Gabe smiled, but it looked rueful more than happy. "Maybe I don't. But do you actually want me to stay?"

Lori laughed lightly, remembering one of their exchanges about Gabe's dislike of that word. "I *actually* do want you to stay." She motioned at the room. "It'd be a shame to waste the use of this hotel room."

Gabe narrowed her eyes as she turned fully to face Lori. "I don't have anywhere to be," she said quietly. "Do you want to watch a movie?"

Lori scoffed. "Is that what you think I want?"

Gabe stuffed her hands in her pockets. "I'm not presuming to know what you might want. I hope that we can still be friends now that you know the truth about my past. Friends watch movies together, right?"

"Don't you remember what I said on Saturday night?" Lori asked as she strode toward Gabe, swaying her hips for maximum effect and feeling the kind of sexy she thought was reserved for movie stars and models.

Gabe's lips parted slightly, and she swallowed so hard Lori heard it as she drew closer.

"Which part?" Gabe asked.

"The part about us being friends and how we both knew it wasn't going to last." Lori raked her nail along Gabe's jawline then rubbed her thumb over Gabe's bottom lip. The short breath Gabe exhaled may as well have been directed between Lori's legs because it damn well had the same effect. Gabe's chest rose and fell with quick, short breaths, and she looked almost drowsy, like she was too weak to stand upright. And her apparent powerlessness ramped up Lori's desperation to finally get her hands on Gabe's body...and her soul.

"Lori..." Gabe murmured. "What do you want?"

Lori smiled, a wicked delight coursing through her veins in anticipation of what was to come. "You, Gabe. I want you; I want us. Every way I can think of. What do *you* want?"

"Everything you just said," Gabe whispered. "It's what I've wanted since we first met, and it's only gotten stronger with every minute I've known you."

Lori tilted her head toward the bedroom door. "This is going to take a while; we should get comfortable."

Gabe tugged at her T-shirt. "Then I should get clean."

Lori wrapped her hand around the back of Gabe's neck and pulled her into a kiss. Though she would've thought it impossible, the promise of desire exceeded their previous kiss. Gabe's lips pressed against hers, and her passion sparked into a raging fire. Her core thrummed a heavy rhythm of craving through her whole body, consuming all logical thought and driving her need to desperation level.

Reluctantly, she pulled back. "Let's get you in the shower."

Gabe wiggled her eyebrows. "I'm pretty filthy from work. Are you going to scrub me down?"

Lori shook her head. "No." She untucked Gabe's shirt and pushed it up her body, revealing inch after inch of rugged muscle, tan skin, and inked art. The sight and feel of it all made her ache for release, but she was determined to take it slow. There could only ever be *one* first time, and she wanted it to last just like her memory of it would.

Gabe shucked off her shirt when Lori couldn't reach all the way up over Gabe's arms, and she tossed it aside.

"Lose that," Lori said, and Gabe quickly removed her sports bra to expose small breasts. Lori stepped back to get a better look. "You are so incredibly sexy." It was stating the obvious, for sure, and for a while, she simply stared at the Greek god-like form standing before her. She'd never seen such symmetry in a fitness magazine, let alone in real life, and she was mere inches away, her eyes pleading with Lori to touch her.

Lori nibbled on her bottom lip and sighed. Gabe was the perfect balance of virgin skin and colorful ink, none of which detracted from the hard, curved lines of her biceps, shoulders, and chest. She had the ridiculous urge to stay just as she was, so that she could appreciate Gabe as if she were a sculpture, wondering how the artist had gotten every detail so flawless.

Lori pointed to the bathroom. "Off you go."

Gabe stuck out her bottom lip but didn't complain. When she turned and Lori followed, Lori saw that God's work had been marred. Gabe had told her about the bombing at her military base, but she hadn't shown Lori the indelible map of the pain it had left behind on her skin.

"My scars?" Gabe asked as she turned around.

Lori thought she'd kept her reaction internal, but apparently she hadn't managed that. "Is it still painful?"

"Sometimes, if I catch it wrong. When it's desensitized enough, I'll have it tattooed to complete my backstory... The story on my back," she said when Lori frowned. "It's a work in progress. Does it bother you?"

Lori took Gabe's hand. "No, of course not. I just wanted to make sure I wouldn't hurt you when I touch you—which I can't wait to do, so please go shower."

Gabe grinned then walked away. "Are you sure you're not joining me?"

Lori's gaze drifted from Gabe's strong back to her tight ass. "I'm sure. I am going to watch though." She sat on the small armchair beside the bathtub and leaned back to enjoy the show. When she was choosing a hotel for Saturday night, she'd wanted one with a wet room, a shower with no glass walls so she could do exactly this.

"I get it," Gabe said.

Then she turned to face Lori and unbuckled her belt. Slowly. She pulled it from the loops of her combat pants with the urgency of a woman who held forever in her hands, then she draped it around Lori's shoulders.

Lori nodded. "You *do* get it."

Gabe opened the button of her pants, unzipped them, and then pulled them open to reveal snug white shorts. She turned around and bent over with her ass in the air facing toward Lori to unlace her boots. Which took an inordinate amount of time, but Lori reminded herself this was what *she* wanted. Even though she hadn't really known it, or more accurately, hadn't wanted to acknowledge it, she'd been waiting for this moment for two long months. Every meeting, every text exchange, every phone call had been a log on their fire, waiting to be ignited. The inevitability of their coming together was almost Biblical, as irresistible a force as the Earth being pulled toward the sun, and Lori was going to savor every single second of the crescendo.

Gabe kicked off her boots, and they were eventually joined by her socks and cargo pants, leaving her standing in just her watch and shorts and looking like she was ready for a Calvin Klein underwear shoot. She hooked her thumb in the waistband and edged them over her hips, low enough for Lori to see just the top of the triangle of hair that pointed down toward the good stuff. She maintained eye contact with Lori as she pushed them down further then shimmied them to the floor and stepped out of them.

Lori smiled widely. In all her naked glory, Gabe was even more magnificent than she could have imagined—and she'd imagined *a lot*.

Gabe backed away and got under the rainforest shower head before turning it on. The blast of cold water hardened her small nipples instantly, and Lori touched her own breast without thinking.

"Hey, that's not fair," Gabe said as she pumped some shower gel and began to lather up.

Slowly.

"You're touching yourself," Lori said. "How is it unfair that I'm doing the same?"

"Because I want it to be the other way around."

Lori unbuttoned her shirt and slipped her hand inside to cup her breast. "And it will be soon enough. Patience is a virtue, Gabe," she said, for herself as much as for Gabe.

Gabe let out a long, breathy sigh. "But I've *never* been virtuous, and I think it's too late for me to start now."

"It's never too late to take the right path." Just like it hadn't been too late for her to venture down this road and rescue them from the hungry mouth of the failed relationships beast. Lori fell silent as the gel became a white foam all over Gabe's skin, and she watched, fascinated, as Gabe paid particular attention between her legs. She turned away from Lori and faced the wall. The water ran over her head and down her back, chasing away the soapy suds to expose her skin again. Gabe turned the shower off, grabbed a towel from the rail, and began to pat herself dry.

Mouth dry, Lori wished she'd brought a drink in with her. Who knew all this voyeurism could be such thirsty work?

Gabe hung the towel back on the rail and approached Lori,

stopping just short of touching distance. She held out her hand. "Can I take you to bed?"

Lori grasped Gabe's hand and stood up. "Only if you promise not to let me sleep."

Gabe lifted Lori up, and she wrapped her legs around Gabe's waist. "That's a promise I'd love to keep."

Lori softened in her arms, more than a little swept away by the effortless show of strength as Gabe walked them into the bedroom. "You can put me down here," Lori said, and Gabe lowered her to her feet slowly. She pushed against Gabe's chest, hoping to push her backward onto the bed, but the muscle in Gabe's chest didn't budge, and she remained standing as solidly as a brick wall.

Gabe winked and jumped back onto the bed as if pushed by an inhumanely strong person. She put her hands behind her head and lay there as boldly as if she were fully clothed. Oh, to have that kind of confidence, Lori thought. But with a body like that, how could she not?

"Is it my turn for a show?" Gabe asked.

"No. You *are* the show." Lori knelt on the floor between Gabe's feet. "Scooch down."

Gabe shuffled closer. Lori hooked her arms under Gabe's powerful legs and placed her hands on the solid slabs of muscle covering Gabe's hips. She kissed the soft skin on the inside of Gabe's right thigh, starting at her knee and working her way closer to the strong scent of Gabe's obvious arousal. Lori skipped over to Gabe's left thigh as she blew a light breath over Gabe's clit, and Gabe pushed her hips up in an attempt to meet Lori's mouth.

Lori pressed Gabe back to the bed and shook her head. "What did I say about patience?" she whispered before returning her lips to Gabe's legs.

"What did I say about not being virtuous?" Gabe gave a wicked smile then reached for a pillow and pulled it under her head.

Lori shifted and rocked back on her butt. "Getting comfortable?"

"Not so much. You're the one in charge of that."

Lori licked her top lip slowly. "And what could I do to make you more comfortable?"

Gabe pushed up onto her elbows and wrapped her hand in Lori's hair, but she didn't apply any pressure. "Putting your mouth on me would be a great start."

Lori pulled Gabe's hand from her head and nibbled her calf. "My mouth *is* on you."

Gabe chuckled, dropped back on the bed, and rested her hand between her legs. "You know what I mean." She began to draw slow and lazy circles over her clit. "I want your mouth here."

Lori let out a slow breath and simply watched. "And is that the way I should move my tongue on you?" she whispered, her intention to take Gabe slowly fading along with the setting sun.

Gabe dipped her finger in the slickness between her lips and then returned to her clit. "I think you should figure that out for yourself."

Lori raked her nails along Gabe's thighs and edged closer. "It doesn't look like you need me..."

Gabe raised her finger and offered it to Lori's mouth. "Then looks have never been so deceptive. I need you more than a desert needs water."

"That's quite poetic for a grease monkey," she said and parted her lips to take Gabe's finger into her mouth. The taste of Gabe's essence made her clench her thighs together—so sweet and fresh—and she moaned softly. Lori sucked it deeper into her mouth and ran her tongue along its length. Gabe's eyes half-lidded in response, and she dropped her head back, muttering something Lori didn't catch.

She withdrew Gabe's finger and pushed herself farther onto the bed so she could take Gabe's hardened nipple into her mouth. She flicked her tongue over it firmly and then traced circles around it. Gabe growled under her touch and snaked her fingers into Lori's hair once more. Lori's light nibble increased the volume of Gabe's response, so she bit a little harder, and Gabe writhed beneath her.

"Aw, fuck..."

Lori eased up and switched to Gabe's other breast while she ran her hand over her other one. They were so small and tight, unlike any woman she'd been with before, and the muscle beneath them seemed to strain for her attention. She lifted her head and moved so that she was lying fully on top of Gabe's body, her heat searing through the thin material of Lori's linen shirt. Gabe was so rock-hard underneath her that it was like lying on a marble table draped with a silk cloth. The combination took Lori's breath away as the softness of her body molded over Gabe's, a feeling as natural as breathing.

She pressed her lips to Gabe's mouth and slipped her tongue inside, probing for a response. Gabe's tongue met hers as they kissed, ramping up the intensity of their passion and deepening their connection. With the taste of Gabe fresh in her memory, she slid down the length of Gabe's body until she was on her knees, her mouth inches from Gabe's pussy. She looked up and met Gabe's eyes, drowsy with desire, a look she was sure was mirrored in her own. "Remind me what you wanted."

Gabe shook her head. "Like you forgot?"

"Okay," Lori said. "*Ask* me to give you what you want."

Gabe's lip curled slightly, and she put both hands behind her head again. "You want to play those games with me?" she whispered hoarsely.

Lori looked deep into Gabe's eyes and nodded. "I want to play *every* game with you," she said, fully committed to exploring her sudden burgeoning sexuality like she was coming out all over again.

"*Please* would you wrap your mouth around me and make me

see stars?"

Lori drew in Gabe's scent. Unable to tease her any longer, she lowered her lips to Gabe's sex and traced her tongue along her length until she reached the tip. Lori drew Gabe's clit into her mouth and ran her tongue in slow circles to the same rhythm she'd watched Gabe touch herself.

Gabe let out a loud and throaty moan then clutched at the bedsheet. "Fuck me."

Lori lifted her head momentarily to say, "We'll get to that," before slipping back into position. She moved her arms under Gabe's thighs and gripped her hips as she quickened her pace slightly to sync with the rise and fall of Gabe's body beneath her. Gabe's breathing became shallow and fast, and she muttered incoherently as Lori continued to take her in.

Gabe put her hand on Lori's head, and this time, there was a light pressure. "Just there... Don't..."

Lori circled and sucked then she moved one hand so that she could slip two fingers deep into Gabe. She grunted hard and moaned lightly as Lori drove hard and fast, matching the pace of her tongue.

"Oh, God, Jesus, and fuck," Gabe shouted as she exploded into Lori's mouth.

Lori didn't lose contact, even when Gabe bucked beneath her and shuddered. She felt Gabe's orgasm run right through her, almost as if she was coming too. Gabe's arousal filled Lori's mouth, and she swallowed thirstily, as if this was something she'd been deprived of for decades. In a way, she had, but she was determined to make up for that now, and she kept driving her fingers inside as Gabe writhed and cried out. The heady sense of control to make Gabe, a woman so hard, soften like putty in her hands was almost overwhelming and so addictive.

She pulled Gabe further into her mouth, wanting and demanding more. And seconds later, Gabe released herself again, moaning and writhing, to Lori's unrelenting desire. Still unsated though, Lori tried for a third until Gabe pulled away from beneath her.

"I can't," Gabe said breathily. "You've already had it all."

Lori tilted her head and stuck out her bottom lip. "That can't be everything you've got."

"It's everything I can take for you, but it's nowhere near what I can give." Gabe sat up, put her hands under Lori's armpits, and lifted her effortlessly onto the bed beside her. She leaned onto her side and began to unbutton Lori's shirt. "I think it's time you got naked too, don't you?"

Lori pressed her hand over Gabe's, suddenly aware of the stark difference in their bodies, something she'd never been self-conscious about until she was lying beside the living, breathing female version of Adonis. "Mm, maybe not."

"Please," Gabe said quietly as if reading her hesitation. "You are the most beautiful woman I've ever seen. Please trust me."

"But...I don't look like you, under these clothes."

"I don't want you to look like me." Gabe kissed her lightly and shook her head. "Your body is stunning." She caressed Lori's cheek. "But if you don't want to, that's okay."

"Oh, I want to. I *really* want to. I just–" she gestured wildly, "y'know, haven't seen perfection in real life before." She pushed up and got off the bed, determined not to let this uncharacteristic stumble keep her from making the most of this connection. Everything that had happened in the past two months had been building up to this moment, and she wasn't about to self-sabotage with an unfamiliar lack of confidence. But then her confidence had never really extended to the bedroom. "I should tell you that I've never really been that into sex." The words were out before she had time to censor them. *Way to kill the mood.*

Gabe sat up and wrinkled her nose. "So...what just happened was?"

"Fantastic." Lori smiled. "I should have said that I've never been that into sex *before*. Before you." She allowed her gaze to drift over Gabe again and throbbed hard in response. "You've kind of made me feel like a horny teenager on spring break."

Gabe grinned. "I don't *think* you want me to apologize for that?"

"God, no," Lori said. "Definitely not." She unbuttoned the rest of her shirt and let it drop to the floor. "It's all just a bit new. Does that make sense?"

Gabe nodded. "So what would you like to do?"

"More of this, with you." She unhooked her bra, slowly gaining in confidence when she saw the hungry look in Gabe's eyes when she uncovered her breasts.

"I'm not sure I've got the self-control to keep asking if you're sure," Gabe said. "You drove me crazy at the pool hall and in that restaurant hallway. I'm desperate to touch you and fucking desperate to be inside you."

Lori threw her bra to the floor and quickly shed the rest of her clothes.

Gabe smiled widely. "You are fucking gorgeous."

Lori moved closer, and Gabe put her hands on Lori's hips and kissed her belly.

"I've wanted you like this so long," Gabe whispered and looked up into Lori's eyes.

She'd felt the same. She still did. And God, did she want to see how much she could take; would she be satiated before Gabe's stamina gave out?

Let's find out. She pushed Gabe back onto the bed and straddled her, and the heat of Gabe's stomach met the heat of the center.

Gabe wiggled her eyebrows. "Feels like someone's ready for this."

Lori rocked her hips back and forth, making Gabe's abs slick with her excitement. She balled her fist into Gabe's short hair. "What're you going do about that?" she asked and got up on all fours, her breast hovering over Gabe's mouth.

Gabe put her hand between Lori's legs, pressed against her opening, then slipped two fingers inside her. "I'm going to do this for as long as you can take it."

Gabe fucked her deep and slow, and Lori drove herself down onto Gabe's hand. Any lingering doubts about anything and everything soon faded into the background as she became hyper-focused on the sensations darting through her body. Every cell sparked to life, every nerve ending tingled in anticipation, and her blood coursed hot and wild through her veins like a stallion running free. With Gabe inside her, she came alive in a way she'd never felt before, never thought possible.

"Gabe..." She moaned, feeling every inch like a woman re-awakened from a sexual slumber. "That's so good," she whispered around each penetrating thrust. But it wasn't just her body; it was like Gabe was piercing the armor around her soul. She looked down at Gabe, who was staring at her intently as if there was nothing else in the world she'd rather be looking at, and her intensity made Lori's heart soar, made her feel like the center of Gabe's universe.

Gabe entangled her other hand in Lori's hair. "Come for me," she murmured.

Gabe's quiet instruction brushed away the last of her resistance to their connection. Whatever had gone before was the past, and all Lori wanted to do was concentrate on the future, their future, and more—so much more—of this.

She rocked against Gabe's fingers, and the wave continued to build inexorably toward its break. Every fiber of her being lost its density, and her body felt like it might float away on her next breath. Heat rushed over every inch of her skin, gathering and flooding to her very core. And through it all, Gabe's eyes were fixed on hers, solidifying their physical and spiritual connection, melding their bodies and souls to become inexplicably linked and forever unbreakable.

And she just let it go and let it be. No more questions. No

more second-guessing. And no more waiting. The rest of her life was here, ready for her to unleash her inhibitions and grab hold of it with both hands.

The wave rolled over her with immeasurable power, and she tumbled gratefully into its energy, washed out and simultaneously reinvigorated on the sands of a new life. She collapsed onto Gabe and moaned against her chest. "That was beautiful."

Gabe wrapped her arms around Lori's back and pulled her closer, her heart beating strong in Lori's ear.

But she said nothing, and they embraced in a soft and steady silence that enveloped them in a protective bubble.

When Lori finally raised her head, she looked up to see tears edging Gabe's eyes.

Gabe swallowed hard and ran her hand through Lori's hair. "I think..." She shook her head, as if the words were alien and might never have passed her lips before. "Lori... I love you."

Lori had heard those words pass the lips of other lovers and then, the lawyer's. But only now, as they emerged from Gabe's mouth, did she ever really feel and truly believe them. She kissed Gabe, crushed their lips together the same way as their lives were now entwined, then pulled away slowly. "I love *you*, Gabe." And as she said it too, she realized it was the first time she'd really ever truly meant it.

Chapter Twenty-Five

Everything that had gone before dissipated like morning dew on a hot summer's day. All memories of the other women Gabe had shared her bed with retreated into the deepest recesses of her mind. All of that now seemed irrelevant, like it had served its purpose and led her to this moment, so now she should let it go. Because this right here, with Lori in her arms, was everything she would need from this moment on. And Gabe would share all of herself, lay bare her vulnerabilities, her fears, the essence of what made her who she was.

The sun had almost fully risen, chasing away the last vestiges of darkness and signaling the first day of the rest of her life—she hoped. Lori's head rested on her chest, and she breathed slow and deep, still held fast in the arms of Morpheus. She laughed inwardly at Lori's comment last night about her being poetic for a grease monkey—Gabe could only blame it on this new and euphoric feeling of being in love. And better yet, of being loved back for exactly who she was for the first time in her life.

She fought the desire to pull Lori from her sleep, particularly since they'd only paused their exploration of each other a couple of hours ago. Gabe should be tired, exhausted probably, after a non-stop first day at the garage followed by hours and hours of the most incredibly intimate and soulful sex. It wasn't just sex though; they'd made love. The moment Lori had stopped Gabe from leaving was the moment she opened the door into what they could be together. If the last eight hours were any indication, they were going to be an epic love story. They'd laid the path to this possible reality over the past couple of months. Revelations, stories shared, and so many tender interactions were pieces of a puzzle waiting to be completed by this. By this connection, the final fragment of their future.

Gabe was drawn back to Lori when she became aware of Lori's fingers tracing her abs. "Morning, beautiful," she said and kissed the top of her head.

Lori shifted and placed her head on the pillow. "Morning, handsome." She wiped her eyes. "*Is* it morning?"

"The sun just came up." Gabe tucked Lori's hair behind her ear and smiled.

"But I feel like we only just got to sleep." Lori narrowed her eyes and prodded Gabe's chest. "What time did you finally let me rest?"

Gabe chuckled. "You're blaming me? I think we were equally reluctant to go to sleep, and it seemed like you were determined to suck the life out of me."

Lori wiggled her eyebrows. "That's your fault for tasting so good. Speaking of which," she said, inching down the bed. She parted Gabe's legs and settled between them again. "I think this is my new happy place."

Gabe didn't have time to respond before Lori locked her lips around Gabe's clit again, robbing her of the ability to form a complete sentence. She dropped her head back onto the pillow and closed her eyes. Images of last night, of Lori's naked body under her hands, played behind her eyelids like a private movie for an audience of one. Lori drew Gabe into her mouth and drove her to the brink of release within minutes. Gabe clutched the sheets as she fell over the precipice and tumbled into yet another wave of pleasure. Lori didn't let up, pulling every drop of arousal from Gabe's body until all her muscles relaxed, and she softened against the bed, fully spent.

Lori raised her head and smiled widely before climbing up Gabe's body to lay on top of her.

"You look pleased with yourself," Gabe whispered when

her breathing evened out, and she regained the ability to communicate. Lori kissed her hard, and Gabe tasted herself on Lori's lips.

"I am." She sighed deeply. "I've finally discovered what all the fuss is about with this sex thing."

Lori pushed herself up to straddle Gabe, and the heat and wetness of her core against Gabe's stomach caused her to sigh in much the same way as Lori just had. Now she understood it was a contentment deeper than the Pacific Ocean. She placed her hands on Lori's hips. "Have I told you how insanely gorgeous you are?"

"You did mention it a few times last night, but you could just have been saying it to have your way with me." Lori dragged her nails along Gabe's collarbone and down her chest. "I wouldn't be averse to hearing it again in the aftermath of our lovemaking."

Gabe grinned. "We were making love, were we?"

"I'm pretty sure that's what it was." Lori raked her nails a little harder over Gabe's skin. "It did seem to get more intense after we both said those three little words, wouldn't you agree?"

Gabe took Lori's hand, but Lori pushed her arms above her head and pinned her to the bed. She eased down a little so her breast hovered over Gabe's mouth. Gabe lifted her head to capture Lori's nipple, but Lori pulled back.

"Nope, you don't get anything else until you—"

"I agree," Gabe said.

Lori shook her head but leaned a little closer to Gabe's mouth. "You could just be saying that to get what you want."

"I *do* agree, *and* I'm saying it to get what I want."

Lori lowered herself enough so that Gabe could kiss her nipple then she eased back up to her sitting position.

"You're gorgeous," Gabe said, remembering Lori's small wobble in confidence last night. "Thank you for letting me see you."

Lori blushed and glanced away briefly.

Gabe took the hint and ran her fingers over the small, inked symbol above her right hip. "So this is the bad tattoo you told me about. It's good work; what's the problem?"

Lori blinked and took a deep breath. "It's not the art, it's what it means. I also told you that it was a bad decision if you remember?"

Gabe nodded but didn't want to pry into its meaning. "The lawyer?"

"The lawyer." Lori caught Gabe's fingers and held them in place over the tattoo. "Would you go with me to have it turned into something else?" She lifted Gabe's hand to her mouth and kissed her knuckles. "It's time."

"I'd be happy to. I had my Metatron work done in New York, but Solo's tattooist here is excellent." Gabe paused, not wanting to push the issue, but she was also ecstatic that Lori wanted to remove any trace of the lawyer's influence from her life and her body. "When would you like to do it?"

"As soon as possible. Do you think I could get it done before the auction?" She looked down at herself. "When this is done and that rust bucket is out of my life, I'll feel like I can finally close that chapter for good."

"I'll give her a call and ask her to let me know if she gets any cancellations. She'll likely be booked a couple of months ahead. The great tattooists always are."

An alarm began to sound beyond the bedroom door, and Lori rolled her eyes. "That's my wake-up alarm. I suppose we should get dressed so that I can take you back to the garage. Or home to change."

"The garage'll be fine. I've got spare clothes in my locker."

Lori arched her eyebrow. "Because you were prepared for unplanned nights out like this?"

"Because I was a soldier, and we always plan for all eventualities: oil spills, paint accidents. It's a dirty job."

"Mm." Lori winked and extricated herself then padded out of the bedroom to retrieve her phone.

Gabe instantly missed the feel of her sex against her skin. "Can we both call in sick? I bet your boss would let you take the day off."

Lori returned, holding the clothes Gabe had strip-teased off in the bathroom, and tossed them onto the bed. "I don't think so. But you should definitely come to my place as soon as you finish work tonight, and the next night, and the night after that."

"I see." Gabe crossed her arms and did her best to look indignant. "The fancy hotel treatment stops now that you've got me hooked, does it?"

"You haven't seen it yet, but I have a wonderful, brand-new Cal king-size bed with a very interesting headboard." Lori pulled on her underwear and linen trousers.

"Interesting how?" Gabe asked, stirring at the possibilities.

"You only get to find out if you swing by tonight...unless you're already tied up?"

Gabe bit her bottom lip at the unsubtle clue. "Oh, I'll be there," she said. "No time to shower?"

"I'm afraid not." She fastened her bra and picked up her shirt from the chair that she'd thrown it on. "I'm already running behind, and I wouldn't want to shower alone. I have a feeling that would make me very late, and Ellery's coming over to check on the clinic renovations this morning. And I've got lots of animals waiting for me as well. Including your boy."

"Boring." Gabe reluctantly dragged herself from the bed but still kept her eyes on Lori as she redressed, which she was somehow making almost as much of a turn-on as she did when she was *un*dressing.

"I thought you'd be excited for the second day of work at your new garage."

Gabe tugged on everything except her shorts, which she stuffed in the leg pocket of her pants—they were way too dirty to put back on. "And you would've been right yesterday, before all this happened. All I want to do is spend the day in bed, making love, talking, and ordering room service. Scratch that. I want to do all of those things for the rest of the week, minimum."

Lori came closer and stood on her tiptoes to kiss her. "I assure you that's exactly what I want to do too, but *thinking* about that all day is going to make tonight even sweeter."

Gabe wrapped her arms around Lori's waist and kissed her deep and hard. "It's going to make concentrating on fixing engines damn near impossible."

Lori pressed her fingers over Gabe's lips then wriggled away. "You'll figure it out." She grabbed Gabe's crotch and squeezed. "And then you'll be *so* ready for me tonight. Right?"

Gabe growled and made a grab for her, but Lori was already out of reach and managed to scoot away.

Lori motioned to the door. "Come on, stud. I need to get on the road."

Gabe glanced back at the bed and the satisfyingly crumpled sheets that told a story of their own. She took Lori's hand and kissed her gently. "Thank you for giving me the chance to explain everything. You should know that I was going crazy not being able to talk to you. I missed you."

Lori pressed her hand against Gabe's chest. "You've got my mom to thank for that." She laughed lightly. "And so do I. It hurt that you didn't tell me about it earlier, but I understand now."

Gabe covered Lori's hand with her own. "I promise I'll tell you everything from now on. No secrets," she said and claimed a last kiss before they left the hotel room. Gabe took one last look around before she followed Lori up the hallway to the door. She might not have the memory Lori had, but she would never forget the special things that happened here last night.

***

"You've been practically floating around on a cloud all morning," Solo said. "I take it Lori did more than just hear you out last night?"

Gabe nodded and grinned. "She did, yeah, and we've moved from friends to something entirely new to me."

"You had sex all night, and for the first time, you want a repeat performance." Solo took a bite from her bagel, and the cream cheese squeezed out onto her shirt. "Ah, shit."

Seeing the mess Solo had just made, Gabe leaned over the engine block table before she munched into hers. "Not exactly. We made love all night, and I'm pretty sure I'd like to see the same show for the rest of my life."

Solo widened her eyes. "You're in love!"

"Looks like it," Gabe said. "I'm starting to see why you're such a big fan of it."

Solo glanced away, busied herself with her lunch, and said nothing.

"You are still a big fan, aren't you?"

They'd gotten straight to work this morning, so Gabe still hadn't gotten to the bottom of Solo's behavior at Lori's birthday dinner.

"Sure I am," Solo said after shoving the last piece of bagel into her mouth. She scrunched up the empty food bag and began to rise from the couch.

Gabe caught hold of her wrist and tugged her back down to the sofa. "What's going on with you and Janie?"

"Everything'll be fine. You don't want to hear about my problems when you're just starting out with Lori."

"Hey, I'm always here for you, Solo. Nothing's going to change that."

Solo gave a short laugh. "We'll see. When I was getting with Janie, I neglected everything else in my life. Ask Shay."

Gabe tilted her head, remembering that she'd been the one to suggest that she and Lori played hooky today, even though the garage had only just opened. She could see how it might happen. "Well, I'm here now, and we only just sat down for lunch, so spill."

Solo looked around as if she was expecting a huge audience of people, but the rest of the team were downstairs working.

"It's just me and you." Gabe patted Solo's knee. "Tell me what's happening."

She rubbed her forehead and huffed out a long breath. "I feel so stupid. I've always known I was punching above my weight. I should've seen it coming."

Gabe frowned. "Seen what coming?"

"Janie's cheating on me."

"She's sleeping with someone else?"

Solo shrugged. "She says she hasn't, that they've just been flirting, but I don't know whether to believe her or not. She says they've just been *talking*, but when people say that now, it means they're having sex."

"Does it?"

"That's what my brother's twenty-year-old kid reckons."

"For them, maybe, but it still just means talking for people our age, Solo." Gabe put the rest of her bagel back in its wrapper, her appetite severely lessened by Solo's news. "How did you find out?" She had a host of questions, but that seemed like a good starting place.

"She told me just before we left for dinner. Hence me getting weird about the cheating thing from your past and mentioning it like an asshole." Solo sank into the couch and put her head in her hands. "It's somebody at work."

"Is it serious?"

Solo dropped her hands to the sofa and made eye contact with Gabe for the first time since they'd started this conversation. "I don't know. *She* doesn't know."

Gabe couldn't get her head around Janie's actions. Everything she'd seen at Solo's house had been picture-perfect. "She's put your whole life together at risk."

"She says that I don't *see* her anymore, not since we had the kids."

Gabe thought back to the night she and Lori babysat the triplets and how Solo didn't register how beautiful Janie looked until she was prompted. It was a fair accusation if that was a regular occurrence. "Why didn't she just talk to you and give you the chance to fix it?"

Solo shrugged and rubbed at the grease on the back of her hand. "If I'm honest, she probably did. I guess I haven't been listening either."

"I'm sorry, buddy." Gabe tried to put herself in Solo's shoes, but she just couldn't imagine neglecting a wife as beautiful as Janie. Solo had clearly thrived in her role as a parent—she loved those little terrors—but it had been at the expense of her role as a lover and partner. Maybe that wasn't unusual in the parenting world. "Is there any way back?"

Solo sighed. "I don't know yet. We both need some time." She looked at her watch and tapped the face. "Recess is over. We should get back to it."

Gabe picked up her bagel and stood. She grabbed Solo's shoulder with her other hand. "We're all here for you. Whatever you need."

"Thanks. And Gabe, I'm happy for you. I'm sorry I nearly messed that up," Solo said and headed to the garage floor. "You just always have your shit so together, and I guess I was feeling jealous and...inept, I guess. It was shitty."

"It's all good, Solo." Gabe still didn't want food, but she needed the energy for the rest of the day, so she ate her lunch in three bites as she followed Solo down to the garage floor. Relationship troubles were difficult enough when they were just between two people but adding kids to the mix ramped up the complication levels to DEFCON 1. And in this case, there were business entanglements too. She couldn't stop the selfish consideration of how Solo's marriage issues might affect the garage. Their dream was finally happening; it couldn't get torpedoed now.

Gabe stopped at the mezzanine and looked across the

garage floor to the Brewster protected by a giant tarp. Woody said they'd gotten interest from collectors all over the world, and Saturday's auction event had sold out within three days of the announcement that the car had originally belonged to Marie Zimmerman. It was a restoration project they were all proud of, and Gabe hoped it wouldn't be their last.

Chapter Twenty-Six

LORI TOOK A LONG drink of the lemonade she'd had clutched in her hands when she started the story. The ice was long gone, and the liquid was room temperature. She'd had a lot to tell Rosie, and it had all come out in a stream of consciousness she could barely make sense of herself. No wonder Rosie looked shell-shocked.

"That's a hell of a story," Rosie said.

Lori smiled. "It was a hell of a night."

"So it looks like you've always had a vamp deep inside just waiting to come out." Rosie shook her head. "I never would've guessed it."

"Nor me. But now that she's out, I don't think I can shove her away again."

Rosie frowned. "Do you want to?"

"No, definitely not." She shivered at the thought of Gabe's hands on her body. "She made me feel things last night that I'd never imagined feeling." She sighed deeply. "It was a maelstrom of *every* sensation possible, every sense coming alive, and then...a perfect peace like I feel at the end of a meditation."

"I just call that an orgasm."

Lori laughed. "Whatever you want to call it, it was like waking up after a deep slumber and discovering life's beau—"

"Oh my God." Rosie rolled her eyes. "Are you in love after one night of halfway decent sex?"

"I was in love way before that. Last night just sealed the deal."

"I was kidding." Rosie sat up suddenly. "Are you seriously in love?"

"I am," Lori said, a little taken aback by Rosie's reaction. "I thought you'd be happy for me."

Rosie took Lori's hand. "I *am*, but I think it's okay for me to worry about you at the same time. I said you should get back on the horse, not buy the ranch. You're still healing from the last person who cheated on you."

Lori withdrew her hand from Rosie's and stiffened. "Gabe didn't cheat on me. It was years ago, in another world almost, and you could even make a case that it was justified."

"Wow, she's got you drinking the Kool-Aid, hasn't she? You'd never have considered *any* cheating justifiable before."

Lori untucked her legs from beneath her butt and sat up straight. "You don't believe her story? Have you asked Shay what happened?"

"Shay shut me down when I raised the issue, but we don't really do much talking when we get together."

Lori relaxed a little, realizing that Rosie's reaction was probably linked to her own situation with Shay. "I'm not a fool, Rosie," she said gently. "I believe she's telling the truth, and I have to go with my instinct. I ignored it for too long with the lawyer, and that brought me nothing but pain. I won't ignore it again and risk a chance at happiness. Gabe...fits." She held out her hand, and Rosie took it. "But I need my best friend beside me too."

Rosie threw her arms around Lori and pulled her into a hug. "I'm not going anywhere. It's just...the lawyer hurt you *so* bad. If there's anything I can do to keep you from going through that again, I will. Even if it means trying to knock down a woman built like a tank."

Lori laughed and withdrew from the embrace. "I don't think you need to worry about Gabe. Her outer shell might be made of titanium, but she's soft and fluffy inside."

Rosie's phone vibrated on the table. She groaned as she picked it up. "I have to go. Fussy clients to handle."

Lori glanced at her watch with a little relief. Gabe had texted to say she'd be there before eight, and it was already past seven.

She wasn't concerned about Rosie and Gabe crossing paths; she just knew that she needed Gabe inside her the moment she got in the house.

She walked Rosie out and saw Gabe's truck coming up the driveway. "Before you go, how's it going with you and Shay?"

Rosie pulled the car keys from her purse. "We're having hours and hours of incredible sex, just like you two."

"Okay. And?"

"And nothing," Rosie said. "It's no-strings fun with a beautiful, young Angela Bassett lookalike. I'm in heaven." She winked and headed to her car, which Gabe had pulled up alongside.

Rosie sounded happy enough, but Lori wasn't fully convinced. "Lunch this week?" she called after her.

Rosie turned. "I'm slammed this week, and you've got final prep on the auction. Let's do dinner next week, okay?"

"Okay. I'll text you." Lori watched Gabe get out of her truck and have a short chat with Rosie. She waved as Rosie pulled away in her sleek sports car.

Gabe jogged toward her and scooped her up to kiss her. "God, I've missed you."

"I've missed you." She inhaled Gabe's fresh scent. "You smell great."

"I showered at the garage." Gabe lowered Lori to the ground and slipped her hands around her waist.

"And you're early."

"Shay kicked me out on account of my 'stench of desperation,'" Gabe said, using air quotes, and grinned. "Is early okay? I should've called. Rosie didn't leave because of me, did she?"

Lori shook her head. "She had clients to deal with. What did she say to you, by the way?"

Gabe chuckled. "She told me that if I don't treat you like the queen you are, I'll have to deal with her wrath."

"And you kept a straight face?"

"Yes, I did. I take all threats to my life very seriously."

Lori raised her eyebrows. "Even when they come from a five-foot-nothing woman who weighs less than you bench press?"

Gabe tilted her head. "*Especially* then. A scorned woman's best friend is probably more lethal than the scorned woman herself."

Lori grasped a handful of Gabe's T-shirt. "Enough about Rosie. I need a reminder of how good you feel inside me."

Gabe swept Lori into her arms and carried her toward the house. "Your wish is my command."

Lori held tight and felt the scarred map of bumps and grooves through Gabe's shirt. She tingled inside with the thought of tracing her tongue over Gabe's skin and getting to know every beautiful inch of her.

She smiled and kissed Gabe's neck, grateful that she'd found the strength to open her heart once again.

***

The tattoo artist, Zed, placed her iPad on the countertop and swiveled it around for them to look at.

Gabe whistled. "That's a beautiful design."

Lori still hadn't told her what the original symbol meant, and Gabe didn't push for it. When she'd first seen it, she'd wondered if it was the ex-wife's initial. Maybe the mysterious woman was a Kate or a Kristen. But Gabe figured it didn't matter since Lori was covering it up anyway.

"I love the way you've incorporated the heather flowers around the butterfly," Lori said. "And the colors you've chosen are gorgeous."

Zed smiled. "Thanks. And thanks for trusting me with that. Most people who came into my last studio either had a very distinct and narrow vision or they chose off-book images I'd already designed."

"Where was your last studio?" Lori asked.

"Vegas. But I got bored of tattooing Cirque performers, so I moved here."

"Really?" Gabe couldn't imagine growing tired of working on bodies like theirs.

Zed laughed. "Nah, I'm kidding. I came back for family reasons."

"I'm glad you did, but I hope everything's okay with your family."

Zed shrugged. "What are you gonna do? Family is family, right?"

Shay huffed from her seat behind them "Truth."

Gabe looked at Shay then at Lori's side profile and smiled. She'd found her family, and she'd do whatever was required to keep it safe, including relocating two thousand miles away.

"You're happy with the size too?" Zed tapped away on her iPad then turned it back to Lori. "Use your fingers to change it, but you can't go much smaller than it is already, or I won't be able to keep that level of detail in the wings."

Lori pushed the tablet back toward Zed. "I think it's a perfect size."

"I'll print it out, and we can put the stencil on your hip for you to get a feel for it in place, okay?"

"Okay." Lori turned to face Gabe after Zed went into the back of the shop. "Do you like it?"

Gabe caressed her cheek. "I love it, but that shouldn't matter. I get the feeling your original tattoo was for someone else; you should get this one because you love it and you want it."

Lori leaned closer to Gabe's ear. "But you're going to be up close and personal with it *a lot*," she whispered.

Gabe moaned quietly. "And I'm going to love every time I get to kiss it," she said, "but it's your decision."

Lori pressed her hand on Gabe's chest. "I know that but thank you for saying it anyway."

"It's bad manners to whisper in company." Shay stood and

bumped Gabe against the desk.

"You're not company; you're family."

Shay rolled her eyes. "When I said that you should get more in touch with your emotions, I didn't mean you should spray them all over the place like a dog marking its territory. You can keep some of the sentimentality to yourself."

Gabe shrugged. "Sorry, buddy. The floodgates are open, and the hinges are busted."

Zed popped her head around the shelving unit that separated the reception area from the tattooing area. "Do you want to come back?"

The three of them followed Zed, and Lori laid back on a tattoo bed covered in plastic wrap while Gabe and Shay pulled up chairs on the opposite side of Zed so they didn't get in the way.

"Could you push your sweats down to about mid-thigh for me?" Zed cleaned and shaved the old tattoo and the surrounding area, then she placed the printed stencil on Lori's hip. "Do you want to go check in the mirror and make sure you're happy with it?"

Lori stood in front of the mirror holding on to her sweats. When Shay tilted her head to the side to clearly get a better look at Lori's ass, Gabe punched her arm. "Cut that shit out. You've got the best friend, remember?" she whispered.

Shay turned to look at Gabe. "I haven't got anyone. I'm a free agent."

"Lori isn't, so keep your eyeballs to yourself."

Shay grinned. "I'm just appreciating what you've got, Gabe, but if it offends you, I'll stop. It's not like she has eyes for anyone but you anyway."

"I'd rather you didn't act like a horny teen, that's all."

Shay held up her hands. "You're right. I'm sorry."

Lori turned to them both, thankfully oblivious to the conversation. "I love it." She got back on the bed and gripped the edges. "Let's do this."

Two pain- and tear-filled hours later, the three of them went back into the reception area.

"We're going for dinner. Do you want to join us?" Gabe asked while Lori was at the desk paying and collecting a bagful of aftercare products.

"No, thanks," Shay said. "You two need some alone time; you're practically combustible together. And I'm staying here a while."

Gabe glanced toward Zed. "Isn't she a bit on the masculine side for you?"

Shay shook her head. "Why would you go there? I told you I had a consultation after Lori's appointment." She touched the shoulder that had taken the brunt of the lightning strike. "I've wanted to get this turned into something for a while. You knew that."

"Oh, yeah. Sorry, I forgot." She tapped her head. "Seems like there's not much room in here for anything but Lori right now. I'll see you at the garage tomorrow."

"Staying out all night again?" Shay chuckled. "We might get someone else to move into your room."

Gabe grinned. "Don't be such a lesbian. I'm not U-Hauling yet."

"You should know we've got bets on when that'll happen. And it *will* happen."

Lori slipped her hand in the back pocket of Gabe's jeans. "I'm all set. And I'm starving. Where are we eating?"

"What are you in the mood for?" Gabe asked.

Lori wiggled her eyebrows, and Shay groaned.

"See what I mean? I'm no one's third wheel." Shay opened the studio door and ushered them out. "Have fun, you kids."

Outside on the sidewalk, Gabe blinked against the evening sun that was low enough to almost blind them. She slipped on her shades and pulled Lori into her arms. "So, what do you want to eat?"

"You."

Gabe laughed. "I like the sound of that, but I can be dessert. What about real food?"

"I want you on your back as soon as possible, so let's get takeout from Tix Pi and go home."

"Home?" Had it only taken four days for Lori's place to become home? Gabe wondered which of her buddies would have guessed closest.

"Did you want to go to your place? We could get enough for everyone, but I'm definitely not sharing dessert," she said and winked.

Gabe shook her head. "That's not what I meant, and no, let's go back to the Sanctuary. We can take Max for a walk before...y'know..."

"Ah, I get it. Home... Did I freak you out?"

"Nope, not at all. It's just something Shay said about U-Hauls."

Lori wrapped her hand around Gabe's neck and kissed her so intensely, it felt like the soft promise of their future.

"I'm in no rush. We've got forever, don't we?"

"We do." Gabe draped her arm over Lori's shoulder, and they headed toward her truck. She'd never really thought of a forever before, never tried to grasp the concept, especially one *with* someone. But Lori had changed that.

Lori had changed *everything*.

And now Gabe couldn't wait to get started on building that forever with the woman she loved more than she'd ever thought possible.

Chapter Twenty-Seven

LORI SHOULD'VE BEEN CONCENTRATING on the ever-increasing price for the rust bucket as the eccentric and fabulously flamboyant auctioneer whipped the crowd into a bidding frenzy.

Instead, her attention was fully focused on Gabe looking every inch the dapper female James Bond-type in a suit that clung to her muscles. As much as she looked insanely hot in that outfit, Lori was mentally removing each garment and feasting on the package held within it. She was already imagining Gabe on her back in just the open shirt and bow tie draped around her neck. The view from where she liked to be, on her knees, was the most exquisite thing of beauty she'd ever seen. And better yet, she could be confident that the reality would far exceed anything her mind could conjure.

She caught their reflection in the wall of mirrors and smiled. They made quite the couple.

Lori gently peeled her dress away from her recently tattooed hip, which was still tender, and gave it some air. With the old and ill-advised tattoo finally obliterated, being naked in front of Gabe had gotten easier, and her brief stumble into body issues was all but forgotten, helped enormously by the lustful look in Gabe's eyes every time she shed her clothes.

Rosie tapped her shoulder lightly. "I can practically hear your thoughts, vampy."

"You should talk," Lori said. "You can't put a piece of paper between you and Shay."

Rosie smiled and licked her lips. "You should be happy about that. I've finally forgotten all about your journalist friend. See, I can't even remember her name."

"I'm sure *her* soldier lover will be ecstatic to discover her competition has given up." She leaned closer to Rosie. "Everything's going okay with you two?"

"No sign of lesbian bed death here, no." Rosie raised her champagne glass and glanced at Shay, who was laughing with RB. "Here's to new beginnings."

Lori clinked her glass to Rosie's then took a sip.

"I have six hundred thousand online," the auctioneer yelled.

Lori almost choked on her alcohol.

"Careful, sweetheart," her mom said as she rubbed her back from behind.

"Are you okay?" Gabe asked.

Lori looked up into Gabe's concerned eyes. She'd always be okay as long as Gabe continued to look at her that way. "I'm fine. I'd zoned out and didn't realize where we were with the numbers. That was a shock."

Gabe smiled. "I told you Woody had been drumming up interest."

"I didn't dare to hope that interest would turn into a figure like that."

Lori's mom put her hand on her shoulder and squeezed gently. "That's a lot of horse and hound food," she said.

"Six-fifty," someone in the room shouted.

Lori grasped Gabe's forearm. "Is this real? Were you expecting this?"

Gabe wrapped her arm around Lori's waist and pulled her in tight. "I was hoping."

Lori looked at the stage. The auctioneer squinted at his assistant, who was monitoring the online bids, then he consulted the computer screen himself. He appeared to have to steady himself before returning to the mic.

He caught her gaze and smiled widely. "I have an online bid for...one and a half million dollars!"

Lori leaned hard into Gabe, and the entire room gasped. The team from the garage looked just as stunned as Lori felt.

"Are there any bids in the room?" he asked, sounding like he didn't expect a response. The room fell completely silent. "Going once for $1.5 million..."

Lori tugged on the lapel of Gabe's jacket. "Did I hear that right?"

"If you heard 1.5 mill, then yeah, you did." Gabe kissed the top of Lori's head.

"Going twice..."

Lori scanned the room. The audience seemed to have been stunned into silence, and she couldn't see a single bidder paddle even halfway to being raised.

"SOLD for $1.5 million to Elodie Fontaine!"

The room erupted into cheers, and there were hugs all around from Gabe's team. Solo stood shaking her head, looking bewildered.

"Wait. What? Who?" Lori almost dropped her glass.

"Pretty sure he said Elodie Fontaine," Gabe said.

"Oscar-winning movie star, Elodie Fontaine?"

Gabe shrugged and grinned. "And ex-Marine. I don't know of any other Elodie Fontaine who could afford to drop that kind of cash for a car."

Her mom enveloped her and Gabe in a hug. "That's over five years of running costs, sweetheart. Well done!" She kissed Gabe's cheek. "Thank you, Gabe. We can't thank you and your team enough."

"It was our privilege, Karen."

"Do you think she'll pick it up in person, or will she want it shipped?" Lori asked as the reality of the situation sank in. She liked the thought of meeting Elodie Fontaine immensely.

"I guess we'll find out." Gabe narrowed her eyes. "Do I need to be worried you'll go back with her if she does pick it up?"

Lori laughed and kissed her hard. "You're more than enough

super soldier for me. I don't need another one." She pulled away and saw that familiar look in Gabe's eyes and then turned to her mom. "We're going home, Mom. Do you mind handling the party?" It didn't matter that they were the guests of honor, or that people might want to chat afterward. All that mattered was getting alone time with Gabe.

Her mom raised both her eyebrows and glanced at Gabe, who looked everywhere in the room rather than meet her mom's gaze. "Of course, sweetheart. That tummy bug's going around, I hear."

Lori hugged her mom and whispered, "Thank you."

"Have a lovely evening," she said.

Lori smiled, and heat flushed through her whole body. She and her mom were closer than sisters for the most part, but she wasn't entirely comfortable with her mom cheerleading for her sex life.

They said quick goodbyes to Rosie, Shay, and the rest of the team. Janie wasn't around, but Gabe had mentioned she and Solo were having some issues and not to expect her. Lori grabbed Gabe's hand, and they exited the hotel.

"Are you sure you want to leave?" Gabe asked as they waited to get her truck from the valet. "This is a big night for you."

"I'm sorry. I should've asked if you wanted to leave." Lori bit her lip. "Do you want to stay?" God, she hoped Gabe wouldn't say yes.

Gabe grinned widely and pulled at the neck of her shirt. "Hell, no. I want to be wherever you are. And I've had about enough of this suit. I can't wait to get it off."

"About that..." Lori said then whispered her plans into Gabe's ear.

Gabe sighed deeply and swallowed hard. "Dessert before dinner again, Miss Turner. You're getting into some bad habits."

"You must be a bad influence," she said and ran a single nail along Gabe's jaw. "I was such a good girl until I met you."

"Lucky me," Gabe said then drew her into a long and passionate kiss.

"Lucky both of us," Lori said when they broke to draw ragged breaths. "What other bad habits can you teach me? I want them all. Just like I want all of you, all of the time."

Gabe pressed her lips to Lori's, and Lori lifted her foot from the ground, almost ready to take off with the magic of their kiss.

"You've got me, babe," Gabe said, "for as long as you want me."

"How's your forever looking?" Lori had never asked a more serious question in her life.

Gabe looked deep into her eyes, and she softened under Lori's hands. "Like it's yours."

Gabe's response couldn't have been any more perfect than if it'd been written for her, and Lori liked the clear promise of eternity in her eyes. "Forever it is then," she said with a belief so strong in the depths of her soul, she knew it could never be broken. Gabe was her sanctuary.

~ THE END ~

AUTHOR'S NOTE

Thank you for reading *Sanctuary*. If you enjoyed Gabe and Lori's friends-to-lovers romance, it would be amazing if you could pop a review on Amazon for me! And if you haven't read any of my other books, maybe you'd like to try my number one US bestseller, *Stunted Heart*?

Sanctuary is the first in the Windy City Romance series. If you're eager to find out who might get their own happily ever after in book two, copy this link into your brower (BookFunnel will take you to a mini eBook of chapter one of book two)::

https://bit.ly/WCR2

www.helenaharte.com
Follow me on Instagram, TikTok, Twitter,
and Facebook at AuthorHelenaHarte

Other Great Butterworth Books

Stunted Heart by Helena Harte
A stunt rider who lives in the fast lane. An ER doctor who can't take chances. A passion that could turn their worlds upside down.
Available on Amazon (ASIN B0C78GSWBV)

Dead Ringer by Robyn Nyx
Three bodies. One killer. No motive?
Available on Amazon (ASIN B0CPQ8HFK7)

Medea by JJ Taylor
Who will Medea become in her battle for freedom?
Available from Amazon (ASIN B0CK2FB7GW)

Virgin Flight by E.V. Bancroft
In the battle between duty and desire, can love win?
Available from Amazon (ASIN B0CKJWQZ45)

Fragments of the Heart by Ally McGuire
Love can be the greatest expedition of all.
Available on Amazon (ASIN B0CHBPHR6M)

Here You Are by Jo Fletcher
.Can they unlock their hearts to find the true happiness they both deserve?
Available on Amazon (ASIN B0CBN935ZB)

Dark Haven by Brey Willows
Even vampires get tired of playing with their food...
Available on Amazon (ASIN B0C5P1HJXC)

Green for Love by E.V. Bancroft
All's fair in love and eco-war.
Available from Amazon (ASIN B0C28F7PX5)

Call of Love by Lee Haven
Separated by fear. Reunited by fate. Will they get a second chance at life and love?
Available from Amazon (ASIN B0BYC83HZD)

Where the Heart Leads by Ally McGuire
A writer. A celebrity. And a secret that could break their hearts.
Available on Amazon (ASIN B0BWFX5W9L)

Stolen Ambition by Robyn Nyx
Daughters of two worlds collide in a dangerous game of ambition and love.
Available on Amazon (ASIN B0BS1PRSCN)

Cabin Fever by Addison M Conley
She goes for the money, but will she stay for something deeper?
Available on Amazon (ASIN B0BQWY45GH)

Breakout for Love by Valden Bush
They're both running from their pasts. Together, they might make a new future.
Available from Amazon (ASIN B0CWHZ4SXL)

The Helion Band by AJ Mason
Rose's only crime was to show kindness to her royal mistress...
Available from Amazon (ASIN B09YM6TYFQ)

That Boy of Yours Wants Looking At by Simon Smalley
A riotously colourful and heart-rending journey of what it takes to live authentically.
Available from Amazon (ASIN B09V3CSQQW)

Sapphic Eclectic Volume Four edited by Nyx & Willows
A little something for everyone...
Available free from Butterworth Books website

Of Light and Love by E.V. Bancroft
The deepest shadows paint the brightest love.
Available from Amazon (ASIN B0B64KJ3NP)

An Art to Love by Helena Harte
Second chances are an art form.
Available on Amazon (ASIN B0B1CD8Y42)

Music City Dreamers by Robyn Nyx
Music brings lovers together. In Music City, it can tear them apart. Available on Amazon (ASIN B0994XVDGR)

Let Love Be Enough by Robyn Nyx
When a killer sets her sights on her target, is there any stopping her?
Available on Amazon (ASIN B09YMMZ8XC)

Dead Pretty by Robyn Nyx
An FBI agent, a TV star, and a serial killer. Love hurts.
Available on Amazon (ASIN B09QRSKBVP)

Nero by Valden Bush
Banished and abandoned. Will destiny reunite her with the love of her life?
Available from Amazon (ASIN B0BHJKHK6S)

Warm Pearls and Paper Cranes by E.V. Bancroft
A family torn apart by secrets. The only way forward is love.
Available from Amazon (ASIN B09DTBCQ92)

Judge Me, Judge Me Not by James Merrick
One man's battle against the world and himself to find it's never too late to find, and use, your voice.
Available from Amazon (ASIN B09CLK91N5)

Scripted Love by Helena Harte
What good is a romance writer who doesn't believe in happy ever after?
Available on Amazon (ASIN B0993QFLNN)

Call to Me by Helena Harte
Sometimes the call you least expect is the one you need the most.
Available on Amazon (ASIN B08D9SR15H)

What's Your Story?

Global Wordsmiths, CIC, provides an all-encompassing service for all writers, ranging from basic proofreading and cover design to development editing, typesetting, and eBook services. A major part of our work is charity and community focused, delivering writing projects to under-served and under-represented groups across Nottinghamshire, giving voice to the voiceless and visibility to the unseen.

To learn more about what we offer, visit: www.globalwords.co.uk

A selection of books by Global Words Press:
Desire, Love, Identity: with the National Justice Museum
Aventuras en México: Farmilo Primary School
Times Past: with The Workhouse, National Trust
Young at Heart with AGE UK
In Different Shoes: Stories of Trans Lives

Self-published authors working with Global Wordsmiths:
Steve Bailey
Ravenna Castle
Jackie D
CJ DeBarra
Dee Griffiths
Iona Kane
Maggie McIntyre
Emma Nichols
Dani Lovelady Ryan
Erin Zak

Printed in Great Britain
by Amazon

49686031R10194